The Flowers of West

By Steve

Second edition.

First published by Amazon: 2020
ISBN: 9798638813598

The thousand injuries of Fortunato I had borne as I best could; but when he ventured upon insult, I vowed revenge. You, who so well know the nature of my soul, will not suppose, however, that I gave utterance to a threat. *At length* I would be avenged; this was a point definitely settled – but the very definitiveness with which it was resolved, precluded the idea of risk. I must not only punish, but punish with impunity. A wrong is unredressed when retribution overtakes its redresser. It is equally unredressed when the avenger fails to make himself felt as such to him who has done the wrong.

– Edgar Allan Poe

Thursday

The scurrying of animals desperate to survive prevented deafening silence in the basement, lasting until a rattrap confirmed its demise. Each trap's ping bringing me one death closer to freedom. Darkness and isolation force time to pace to a distorted rhythm. The final ping charms around the room, and after I dispose of the body, I'm free to leave behind this carcass-infested dungeon for good.

My hand falls against solid wood, exhaustion preventing the knock. Fatigue showers my body and drowns me with its smell. The decaying corpses barely noticeable. Two more thuds bring Mother to release me, with the door allowing the kitchen's light to engulf the basement; allowing my eyes one last longing glance at a life free from worries, before completing my ascension back to the world.

'You took your time,' Mother says, rushing me into the kitchen before closing the black door which guards a torturous Hell. Its blackness isolated in a room brimming with white décor. Even Mother's eyes, normally a pale blue, near white. Mother once told me Ms Woodfield, who left this house to her, believed the kitchen should always be the purest of white; from the

4

units to the flooring and the walls, a tradition Mother continues to honour. The only slight colour changes have grown from the smoke of Mother's cigarettes greying the tiled walls.

'Yeah, sorry,' I mutter. Calmness washes away fatigue as keys confine the part-time villain of my nightmares to its dungeon. The mouth of the beast screeching as the key turns. 'There were more bodies than normal,' my eyes descend to my crimson hands. 'More blood.' My words quiet; Mother makes no notion of hearing them. The paint covering my hands languishes between fresh and stale. 'I'm sorry.'

'No need to apologise, Lilian. I was just making an observation.' Only Mother calls me Lilian; as a kid, I loved it: it sounded so grown up, yet as time passed, it became synonymous with punishment. 'Right, better eat your dinner soon, it'll be going cold.' She retrieves a plate of spaghetti and meatballs from the microwave and places it on the table with a fork. 'I made your favourite.' She leans back against the counter and lights a cigarette, despite the aroma of a deceased cigarette's smoke filling the room. New smoke pumps into the air with every drag Mother takes. This time it's nostalgic: warm, kind, welcoming.

I fake a smile. 'Thanks, but I'm not that hungry,' my eyes close awaiting the response. 'Sorry.'

'No need to apologise; it's probably cold by now, anyway.' The part-smoked cigarette sits on the brim of the ashtray, desperate to fulfil its purpose. Mother grabs the plate and scrapes the food into the bin; each scrape coarser than its predecessor. Her words act as a ruse, a prelude to the main course: the lecture. Families such as ours should be grateful for the food we have on our tables. The same lecture every time. This time, though, no lecture comes. 'I assume you know why you're not hungry?' Her words walk the tightrope between serious and playful. The cigarette jumps back between Mother's open lips.

'Yes, I know.' Confusion and fear reign.

'Good,' the plate clatters against its unwashed brethren in the sink. 'Let's play Guess-Guess.' Her smile honest: the past four years forgotten. 'Guess-Guess who's upstairs?' Her question met with nothing more than bemusement.

The rules of Guess-Guess, a game invented to pass the time on long trips, are straightforward: the guesser must ask yes-or-no questions to find the mystery identity. It's a version of 20 Questions, but it's ours. It retired the day of my first period; the day Mother stopped seeing me as a child. The day the sands of time allow you to begin maturity should be a joyous occasion. Instead, sadness will forever tinge that day's memory.

'You're not a child anymore, Lily,' Mother said. 'So, let's leave childish games to the past, shall we?' In the years since, Mother has scorned me for a variety of reasons, with each followed by the same procedure: I run upstairs, hide under my quilt and imagine a world where Guess-Guess has no age restriction, a world where Mother would run upstairs and apologise in the form of offering a game, and we would laugh and joke until their identities came to light. The game would quench my heart of its thirst for anger. Yet Mother would never come.

Mother's impatience led me back into the moment. 'I'm not sure.' The tone in my voice honest, but scared. A thick, dark cloud forms over my mind: anticipation.

'Lily, you're better than that.' Her tone playful. Her smile demanding. The cigarette nearing the end of its life.

The cloud on my mind parts and allows a thought through: someone is upstairs. Mother hasn't specified, yet my mind places them in my room, waiting for me. Maybe it's a local celebrity coming as part of a charity event. Perhaps it's a long-lost family member who has contacted Mother and wants to see me. The possibilities excite, which wash away the fear. 'Okay. Male or female?' Always start with a question which eliminates fifty-per cent of answers.

'Female. All of them.' *All* of them? Why would a group of females be visiting me? I'm not the social type, anymore.

'Have I met them before?' Maybe a local girl-group has heard my history. Perhaps Mother reached out to them and begged them to come. Begged four strangers to pity the freak.

'Yes; plenty of times.' The ashtray welcomes the dying flame of the cigarette, signalling the end of its lifespan. Mother grabs the green packet and sits them next to the ashtray. The window stands watch, opened enough to suck out Mother's smoke; Ms Woodfield's hatred of smoking forced Mother to sneak out during the early hours for a quick drag, before allowing the night to wash away the smells of cigarette and shame.

Mother has never remembered when she started smoking, yet she's always said the stress of pregnancy turned it from a casual hobby to a severe addiction. We all have our addictions. Despite being underage, a cashier at the time fancied her and served her. And she'd visit him in revealing attires (push-up bras teaming with low-cut tops, worn atop a mini skirt), bought solely to get cigarettes. He'd flirt with a pretty girl; she'd get cigarettes. Everyone was a winner. He still works there, and once I used Mother's technique (and clothes) to buy my one-and-only pack of cigarettes from him. It was one of the most uncomfortable things I've ever done; I could've vomited after the wink I attached to the name on his badge: Sebastian. He's handsome, even still in his mid-to-late thirties. His ring finger sat empty, ashamed of the dent forced upon it. It wasn't empty for long, as the next time I tried, a ring hugged his finger like a long-lost friend. A ring which blinded him to me (although my long-sleeve shirt and baggy trousers helped, too), and informed me against trying for a second pack.

Faces and names race through my brain, trying to find a group of girls whom Mother would welcome into our home. 'Have they come here to see me?'

Feeling the need to aid my guessing, Mother walks over to the drinks cabinet and pulls out a bottle of wine and a corkscrew, and places them on the table. 'They've come to see you.' Mother, the bottle and its partner wait for my mind to put the pieces of the puzzle together, but only after my eyes drift upwards towards the calendar did things make sense: it's Thursday. I take a half-step back as another cigarette begins its demise in Mother's mouth. She always smokes more in the evening.

'Mother?' My voice coarse, struggling to settle on an emotion. 'You don't mean?' My body froze.

'I sure do. The Flowers are here. How great is that?' While Mother's tone matches her words, I cannot follow in her excitement. The last time Mother mentioned The Flowers was as she vowed never to entertain them in our home again. The Flowers are, or were, the only real friends I've ever had: Poppy, Ivy and

10

Rose. We named ourselves The Flowers, and we were inseparable at our group's height. Poppy was the first to take pity on me when I was fifteen and skiving school; until the police caught me. The police's intervention forced Mother to free me from school by telling them I was being home-schooled. The Flowers never attended my school, and they're a year older, yet during my life's darkest spell, they offered light. A reason to be excited every time the school's bell sounded off at 3:20; on the rare days I went.

Age, boyfriends and jobs soon took over, and our group resigned itself to meeting every Thursday. They'd come to my house; we'd drink wine and gossip about their crazy lives. They always had such wonderful stories to tell, stories which I loved hearing. Stories I could never match.

The last time I saw them, Ivy and Poppy had started university (Ivy studying English Literature and Poppy studying Classical Art), and Rose was working her way up the career ladder (the last time we spoke she was the assistant manager of a small store).

Despite how much I loved The Flowers, Mother detested our friendship. She'd always lie and say they

11

were using me for my home and the free wine ('They never even bloody pay for the wine,' she'd say *every* week as if it were her catchphrase) while lambasting how they weren't 'true' friends, whatever that meant. I never questioned The Flowers on Mother's allegations, because even if they were using me, I didn't care: I *had* friends. Then one week Mother got her wish, and The Flowers didn't come. No messages. No reasons. They never came the following week, nor the week after, and they always ignored my pleas. That was nine months ago.

Mother's tears of joy contrasted with my tears of sorrow in the ensuing weeks and months which followed, as the realisation I was alone once more nestled in my brain. She pretended to be sympathetic in her way: 'I'm sorry, but I told you they were bad news,' she'd say while hugging me as I sat at the window; a dog waiting for its owner. 'They've probably found another poor girl so desperate for friendship she's blind to their manipulative behaviour.' *That* was Mother on nice days.

'We'll need more wine,' I jest, still unsure of the whole situation. My eyes lead Mother's to the lone bottle stood on the table.

'You know where my purse is, take some money and get yourselves more later. I'm sure they won't mind waiting an extra ten minutes.' She *hates* giving me money.

'Are you sure? We don't have to drink wine; I'm sure they'll understand if-'

'Nonsense,' she interrupts. 'It's Thursday, so you need wine. Now, you've kept them waiting long enough, go enjoy yourself.' She leans back against the counter, folds one cigarette-less arm across her chest and smiles. 'You've earned it.'

'Hey, Sis,' in strides Alexa, my baby sister; well, in my head she's a baby, but she's getting bigger and bigger. 'Do you have a spare copy of Wuthering Heights? We're studying it in school.' She's everything I wish I was at her age: thin (but not too thin), pretty, confident, athletic. She's nearly the same height as me, which, from a big-sister point-of-view, is annoying.

'Alexa? I can't believe how big you're getting.'

'Well, I am thirteen, now,' she clicks her fingers and poses. The behaviours of teenagers confound me; despite my retirement from being one still fresh. 'So, Wuthering Heights?' Her eyebrows display impatience.

13

'Yes, yes, come up and I'll grab you my copy.'

Alexa skips up the stairs; she has such love of life. She's yet to meet the perils life will have, nor has she ever been desperate enough to wear revealing outfits to charm a grown man: long may that continue; there's *enough* trouble in our family's history. I smile back at Mother, who takes one final drag of her cigarette and crushes it next to its Lambert and Butler brother. She nods, and I head upstairs, wine and corkscrew in hand. My pace more sombre than Alexa's; I'm walking into the unknown. Nine months of complete silence.

My brain highlights every seed of doubt and tries to cut it; maybe friends disappear for a while with no major reason. Plus, if nothing else, the last nine months will have plenty of stories (from their side). Stories of school, and men, and work. Stories of adventures, because they had adventures. None I featured in, yet the way they told the stories made me feel like I was there. I was there when they went camping, and Ivy peed in an empty wine bottle and served it to Poppy. I was there when they drove for five hours across the country just to buy a packet of crisps. I was there when they broke into the old, abandoned house on Coedroad Lane, but ran away scared when an army of rats came charging towards them.

Halfway up the stairs, my eyes capture the image of Mother, hand-washing the dishes while humming away The Penguins' Earth Angel. Her singing voice is shy, however, it's better than what you'll hear on the radio. The whole picture an artist's dream scene.

'Hurry up, Sis, haven't got all day,' Alexa's impatient words bring me back to the moment, and I finish ascending the stairs, forgetting for a moment the group of girls who await my arrival.

Every Thursday I clamoured for The Flowers to include me once again in their group: I would listen for the doorbell to ring for hours, scaring the postman on multiple occasions; Mother hated Thursdays because of it. A keen eye could detect the day of the week by the smile etched on Mother's face: on a Friday it borderline covered her whole chin; by Wednesday you needed a pirate's map to find it.

My eyes embrace the image as I enter the room: Poppy sitting with her legs crossed texting away on her phone (telling her mother she'll be out late tonight), Rose sitting on the bed with the television remote in hand, flicking through the music channels (she always has control of the television) and Ivy testing my makeup by my mirror. This picture is how Thursdays should be. It happened so frequent it became the norm; a sight which I could've explained to Alexa before entering. Today, though, there's confusion wafting in the air: theirs caused by my lateness, mine caused by their presence.

'There you are,' Rose chirps as I enter the room. 'We've been waiting here for ages.' Abandonment dominated Rose's childhood; from her parents to countless foster-families which followed. From time to time her personality has rubbed us the wrong way (the first time Ivy slept with a man he dumped her the following day, yet Rose's words angered Ivy more than helped ease her hurt), however, we've always given her the benefit of the doubt. The constant string of abandonment *must* have had some psychological effect on how you interact with others. Her domineering behaviour granted her the leader's throne. 'Who's the kid?' She glances over at Alexa.

'Oh, guys, this is my younger sister, Alexa.' Alexa bows; such confidence and showmanship. 'She's not staying; I'm just getting a book for her.' I walk to the bookshelf and find my copy of Emily Brontë's novel. 'Here, now, clear off.'

'Thanks, Sis,' she smiles and skips off back to her room. The door closes, hiding our secret club away from any watching eyes.

'She's cute,' Poppy the first to speak. 'I'm assuming she doesn't go to West Drive High?' West Drive High School was my old school and not one I would *ever* allow Alexa to attend.

'Of course not,' I try to make light of her remark. 'She goes to your old school.' The Flowers were lucky enough to attend St. Andrews High on the other side of West Drive; its reputation much more positive, and none of The Flowers ever badmouthed too much about their old stomping ground.

'Nice. So, where've ya been? It's like twenty-past six,' Rose interrupts, eager to get the conversation back on track.

'Yeah, yeah, sorry, I had to clean the basement. It was full of rats, and,' my bloodied hands a siren across the room. 'I better go clean.' I place the sole bottle of wine on my table. Rose the first to notice its lack of company.

'We will need more than *that*.'

'I know, I know, I just wasn't expecting company,' a cloud of awkwardness rears its head. Silence. 'Mother's given me money, so I'll be heading to the shops later to get more.'

After Rose had time to deliberate, she nods and accepts the plan, which allows me the opportunity to leave and wash my hands in the upstairs bathroom. A little water cleans me of this deed. I scrub and scrub, yet the red stains prove a challenge. The water's temperature rising with every passing second: cold, mild, lukewarm, warm, hot, boiling. My body ignorant to the burning heat of the water until it reaches boiling point, snapping me back to the moment with its sting. I jolt back, my hands clean. Spotless. Notice-me clean. Notice-the-freckles clean.

I ignore the returning freckles (where have they been?), wrap a cold hand-towel around my hand and return to my room. 'Well,' Ivy says the second my body passes the threshold. My eyes ask her to elaborate. 'Are you going to open the *one* bottle or not?' She smiles. Whenever she acts Rose-ish, she always follows her orders with a smile. I've never worked out if it's to calm anyone annoyed by her domineering behaviour, or an extra layer on top of her game, however, I appreciate the smile.

During our group's infancy, we used to hang around and gossip; they'd tell me the goings-on at their school: what boys looked fine, what girls were letting themselves go, what *teachers* acted human. I knew their school more than mine. But, one day, Ivy brought along a bottle of wine: and so, a Thursday staple began. Ivy has long been far more interested in drinking alcohol than socialising; sure, she'd contribute her part by offering stories on which bed she woke in on the prior weekend, or how many beds (what she calls a 'special' weekend), yet she'd be the first to get drunk. The sheer number of messages she received every Thursday was amazing, all from lads believing their one night with her to be something more. She had such confidence with men. They didn't say no. And they *always* wanted more.

I offer a slight giggle, still unsure why they've returned, yet I oblige and open the wine, pouring four glasses. There wasn't much left in the bottle afterwards, which allows Rose to offer one of her famous looks. Sometimes Rose's eyes spoke the words her throat didn't

19

have to say. And they were clear. We're powerless to do anything about her looks. And it's not just us: men have abandoned their date because of her eyes. They have their superpower; the ability to manipulate your mind into doing her bidding or supplying a service she requires. Whatever she wanted, from whomever she wanted.

'I know, I know,' I answer her eyes. 'I'll have mine then I'll nip to the shop for more.' I sit, crossing my legs, and fight back every urge to demand an answer to their disappearance. I may not like the answer. Maybe they *had* found someone else, though she became strong enough to rebuff their manipulative behaviour. I'm not that strong.

'So, how are you, Lily?' Poppy asks, eager to kill a forming silence. Are they as uncomfortable as me?

'I'm good. Well, I'm okay,' I struggle for the right adjective; my mind reasons to use a variety. It was always Poppy who questioned how I'm feeling or what I've been up to (the others latched onto anything considered worthy, yet they'd never be the ones to instigate the topic). Of The Flowers, Mother only liked Poppy. She had this way of making girls like her. Boys, not so much. I think she's gorgeous, we all think she's lovely, however, boys don't. Before their disappearance, she was the only virgin of the group. She probably still is.

My response isn't a great way to engage in conversation, and soon another lull threatens; Ivy defeats it by telling us about John. 'He's a solid 7/10,' she always starts by scoring their looks. 'His flat was an absolute mess, but I let that slide,' there's always something she lets slide. I drift in and out of her story, unlike Poppy and Rose who interrupt various scenes with questions, ranging from the specificity of the mess to how good he was in bed (another category she scores them on: John got a six). She has such passion when she's detailing her exploits; a passion I've never had. What makes her so carefree and passionate about sex? I wish *I* had it. In the early days, I assumed the stories were all lies. Afterwards, I thought she sought encounters to please us with a story. Speaking to her, though, you can tell she loves the whole adventure, from the seduction to the kiss goodbye. 'The first time I was bent over the living room sofa,' she says with such excitement, despite never wanting to see John again. I've always dreamed of being

21

able to find a story like hers to offer. 'And, as like all men,' her passion turns to mock-annoyance. 'He wanted me to go down on him *without* him repaying the favour.' Rose and Poppy laugh at John's intrepidness. I laugh because I have to.

'Men,' Rose shakes her head. 'Me, me, me. That's all they care about.' Mischief wears her face. 'Did you do it?'

'Of course, I did.' Her smile shows satisfaction, regardless of her complaints, and we laugh again.

As Ivy's most recent escapade finishes, the bottle tips out the last of its wine. Rose's eyes meet mine.

'Well, I guess it's time I get more wine,' I interject, and Rose's eyes congratulate me on following their rules.

'Fancy some company?' Poppy always asks if I want company, however, the evening has lulled her too much to have meant it.

'It's fine; it's only a short walk.'

I grab my jacket from the cupboard, but Ivy stops me before I could leave. 'Don't be too long, babe,' she says. 'I don't know how long I can delay talking abo⸍

Anthony.' A second lad. A *special* weekend. A gentle laugh escapes my throat.

'I'll try,' I jest, and leave.

Mother's still washing the dishes as I reach the bottom of the stairs; the water a thick red from the washing-up liquid. 'How is it,' she began, 'seeing them after all this time? Must be strange.' Had her eyes lifted from the plate, she would've seen the honest answer in my face.

'It is, yeah, but it's nice. Anyway, I'm going to the shop,' I wait for the refusal of money, despite Mother's offer. Yet it doesn't come. Every step towards her purse nerve-wracking, yet no argument or denial comes.

'There should be £30 in my purse, use that.' There's a strange tinge of sadness taking the money, however, it's Thursday: Thursdays *need* wine. I turn and make my way.

The walk itself is not too long, with enough images to keep my eyes satisfied. First, there's the park; it's only small, no doubt built to fill a spare bit of land and to give the houses nearby something to smile about. Should they have children, that is. I loved playing there as a kid. I'd spend hours and hours climbing and running and laughing. Mother and I would walk to the park together, we'd walk through the gate together, and then she'd unleash me onto a world of make-believe and adventures. I always adventured solo. Mother would go straight to the tables and cackle with other mothers who'd also unleashed their children.

I loved playing in the park *too much*. 'Clean your room, or we won't be going to the park on Saturday,' she'd order. 'Eat your carrots, or you'll be coming straight home tomorrow after school,' she'd threaten. 'How about setting some rattraps in the basement, and we'll have an extra hour in the park?' She'd bargain. She went through with everything: if my clothes lay sprawled across the floor, we didn't go to the park that Saturday; if one carrot resisted me, we came straight home after school the next day; after the first time ridding the basement of rats, I got that extra hour.

Nostalgia is a funny thing. As many bad memories as good haunt the park: me, the poor little pigtailed girl, begging in vain for others to join her adventures; the rain stopping me from the outside world; Mother using the park as reason to rid me for an hour, while she got to spend quality time with other adults. But still, it warms my heart: it feels like home.

The park near bereft of life; dusk scares away the wants of playing children. The only body inside a youngish man rocking on the swing. There is something sad about his demeanour. Mother warns me about strangers; Mother warns me about a lot of things. So, he'll be a mystery I may never understand.

The next road divides the park and the town's castle. It's not the grandest of castles, however, it still presents a historic shine to our otherwise forgettable town. More childhood memories explode into my mind, starting with the young pigtailed girl sliding down the castle's moat on those fantastically snowy days. The angle of the moat languishing between dangerous and safe. The pigtailed girl doesn't care about the risks; she slides on homemade sledges. Age allows eyes to see the ways of getting hurt: a slight hole in the floor, a misplaced rock, other kids. To children, that stuff is meaningless. Once I hit a rock and fractured my arm, and Mother banned me from the castle for two months. I healed, I served my time and I returned.

Terraced houses accompany the rest of the walk; built during the industrial revolution for local workers (or so the story goes): all two-up, two-down and circle where the paper factory used to be. Two empty buildings lay dormant next to it; however, I've never researched what West Drive made during its history. Mother's parents used to live on one of those streets (and true to the story, Mother's father worked at the paper factory). I've never seen Mother's parents (they severed contact with her months before I was born), so I'm not sure if they still live there. I hope they don't: it'd be too sad to think of a family split by mere metres. Only when defending herself in arguments, would Mother mention her parents: 'You should consider my punishments lenient, I used to get the belt.' And she *never* mentions them in a positive light. The tone of the argument always dictated who got the blame for their falling out: sometimes it was my fault, other times it was theirs. However, it was *never* Mother's.

After the rows of terraced houses comes the bridge, and through there the little local shop. It's one of those shops where you can memorise the entirety of their staff. Likewise, they know their clientele; they greet you as you walk in, and they're always willing to have a friendly little chat while you paid. My favourite colleague is Natasha; I used to time when I went to the shop so I could see her. Any excitement at seeing Natasha again fades as the bridge's walls clear, revealing a man behind the kiosk. A man I've not seen before.

He smiles at me as I enter the shop, switching from leaning against the counter to standing to attention. I half-smile back, take a deep gulp and head over to the wine section. His eyes cast a cold shadow which crawls along the floor and greets me. I scan over the New Zealand section and find a decent priced (yet not too cheap) bottle, from a company called Gunn's Lake. They're new, but they'll do. I approach the unknown man at the kiosk with four bottles.

'Evening,' he offers, before even looking at my shopping. His gaze an insect crawling across my face. An insect I can't swat away.

'Hi,' I mutter, placing the four bottles on the counter.

'Four bottles on a school night? I like it.' He scans the first bottle and offers a tooth-filled grin. His gaze crawls over my body and nestles on my bandage-covered hand. I should leave. I should run. I should scream for help.

'I've got friends round,' my tone matter-of-fact. My hands clench, desperate to scratch at my skin, to take away the sting from his gaze.

'Nice. Where's the party at?' He scans the bottle a further three times and doesn't ask for my I.D. Is he fishing for my address? Why would he want my address? I don't know what makes him think there's a party. Why would he even want to come? I don't know who he is, and he doesn't know who I am. I smile, as if what he said was funny, and pull the money from my purse without asking him the price. 'That's £19.96, please,' he says on cue. *Where's the party at?* What party? 'What's the weather like outside?' Why is he asking so many questions? I interlock the fingers on my hands and rest them against my stomach. Each finger presses into the back of my fists. 'I finish in just over an hour, but I've forgotten my coat.' He laughs, am I supposed to laugh? I offer that same smile again.

'It's not too cold.' I must answer. His gaze's crawl retreats a little. I so desperately want to swat it away.

'Sweet. Here's your change.' He hands over the 4p. Money I would've sacrificed to have avoided his gaze those extra few seconds. 'Enjoy your evening. And don't drink too much.' He laughs again. I smile, grab my shopping and leave. The insects loosening their grip the closer I get to the exit. Natasha always offers a warm and welcoming shopping environment. He offered nothing but gloom and darkness.

I'm desperate to get home, back to my haven. This time, there's no pondering about Mother's parents, no reminiscing about sliding the castle's moat on merrier days, no excitement about The Flowers' return. The thump of heavy footsteps appear behind me, freezing my body on the spot. I turn and see a figure.

I race off, walking a near-jogging pace. With every entrance to a new row of terraced houses I pass, my neck spins: the figure's still there. I scan each street, looking for a person to save me, but they're hiding. I could be on the news tomorrow morning: another missing person in West Drive, because of their hiding. And they wouldn't care.

Those same insects from the shop return, crawling along my spine.

My heavy breath partners the clanging bottles. The empty evening allows the sound to reverberate; I'd even laugh at the sound on a merrier journey. Each clang separated by a stomping footstep. 'You know what you've done,' the figure calls out. My pace quickens.

My mind fills with nightmarish thoughts of what this man will do upon reaching me; each footstep he slams brings those nightmares closer. His shadow comes into view, towering over mine. A ghastly shadow. A sinister shadow. 'You know what you've done.' The insects crawl from my spine to my neck. The arms of the shadow stretch. I'm in his reach.

Without thinking, I race into the park and ready my voice for the biggest scream I've offered in years. Then he appears: the stranger on the swings.

In the lone light of the park, he's more handsome than I should think, but I was right: sadness consumes him. The scene a black-and-white photograph; with light and shading used to illustrate the thoughts and feelings of its subject to perfection. If only I could capture this moment. I walk towards him, trying to silence the bottles.

'Hey,' I offer.

He looks up, not even noticing my presence before, offers a wry smile and gives me a 'hey' back. It's rare I focus on the looks of someone I meet, yet there's something about him which attracts me to it. As I get closer, details of him become clearer: from his face's unshaven chin and heavy eyes to his choice of expensive-looking clothes. His eyes could tell their own story of a man who's kind and understanding, yet vulnerable. Sadness radiates from him, assuring me of my safety.

'I'm sorry to intrude,' the bottles silence. 'But is anything the matter?' When I was at my lowest ebb, I hated when people *pretended* to be interested in you. Teachers would pull me into a room and question how I'm feeling in myself, how I'm coping with schoolwork, how my family life is back home. Yet all they wanted to know is why I slammed Charlotte's head into her locker. My questioning could come across as insensitive, but it's honest. I don't play games with their emotions to get to the root of their sadness.

'My mother died today.' The air cools, and I struggle to inhale. For a moment, my body convulses, and my pupils shake.

31

'Oh, oh god,' I say as my body calms. 'I'm so sorry to hear that.' The air slow in its return to the spring evening temperature. The taste of oxygen in my lungs delicious.

'You don't need to be,' he reassures. 'We weren't that close.' His fingers interlock; there's more to this story.

'Still, it's your mother.'

'Yeah,' he sighs. I can't help but fight off the thoughts to compliment his face. 'I'm sorry, if it's all the same with you, I'd rather not go into it too much.' His outward expression tries to switch to one of bravery, yet his eyes cannot hide anguish. I offer a comforting smile, unsure how to act.

The only time I've ever met death was with Richard, the elderly neighbour next door. His wife had passed away five months prior, and I had to ask Mother what to say because I was afraid of speaking out-of-turn. Thankfully, the five months which had elapsed healed him enough of the pain to find the funny side of me stumbling through words. I dread to think about a conversation the morning after her passing. He committed suicide a few days later, he couldn't live without her, and as much as I liked him, I couldn't go anywhere near the family members passing in and out of his home.

'Sure. I'm Lily, by the way.' My body sways in search of a way to act.

'Hey,' he offers out his steady hand for me to shake. 'I'm Brad.'

'Mind if I sit?' I gesture to the empty swing next to him, and he accepts. We sit in silence, watching the world pass by. I've grown to appreciate the night over the last three-to-four years, thanks to my abnormal sleeping pattern. The way the moonlight glows everything in a black-and-white hue. The way the streets quieten, allowing peace. A full moon shines its light on the park. At least he's not a werewolf.

In view the castle stands, guarding over the town. Guarding over the families doing their family things, with lights on here and there, and the occasional body moving about their home.

As a child, I loved the colour violet, so much so I begged Mother to send me to Athertyn Primary, despite it being much further away than St. Victoria's, purely because of their uniform. In St. Victoria's we wore navy blue. 'It's basically the same colour,' Mother used to say. However, as I've got older, I've grown to appreciate grey. The way it rests between white and black, between life and death, between Heaven and Hell.

'Are you from round here?'

'Yeah, Dolphin Street,' he points towards the middle row of the terraced houses. 'When I was younger, anyway. My mother used to bring me here, before, well, it doesn't matter. After I found out, I felt I had to come here to reminisce, you know?' He's trying to smile, and I long to reassure him he needn't maintain a false emotion for my sake, even if his smile is cute.

'I live over there,' I'm not sure if he cares, and his eyes don't linger too long where I point. 'My mother used to bring me here, too. Maybe they used to talk to one another.' We're the same age, so we would've met each other here.

'That's a nice thought, but my mother wasn't the nicest of people, so I can't imagine they would've talked for long,' he laughs. His fingers release each other, revealing a photograph of a beautiful woman with a beautiful young boy in this park on a bright, sun-filled day. The young boy smiles, the woman cherishes motherhood. What happened?

'How did she, you know?' I can't say the word; it sounds too final, too grotesque.

'I'm not sure. We haven't had much contact lately. It was my aunt who told me.' He folds the picture and tucks it into his jacket pocket. There's something alluring about the mere way he carries out every action. As if each rehearsed to perfection. 'So, what brings you here?' His voice desperate to change the topic.

'Some friends came around, and we didn't have enough wine,' I relax the bag onto the floor; the bottles mock me by making their presence known. 'I haven't seen them for a while, so we've got some catching up to do.'

He's intrigued: never has a boy been genuinely interested in what I have to say. In high school, a few mocked me with pretence, however, I was far too inexperienced in the world to spot the difference between interest and sarcasm. They pretended to care, yet they just wanted something from me, often to humiliate me, as Henry did before our year nine prom. After inviting me and getting my hopes up, I arrived at his house as agreed, yet there everyone stood. Laughing. He would never slum with the likes of me. To rub it in further, he kissed his actual date in front of me. Mother warned me about high school boys, but I didn't listen. And she was right. However, Brad's eyes confirm he's different from Henry.

'It's nice that you're all still friends despite the gaps in seeing each other.' His tone keeps secrets, yet again I refuse to pry. 'So,' the subject once again switching. 'What was your favourite thing here?'

He nods his head out towards the park and has a look of apathy. It's small, housing four swings (two adult, two baby, the latter of which I can still squeeze in to), two animal-shaped rocking seats, a pair of slides (one for the small kids, one for the big ones) and a seesaw. Despite its limited choice in the eyes of adults, to children, they offer a diverse choice of activities. Still, as I got older, I became more fascinated with the real challenge which the park offers: scaling the random building sat on the edge of the park's grounds. The challenge all big kids want to conquer. It wasn't straightforward: first, you had to be small enough to climb under the gated fence (it's far too tall to climb over

36

it), then use the pipes and cracks and ventilation shafts to climb, at an awkward angle, before leaping to grab hold of the roof. Mother hated seeing me up there and always warned me about it beforehand. However, when she was with other adults, her threats offered no meaning.

'The swings,' I say to his eyes, hoping mine hide the lie. 'Getting higher and higher, you know? Watching the world zip back-and-forth.'

His laugh is cute. 'Wanna see who can swing higher?' He smiles back. I think I'd do anything those eyes of his ask.

'Game on.' Despite my body demanding rules and regulations, we set no real parameters for the battle. We each use different techniques, with Brad's terrific physique allowing him to scale to great heights early on, while I rise inch-by-inch.

'Slow and steady wins the race', Mother would always say when she and I raced. When no other parents demanded her attention, that is.

'Catch up,' he teases.

Feeling the urge for victory, I push my legs harder and harder to close the gap. The buildings and views become nothing more than streaks of varying dark colours zipping back-and-forth. My body desperate to stop, yet determination forces my legs to kick. As I get within reaching distance, though, Brad jumps. I'm still swinging, and each of his movements become photographs: the picture of him landing, him standing tall against the moonlight, him turning around. The final image him watching, waiting, for *me*. There's genuine happiness on the face of the man in these mental pictures I'm taking.

Despite my fear, I allow the girlish urge to impress the cute boy overtake every logical part of my body, and I imitate his jump. I don't mimic his landing. My face crashes against the floor, the grass softening the blow, and Brad comes rushing to my aid. The pain worth seeing him care for me. He sits me up and helps dust off blades of grass.

'I'm assuming you often slowed down,' he mocks as the rusty metal holding the two swings creaks. '*Before* getting off.' That smile again.

'Most of the time, yeah,' I admit. There's no use in even trying to lie after offering such a poor effort. We each laugh, still sitting with him guarding over me, like a father over his child or a bodyguard over his celebrity. Each scenario brings warmth and safety. There's a longing inside me to stay here for the rest of the evening, though a quick flash of The Flowers waiting for me snaps me back to reality. 'I should probably get going,' my voice a mixture of nervousness and regret.

'No worries, I understand,' he stands and helps me to my feet. 'Thanks for this.' I'm not sure what he's thanking me for, but I smile.

I wipe away the remaining blades of grass and dust off my clothes – under no circumstance must Mother see them – and grab the bag and wave at him goodbye. The otherwise silent evening accompanied by the rusty swing still rocking and the bottles of wine dancing with each other.

'Hey, Lily,' Brad calls over and jogs to the gate. 'Mind if I leave you my number?' A tingling rises up my spine and flushes heat into my forehead. 'So, we can battle again after you've had some practice.' He looks over towards the swings and back at me. My face burns – he must be blind if he cannot notice – yet I smile as if to say yes. He grabs a pen and paper out of his jacket and writes his number; I can't help but admire his face in the moonlight. 'Here,' he hands over the paper, and I look at the eleven beautiful numbers with a cross below them. 'You don't have to message me,' his demeanour copies my shyness. 'But if you want to.' He smiles into my eyes. He *is* interested in *me*. To him, I'm not the victim of a prank in the making. To him, I'm not the home-schooled girl with no friends. To him, I'm not the pathetic mess who only cries wolf to those unable to affect anything. To him, I'm a clean slate. Which means I can be whatever I want to be. I can be *whoever* I want. Instead of the victim, I can be the victor. I smile, pocket his number and walk away. There's a fine line between creepy and charming when someone watches you; he cushions himself on the side of the latter.

I urge to take far too many longing looks back at him. My eyes desperate to catch even the slightest glimpse of his face. The park soon becomes blocked by houses in my street, and with that, his face fades. It's annoying the way I'm acting is the way those high school girls acted, the ones I hate, yet I can't help myself. I allow myself a cute smile at the thought of his number in my jacket. However, flashing lights soon wipe away that smile.

40

I come to a halt three doors away from my house as an ambulance drives towards me from the other end of the street. Its light gets closer and closer as my heart beats faster and faster. Anxiety. Relief. Fear. 'No, no, no,' I shake my head with vigour. The ambulance nears. I fall to my knees, clutching my chest to calm my racing heart its thumping drowns out the sirens. The ambulance races towards me. Flashes of images plough through my mind: a hammer, the dishes, rats, a swinging lamp. The ambulance getting closer. A hammer, the dishes, rats, a swinging lamp. Closer and closer. Hammer, the dishes, rats, a swinging lamp. Blood drips to the floor from where I burnt myself. Hammer, dishes, rats, lamp, blood. The lights of the ambulance near, faster, faster, hammer, dishes, closer, closer, rats, lamp, faster, closer, blood.

Then it turns off into a connecting street and disappears.

My heartbeat returns to a semi-normal rhythm, and I wipe the blood away from my hand.

'Where on God's green Earth have you been, young lady?' Mother scorns as I enter, still washing the dishes.

41

'I went to the shop to get some wine, remember?' My speech quickens.

'Since when has it taken *that* long?' Her voice balancing aggression and calm, unable to decide. My body shakes in fear.

'It was really busy, Mother, I swear. I'm sorry, I'm sorry.'

'No need to apologise,' her voice calms, stopping me from repeating apologies. 'So, how many bottles did you get? Oh, did you get my washing-up liquid?'

'Washing-up liquid?'

'Yeah, I asked you to get me some when I gave you the money.'

'Sorry,' my brain searches for the memory, but it comes up short. 'I guess I didn't hear you.'

'Really?' She smiles. 'Never mind, no need to apologise. So, who was working?'

'Someone new.'

'That's a shame, I know how much you like Natasha. So, what was this new *girl* like?'

'I didn't speak too much,' the fridge houses three bottles. 'I got four,' desperate to change the subject. 'With the one we've drunk; it should last the night.'

'I should hope so,' she turns and grins. Her voice layered with sarcasm. 'And, you haven't drunk in a few months, so take it easy.' My pupils shake as we stand staring at each other, each momentarily afraid to speak; the elephant an ignored third member of the conversation. 'Anyway, go on,' Mother breaks the tension. 'They're waiting.'

I leave, saying nothing else, though offer a smile of fake thankfulness. I grab the bottle which evaded the fridge's cool life and head upstairs. A moment's peace on the upstairs landing allows me to save Brad's number into my phone under the name 'B'. I'm sure I can pass it off as someone else if Mother or Alexa spot it.

'Where's my chocolate?'

I shake my head, the discomfort of that shopkeeper's watching gaze fills my body. I fight off the urge to shudder, to scratch away a surviving insect from my back. 'I'm so sorry, Alexa, I completely forgot.'

'You're such a disappointment. Move,' Alexa's frustrated body barges passed en route the bathroom, and a large thud shakes me on the spot.

'You can't please everyone,' I mutter.

'Better late than never,' Rose speaks first, holding her empty glass aloft.

'Sorry, ladies,' I open the bottle and begin pouring into Rose's glass. 'There was a large queue. And fear not, we have three more bottles downstairs just chilling. So, tonight can begin.'

'Did you meet anyone cute in the queue?' Ivy offers while licking her lips, an action I hope is for the wine entering her glass.

'No.' I've read many stories over the years about lie detectors and their uses, and why they're not used in a court of law to find the truth. "Many people think using a polygraph is as bad as dunking putative witches in a pond," one article read. "It wouldn't be a justice system," argued another. Accurate lie detectors could grant guilty/not-guilty verdicts in moments. Punishments would fall on wicked men. However, some bad men know how to trick the test. Wicked men like *him*. Every single tell a lie detector notices in a lying person; I display when I lie. I pray nobody notices. The wine diverts their attention from the definite colour change of my skin, as Brad's face enters my mind.

'The question is,' Rose says before taking a sip. 'Were you *looking*?'

My glass fills last yet empties first. 'No, I, just,' little beads of sweat come to life, screaming Brad's name at the top of their voices. 'Waited and queued and left.'

'The last time we spoke, you wanted a relationship. You felt you needed one as a way of coping.' I hoped they wouldn't remember this.

The week before The Flowers disappeared, I was at my emotional lowest. Mother and I were arguing more, and everywhere we went were romantic couples; they were teasing me with their love. I wanted that. I *needed* that. To feel loved, to feel wanted, to feel happy. To *feel*.

This boiled over on their last visit, which ended with Mother kicking and screaming at me about how they weren't real friends. I drank too much, and romance came flooding out of my mouth to them. 'You, like us all, deserve love,' they'd say. They even offered a shortlist of candidates who met their approval. Mother, however, was steadfast in saying no.

My begging for love didn't cease when my body reached sobriety. I asked, I begged, I pleaded every single day. And then The Flowers never returned.

'I was in an awful place.' Honesty. 'But, I'm better now.' Lies.

'So,' Ivy interrupts. 'Anthony was a pretty sweet 8/10.' Tension fades as our minds fill with the animated adventures of Ivy Lorraine.

The rest of the night was perfect. It didn't take too long for my mind to ignore the lapsed time as I became absorbed in the countless stories which I had missed; stories which The Flowers were all-too-willing to repeat with never-ending laughter. Ivy followed Anthony's chapter in her love life with one man after another; some even brought on chuckles from Rose and Poppy, each aware of that escapade's end. She even talked about a threesome she had when she bumped into a couple seeking a third partner (a story which *really* embarrassed Poppy). The more alcohol she drank, the more details she revealed.

Rose's stories centred around her newfound love of football (her family had always been *huge* football fans, yet she had never taken to it). She's got herself in West Drive's women's team and soon became captain. Her most detailed story focused on a tense-sounding match where she won the best player award and scored the winning goal in a 5-4 victory over their fiercest rivals. She offered stories of their wild nights out, yet they felt tame by the standard Ivy set.

Poppy, meanwhile, couldn't even hope to offer anything as dramatic, with her choosing to focus on her university studies (despite Ivy's insistence on the first year 'doesn't count' and she should 'live a little'). She's found a career passion she wants to follow, and I admire that more than any success Ivy or Rose have had. She wants to be a teacher. Awkwardness floated in the air when she said this, however, it soon washed away with the mention of a boy she's crushing on.

'Details, now,' Ivy demanded.

'Cute or sexy? Fit or fat? Brainy or braindead?' Rose questioned.

'He's nice' was as much as they got, despite their pestering for more. They knew 'nice' meant fat. Ivy has dated her fair share of chubby men, yet they don't score high on her system. The guys would be 'a cute 4/10' or 'a sweet 3.5/10'. She'd point out with precise enunciation *she* was on top, and we'd laugh with her. Poppy was more reserved in talking about boys because the guys she's likely to date differ from the ones sniffing around Ivy and Rose's heels. Poppy doesn't get random Facebook requests with comments praising her looks. Poppy doesn't have thousands follow her on Instagram waiting for the latest bikini selfie.

Despite it being my house, I wasn't the centre of attention. They remembered my butterfly collecting (although there's a big board hanging above my wall with the butterflies I've caught). Butterfly collecting became a major hobby of mine a few years ago after I left school. They offered comfort and beauty in an otherwise disgusting and ugly world. Mother was very much against me starting to collect butterflies (not only due to the cost, but because I was 'murdering God's creatures'), yet she soon conceded. It brought me joy at a rough time, and that was worth every penny for her. My eyes glossed towards the collection when they asked, and I scanned straight for the middle one: a green and white striped butterfly: the first one I collected. I was sick for a week after killing and framing it. Killing it was one thing, yet sticking pins in it to flatten it out and waiting was a whole different field. I vomited daily, more in the mornings, however, the guilt soon faded.

The size of the collection impressed them (with it more-than-doubling since their last visit), yet Poppy had to fight back the tears after seeing the killing jar sat on the windowsill. She objected against me collecting them, citing how it's inhumane to kill them for my selfish wants. She hated it so much I used to hide the jar when she came in, and she shuffled her seat to face away from the butterflies.

I know what she means: killing butterflies *is* horrible. And I feel horrible for doing it, though the act of fury is brief. And they're beautiful. And they will always be beautiful, forever flying above my bed. Preserved forever. And that makes killing worth it.

Mother even joined us for twenty minutes at one point, before she went to bed. She *never* used to pop by and chat. Alexa forced her way into the room as well and introduced her personality in the most Alexa-way possible. We laughed and joked together, and everything I've ever wanted was in that moment.

In the worlds of *Doctor Who* or *Harry Potter*, I could capture memories and store them as paintings. These magical pictures offer much more than your usual photograph: they offer emotion. They offer life. If one of those magical photographers captured this moment, I would buy a million copies and hang one in every room in every house I'd ever visit. I'd look at the picture, it'd repeat the memory of Mother joking with The Flowers and Alexa over-acting to impress, and I'd be happy everywhere I went.

Mother helped with the bottles, and four was *just* enough. The Flowers took off about 1am, long after Mother had collapsed in her bed, and they all hugged and kissed me goodbye, before skipping down the street. They ricocheted their voices off every surface as they repeated the lyrics to a song I didn't know. After their drunken bodies fade into darkness, I pull out my phone and message Brad. "Hey, it's Lily x". Ten minutes elapsed while I waited for a response, yet nothing came.

I undress and tuck myself into bed, switching off my phone after one last check for a reply. The effects of the alcohol helping Planet Lilian swirl around the planets and stars floating on my ceiling.

Friday

I expected more nightmares throughout the night or the post-nightmare headache upon waking, yet neither of those things greet me. A rare morning of feeling great.

The sound of Duran Duran's *The Reflex*, sung by Mother, echoes throughout the house and into my ears as I walk down the stairs. As she came into view, her singing and dancing bring a smile to my face. I once got a video camera for Christmas, as I wanted to document everything, as Mother did for me during my early years. On Boxing Day, I was recording as I walked down the stairs and caught Mother singing along to Band Aid while preparing breakfast. She caught me recording, and we both fell into a pit of laughter. I wish I had a camera with me.

'Good morning, Sleepyhead,' she broke the lyrics to speak to me. 'Join me.' Her dancing isn't career-worthy, yet it provides her with an abundance of joy. And I feel that same joy as I join in; we dance through the greatest pop hits of the 1980s (Mother's favourite musical decade): Duran Duran (Planet Earth), Michael Jackson (Smooth Criminal), Bon Jovi (Living on a Prayer). We danced, we jived, we vogued, we laughed.

Mother and I haven't had a morning dancing session for years.

It started as a way of getting me out of bed early on weekends; Mother even bought a video game featuring dancing to help inspire me. However, after what happened, Mother's dancing became sporadic. Mine became retired. The laughter hid away with her emotions — the smile a prize to earn.

I would've danced the entire day away, though last night's alcohol didn't pair well with the spinning.

'So,' Mother says, resting against the counter, wiping the sweat from her forehead. 'Any plans for today?'

I don't have any plans. I *never* have plans. 'I'm not sure. I suppose I could do with a new hobby,' something which Mother has been trying to force on me for months. 'I might check out the new catalogue to see if anything takes my fancy.'

'That is wonderful news. Maybe it'll be something we can do together.' Mother lowers the volume on the radio, allowing speech without needing to shout.

I smile, my soul soothes. 'I'd like that.'

'Excellent, I'll fetch the catalogue,' she stops for a moment, 'if I can remember where I put it.' I laugh at her memory, and she takes off with a spring in her step. A few minutes pass before she returns and drops it in front of me. 'We could build models. Your grandfather used to love building model ships when I was younger. For hours he'd lock himself away in his model-room with a No Entry sign on the door.' The smile retreats. 'I hated that sign.' It's rare for Mother to voluntarily talk about her parents. 'I remember this one time,' a nervous laugh interrupts her, 'I must have been about 13. Your grandparents had gone out for a meal, leaving me alone in the house. I can't remember why I didn't go,' she trails off. 'Anyway, I was feeling mischievous, as you do at that age, and I snuck into your grandfather's model-room, and there they all were: The Titanic, HMS Victory, World War I and II ships and God-knows-what else. Each one put together with such skill and precision,' the awe in her voice screams as she speaks. 'And just being there gave me that feeling of rebellion, you know?' I nod. I don't know. 'Everything was going great until I found this ship I liked. You should have seen it, Lils, the painting, the design, it was amazing. And so, I picked it up.' Mother's eyes close. 'Then Tony knocked on the front door.' Mother *never* mentions Tony. Her voice bereft of awe and admiration. 'Because of how nervous I was being there, his knocking startled me, and I dropped the ship.' Her eyes slam shut. 'I was so scared. Your grandfather wasn't the nicest of people when someone crossed him, regardless of who you were. So, I took the ship and the pieces that fell and hid it in my room. I was a wreck every time I saw your grandfather, just waiting for him to notice.'

'What happened when he found out?' I regret asking straight away; I know what followed.

'I got the belt.' The pain returns to her face. 'He never even told me he knew about the ship to give me a chance to defend myself or apologise. He just came into the living room one day when your grandmother and I were watching telly, and he pulled me upstairs and closed the door.' Her eyes fighting the urge to close for good. 'Whenever I think back about that day, I can't help but think about your grandmother, you know? I,' her voice tries to retreat and silence. 'I screamed in agony. She must have heard. She never even asked me if I was okay.'

I rush to hug Mother. 'Thanks,' she whispers. Never has Mother felt so human. Never has Mother been the victim. Like me. I read about this incident in her diary when I found them in the attic last year. Afterwards, she locked herself away for two days, only ever coming out of her room when necessary. The whippings only ever happened a few times, with what happened with the ship marking the last whipping she received. Her father had no problem stripping her waist down and attacking her bottom. Her bottom still wears the scars. For everything Mother has done to me, she's never resorted to that.

She didn't live long with her parents afterwards, and for that time she never stepped foot inside the model-room. As we part, I look in her eyes and see all the pain she's gone through. Every argument, every punishment, every lecture ceases to be of any concern. *This* is my mother.

'Anyway,' she says, wiping the straggling tears away. 'I've probably got ironing or whatever that needs doing. Let me know what hobby you've chosen.' She takes off without allowing me much chance to offer any meaningful form of reply. I sit in silence; her past a sorrow tale, one I'm thankful to be a part of. She knows all of my horrific moments, so we're on an equal plane.

My mind switches from Mother to Brad, and I return to my room to check my phone. A little green text light greets my entrance and the possibilities flood my mind. What I didn't expect is *four* messages from him.

"Hey, it's Brad. Ha-ha."

"How are you?"

"I'm free later today if you fancy a drink or whatever?"

"Thanks again for comforting me last night. I needed it. X."

I've read many stories and heard so many clichés about butterflies in your stomach when you're in love. I've always assumed it to be some made-up Hollywood rubbish which somehow became a staple in romance fiction, yet I feel it. A flight of butterflies could flutter around inside of me. I could've been the last person he thought of before sleep. And the first after waking. Much like he has inhabited my mind, maybe I've inhabited his. I bring my phone to my chest, and it kisses my beating heart.

"Sorry, I had my phone off last night. That'd be nice. I'll try to sneak away around 2pm, if that's good for you? No worries if not." I hesitate on sending it, debating on whether to return the kiss. Thankfully, this isn't a conversation we're having in person, as texting allows me to filter out these fears and worries. I send without the kiss.

"2pm. See you then. X." My body lets out a small jump of happiness, but then it's enthused with annoyance at my not sending the kiss back.

'Hey,' Mother interrupts my jumping, which she doesn't question. 'Have you seen the ironing board?' I shake my head and offer a confused look. 'That's strange. Maybe it's in the basement.' We both freeze, the word a Russian Roulette gun debating on who gets the first pull of the trigger. The sounds of the world fade away to a blur, with just my racing heartbeat allowed presence in my ears. The saliva in my throat solidifies. My eyes burn from their inability to blink.

Seconds, minutes, hours, any length of time could've passed by the time my eyes break through the barrier and close, forcing the pieces of the world to return to their original place. 'Have you checked your room?'

'You know what, you're probably right. I guess I was in a world of my own. What am I like? Anyway, enjoy your day.' She retreats from my doorway, and I pull out Brad's message thread again and read over and over those three wonderful words: "See you then."

The old clock on the wall informs me three hours separate loneliness from happiness. Three hours until we meet again. Three hours until I have to lie to Mother about why I'm leaving the house. That thought tried to bring my spirits down, but I soldiered on and began the arduous journey of getting myself ready. Ready to meet Brad.

Today isn't the day to start a new hobby. Today's hobby is Brad. A hobby Mother and I cannot share. I skip along the hallway to the bathroom, receiving and ignoring a sceptical look from a groggy-looking Alexa, and instinctively run the bath.

The steam from the scalding water blocks my image from the mirrors, the slow rise of water intersperses with flashing images. Images of tears; of pain; of red. A sharp pain greets my body, and I turn off the water. Today I resist the bath's call. I spin around and instead turn on the shower.

The shower's quieter; quiet enough to hear Mother's humming to an old wartime song (every-now-and-then she spends entire days listening to war songs, I never ask why). Vague recognition comes during the chorus, yet not enough for me to place a name and artist next to it.

As Mother's volume decreases, the dripping water from the tap still attacks the pool. My eyes watch the water. Calling me to take a bath. I reach in to remove the plug, freeing the water from its trap, but it tries to pull my hand in. The hole showing teeth, ready and waiting for a taste of my wrist. The water its soldier holding me in place.

With unexpected strength, I force my hand back to dry land and fall backwards against the floor. The mouth sucks up the remaining water, and I de-clothe and take a shower.

I rarely close the cubicle door, but today it feels needed. I stand and watch the pouring of water from the showerhead soothe my naked body. The relaxing atmosphere keeps me longer than intended. Still, I feel amazing as I step out (helped by avoiding the gaze of the bath when drying).

As I open my wardrobe I'm confronted with another dilemma: is this a date? Is this two friends spending time together? Is this one guy wanting to thank someone for helping him out? Each scenario demands different attires. I choose nice-casual; a comfortable (not tight) pair of jeans and a humorous shirt (one with five commas in a row followed by a chameleon. I love shirts with humour on them, this being one of *many*, so hopefully he'll appreciate it, too). Mother doesn't question the outfits sprawled across my room (nor the fact she's seen me in at least three different shirts throughout the day), so for once, I don't have to lie. Yet. She ignored most of my dressing as she spent the afternoon locked away in her room doing the ironing (she found the ironing board in her room, where it always is).

Happy screams and excited children greet my eyes as I near the park earlier than we agreed. It must be the school holidays. Instead of school, the children are running; they are sliding, seesawing and laughing. But no children climbing. No children brave enough to conquer the building.

It doesn't take long for mothers to offer me suspicious looks. It's not helped by my nervous appearance (and a lone stranger is watching children play). If I were in their shoes, I'd be cautious, too. Despite my body urging me to leave, a young girl, no older than eight, catches my attention. She's playing on her own without a care in the world, and she has the cutest pigtails. And her smile is so infectious. Her parents must be so proud. I scan around to see who the lucky parent is and find a dark-haired lady who seems to be the closest fit, and she's acting in a way all too familiar to me: distant.

'Mummy, Mummy,' the girl shouts, and as I suspected, the dark-haired lady looks. 'Play with me.'

'In a minute, Gorgeous, I'm just talking with Mrs Carmichael.' The isolation and hairstyle resonate so much with me, and the careless mother compounds the similarities. It wasn't Mrs Carmichael, but it was always a Mrs Somebody which kept Mother away from playing with me. She's not even one of the mothers suspicious about my behaviour. I could be here ready and willing to abduct her child, raise her as my own and play with her in every park in every county we ever visit. The mother would plead and cry. She would say how much she loves and misses her daughter, and she'd do anything to have her back. Other mothers would describe me: they'd call me skinny; they'd note my casual clothes; they'd point out my hair, which falls to my shoulder blades; they'd call me odd. They'd know it was me who stole her; because they're protecting their children by watching me. This mother couldn't care less.

Brad arrives before my mind allows too much anger to seep through; seeing his face again calms me. I've let my mind exaggerate someone before, but I'm thankful this time it didn't: he's gorgeous, even without the moonlight glossing across his face. Brad went for the same approach as me: casual. Should this upset me? If he arrived dressed for a date, I could apologise and run and put on a dress. Arriving in casual clothing means he doesn't see this as a date.

'Hey,' he says, breaking the thoughts beginning to spiral in my mind. I smile back. I'm every girl I ever hated in high school. I watched them on breaks, the cute boy talked to them, and they'd smile without saying anything, do the stereotypical thing of playing with their hair (why do *I* want to do that?) and still get the boy. The boys weren't falling for their personalities; the robots didn't have any. I did. But they never fell for me. 'Friend of yours?' He again breaks my mind's thoughts.

'I'm sorry?'

'That woman; I saw you looking.'

'Oh, no she's not,' I don't need another figure like her in my life. 'Her daughter, that little girl there, reminds me of myself at her age. Although cuter, happier and more carefree.'

'Were you not cute, happy and-or carefree?'

'Well, Mother always told me I was cute, but parents have to say that, don't they?'

'Ain't that the truth. I was my mother's "Handsome little man" at that age. I think they called me that more than Brad.' The difference is my mother said it to be kind. Brad *is* handsome. That thought needs washing away before I say something stupid.

'Suppose we'll do the same should either of us have kids.'

'I won't. All the depression in the world, I believe, stems from kids having their over-inflated ego crushed. Parents build this mirage which makes the kid think they're irresistible because all their lives they're called cute or handsome, or whatever. But when it matters, when they need to be cute or handsome, it's revealed to be a lie and breaks their soul.' I've never been a follower of conspiracy theories or languishing every problem under the same umbrella, but he has a point. 'Unless you are cute or handsome, in which case you get the guy and girl and live happily ever after.' He smiles. Does he know he's the handsome guy in this scenario? Am I the girl to grant him the happy ever after?

'Possibly,' I concede. 'But that little girl *is* cute. So, if she were mine, I'd have no problem calling her it.'

'Anyway,' he rises like a soldier to his sergeant. 'Where shall we venture to, my lady?' He bows like a prince. He's cute. Am I *his* lady?

'How about the castle? It's been a while since I've walked around the grounds.' He accepts and offers out an arm to lead the way.

67

We walk in silence, each still trying to figure the other out. 'I like your shirt,' he remarks. 'It's funny.'

'Thanks,' a wave of satisfaction washes over me. 'I collect funny shirts. To me, they're better than plain old black with the company's name on.' A smile escapes.

'True. Although I'm a sucker for those plain old black shirts with the company's name on,' he unzips his jacket to reveal one.

'Sorry,' this time a giggle escapes. I love irony.

'So, what other better shirts do you have?' He's laughing, too. There's a sound which accompanies his soft laughter. I don't think I could ever be tired of hearing it.

We cross the road leading towards the castle's entrance. 'Well, I have a plain black shirt,' I leave the sentence hanging in the air. He's waiting for more. 'Although it has the word "You're" written across it.'

'So close to being a hypocrite.' That laughter sound again.

'Another which says, "I've CDO: It's like OCD, but the letters are the correct way" and another which has a picture of a cactus asking for hugs.' He's hanging on to every word I say. 'There's more, but, you know, spoilers.' I smile before realising what I've done. I've already decided there will be another meeting. The moment between the last word exiting my mouth and the first from his in response drags. Scenarios flood my head: one where he says this is just a thank you meet with no tomorrow; one where he kisses me and wants to see them all; one where he asks me how I'm feeling about us; one where he runs.

'I can't wait to see them.' Is there a tomorrow for us? 'Anyway, like you, I haven't been to the castle in years. I suppose I've always taken it for granted, with it being right here in our hometown, you know?' The sign leading in details every known reference of it and knowledge of its creation, even bragging about how a Shakespearean play features it as a location. Each town has to be famous for something, I suppose. We didn't create rugby. We don't have a haunted apple tree. We aren't the birthplace of Olympic heroes. We have a decrepit castle. It stands and waits for time to finish the job; an old guard whose career winds.

'Yeah, same,' we cross the bridge and enter the main castle grounds. 'So, which one first?' West Drive's castle is square in design with four round dungeon-like rooms in each corner, at varying levels of life. One building stands taller and thinner than the rest, which I assume to be the watchtower, two have chamber-like prisons in them (prisons or bedrooms, perhaps) and the fourth is barely serviceable as anything more than rubble. Whatever ruined this castle, that corner took the brunt of it.

Our first port of call is the watchtower, and we climb up the steep steps to the top. With the castle being at the edge of West Drive, standing on the highest point of the castle allows for a beautiful view of everything. West Drive, outside this little industrial revolution built area, is a pretty town; rivers and fields protecting us from all sides adds to its secluded beauty. Parks and shops and houses and restaurants and schools are visible from this spot. Back at my lowest, I often came here and watched over the town throughout the evening. I was Batman, without the crime-fighting ability. I'd look at the terraced houses full of families living their lives, unaware of me watching. Protecting. Crying.

In the park, the little girl with pigtails still runs in circles. The mother still talking to Mrs Somebody. So much for 'In a minute.' I glance over at the terraced houses and wonder if Mother's parents are still there. They must be ageing heavily. Perhaps they still work. Perhaps they're returning home with their shopping. Perhaps they've moved, and I'm looking over at nothing more than a shadow of a life I've never known. Back at my lowest, I watched out for the older people who walked in and around the terraced houses, hoping to spot anyone who resembled Mother, but I never found them. I wouldn't have done anything about it even if I did. They wouldn't have understood. They never did with Mother.

Brad wears the same expression as me, and I can't help but wonder if he imagines his mother still alive and walking throughout the town. We watch the world in silence.

'Good day for it,' he eventually says. The weather has blessed our friendship by providing some much-needed sun in an otherwise damp spring week. 'So,' he turns to me. 'Tell me about yourself.'

'Honestly, there's not much to tell.'

'Well that's just not true, everyone's got a story.'

'Well, I enjoy reading.'

'Fair enough. I'm not much of a reader, although I enjoy the occasional Stephen King.'

'He's okay, but I prefer female writers: Mary Shelley, the Bronte sisters, Jane Austen, Mary Ann Evans, George Eliot. They're all wonderful.'

'George Eliot?' His lack of knowledge is charming. 'I think I studied one of the Bronte sisters, Emma or Emily is it? Wuthering Heights with Heathcliff and the woman whose name I've forgotten.'

'Catherine. Yeah, Emily Bronte,' we share a laugh. That cute sound again. 'I suppose my favourite male author is Edgar Allan Poe.' He nods, but it's there in his eyes; he has no idea who Edgar Allan Poe is. Well, he would if I were to mention The Tell-Tale Heart, or The Pit and the Pendulum, or The Masque of the Red Death. I've always loved 19th-century literature; when everyone in primary school brought various instalments of the Harry Potter franchise for reading, I was engrossing myself in Pride and Prejudice. When The Hunger Games series became popular, I absorbed myself in Jane Eyre. When the Twilight sage came around, I was onto Frankenstein, or the Modern Prometheus. I was always the one to complain if the teachers quoted a scene from a movie adaptation rather than the source material. I would've studied 19th-century literature had I gone to university. A world of books I'm yet to discover. Instead, my knowledge is restricted to West Drive's classical section at the library.

An old English teacher introduced me to Edgar Allan Poe (as the teacher cited him as his favourite). He gave me his copy of The Black Cat, and I loved it. I've not since mastered all of Poe's work, but I've gone over the major releases.

'He wrote The Tell-Tale Heart,' I offer.

'Yeah, sure, I know,' he tries to play it off, but we both know. The conversation enters a lull, our minds scrambling for what to say. Maybe *this* is why personalities didn't matter to those high school girls. They'd smile, flutter their eyes, get the dick and move on to the next. They didn't need to concern themselves with conversational lulls between people who want to care for each other. 'Oh, I forgot to ask,' there's excitement in his voice as he defeats the lull. 'How was your evening last night with your friends?'

'It was great, thanks,' my heart tingles at the thought of him remembering things I say. 'We drank, a lot, and talked, just like old times.'

'Ace. My friends and I never have evenings like that anymore,' sadness replaces excitement. 'I suppose it happens, though. Some have kids, some got married, others off hooking up with girls in clubs.' The last remark forces my eyes shut, trying to hide the image of him meeting other girls in clubs. 'I suppose there's always one who gets left behind, who wants unique experiences from the world.'

With The Flowers, I was that friend. I couldn't go to clubs and meet guys like Ivy. I couldn't play sports like Rose. 'What experiences do you want?' My mind fretting over his answer.

'To travel.' The answer I didn't want. His eyes scan over the town. 'I've lived all my life here; I've never even gone abroad for a holiday.' A line straight from my life. 'I don't know; I guess I want to see the world before I settle down, you know?' I nod. I know.

'Do you feel trapped here?' I do.

'I don't know if I'm trapped or scared. I live with my aunt, and she always tells me to apply for jobs across the country and move if I've to, but I always lie to her and say I'm not getting interviews when I'm not even applying. I've got nothing keeping me here, yet I cannot leave.' He's kept here for me. I'm kept here for him.

My mind floats off to a world where destiny presents itself and reveals it forced him to stay here, to live out his life with me. The clang of wedding bells and the screams of newborn children. Him saying I do. Him making love to me. All thanks to destiny. My eyes scan over his perfect body, adding colour to the world my mind is creating. Dialogue from our first real date, the romantic way he proposes, his soft voice comforting me on those dark days, how handsome he would look in a tight suit. His hands make sure I'm safe. All thanks to destiny. By the time my mind returns to my body, he's nearing the end of a story and laughs. Despite being clueless, I return the laugh. Anything those lips of his do I would copy. Anything they say I would accept.

'Shall we go to a different chamber?' He asks, and we set off towards one of the dungeon-like rooms. 'So,' he starts as we reach the railings protecting us from falling. 'Dungeon or bedroom?'

'Dungeon?' My voice confused.

'I suppose. After all, it's not big enough for a king-sized bed for King Edward. However, where else would he sleep? I can't imagine him building this castle and kipping down Dolphin Street with the peasants, can you?' He's so charming.

'Well, there's no safe way in or out,' I raise my finger to my chin, the best detective caricature I could muster. 'So, it must be a dungeon.'

'True, but the drop is what, only eight-feet? A tall person with a solid jump could escape.' His detective caricature betters mine.

'Perhaps it was a kitchen, and we're both wrong.' We both smile, and I make my way around the railing covering the circular room. 'Soldiers had to eat, and Wong Palace won't be open for a good 700 years.' Mother and I would have a takeaway from Wong Palace every Friday night, but like my Thursday meetings with The Flowers, that fell away.

'I love Wong Palace. If King Edward had any sense, he would've ensured a Chinese was nearby.' He follows my direction and begins circling the railing, his hand gliding across the steel. 'It could've been where they kept their livestock.' The thought of a room full of chickens and other animals forced to sit and wait for their death adds a damaging aroma to the otherwise healthy atmosphere.

'That would be cruel.' I should make a joke about them being free range or something, but it's too sad. 'Fancy walking along the footpath?'

The footpath is a forest-like area next to the castle which leads to a small shore. It's one of the best places in West Drive to go for a walk. In the mornings, dozens of dog walkers enjoy the view. The river to the north, the castle to the east and beautiful trees surrounding south and west made it a special treat for me as a child to come here (it was a 'special' treat as Mother knew the second we began we'd have to commit to walking for hours because as a child I wanted to see everything).

'So, tell me about your childhood with your mother,' I say as we take off. He doesn't want to speak about her, but she's just passed away, and it could help.

'Well, we were close when I was a child,' there's a real fight in him to carry on. 'She was an actual parent back then.'

'What about your father?'

'Just some loser who knocked her up and vanished. It was around the time I started high school that Mother started acting strange. She shouted more, closed herself off in her room. I needed to get away; I needed a mother-figure, not the empty vessel she became. I don't hate her; I mean that, I never did, I just hated what she became. And she never got better.' His eyes long for freedom. 'She was sick. She wasn't a maniac; she just went a little mad sometimes.'

'We all go a little mad sometimes.'

'Anyway, there's no benefit in reliving it. So, changing the subject ever so slightly if you don't mind, what's the worst thing you've seen down these woods?'

While it's beautiful, it has a somewhat seedy reputation. The car park is quite a hassle to get into, meaning police officers wouldn't waste their time even trying to stop anything from happening. Which meant people would meet for sex, deal drugs, drink underage or anything else illegal. That's also the reason so many dog walkers come in the morning. Beauty without sin.

'I've seen people having sex, but that's not rare, is it?'

'I can top that; I saw two guys doing it once. They both put their hoods up and legged it when they saw me. Guess they weren't ready to reveal themselves to the world.'

'I remember one evening when I begged Mother to let me come here; I cleaned the house to the best of my ability, I even cleaned her car, but she point-blank refused. Funny how as children we think they're punishing us when they know the truth.'

It is a perfect day for it. It may be my imagination, but the birds appear as they do in those fairy tales; hopping around in the trees making sounds, serenading our friendship.

'I'm glad I've met you,' he breaks the birds' serenade. 'To be honest, I've needed a friend.' I smile, too embarrassed to respond. His eyes copy the actions of mine and etch my face in his mind forever. This is one of those moments on my death bed where I'll look back on and think happy thoughts: the birds chirping, the soft wind whistling, the trees dancing and the sun shining. Everything is perfect. He takes my left cheek in his right hand, leans in and kisses me.

Elation turns sour. The wind and the trees go silent — the birds screech. The river crashes against the shore to help. Without thinking, without realising, I slap him as hard as my body allows, knocking him from the bench to the floor, and I run home. I'm speedy when I need to be, and it doesn't take long to lose him. I can hear him calling out. He wants to explain, to calm me, to stop me going to the police. But I don't want to listen. He begs and begs until his voice is but a faint sound in the background.

The castle is so close to home it doesn't take too long for me to return, but knowing Mother, she would be cross if she sees me like this, so I hide in the back garden behind the bins. Mother cannot see me like this. Not again. Not anymore. I assume the foetal position and cry. My breathing heavy. My life racing.

My phone buzzes and I know it's him. I fling the phone across the garden, and my teeth clatter against each other. He's no longer Brad: he's The Teacher. Floods of visions fill my mind of those dark days. I slap my head, harder and harder, hoping to turn my brain off for just a second of peace. Peace doesn't come; just a merry dance between the physical and emotional pain.

By the time my mind settles into some form of normality, more clouds fill the sky. Time once again ceasing to flow on its natural and linear path. I retrieve my phone, careful to make sure Mother doesn't spot me and notice three messages from Brad.

"I'm sorry." They always are.

"I didn't mean to startle you. I thought we were . . . doesn't matter. Please don't hate me." I never could.

"Please talk to me. I'm worried."

Over an hour elapsed between the first and last message, hammering home how long I've been out here. I sneak out of the garden and make my way to the front door, dust myself down and ready to pretend to be normal. Mother cannot suspect a thing.

No chance of sneaking to my room. No chance of crying into my pillow. Mother stands in line with the front door, washing the dishes.

'Oh, there you are, I was getting worried.'

'Sorry, I got distracted; and time just got away from me. And-'

'No need to apologise, you're home and safe, that's all that matters.'

Alexa comes hopping down the stairs with her hair up sporting one of my pretty orange dresses. She's one of those girls who suits her hair being up. 'Hey, Sis,' she stops in front of me. 'I found this in your cupboard, I hope you don't mind me borrowing it,' she does a twirl to reveal how well it fits. I should have burned that dress, to stop it ever manifesting itself back into my life.

'Of course, it's too small for me, anyway.' She thanks me and bounces off into the living room, the sound of adverts appearing within seconds. Neither Mother nor Alexa knows that dress' history. Neither Mother nor Alexa *will* know that dress' history. I peek into the kitchen and grab a bottle of water from the fridge.

'Water?' Mother knows when something is wrong.

'It's hot outside, and I fancy water for a change.' Part of that is true. I take a mouthful of the cold liquid but spit it back after seeing the bottle labelled "Poison".

'Lily,' Mother scorns. 'What the hell? I've just cleaned this floor.' She hasn't, even I can tell that, but she loves adding extra layers of guilt. 'Are you okay?'

'Yeah, I'll clean it, sorry, I just, never mind.' I grab the towel and wipe away the mess from the floor — Hill Springs, not Poison.

'No need to apologise. Clean it up, and we'll say nothing more.'

I turn the heating on for an hour; despite it being warm outside our house is always freezing. We spend so much money on heating. A plumbing issue never fixed. And never will be. It always made visitors confused when they walked in wearing shirts and shorts to be in a house with the radiators on. When I was younger, I rearranged my bedroom, so my bed was right next to the radiator and I'd spend days lying in bed naked with my skin pressed against the warmth. Vengeful air, restricted from the radiator's warmth, would greet me daily when I finally left my bed's comfort. There were days I was so afraid of the air I'd hold my bladder in for hours. It wasn't healthy, but it kept me safe in the comfort of my bed.

I arrive in my room, undress down to my underwear, position myself close to the radiator and wait for its warmth. The pillow a shoulder to catch my tears. "I'm okay." I message Brad. My eyes finally allowed peace.

The screams of Isabel Emrich's In the Moment brings me out of my sleep. The sweat from the nightmare soaking my pillow. The clock informs me two hours have passed; the need for sleep beforehand fighting the headache which has followed.

A green light flashes from my phone. Fighting back the fear, I reach over and see eight texts and four missed calls from Brad. They occupy my front screen, but my mind switches to Mother and how she will react to hearing my phone ringing so much. Its ring fires again, and this time I answer.

'Oh, thank God,' Brad says with relief in his voice. 'I've been so worried.' I can't speak. I don't even know what I'd say if I could. 'Look, I'm sorry, please don't hate me.' The arsenal of messages on my phone all point out his sorrow. 'If I overstepped, please just tell me.' My knees bang together, my body ignoring the pain of bones colliding. 'Lily, please.'

'It's okay,' I cave. 'I'm fine.' There's no conviction in my voice.

'Can we meet?' My body shudders at the thought, but I resist it and accept. Too many times I run away. Too many times I've been too weak to fight back. This time I'm going to confront my demon.

Mother is mid-conversation with Alexa as I walk downstairs. 'Hey, Sleepyhead,' Mother mocks. 'We're thinking of going to the cinema tonight. You in?' I nod, wearing the cheerful face of a stranger. 'Are you okay? You look a little pale.'

'I've just woke with a headache. I'm going to walk it off; I won't be too long.'

'Fair enough, perhaps fresh air will do you good.'

My walk to meet Brad at the castle, who has waited there since I left him, is strange. My body aches to see his face, but my mind fears his actions.

'Hey,' he stands as I arrive, but I come to a halt and stop him from speaking.

'I've been mistreated.'

'What-'

'Please.' My eyes close as my head tilts to the floor. 'A few years ago, someone abused me. I'm sorry, but I guess it's left a bigger scar than I thought. I didn't mean to offend you.' I open my eyes; he's eager to hug me as a way of apologising, but I wrap my arms around my stomach as a way of warning against contact. 'It's nothing personal-'

'No, no, it's me who should apologise. I shouldn't have been so forward. I like you, and I misread the situation. But if you're not ready, that's fine with me. I promise I won't push it.' Now he's in control of this *relationship*.

'You're better off walking away. I'm a mess and not worth the trouble.' More control surrendered to him. This isn't me copying those silly high school girls who put themselves down for the lad to pick them up, this was me being honest. For once. He deserves better than me.

'Don't be silly,' seriousness replaced by a comical sternness. 'You were there for me as a friend, so I'm going to be here for you.' I look to the ground, avoiding his gaze. Maybe Mother was right about men. 'Can we please start over and ignore how stupid I was?' His voice vulnerable. He needs a friend, I'm aware of that, but I can't help but enjoy his begging. For *me*. For *my* friendship. Maybe I'm more like those stupid high school girls than I realised. I nod and raise my eyes to meet his, as if for the first time. 'Hi, I'm Brad, nice to meet you,' he offers out a hand to shake.

'I'm Lily,' I accept his hand. Neither of us speaks, allowing laughter its presence. Starting over brings back the floods of feelings of longing on my part. For *him*. For *his* friendship. 'I can't stay out too late, I'm going the cinema with my mother and sister, girly-family evening, you know?' His face no longer the villain, but the prince. 'But maybe tomorrow we can do something?' Now I'm the one begging. Ceasing more control of this *relationship* to him. Perhaps I like it that way.

'I'd like that,' his eyes study mine. He's far more assured when speaking than me. He's not fighting back waves of emotions and secrets, ensuring every word is the correct one without revealing too much.

'Well then, until tomorrow.' I smile like an idiot (I *am* all those high school girls) and back away from him. He mouths goodbye back, and I turn and walk away. I can't hear his feet moving, and I imagine all the silly romantic pictures of him watching me walk away; which brings on itself nerves (falling on the grass could cause embarrassment our *relationship* is too young to overcome). I take one last longing look back, half-wave and disappear behind the castle's walls.

Brad isn't the enemy. Especially not now. Not now I'm safe inside *my* castle. While Edward's castle is metres away, I've always considered this house to be my castle. Nobody ever breaks in. Like vampires, they need permission. The garden a moat, warning potential wrongdoers about this land. The front door's locks the guards, the first line of defence. The peephole a periscope, to watch the outside world. The walls hide our strategies and secrets away from the enemy's view. Then there's Mother: the queen. Like chess, the queen is more useful than the king; she is more agile, more offensive, more ruthless and more valuable (the queen wins the battles, the king loses them). *My* mother would do anything to protect me within these walls. If she hurts a would-be intruder, we've won. If he hurts me, we've lost.

I stand by the door for a couple of minutes, waiting for any intruders, but none come. And my body relaxes.

I walk into the living room where Mother and Alexa watch nonsense programmes before Mother mutes it and turns to me. 'We've had a look, and there's a new sci-fi film showing tonight; I know how much you love sci-fi films. And Alexa says it looks quite good.' I don't love sci-fi films; once I begged and pleaded to watch one in the cinema, begs and pleas which went unacknowledged, but that aside, I've never taken to them. 'We'll go the chippy on the way home. Make a right girl's night of it.' Alexa sits like a dog waiting for the leads to come out after hearing it's going for a walk. Waiting for my say-so.

'That sounds lovely,' I respond, relaxing Mother and Alexa.

It has been so long since we've done anything as a family. Over the last year, Mother's behaviour has deteriorated. It's no longer a surprise to come downstairs in the morning to see her watching the television with a vodka on the rocks in one hand and a cigarette in the other, judging and berating everyone. I received many of those same judgements. She'd apologise, sometimes, in the afternoon, and blame the alcohol and sleep depravity, but I knew she always meant it. When she called me ugly, that wasn't just the vodka talking. When she called me weird, that wasn't a tired mind making

90

stuff up. The Monday-Lady feels the same way. I know they talk about me. They tell me they don't, but they do. The Monday-Lady also thinks I'm weird and ugly. And weak.

The evening was perfect.

The film itself was quite boring (the plot centred around a female robot who fell in love with a male human in a time where robots were revolting against their owners), but I suppose the quality of the film didn't matter. The company did.

On our way home we stopped by our favourite chippy (although the 'Under new ownership' sign bragging in the window annoyed us) and chatted away as mother and daughters through the night. Mother told many stories of my childhood, ones I knew of but couldn't quite remember, such as the time I climbed a tree while out playing and went too far. Mother has always said my fear of heights didn't exist before I climbed that tree. I don't remember too much about it, but Mother said I was stuck there for over two hours. She banned me from climbing trees afterwards. That rule I accepted.

It's a memory we all look back on and laugh as a trio, but the urine-soaked, frightened girl weeping from the sky was no joke. We even reminisced about when Gnarls Barkley's song *Crazy* topped the charts, and how excited I was. She told me I once started singing it in the middle of a supermarket, without a care for the eyes of judging people. I even created a dance to accompany the song, which ended in me spinning around, my pigtails act like a propeller readying itself for lift-off. The three of us attempted the dance routine. We failed.

I bathe in all the stories she tells, all the jokes she makes, all the anecdotes, all the laughter. I am her daughter. And she is my mother.

As a lull creeps into the night, I excuse myself and check on my phone. Seven messages from Brad. Granted, a couple were correcting some spelling mistake, but that didn't matter. He messaged me *seven* times. I reply with a smiley face and hide my phone away; tonight, I'm not Brad's Lily, I'm Mother's daughter.

'What was I like as a kid?' Alexa asks as I return to the room. A question which chills Mother and me on the spot. Each of us unable to answer. 'Any stories? I don't remember too much.' The sound of the television fades, the light dims; Mother and I engulfed in silence. 'Do we have any pop?'

'Yes, of course,' Mother says, returning senses to our bodies. I offer to get us all a drink and near collapse on the kitchen floor.

You can tell when Mother's done the shopping because all the food and drinks are off-branded (Koki Kola cans and Swix chocolate bars and Gerry and Benjamin ice cream). Mother let me go shopping once, and finally, our home was not full of Best Price or Supermarket's Own, but actual proper brands. Mother grounded me when she saw the bill.

'Do we have any wine, Lils?' Mother calls out.

'No,' I return, three cans of Koki Kola in hand. 'We drank it all last night. But pop is fine.' Pop isn't fine. Pop doesn't help you forget.

'Come on,' she stands, rejecting the can. 'You and I need wine.' She gulps down the last of her vodka and cola, slams the glass and leads us to the door.

'I will never say no to wine,' I joke as we grab our coats. The Monday-Lady hates me drinking wine, so much so I used to steal Mother's vodka when she listened to her. I hated vodka, but I needed that kick.

Mother would often drive everywhere, but tonight we walk. We walked to the cinema, the chippy and the shop. It's nice, it's sweet. And Mother's amazed by all the sites she passes (the park, which brought on a story about me falling from the top of the slide, which resulted in the scar I have just below my right eye; the castle, which brought on a story about an evening we heard a voice coming from one chamber and ran away screaming; the terraced houses, which brought on a story of the shenanigans she and Tony would cause).

As we walk under the bridge and come into view of the shop, Mother grinds to a halt. 'What's the matter, Mother?' I ask, my voice trembling.

'There's a *man* working.' We all look towards the shop; it's the same man as yesterday. There's a pretty girl in the shop buying stuff, and that predator is no doubt planning the same conversational assault he gave me.

'Yeah, he's new.' Something I shouldn't have said.

'Lily, tell me this is not the person who served you yesterday?'

'I didn't talk to him, Mother, I promise. I bought my wine and left. He said nothing to me. I'm sorry, I'm sorry. Honestly-'

'It's fine, there's no need to apologise. But you shouldn't have gone in there,' her hand clenches. 'You have no idea what *he's* like. *He* could be a serial killer, for all you know, and you walked right into *his* chamber. I taught you better than that.' Such venom in her words.

'I was quick. I needed wine. I didn't speak, I promise. Honest, Mummy, I'm sorry.' Her stature towers over mine, despite our similar height. I'm no longer an adult, no longer her equal. My whimpering attracts the attention of passers-by, none of whom want to help. People detest the freak. Freaks should be in cages. Locked away. Their precious life protected from them. 'I'm sorry, I'm sorry,' I repeat as if broken.

'It's fine, there's no need to apologise, you're safe.' Her words break the record I was stuck playing. 'Right,' her entire demeanour switches. 'Let's walk to the other shop.'

Neither Alexa, who remained quiet and ashamed of me, nor I objected to walking another ten minutes to find the nearest shop. The walk aided by an uncomfortable shadow, a memory of my behaviour. My voice frightened to say anything, for fear of repercussion. Mother often silences me. After the incident, I pointed out a good looking man on the television and the venom she spat belittled me so much I locked myself away for a week. We arrive at the store and Mother scans to ensure only women were manning the store.

'Plenty of customers, too,' I point out, hoping to prove she's taught me well.

'Word of advice, Lily: never, and I mean *never*, rely on the kindness of strangers.' Her voice quietens to not grab anyone's attention. 'Unless there's a gun to their head or a reward in it for them, they would sooner you bleed to death in the middle of the aisle than help. Never trust anyone. You too, Alexa.' Alexa nods and agrees, but I still hope humanity *would* help me in such circumstances. Despite all the evidence to the contrary.

The shop had one male customer (an elderly gentleman), and we circled one aisle three times before he left and allowed us to visit the wine section. We bought three bottles and left without any aggravation.

Back home, we resume our positions, and the stories carry on. 'Tell us about your childhood,' Alexa asks.

About three years ago, I snuck into the attic, despite Mother's warnings and my fear of heights, and stumbled across a bunch of old diaries Mother used to keep. She's never even mentioned them, so it was a surprise to find them. I borrowed them, hid them in my room and over the next few weeks I read them all. They detailed her life, the ups and downs, from twelve to twenty, when I guess she stopped (or they're hidden somewhere else). The woman in the diaries someone I wanted to meet; much happier than the woman I lived with.

'When I was your age, I was best friends with a guy called Tony; we were thick as thieves.' She's mentioning him again. 'Your grandfather didn't care much for us, because we were always so loud. But he knew Tony was a good guy deep down. His family moved in when he was about seven, I think I was about six. From there on we were inseparable.'

I've never met Tony; Mother's contact with him faded before I was born, and she only brought him up in anger. If it wasn't for me reading her diary, I wouldn't have had a clue how close friends they were. All the stuff they did, especially in their teenage years, were naughty, but in a cute way. They'd ask each parent for money, or they'd stay out past curfew but within earshot.

Much like with The Flowers, I became invested in Mother's diaries and the stories they told. Every adventure they went on, from Tony running into a clothesline and hurting his neck to them bike riding to a strange part of West Drive and getting lost, I was there. In my draw, hidden at the back, are pictures of Mother, me and Tony, all holding hands and all playing. They weren't just a twosome; we were a threesome. In my teenage years, I clamoured for a friend as good as Tony was to Mother. A friend as wild and adventurous as Tony. A friend who respected me as much as Tony respected Mother. At first, anyway.

'You two would've liked Tony,' Mother says. 'He was a good kid; he just went a little mad.'

Mother's demeanour shows the stories of her youth are over, and neither Alexa nor I object.

We watched rubbish on the television, drank wine and chatted until 2am. She never brought up Tony again. She mentioned a few things she used to do with her high school friends, but her diaries never explained what happened to them.

'What's that sound?' Tiredness screeches out of my voice. 'Like, wind? Or something.'

'Didn't I tell you?' Mother sounds surprised. 'We've got a little crack in the window.' I open the curtains to see a chipped pane of glass. The crack but an ant on the glass; seeping wind in at a rate contradictory to its size; muting the sounds of the outside world. 'Is that the sound?'

'Yeah,' I reply. 'There's a bit of wind coming through; we should get that looked at. Any idea what happened?'

'No idea. I came in here yesterday and there it was.'

The whistling of the wind tickles my ear as it squeezes through the crack en route to invading our home. It's a pretty sound. Then it speaks. 'You know what you've done.'

I recoil back, confusing Mother and Alexa, but they don't press on for an explanation. The sound of the wind still whistling in the background.

The three bottles of wine didn't last the night (despite Mother being a vodka drinker, she was helping put away the wine). A lack of energy and a spinning room resorted in us all deciding to sleep on the couches. Mother grabs a blanket and wraps it around me as the room fades into night.

A baby's cry wakes me to a cold, empty room. A pendulum ticking away. The baby is upstairs, and without thinking, I rise. The cry is young, incredibly young, perhaps the first cry it's ever let out. But it's scared. Frightened. Alone.

I creep upstairs and listen for which room it comes from: Alexa's. Her room is empty, except her bed and a copy of Van Gogh's Chair. The cry louder, begging for my help, but there's no baby. The pendulum's ticking rising in volume, following me upstairs. The cry's in the walls. I search the wall, trying to find any way of rescuing the baby, but the pendulum's ticking catches up to me. Each tick of the pendulum spaced between a quick cry. Tick. Cry. Tock. Cry. Tick. Cry. Tock. Cry.

The sounds force me out of the room, slamming the door shut.

'Get out of my head,' I scream, rocking myself on the landing floor. A creek from behind me welcomes me into my room, and I follow without thinking.

Everything's out of focus in my room. Everything bar the mirror. I walk to it, and I'm greeted with no reflection. Just my room, devoid of life. I wave my hand from side-to-side in a fruitless bid to bring my shadow back, but nothing appears.

'Hello?' I call out as loud as possible. 'Is anyone there?' I'm shaking the mirror.

The cry returns, as does the pendulum's ticking, each watching me. I lift the mirror from the wall and see a body in the distance, going into Alexa's room. The crying following it. The pendulum's ticking following that.

I walk, mirror in hand, angled to see what my eyes cannot, to Alexa's room. I open the door, and the mirror shows me a girl holding a baby. Her dark hair covers her face. She's singing a lullaby to soothe the crying baby. She walks towards the door, passes me and goes to my room.

As she returns to the doorway, she looks up straight at me. The girl *is* me. 'You know what you've done,' she says.

'You know what you've done,' the baby says.

The pendulum's ticking stops as darkness takes over.

Saturday

I wake panting. Mother's heavy breathing reassures me she's still asleep and unaware of the latest rough night. The nightmares have become far too regular, with their meanings not decipherable by websites proclaiming to understand them.

I walk to the kitchen, fighting every step against the cold in my bed-shorts and bra, and down a bottle of water in one go. My stomach roars with delight with every gulp. I make sure Mother's still sleeping before going upstairs to check on my phone: three more messages from Brad. They're all sweet; checking how I am and what I was up to. I hope he doesn't think I've been ignoring him; I just needed last night. I reply with another smiley face and an instant response asks me to dinner this evening. A dread sets over me, but I accept. He doesn't specify whether it's a date, an apology, friendship or a meal goodbye. But I know the only way to find out what the future holds is by attending, even if it's against my body's better judgement.

On my way back downstairs, I called into Alexa's room; the nightmare's fading away from my memory, but the image of her door brings about recognition. Her walls decorated with various pop singers and film posters (something Mother banned me from having at her age). Alexa has always stated they're to cover up the babyish wallpaper, and nothing more. I like the wallpaper.

As I return to the living room a scornful Mother stands and waits. 'And where have you been?' She demands.

'I-I just went to the-the toilet.'

'That's funny,' she walks closer, again towering over me. 'I didn't hear a flush.'

'I didn't want to-to flush with it being so-so loud in the morning, and-and wake everyone.'

'And I suppose you didn't want to wash your hands for the same reason?' She doesn't need to inspect my hands to know they're bone-dry. She is right, though; our taps are notorious for being squeaky (Mother always says warm water against cold pipes causes it, or something). Richard once knocked on our door and complained to Mother about the taps first-thing in the morning, and she banned me from using them until at least midday out of respect.

'I'm sorry, I went to put my phone on charge, too.'

'Why? Why was your first thought after waking to put your phone on charge? Who are you expecting a message from?'

'Nobody, I swear, I promise. I'm sorry. I just-just didn't charge it last night, and I-I wanted to make sure it-it was ready, just in case, you know? I'm not texting anyone, I promise. I'm sorry.'

'No need to apologise, I just don't appreciate lying. I'm your mother, you can be open with me about anything.' No, I can't. 'And I'll always respect what you have to say.' No, you won't. 'You don't need to lie your way through life.' I do. Like you. I offer a smile, and her body shrinks back to its normal size. 'So, what are your plans for today?' She opens the curtains and lets life brighten the room, which would have remained consumed by darkness otherwise. 'Did you think of a hobby? You know your uncle played a competitive card game; we could give that a shot?' She's never told me about Kevin, her brother. From what I found out in her diaries, he's twenty years older than her and moved out while she was a baby. He'd come home once a month and spend the night, but they never had that brother-sister relationship.

'That sounds fun.' More lies. 'But they can be quite expensive. I didn't find anything,' such shame in my voice. 'But I'll keep looking.'

'There's no rush, you're only young. Do you want any breakfast?'

I shake my head, knowing any food will not sit well with last night's alcohol consumption (the water is trying its best to fight away the urge to vomit as we speak). 'Maybe later.'

As the last of Mother's beautiful blonde hair disappears into the kitchen's lair, I slump back into the couch and turn on the television. After I left school, I'd spend hours scrolling from one channel to another in search of something to watch, anything which could fill half-an-hour of my life. Mother initially accepted the chaotic channel surfing (as long as she had her vodka she didn't care), but even she had a limit. 'Stop *fucking* changing the channel,' she spit out one day. 'You should have *something* you like by now.'

It upset me, but I understood her anger; I'd feel the same. Not long afterwards I stopped watching television altogether and started reading more seriously. It started as a way to be closer to Mother, who was obsessed with child abuse biographies, but my love of books as a kid soon resurfaced and I read every day. Their worlds were so fascinating to me, and I'd picture myself with them on their journeys (not *as* one of the characters, but *with* them). I adventured with Alice. I was Elizabeth Bennet's confident. I befriended Frankenstein's monster. I stood alongside Harry, Ron and Hermione in the Battle of Hogwarts. I never changed the outcome, I just wanted to be in their world. Not mine.

The idea of me being with them stems from Mother, who read bedtime stories and always replaced a lesser-used character with someone called Lily (it took me far too long to realise not every story featured a Lily in it). But I loved hearing the heroes fighting alongside Lily.

Once again, though, I'm channel surfing. The cartoons offer a poor selection, the daytime reality shows annoy me. Maybe the rubbish is to encourage children to stay in school? Or parents to go to work? Who wants to watch someone reveal the results of a pregnancy test? Who would even go on that show? Not even an hour passes before I give up with the television's pathetic offerings and head upstairs and relax.

Mother wears a gentle laugh as I tell her about my plan to relax; she has this attitude of 'Once you're up, you're up,' but today that lecture doesn't come, and I trudge my way upstairs.

A quick check reveals Brad's only sent one follow-up message (should I be happy or sad?), but I mute my phone without replying and stare at Planet Lilian filling the ceiling. Planet Lilian sits between Jupiter and Saturn, but there's a secret path which allows humanity to send rocket ships to it. Its inhabitants live beautiful lives. Its inhabitants are free from violence, abuse, anger and madness. I told Mother about Planet Lilian and she said I'd invented a planet full of robots with no emotion or freedom, but she was wrong. They were free from worries. Freedom I'm jealous of.

My body floats away from my bed and I'm transported to Planet Lilian, where I assume my place at the head of the President's table.

'Welcome back, your Majesty,' a soldier says with a bow. I permit him to continue speaking. 'During your absence, not a single smile has dropped. However, Earth has plans to send an Earthling here to propose sharing the land.'

'Inform them we will not entertain their ideas.' The Presidents applaud. 'Earthlings are selfish creatures, who will want a deal to benefit them, not us.'

I excuse myself and walk through Wildewater, the capital city of Lilyland (the biggest region on the planet) and admire its beauty. Buildings shine an array of colours, each reflecting different stars and planets which rotate around the sky. The city's picture enhanced by a sea of smiling faces. Not an insult in sight.

As I reach the city's main park (I accept we copied Central Park's layout for it), a grating noise from the red siren at the heart of the planet sounds off. People rush around in panic as the sound roars. The two-minute warning in full effect. Two soldiers come rushing towards me and forgo the customary bow.

'I'm sorry, your Majesty, but we have reasons to believe an attack is being planned against you.'

'An attack? How is this so?'

'Yes, ma'am. And the attacker bears your reflection.'

The soldiers and the planet melt away, ejecting me from my sanctuary. Back to my bedroom.

I wake two hours later to a note from Mother informing me she and Alexa have gone out. It doesn't specify where, but I'm grateful for the temporary isolation. I creep downstairs and have a breakfast of crisps; a churning from my stomach prevents anything heavier.

I return upstairs and head to the bathroom, feeling the need to clean myself in preparation for meeting Brad. As always, the dilemma between bath or showers rages on, but I opt for the shower. I sit in it, my body not feeling the lengthy standing, and watch the water drop against my skin. As a child, I used to sit on the windowsill listening to torrential downpours with a satisfied grin. While they banned me from the park, they at least brought beauty. So, I sit, watch and listen to the droplets crashing against me. Washing becomes a distant aim as I relax more and more into the moment.

The barrage of droplets sparkle and glisten; a cartoon cave made of the rarest crystals. At the centre of the droplets, my eyes picture Brad's face. He's smiling with that cute smile of his. Looking deeply into my eyes. I smile back, wishing so desperately he was here for real. My body moves on its own, and my hand reaches between my thighs. My spare hand offers a finger for me to bite to keep silent.

My soul leaves my body and floats into the droplets with Brad's face, and we stare into each other's eyes. The water droplets crashing against my knees offering a Hollywood-style clichéd scene where the guy and the girl get together at the end and allow our souls to intertwine for the rest of humanity. My body fights to repel the urges of my mind; poisoned in a fit of madness. They're each pulling for control. My mind winning. My body willing to embrace its desires.

The front door slams, retreating my soul into my body, as Brad's face evaporates.

'Lily?' Mother calls.

Thuds get closer and closer. The bathroom door soon hounded by Alexa. 'Hurry up, I need the toilet.'

'Use the one downstairs,' I try my best to disguise the panting.

'With Colin in the corner? You must be joking. Hurry up.'

Colin: The spider. His size isn't much more than a penny coin, but he's been bullying those who have desired to use the downstairs toilet since Thursday. If it is true they're more afraid of us than we are of them, that doesn't apply to Colin. His cobweb woven to perfection, resting above the toilet; Mother said it once dangled itself down to scare her away. That would be funny if it were true. She screamed so loud I feared something disastrous had happened.

Their presence has returned me to Earth, but my body yearns to return to my utopia.

'Lily? Are you in there?' Mother shouts, her knock and tone lighter than Alexa's. I scramble to grab a towel and wrap it around my body as she barges her way in. 'You'll never guess who I bumped into downtown?' She doesn't care about how bad her timing is. Mother tells a lengthy story about an old next-door neighbour from when she lived with her parents. This old neighbour had moved away, so Mother couldn't find out if her parents were alive or not. 'Get this, she had no idea I had a daughter.' She demands a shocked expression, and I oblige. She finishes the story by saying how they went for lunch (much to Alexa's annoyance) and the food she ordered.

'Sounds like you've had a nice time.' The only words I could offer.

113

'I did. It was nice to catch up, you know. You can shower while we talk, Lils, I have seen you naked before.'

'I know, I'm pretty much done, anyway.' Lies.

Mother sets off, leaving me to clean and dry. Brad's face vanished. My finishing allows Alexa to release her bladder (she doesn't swear around Mother, but she had a few choice words for me as I left the bathroom).

Mother's hand-washing the dishes again as I reach the bottom of the stairs (why?). 'Sorry I was in there so long, my hangover's kicking in.' She offers a sympathetic look. She believes me.

'Want any food?' She offers, but again I refuse. I grab a bottle of water and head back upstairs.

As I crash into my bed, my mind races around. My body exhausted; my mind pumped. Insignificant events become mountainous in my mind. Every little thing over-analysed. Depression can cause that. So can anger.

My phone reveals no messages from Brad, as a wave of sadness fills my body. Is it my fault for not messaging back? Is he not interested anymore? His crazy over-the-top number of messages told me he cares. Do no messages mean he no longer cares? Every word, every action over-analysed. Every scenario has a negative outcome.

Laughter enters the room. I scan around and see it's from the mirror. 'He doesn't like you. He doesn't care about you. He doesn't want you.'

'Shut up, shut up, shut up, shut up, shut up.' I slap myself seven times, but her face still mocks me.

'Why would anyone want you? Even I don't want to be *your* reflection. Such a pathetic mess.'

Tears pour down my cheeks as the reflection shakes her head. 'Leave me alone, leave me alone, leave me alone.' I rub my eyes with every muscle in my hands and as they release, the reflection still mimics me. Back doing her job. Tiredness washes over me and my eyes fall back into darkness.

An hour had escaped during my incarceration. An hour which bought into time reserved for changing. I rise and stare at my wardrobe; each scenario of what tonight presents a different outfit. I settle on smart-casual (a dark-blue skirt with a plain, black shirt and a grey cardigan). I like it. I can hear Mother's feet moving downstairs, as my mind plans its next lie.

'Excuse me,' Mother spots me the second I reach the bottom of the stairs. 'You seem awfully dressed up for an evening in front of the television. Am I missing something?' She folds her arms; she's the warden. In the evening, this house no longer stands as a castle, but a prison. My cage.

'The Flowers, they-they messaged me and want to-to hang out,' activating the best puppy dog eyes I could offer. The power it possesses has faded away as the years have gone on, with it last used in effect when I was 12 and wanted a second ice cream. Today I pray she's more kind to my magic. 'I-I don't know where we're g-going. Or-or what we're doing.' She pauses, analysing everything to dissect the truth. The walls wait, eager-eyed, for Mother's staunch refusal to permit me to leave. The windows locked. The doors bolted. But Mother's facial expression softens.

'Okay. I have no reason not to trust you.'

'Thanks-'

'Tell the girls I'm asking for them.' She backs away, her feet lighter. I've never understood how she manages to add extra weight to her body when she's angry. A psychiatrist may attribute it to her father, who had heavy feet, but psychiatrists try to attribute everything to someone's parents.

'I will do, thanks.' Guilt.

There's something about Brad I need to explore. Mother would disapprove; 'It's too risky,' 'you know what boys are like,' 'he'll use you for sex.' I don't need her vengeful tone anymore. Brad is a risk, I know that, but it's a risk worth pursuing. With proof, I can introduce him to Mother and guarantee his decency. And if he *does* hurt me. No. He won't. He can't.

I sulk out the door, ignoring all the photographs and the mirror in doing so. Mother watching every step; she must know something's not quite right. It's Saturday, not Thursday, for a start. Since when did I dress up to meet The Flowers? Since when did I go

117

anywhere to meet The Flowers? She knows. She's setting a trap.

I arrive at the restaurant before Brad, and the waiter escorts me to my seat. He offers me a variety of menus, reads out the specials and takes my drinks order: two glasses of wine, one glass of water. No identification needed. Perhaps age-restrictions are more lenient in restaurants than shops. He returns with the two drinks and asks if they're both for me. 'No, my partner will be here shortly.' Partner? I could have said colleague, friend, brother, psychiatrist, anything. But I said partner. A shiver rises through me at the word.

Brad arrives and we shake hands (I hope the waiter isn't watching as this could look quite strange), and he sits, apologising for being late (it's only five minutes).

'I ordered us both wine,' I interrupt another apology. 'I didn't know what you drank.'

'I don't love wine, but I'll drink it.' Relief fills my chest, preventing me from blubbering on about *why* I ordered wine. I should've ordered a beer, or a cider, or a vodka. 'So, about yesterday-'

'There's no need to drudge it up again. What's done is done.' A lady to Brad's left offers me a strange look; one of either fear or hatred. Another who believes the freak belongs in a cage. 'There are a few things in my past which haunt me, but I'm trying to deal with them.' I take a large mouthful of the sweet wine. 'If they can be dealt with, that is.'

'I'm willing to help any way I can; I want you to know that.' He's genuine, I can tell. This isn't a clichéd phrase spoken by every man trying to win over the woman, it's as if he's invented the words, and only he can speak them honestly.

'So,' my tone rises from serious to playful. 'If a crystal ball could tell you any one thing about your future, what would you want to know?'

'That's random.'

'Where's the fun in being formulaic?' We both giggle and sip more wine.

'Right, *one* thing about my future?' I nod. 'I'd like to know so many things, like the name of the woman I marry or how many children I have. But if I have to choose one thing: I'd want to know if I pay for all my sins before I die.'

'Pay for your sins?' His answer shocks me.

'Yeah,' he takes more wine. 'When people die, the focus is on negative things. Like, for instance, I told you almost immediately my mother was not a nice person. She never paid for her sins. I don't want that from me; I want to make sure I've paid all my sins and that I'm forgiven before my soul leaves my body.'

Never have I met someone so deep, so connected to his feelings. My desire for him rises with every word. 'Wow,' I whisper, unsure how to react. I've never thought about that, but I agree. Mother's parents never atoned. The Teacher never atoned. All the bad outweighing the good.

'So,' again his tone switches. He has such control over how he speaks. 'Food?' I'm relieved to be out of that serious conversation. After the incident, I never told Mother straight away, nor the police, and that's probably fear of having a serious conversation. I spent weeks with The Monday-Lady cowering because my brain didn't want to speak the words she so longed to hear.

We couldn't decide on what to eat (why does everything look so good on a menu?), so instead, we close our eyes and pick an item at random with our fingers. We both land on pizza. Cute. I call the waiter over and he pulls out his notepad. 'Have you decided, ma'am?'

'Yes, can I have the Meat Lovers Round 2, please?' I read back over the ingredients (I always go for a meat feast style pizza, but this one's different). 'Yes, that, please.' Brad ordered his food, and the waiter took off with our menus. He's wearing a look of pity. I disregard it and return to Brad.

'There's something in the water tonight,' I joke, gesturing to the woman who still shot occasional looks of disgust.

'Maybe they're all admiring how pretty you look.' My cheeks flush; he *really* does like me.

The rest of the evening passed by with a heart-pleasing atmosphere. We laughed about stories of our youths. He went into detail about his high school story about zombies; it was a zombie-invasion story for an assignment with a strong comedic element. One character, Carl I think, died about three times but kept coming back to help the protagonists. He also told of his love of football; I made a mental note to tell Rose about that. Anything he has in common with my friends is a plus. They'll act similar to Mother when they find out, so I need ammunition to please them with. He has a full life: a full-time job, a season ticket to his football team, marathon training in the gym, writing film reviews when he has a minute (he's trying to start a career as a film journalist) as well as seeing me. Each offers a better picture of himself. A picture Mother *might* accept.

After the meal Brad walks me home, soaking in the moonlight shining on us. We come to a stop at the top of my street, with me still conscious of showing him my exact home. 'Thanks,' I say, indicating this is far enough.

'No need to thank me, I had a lovely time.' He smiles. That smile from the shower.

'Me too,' I return it. The only thing missing is the camera crew and the director ready to yell 'Cut'; that's how well we played the roles of young lovers in the infancy of their blossoming romance. And possibly rain. Hollywood likes those rain scenes. But, for once I don't care how stupid I'm acting, how I'm like every stupid girl in the movies; all that matters were Brad's eyes, looking at mine.

He takes a half-step forward and fear sinks in. 'I meant it, you know,' he grabs my right hand and holds it within his. 'I care for you, and I'm not willing to throw us away.' Fear and excitement swing the pendulum back-and-forth to one another. I want my hand back. 'Whatever and however long it takes.' My eyes gaze at how trapped I am, pleading silently for him to set it free. His words reassure, but his actions frighten. Is this the big prank? Is Mother watching? I'm powerless to gain control of my hand. That's what *he* did. This is how it started.

Hours could have passed as we stood watching each other before I plucked up the courage to leave. He releases my hand and I walk away, safe knowing he's watching me. He's protecting me. He wants me. Baggage and all. My body desperate to skip, but it's too soon to be acting immature around him. One day he'll have to rummage through *all* the baggage I carry with me, but that day isn't today. I take one last look back, wave and disappear into my garden.

'Lily,' a voice whispers. 'Lily, return to us.'

'Are you okay, love?' A woman's voice calls out. A middle-aged woman looks at me, with pity. 'Want me to call someone?'

It takes a second for my functions to return and realise I'm just staring at the wall on the side of my house. 'I'm fine.' Lies. 'I think I must have been sleepwalking or something.' Lies. 'Thank you, anyway.'

'Okay, as long as you're fine.' She and her dog set off; she's done her good deed for the day.

A voice calls out as I approach the door. 'Go, go.' The letterbox. It's speaking to me. 'Run.' Its voice frantic. 'This house is poisonous. Run.'

I quickly unlock the front door and run in. My heart's racing. An embracing light emanates from the living room. Welcoming me in. I oblige to its request.

'Where the fuck have you been?' Mother releases as soon as I step into view. She storms over to me, grabs my hair and drops me to my knees.

'Mummy, please.'

'Shut up.' She drags me to a chair and slams me down; I look around, The Flowers all stand, arms crossed, supporting her actions.

'Mummy, I'm sorry, I'm-'

'Shut up, shut up, shut up, shut up, shut up.' Each raised in volume. She frantically scratches against each side of her head. 'Off to see the girls, are you? Off to the pub, are you? All dressed up for them, are you?' She's never looked so cross. She's never looked so disappointed. 'I didn't believe you. Just think about that: a mother didn't believe her own daughter. So, I'll ask again,' she leans in, her face near pressed against mine. 'Where the *fuck* have you been?'

I look around to avoid the gaze she's throwing and see The Flowers; their expression only a few levels weaker than Mother's. Everyone's disappointed. The air glues me down to the seat; there's no escape. The television's silence screams across the room. The lamp's light the difference between visibility and darkness. I'd prefer total darkness. 'I've met someone,' I say.

Mother stands, readying her hands for violence. 'You've what?'

As a child I played a video game where you could see emotions on people; they radiated as smoke coming from their backs, and you had to use this ability to solve crimes based on their emotions. Anger came as a red smoke, and Mother glows head-to-toe with thick, red smoke.

'His name-'

'*His*?' She slaps me with the back of her hand, the ring cutting open my cheek. '*His*?' Her voice angry. The hand swings back and slaps my other cheek. '*His*?' Her voice raised in volume. Another slap. '*His*?' A barrage of slaps released as I cower. The final slap knocks me from my chair. 'I thought you'd learned your lesson,' disappointment nestles in her voice. 'Have you not suffered enough already? Have *I* not suffered enough already?' She falls to a knee, panting from her assault. 'I guess all that meant nothing inside that thick skull of yours.'

'But, but, but,' tears race against blood to the floor. 'The Flowers sleep-'

She grabs me by my throat, cutting me off, her face millimetres away from mine. 'I don't care if they fuck every man, woman or animal on this planet. *They're* not my responsibility: *you* are.' My words refuse to leave my throat, her strangle tightens.

Mother lets silence fills the room. She steps back, her eyes retreat to look at the ground; anything other than her daughter. The Flowers all stand side-by-side, disgusted with me. Mother paces; light steps with such weight behind them.

'You'll never see him again.' I nod, like a coward. 'You'll forget he ever existed.' I nod, like a child. 'You'll start behaving yourself from now on.' I nod, like a victim.

The blood inside my body rejects the ban on men she sticks against my heart, but I know she's right. Too much has happened to us. She shakes her head and looks towards the door. 'Go,' she says. I stand and leave, taking one last look at the four bitter faces.

In my room I cuddle my pillow; it absorbs the tears still streaming down my face. I hear The Flowers setting off and a bottle (probably vodka) opened. The stars above have never looked so distant. Planet Lilian rejects my leadership. My anger prevents sanctuary there.

Like a swipe transition, a blink takes me away from the protection of my room to the cold, hard geography classroom. I'm stood alongside *him*. The classroom of students not paying any attention to the inner workings of tectonic plates, despite their upcoming exam. Most of them will cheat, the rest will be the victim of answer theft. All bar one. All bar the quiet girl at the back. Me.

She fails her exam.

The bell rings as the clock strikes 3:20 and an army of students rise from their seats and ignore The Teacher's advice on what to study over the weekend. They don't care; they're keener on the mischief and mayhem they're no doubt going to cause. Face after face passes me by as I stand by the door, none noticing me (they never did). The boy who pretended he caught cancer after hugging me. The girl who pulled down my trousers in the canteen. The boy who distracted me long enough for others to graffiti one of my textbooks with unpleasant pictures. None the worst crime inflicted on me.

Lily's the last to get up; she's hoping everyone leaves the premises to allow her a safe journey home. It wasn't always the case. The Teacher calls her back as she reaches the door. I've never been able to leave this room; each time I pass the threshold of the door, I return through it. I've tried smashing windows, kicking down the walls, smashing the ceiling apart. Nothing works. I'm always trapped here. Like she is. Like I was.

'Lily, I marked your homework.' That tone of disappointment she's all too used to. 'Please sit,' she obliges. He walks to his drawer and retrieves her homework and places it on his desk.

'I didn't understand it, sir,' she tries. She didn't understand it because of the distractions from other kids. Because Stacey thought it would be funny to touch her throughout class. The outside world mocks me by preventing my escape.

'Is this because of the subject matter, or are you distracted by your peers?' He sits down on the desk.

'Both,' she replies. Her hands interlock, allowing an arena for her thumbs to wrestle. 'They bully me, sir.' Honesty.

'I've seen,' he crosses his arms. If he did see, he never did anything about it. He never mentioned it to other teachers. He never punished the bullies. He never even tried separating her from them in class. 'Okay, my family are always out-of-town on Thursdays; something to do with one of my daughter's clubs. So, I always stay behind after school. If you want, and if your mother allows it, you can come here after school and I'll go over any work again, one-on-one. No distractions.'

'I don't know. Maybe. Perhaps I'm just not good at geography.'

I remember how she feels: elated. A teacher is trying to help her for *her* benefit. Some teachers (the music one in particular) were known to help failing students in their exams to boost their grade average. To her, a grade below a C is a fail. To him, anything above complete failure is a success. Genuine teachers are rare. And she has one.

'I know it can be daunting at times, but I've seen enough in bits over the year to know there's potential, and I want you to get the most out of your time here to give you the best possible start and the most options when you leave school.'

'I suppose.'

'Okay, I'll prove it: what's the capital city of Brazil?'

'Rio?'

'Correct. What's the tallest volcano in the world?'

'Mount Fuji?'

'Correct. See, there are parts of geography you're good at. It's up to you, I don't want to force you, but the offer's there.'

She smiles. She's putty in his hands. And he knows it.

The moment freezes, the characters rendered as mannequins on a set. I walk towards their bodies and see their smiles. Each telling its own story: hers of thankfulness; his of predatory success. I stroke her hair and pity the journey she's about to go on. To her, life still has hope, it still has meaning. Sure, she's bullied in school, but plenty of kids get bullied. She'll grow, get a job and work her way through the company. She'll meet a man. They'll have children. Their children will continue life's cycle of bullying. To her, she still has a future.

Another blink and a transition replaces the scene with another, three weeks later. The one I long to escape from. The doors and windows still keep me prisoner.

'It seems a lot easier, sir,' she says, alone with him after school on a Thursday. Geography is rising to challenge English as her favourite subject (English held the crown as her class is free from the major bullies). There's passion in her eyes, a keenness to learn.

'At its core, it's a simple subject,' he winks at his joke. She laughs back, happy for once to understand the reference. 'When there are fewer distractions, anyway.'

Her grade, according to him, has risen from an F to a D in a matter of weeks; and she loves that. She wants more after school sessions with other teachers. If nothing else, to avoid her life at home. Her mother's working more. Her mother's drinking more. And when she's not working or drinking they argue. Despite their arguing, she still tries to see the good in people. She still tries to please people. She loses that.

'Let's put geography to one side for a moment,' he places his pen on the desk and walks to sit on the front of it. 'How's your home life?' He picks the right week to question.

'Erm, not great, I suppose.'

He pulls out a chair and sits opposite her. 'Anything you want to talk about? I'm a parent as well as a teacher, you know.' He's good. He's a professional playing against an amateur. Every move he does to a beat. Every beat played to a rhythm. Every rhythm well-rehearsed.

'It's okay, sir, I'm used to it.'

'A young girl shouldn't have to face these things alone. We have staff here, whether you need nurses or counsellors, ready and willing to help you, if you don't want to talk to me, that is.'

'Thanks.' In her mind, she's considering speaking to a counsellor. She would explain how her mother would neglect paying bills, allowing the house to freeze while she worked, leaving poor Lily to feel the effect. She would explain how her mother would order her around while she sat on the sofa and drank. She would explain how her mother would banish her to the basement for hours at a time because she kept dirty plates in her room; a punishment where she urinated on herself while sat on the top step, too afraid to venture any further down after she once heard a voice speaking from the wall. The counsellor would help, and maybe even her mother would take up counselling. And their life could return.

He stands, pats her on the back; he's a father to girls, he knows when something's wrong. 'Have you ever tried wine?' He walks off and brings back a bottle.

'No, sir, I'm only 14.' Only 14. She's *only* 14. He didn't listen. He didn't care.

'That's fine, I'll pour you a small glass,' he smirks. In this battle of wits, he's won. And he'll continue winning. The two glasses poured to their brim. 'I find when I'm a little stressed, and bear in mind I'm a teacher, a glass of wine helps me relax. Here,' he hands her the glass, and she takes her first sip of wine. Her first of many. Its taste hooks itself to her heart's list of desires. 'Well?' He questions, but her face gives away the answer.

'It's nice, but I don't know if my mum will-'

'I won't tell if you don't? It can be our little secret.' That well-executed rhythm playing. 'Besides, you shouldn't worry about what other people think.' His eyes watch her take bigger sips. 'The school tells me I shouldn't keep alcohol on the premises, but do I listen?' He giggles.

'I guess not, but should you be giving a student wine?' She tries to play the moral high ground, but she would reject any notion of returning the wine.

He nods. 'I don't see us as teacher and student, I see us as friends. And two friends can have a drink

135

together, can't they? Unless you don't see me as a friend?' He's good. He's playing her to perfection.

'I do, I just didn't think you did.' She's everything he wants: broken and gullible. 'Why would you want to be friends with me?' My eyes slam shut. She could have accepted their friendship, but she couldn't. She needs more. She needs patting on the back. She needs her ego stroked.

'Because you're smart, because you're funny,' he places the wine glass down and leans forward. 'Because you're sweet, because you're pretty, because you're kind.'

Pretty. He said *pretty*. Run away. A 30-something man shouldn't say that to a child. 'I'm none of those things,' more wine. Led by a master. And she's assisting him every step of the way.

'You are all of them, and more. Don't put yourself down.' He finishes the wine in his glass in one mouthful and refills both glasses. He doesn't ask if she wants more, but she doesn't object.

'How? If everyone bullies me.' So many ways of changing the subject and to be free. Instead, she wants more. She *needs* more. She's the one to blame.

'Everyone bullies you because they're immature little shits.' They smile together. 'I, on the other hand, appreciate your humour and personality.' He leans back and takes another large mouthful of wine. I know it's coming, but the door won't open. It never opens. 'Maybe you need the company of more mature people.'

'Thank you, sir. You've really made geography fun.' He leans in, she suspects nothing. 'And I know I don't deserve your kindness, but-'

He kisses her. I close my eyes.

Her pleas are nothing shy of pathetic. Her attempts to rebuff him physically nothing shy of pathetic. Her tiny frame doesn't stand a chance against the might he possesses. She's an embarrassment. His hand explores her chest. His belt clicks; she still tries to argue. But there's no escape for her.

'Lie on the floor,' he whispers. Words which shudder down my spine.

He's not gentle with her. Her body slammed against the tiled floor after any attempt to flee. I'm smashing against the door to be free, but my words, like hers, fall on deaf ears. Grunting and sweet nothings rise in volume. Tears run down my face. As they do hers.

137

She's wondering why her. Why today? Why him? She fixates on the setting sun in the distance, trying to ignore all the strange and painful things happening. She pleads with gods she doesn't believe in for someone to come to her rescue.

After a few minutes, he unbuttons her shirt and finishes on her chest. 'Wow,' he whispers between heavy breaths. I can't even look at them. I need to leave. I need to be free.

She stays motionless on the ground as he puts his clothes back on. He doesn't appreciate her frozen body. 'Come on, you best clean yourself up.' That means, go away, Lily, I've had my way.

She cowers as she puts her clothes back on, and I walk over to her and try my best to comfort her. To tell her it will be okay. She can't hear my lies, but she needs some mothering. He turns his back; is he ashamed? Is he proud? There are scissors in a draw nearby, a stronger woman would have grabbed them and ended his tyranny there and then.

'Sir?' Her voice barely a whimper. His face returns; the mask he wore to befriend her gone to reveal the true heinous man underneath.

138

'Look, sweetheart, I think it's best if this little bit of fun was kept between us.'

'But, sir,' her lips quiver, her hands positioned over her crotch and breasts. 'This was wrong.'

He sighs. 'And here's me thinking we were close friends; *this* is what mature friends do.' The belt buckle completed his dressing. 'Perhaps you just aren't as mature as I thought.' Classic.

'I am mature,' her words hold no weight. She's trapped, begging for his forgiveness. 'I just-'

'Don't tell anyone and everything will be all right.' His patience waning.

'But-but Mother-'

He's had enough of this whiny child. He storms over, grabs her by the throat and forces her against a wall. Her semi-naked body flailing around. 'Look, sweetheart,' he's unable to look her in the eye. I've never understood that; he's had total control over her, more control than any man should hold over any woman, and he can't look her in the eye. 'I've been nice to you, now you need to be nice to me.' His grip tightens. 'Friends do each other favours, so do me a favour and keep this between you, me and the walls.' A nod from her releases his grip, and silence accompanies her redressing.

If she goes to the police, she has evidence on her. He'd be the freak in the cage. She'd be free. I long to walk her there myself, to end this nightmare before it gets worse. But shame accepts his demands on her behalf.

He walks over to his glass and drinks it all in one, before filling it up again and repeating. 'Same time next week?' He smirks. That victorious smirk. 'Oh, and Lily,' we both turn around. 'Remember, don't tell anyone.' He pauses, we know he's not done. 'Or else.'

Those words haunt her evening. But they serve as permission for me to leave, and a transition brings me back to my room. I drink a bottle of water in one go, hoping it soothes my heavy breaths. I rub my eyes. It's a dream I'm all too used to. But it's a dream which still saddens me.

I head over to the wardrobe and rummage through the bottom drawer until I find a light-pink bra. The same bra I wore that day. I never washed it.

It still fits me, although it's a little tighter, and I stand facing the mirror wearing it. The reflection kisses the bra and smirks. I close my eyes, and when they reopen the reflection is back to being that of a sad, lonely girl.

Sunday

Shoots of Alexa's breath greet me as I wake; her arms wrapped around me. 'Alexa?' I say.

'Oh, good morning.'

'Why are you in my bed?' More features of the room form as the sleep in my eyes fade.

'You were having a nightmare, so I came to comfort you.' She leaps out of bed, quicker to adjust to the waking world than me, and hops off to her room. She returns fully dressed, ready to embrace the day. 'We should spend the entire day together.' Where was Alexa last night? Did she hear?

'Sure, sure,' I say before the sight of the pink bra distracts me. 'Let me get dressed first, yeah?' She smiles and sets off downstairs. I return the bra to its prison, swearing to never wear it again.

'Good morning,' Mother says as I enter the kitchen. Mother is cleaning the dishes while Alexa sits at the table, her legs agitated for the day ahead. 'What have you two got planned for today?'

'Not sure, yet,' Alexa responds, her voice almost chirping. 'We could go to the cinema. Or the park?. Oh, we could go to that new spa place that's opened. Or we could go bike riding?' Such excitement.

143

Alexa excuses herself, which switches Mother's demeanour. 'I hope you listened to what we said last night.'

'I did,' I say, fighting back floods of tears. 'I'm going to see Brad today to tell him it's over. I was going to do it by text, but it seems harsh considering-'

'Harsh? He's a man; it's the least he deserves.' Her eyes refuse to leave the dirty dishes.

'Even so, his mother's just died, and,' my voice trails off. An unease makes itself known to the room, stroking both of our hair. It retreats to the basement as my words return. 'And he's been helpful lately.'

'Do it however you want; but if he hurts you, don't come crying to me.'

I nod, not knowing or caring to see if she looks, and grab a bottle of water in place of food. My body cries out for food, roaring for some, but any more time in this atmosphere will lessen my spirits more than they already are.

I make my way upstairs to fix myself and come to a halt as my phone rings. In a flurry, I answer it. 'Hey,' my voice quiet.

'Hey, are you okay? You sound a little flustered,' Brad's sweet voice returns.

'I'm fine. Can we meet later? I,' my voice struggling. 'I think we should talk.'

'I'm free later, so that's fine. Is everything okay?'

'I'll explain later. I'm sorry, I've got to go.' I hang up the phone, not giving him the chance to reply. Seven messages lie unanswered on my phone from him; thanks to Mother's warnings, seven comes across as creepy; not sweet.

'So, Sis,' Alexa bounces to the top of the stairs. 'We could go to the arcades. Or swimming in the leisure centre?' An excitement I long for.

'Let's just walk around town and see where we end up.' Her acceptance of the plan dims her enthusiasm a little, but she still races off to wait by the front door. A dog waiting for its owner to take it for a walk.

I rush through the last stages of getting myself ready, not wanting to further hurt her enthusiasm, and only deviating from the task to message Brad, apologising for the abrupt end to the phone call. He must know I'm ending it today. Have I given him power by revealing it this early? Now he can plan his assault.

145

Without my phone, Alexa and I take off and walk around town. West Drive is a reasonably competent town, with enough diversity in its features to entertain even the most stone-walled of teenagers. Two high schools and three primary schools offer competition, and each has a rugby and football field for their teams (the high schools also having a cricket ground, a basketball court and an athletics track). The leisure centre has a variety of activities and gyms. A small cinema, plenty of restaurants and takeaways, a retail park full of shops and many parks of varying sizes (the one by our house tiny compared to some others).

Any time we hear of a new place opening, like the Indian on the high street, Mother promises to take me, but as we pass it I realise I've yet to go. She never has the time. Mondays are perfect, but she wouldn't let me avoid The Monday-Lady. There are also plenty of routes for dog walkers, not just the castle. Mother never allowed me a dog: 'You'll just abandon it as you did with the gerbils, and I'll be left cleaning the mess once they die.'

It was an argument I hated hearing; I loved Road and Farm (my gerbils). After the incident, I neglected

146

them a little bit, until flies circulated their rotting bodies. But I wasn't in the right frame of mind then. I am now.

'I heard Mother and The Flowers last night,' Alexa says. 'They were saying you lied about who you were going out with.'

'Did you hear everything?'

'Not really; Mother brought me a drink, and I fell asleep soon afterwards. So, who were you out with? I assume it was a boy.'

'What makes you assume that?' Did Mother drug her to put her to sleep?

'You've been behaving differently since Thursday, I can tell something's up, and now you're lying to Mother and she's angry? It *has* to be a boy.'

Her mind is amazing. 'It *was* a boy, but I'm ending it today.'

'How come?' We sit on a nearby bench, watching families feed pigeons.

'Mother doesn't want me to see a boy after what happened.' Alexa knows the story, Mother made sure she didn't follow in my footsteps. 'Which I can understand.' More pandering to the will of the dominant.

147

'Well, that sucks. Tell me about him.' Her behaviour everything I've wanted in a sister; a girl-girl closeness to gossip with. I want to talk to her about boys, and have her talk to me about boys she's crushing on in school.

'He's cute,' I smile; the sky a gorgeous blue. 'He's kind, he's sensitive.' I wonder if Alexa can tell I'm every teen-girl trope in Hollywood movies. I hate it myself, but there's something about Brad which brings it out in me.

Two benches sit adjacent to one another, and we switch over to watch the ducks frolicking in the pond. 'I'd like to be like that someday,' Alexa says, looking out at a mother helping her two daughters feed bread to the ducks. The father waiting with the pram. 'Maybe you should introduce her to him because he sounds nice. And if he's nice, maybe she'll like him.'

A loud, inescapable laugh fleets from my mouth, forcing onlookers to direct their attention away from the ducks. My skin reddens more with every passing second until all lies leave me alone. 'She'll never accept any man in our lives, not after The Teacher and Tony.' I stop, aware Alexa doesn't know the ins-and-outs regarding

Tony (*I* shouldn't even know the ins-and-outs regarding Tony).

'Tony?'

'Doesn't matter, forget I spoke.' The distant sky to the right wears a dark cloud, while the left shines down blue. An oil painting of warring sides ready to battle; good vs evil; hero vs villain; sunshine vs rain. One side bright and cheerful, the other dark and destructive. The land below caught in between. 'We should get going before the storm hits,' I say, more to myself than Alexa.

She disagrees, and we remain watching the ducks eat the bread given to them before the family takes shelter from the oncoming storm. The ducks don't care about the weather, dancing around the pond; a mother protecting her babies, friends swimming side-by-side. Careless. Fearless.

'Lils,' Alexa says, breaking our smiles. 'Have you noticed the weird smell in our house lately?'

My face contorts to form a confused expression. 'No. What type of smell?'

'I don't know, it's hard to describe. I was sort of hoping you'd noticed it. It's horrible, though.'

'I'll have a sniff around later; it's probably some food rotting in the bin or something. Don't worry,' I put my arm around her. 'Your big sister will take care of it.' I wink and we both laugh.

'Anyway,' she releases herself from my grip. 'Your mystery boyfriend. Are you definitely ending it?'

'I've got to. Mother's orders.' She must feel the hurt in my voice.

'You're a grown-up, make your own orders.'

Despite her youth, she has a point, but I fail to continue the conversation. I love Alexa, but The Flowers sided with Mother on this, so I'm all-too-aware she may be working as a double-agent, hoping to suss out my true intentions.

Grey clouds march across the battlefield, retreating the blue sky: its territory overrun. One daughter from the family looks in my direction, raises her index finger to her mouth and mouths 'Be quiet' to me. I understand. Alexa *is* working with Mother. They all are. Grey and blue skies dig into their trenches, as No-man's-land opens and drops gallons of water on all those remaining in the park.

Alexa jumps in a series of puddles, without a care in the world. It's been so long since I've had that feeling. I must have been about Alexa's age when mother and I went out for the day to Roskell, with the weatherman predicting sunshine. He was wrong. Mother was fuming (it's a lengthy drive from West Drive to Roskell for a ruined day) and demanded we retreated to a nearby café to keep out of the storm. But I was stubborn and decided that plan sucked. I didn't want to be stuck inside a shop. Not on a day I'd been looking forward to for months. So, I begged, and I pleaded to stay out. She had a hood, so she agreed after a lengthy spell of me pestering and we stayed out as if the weather wasn't a thing.

After Mother's hypothermia diagnosis roared its head, I blamed myself for weeks afterwards, even ignoring Mother's attempts to calm me by saying it wasn't my fault. I know it was. I hospitalised my mother. What sort of daughter does that? It was about six months before I could look myself in the eye with any respect, long after Mother had made a quick recovery.

'Come on, Lils, let's play. We've got the entire field to ourselves.' We look out at the empty field, with only the remnants of life left behind in the form of rubbish they didn't clear away.

We compromise on going to the nearby arcade; I couldn't hospitalise Alexa, too. West Drive isn't much of a tourist destination (aside from those who castle-hunt), but about five miles down the road in either direction are caravan parks, which garner traction. The arcades are our town's way of trying to poach some of those tourists. There was even a committee against their presence here. Mother was a part of it. That was three years ago, and not much has happened since.

We arrive with a £20 note between us, and a long game on the penny machines soon commences. My £10 ran out quicker than Alexa's, and I restrain from rushing her. She's enjoying herself. And she needs some time away from the ills of the world.

An hour had crawled by before Alexa *finally* told me she was out of money and we were free to leave. I'd saved a couple of pounds for two bags of chips, and we ate them against the rain walking home.

'You two look like you've had fun,' Mother says as we walk into the house, exhausted smiles across our faces. 'That's good to see.'

Mother helps finish the last few chips from Alexa's bag. 'Yeah, it was amazing,' Alexa buzzes off upstairs.

'See, you don't need men. You have me, you have her.' She resumes washing dishes as I subtly try to sniff the air, hoping to locate whatever smell Alexa has noticed.

It's there; it's faint, but it's there. A unique smell, nothing I could place it against. It must be rotten food. I'll take the bins out later; it obviously emanates from there. 'I know,' I say, Mother not caring about the delay it took. 'I don't need anyone else.'

I excuse myself and go upstairs, the world finally granting me time to relax. The furniture in the room blurs as the world fades away.

'We all go a little mad.'

Competing inaudible whispers wake my mind, as the sky outside shines a thick, blood-red shade.

'Mother?' I call as I step out of my room.

'Alexa?' I call as I tip-toe down the stairs.

'Anyone?' I call as I enter the living room.

My words bounce off mannequins, which fill the room. All erected with anger in their faces. The whispers retreat to the mannequins, replaced by mumbled laughter from the kitchen.

The eyes of the mannequins look towards the kitchen, beckoning me to leave. Against better judgement, I accept. Fear engulfs my body as The Teacher stands in the kitchen as I enter.

'Ah, Lily, my sweet child.' My teeth clatter, fear gluing me to the spot. 'Long time no speak. Oh, how I've missed you so.' His frame seems bigger, filling up more space in the room. Every passing second accompanying a bang from the clock. 'I know what you think of me, and I completely agree. I'm a bad man. A bad, bad man.' The sky still seeps through the room, shading over him. 'But you know that already, don't you, my sweet, sweet Lilian?' He slaps himself, leaving a mark. 'You poor

154

child.' Two more slaps, knocking his head from side to side. 'Alas,' he holds up his hands. 'Fear no more. For my body shall be cleaned of all ill blood.' A pair of pliers appear and meet his teeth. 'I know what I've done, Lilian.' The two front teeth forced out, spitting blood across the floor. My body still stuck. 'I know what I've done,' he screams, seven teeth down. Each one patters against the tiled floor, each filling more of the floor with blood. By the last 'I know what I've done' leaves his mouth, no teeth aid its coherence. He collapses to his knees, his mouth drowning in his blood.

Tears leak from each of us as his bloodied body struggles to maintain being upright. His eyes pierce mine. 'You know what you've done.'

I suck in the sweet air of my room as my body jolts awake. My breasts rise and fall, my teeth clatter, my knees shake. The fears of the nightmare still linger. A flashing green light returns my spirit, as a message from Brad calms the fears.

Brad's wondering when we're meeting, and I message back asking if soon is okay. I need to end this. The sooner the better. I change my clothes, which still retain water from the rain, and put on a more formal attire; this is *not* a date. This is not two friends catching up. This is not someone comforting a friend in grief. This is a break-up.

If there is anything to break up, anyway.

Judging eyes greet me at the bottom of the stairs, and my body quickly scrambles for reassurance. 'I'm going to end it,' I try. A slight shrug is my reply. 'Just so you know.' My body begs for a response. It doesn't come.

The walk to the castle is quiet; everyone probably enjoying their Sunday dinners, readying themselves for a new working week. Everyone bar me. The sun dims a blood-red: a war veteran on his last legs.

'Hey,' I call out as I see Brad, looking into the prison-like chamber.

'Hi,' relief screams from his voice. 'Before you say anything, I lied to you.'

'What?'

'You know I said my father vanished?' I nod. 'Well, I was about four or five, I can't remember exactly what age, but I walked downstairs in the middle of the night. I think I wanted a glass of water or something.' He's doing what I do; add minor details to delay the inevitable truth. 'Anyway, this night he was acting really strange.'

'Strange how?'

'Like, babbling nonsense to himself, rambling on and on. I couldn't make out what he was saying, and to be honest, I'm not even sure if he knew I was there. There was vomit everywhere, and the room smelled horrible.' He walks around in circles. 'He and my mother weren't together but he still used to spend the night once a week, hanging out with me and whatever. The way she spoke, she hated him, but she always allowed him to spend the night.' He rubs his eyes with the palm of his

157

hands. 'Anyway, this night he'd scribbled "Go to Hell" on the walls.'

'"Go to Hell"?'

'Yeah. In red paint. His babbling almost seemed like he was arguing with himself, before,' Brad's eyes slam shut. 'Before he pulled out a shotgun and killed himself.'

My tongue retires. Such pain in his words. My body yearns to hug him, but fear restricts my movement. 'Why are you telling me this?'

'Because my grandfather also killed himself, before I was born, anyway. He deliberately ate a poisoned sandwich, of all things.' His walking around the room continues, free from the shackles of grief. 'There's a history of mental illness in my family, and you've been honest, so I should.' His eyes long to topple over the railings to resume the family tradition. 'And I know you want to break up with me, so I'm giving you an out. No hard feelings.'

His words catch me by surprise, resulting in a step-back needed to maintain my balance. 'What makes you say that?'

'I can tell when I'm being brushed off,' he leans against the railings, his ocean-blue eyes look across at me.

'It's not that,' my body mirrors his. 'I was raped when I was fourteen.' His eyes widen, asking for me to continue. 'He was a teacher at my school. He offered me extra tuition after school because I was falling behind, and I thought he was being kind. Instead, he trapped me and raped me.'

'Shit.'

'That's why, despite how crazy I am about you; my body desperately wants to run away. I'm afraid of suffering abuse again. And Mother feels the same.'

'So, it's your mother who wants rid of me?'

I nod, the break-up dangling in the air between us, unsure on its purpose. My words want to blame Mother, to say how everything is her fault, from her shitty parenting to her alcoholism and depression, but she holds such power over me. My body would sooner absorb the responsibility to spare any ill-feelings towards Mother. He walks over and offers a hug, a hug I don't refuse. We both need it. 'My poor sweetheart,' he whispers into my ear.

His sweetheart. I'm *his* sweetheart. I smile. Just being with him warms me up, even if there is a voice screaming to run. Just seeing his face erases all desires to end this. I'm intoxicated by him. He pulls away and looks into my eyes, our noses touch. 'I want to be the reason you trust again.'

'And I want to be the reason you don't end your life,' I say back. His aroma, his stubble, his everything sucks me into a happy place which I never want to leave. Planet Lilian has its queen, but it would be a much brighter place were Brad to take the mantle beside me, ripping the decree which forbade the anointment of a king. Peace and harmony would fill the land. Little princes and princesses would soon appear, loved by all. Everyone waiting for our retirement and their succession. Mother doesn't exist on Planet Lilian, though. For better or worse.

Brad releases me from his grasp, probably aware of the slight shaking of my body, and steps away. 'I assume he's in prison?' I shake my head. 'What? You're not telling me that bastard got away with it?'

'I never reported it.' I've never felt so small in my life.

'Why? That monster is still out there. Still teaching children. He could be still-'

'I know, I know. I just didn't want to be *that* girl. The girl who cries rape. Besides, half the school wouldn't believe me, anyway. He was the handsome teacher, the one whom all the girls made sexual fantasies about in the toilets. Why would they believe he'd choose me over them?' I know why: I'm weak and pathetic. Popular girls talk. Popular girls have people who care for them. I'm thankful for Brad not answering.

'I can't believe he got away with it, though.'

'He didn't get away completely; Mother gave him a bloody good smack in the eye.' We share an awkward laugh. In the pantheon of memories inside my head, Mother punching The Teacher is one of my all-time favourites. It wasn't until after the fourth time I finally confessed to Mother, who, like Brad, immediately suggested we went to the police. But I'd read up on what happens, what victims have to do, what victims become. I didn't want to be the poster child for West Drive. Visit the arcades and castles, but don't get raped. I begged and pleaded with Mother to accept my plan. She withdrew me from school, straight away, and so began many months of lying around, feeling sorry for myself.

About a month later, Mother had enough wine in her system to go to his house on a Thursday. She spat vile words at him, and he couldn't say anything. She threatened the police, of course, and he believed her. We still had the bra with his stain on. He didn't have a leg to stand on, so he stood there and took the abuse. Mother did not hold back, while I stood behind licking my lips at every word. She behaved in ways I could only ever dream of. She warned him to steer clear of us and any other underage girl, before she punched him. I don't know for certain, but she definitely broke his nose. That image started a new line of fantasies in my dreams: Mother hurting The Teacher to please me (sometimes she castrated him, others *she* raped *him* with a series of sharp, pointy objects), but he always wore that face. That bloodied, broken face.

I've often wondered if he would have come back for more had it not been for Mother's attack. The lack of police would have clued him to the fact I was weaker than he could have hoped for. Brad and I sit against the pit, dangling our feet over the edge.

'I can't imagine how anyone could get over such a thing.'

'I suppose I've had years of practice.' The spare room held me prisoner for just under a year afterwards and gave me plenty of time to reflect and mourn. At a time when The Flowers were a dream yet unfulfilled. I told them straight away when our Thursdays started, and they helped, too. But Mother felt like I still needed more, so she paid The Monday-Lady to listen to me. She'd always nag at me to go over certain things again and again, as well as making me read countless books by other victims. I could have authored my own book; although it still haunting my dreams presents a spanner to the idea my coping method works.

Brad doesn't speak; instead, each of us tries sneaking looks at each other without making it too obvious. Neither of us knows what to do. If nothing else, the season has blessed our friendship, with the sun's light beaming into the chamber, defending against oncoming grey clouds. Brad's everything I could want in a man, and he's everything Mother could have hoped he'd be, but she won't give him the chance to prove his honesty. She'll just see another man. Another Tony.

Another Teacher. Another nightmare waiting to happen. But Brad would never threaten me, pin me to the ground against my will, degrade me or control me. But Mother won't believe that. She'll say he's playing me and all of this is an act. Maybe she's right. Maybe in four years, I'll meet another man who appears perfect. A man who'll restore the confidence which Brad built and shattered. I'll explain everything to this new man, who will be sympathetic and understanding.

Maybe.

Maybe he's worth the risk. Maybe in four years, I'll still be with Brad, and we'll be in love. Maybe we'll have a daughter of our own.

With each moment my mind accepts Brad and I have no future, a quick look at his smile and I melt into a world of desire. Mother's too smart for my lies, or I'm too dumb to be able to lie effectively, so she'll know straight away. Mother on the right of me, Brad on the left, each waging a war for my heart.

'Has your mother sworn off all men, then?'

'She sure has, for both of us. If your family tradition is suicide, ours is rape.' His eyes know there's more to the story, I take a deep breath ready to reveal. 'I'm a rape baby.'

'Shit. So, so your mother?'

'Was raped at fifteen. Yep.' The raped daughter of a raped mother. The title of a book I'll never write. 'Afterwards, she vowed never to be fooled by a man again, but it still happened to me.' I loathed Mother for long periods after my abuse, as she always promised she'd protect me from the world. Instead, she sent me straight to him. I suppose she felt bad, too. She chose the school, after all. And it soon happened under her very roof. But it still took years to build trust with Mother again.

'Well, aren't we a mess of a couple?' The last word hung in the air, a bad smell we each wave away. 'I suppose we should go our separate ways, otherwise, our son would kill himself and our daughter would be raped.' We each offer a laugh, all-too-aware of its real-life possibility.

Queen Lily and King Brad would live in perfect harmony on Planet Lilian, with rape and suicide forbidden in thoughts or actions. If only.

'I need time to think.'

'I understand.' I know he really does. 'I know it's just words, but I'm nothing like him. And, for as long as you need, just consider me nothing more than one of your girlfriends. Albeit minus the boobs,' a laugh more friendly lets out. 'Although,' he looks down. 'A few takeaways here and there and I can grow a pair if needed.' I'd much sooner him without.

'Great, now I'm going to have that image in my head all evening, thanks a lot.' My words accompanied by a smile.

'Nothing too racy I hope,' he winks.

I stand and he follows my lead as we walk to the castle's entrance. His body glistens against the evening sunlight; how am I supposed to give up this man? How am I supposed to reject the one chance I have at happiness?

'If you need to talk, you have my number.' He offers another hug, and I accept. When God created humanity, I doubt he planned for everyone to have an exact physical match when it came to hugging, but Brad is mine. We didn't even have that awkward moment you see in romantic comedies where the two protagonists get confused about which arm to use, or whether to kiss; we know exactly where we are going. How am I supposed to give up this man?

He smiles as he pulls away. Each time he's touched me, I've wanted to run. This time, that desire doesn't appear. There's hope for a future. Hope shattered by the need to go home. To decide whether the truth is worth telling.

My mind see-sawed back-and-forth on whether to tell the truth on my walk home, and I sneak in the house hoping to delay telling Mother for as long as possible. But there she is. She grabs me by the throat and pins me against the door, such hatred in her eyes. Her spare hand rises, ready to slap on cue.

'Well?' She demands. Releasing enough of her grip to allow my throat to speak.

'Mummy, please, he-'

The spare arm crashes against my face. My body wants nothing more than to fall against the floor in a ball, but her hand remains gripped against my throat. 'I'll ask again: well?'

'Please, Mummy, if you give-'

The hand crashes a second time. This time opening the floodgates, allowing tears to stream down my face. 'Tell me you told him to fuck off, or else.'

I can't lie to Mother. And even if I tried to, she'd see right through it. Mother understands the silence locking my mouth shut and drags me down the hallway. I kick and scream with each step. I glimpse Alexa's face as I cross the living room's viewpoint; she shouldn't have to see this.

She slams me against the solid kitchen floor while she unlocks the basement. My eyes widen. 'Get in.' She orders. I shake my head and she wraps her arms around me and throws me in before she slams the door shut.

'Mother, Mum, Mummy, please.' I scream and shout, banging the door with each syllable. Nothing returns other than the sound of locks confining me here. Cold air nestles on my body, tickling me with its presence.

When I'm here to clean, I'm given lights and extra clothing, anything I need; when I'm here as a punishment, I get nothing. Just me, my bouncing heart and my breath.

Left to right, above and below, all that greets my eyes is black. Black and silence. I sit and wrap my arms around my legs. Black, silence and cold.

A brick falls onto the floor in the distance, bringing my stoic demeanour to an end. My breath retreats inside my lungs. A second brick falls off. My heart pounds for freedom. I hammer at the door again. Two more bricks fall against the floor.

'Lily,' a voice whispers.

My thumping hits harder. 'For God's sake, Mother,' I plea. I'll do anything to be free. 'I'm your daughter. Let me go. Please.'

'Lily,' the whisper closer. More bricks fall. 'You know what you've done.' Rats scurry away from the voice, back to their sanctuary; Mother still refuses to grant me the same luxury.

'Mummy, Mummy, Mummy,' my voice screams on repeat. Punches, kicks, headbutts, anything to be free.

'Lily,' the voice at the bottom of the stairs.

Finally, the door to the kitchen opens and beckons me to safety.

I race to the other end of the kitchen and wrap myself into a ball in the corner. Mother looks in the kitchen. 'You know if there's anything down there, you failed to clean it properly.' Her words cannot break my body's shield, and I rock back-and-forth on the floor. Alexa soon comes in and hugs me, helping soothe my heart. My eyes refusing to leave the now-locked basement. 'So, girls, how about a trilogy night? I'll let you two pick.'

When I was younger, we used to have these trilogy-nights where we'd buy or rent a trilogy of films and watch them back-to-back. I think it stems from Mother's father idolising the Star Wars trilogy (although Mother refuses to let me watch Star Wars). I loved trilogy nights; we'd get in our pyjamas, whatever the time, and we'd watch until we fell asleep. It started when I was ill one day, and with Mother never working Sundays she offered it to me as an alternative to the park. It soon became a once-a-month thing with us taking turns in picking the film series. It stopped about a year ago.

'How about Back to the Future?' Alexa answers. She's only seen the first one and has always wanted to watch the rest. Mother agrees and sets off upstairs for the DVDs. I've never understood why Mother keeps the DVDs in her room.

Alexa releases my body as colour sinks back into my skin, relaxing my mind. The basement door fading away into the background as best it can.

Last time Mother and I watched the Back to the Future trilogy was in 2015 as the date in the second film neared, and we spotted what was and wasn't real about their predictions. I suppose watching it in 2020 we can again laugh at how wrong they were.

171

I always wanted a hoverboard.

'We'll order pizzas later,' Mother says as she arrives, DVDs in hand. Alexa runs off to the living room to grab her seat (no one ever sat in it, but that didn't stop her panicking about it) while I grab my lazy Sunday blanket. 'Saves using up any more dishes.' My eyes glance over towards the sink full of unwashed dishes. Confusion compounds me to stand and solve the mystery.

'Hurry up, Lils,' Alexa shouts, which brings me out of a momentary trance and into the living room.

'What did you want to become when you were younger?' I ask as Marty meets his younger mother.

'I never really had a career set out.' And because of me, she never needed one. 'Your grandfather wanted me to join the forces, as he was in the army, but it wasn't something I was keen on. I flirted with the police for a year or so in my early twenties, but nothing ever came of it.' Because you had a daughter, right? All those doors closed because you had a child, right? 'I guess I just fell into admin and never really left. Do you have any career dreams?'

Since the incident, I've not thought about a career. I shake my head, unable to even contemplate a job I once wanted as a kid. No hobbies, no career choices, a mess of history; maybe I should end things with Brad for his sake. It would please both Mother and Brad in the long-run. And I'm used to rejection and disappointment.

'Of course,' she sits up, excitement painted on her face. 'When I was young-young, I always dreamt of becoming a famous singer.'

'Really?'

'Oh, yeah. I used to force Tony to listen to me singing for hours; he'd judge each performance on a score out of ten. I used to build up a repertoire of songs to perform for him; I even made up my own song once. It wasn't very good. Bless Tony, though, he scored it quite high. I had visions of touring the world and topping charts in country after country. Pipe dreams which your grandparents thought of as stupid and immature to have, but they're exciting, you know?' I nod. When I was about ten, I wanted to be an astronaut. I hunted down anything space-related whenever we went shopping, and that's where the planet stickers came from on my ceiling. Ten-year-old me discovered and named Planet Lilian on a voyage, and left it empty until a more mature mind could fill it with civilisation. I also wanted to be an actor at one point, but I think that was because I had a crush on Zac Efron at the time and knew it was the best route to him falling in love with me. He would be the lead; I'd be the unknown rookie who dazzled the director during an audition. The story would feature an unlikely romance between the hugely successful character, portrayed by Zac, and a peasant, portrayed by me. And as the love between our characters blossomed, so did the love between us. The tabloids would be littered with unauthorised pictures of us walking along the Santa Monica pier, and speculation would be rife in all the gossip magazines. We would keep the romance low-key until the film debuts. Adding a genuine romance to a romance film would create a buzz, and the film would land us both an Oscar.

'You're a beautiful singer,' I finally reply.

'Thanks, that's sweet but I'm too long in the tooth to get into that game now.' I never said anything; it *is* too late for her, but I can't tell her that. Nor can I lie.

Marty's crazy time-travelling adventures distract my mind from Brad for a few hours. He made a guest appearance when *I* obtained the time machine at the end of the film; assisting in the removal of The Teacher as a child (year 1324BC seems like a good enough place to drop him). In that world, Mother allows Brad to love me.

'Thanks, girls,' Mother says as the films come to a finish. 'We need more nights like this.' We both agree, but we all know it's Mother's fault. She's always packing me off to The Monday-Lady or going to work or sitting in a corner drinking on her own. We tried a movie night once when she was drunk, and she criticised almost everything. Perhaps she's changing. Hopefully, she's changing.

After we bid each other goodnight and retreat to our rooms, I pull out my phone and see a message from Brad. "I'm here if you need me. B. Xx"

My mind scares me. I need him.

Butterflies flapping around my room grants my body consciousness. My collection stands at thirteen, but hundreds flutter out of the framed picture on the wall, flying around my room. I marvel at the multitude of colours coming to life.

They urge me out of bed, and I follow as they lead me downstairs and into the living room, where more colours fly around the room. The colours sparkle as they pass one another. One flies to my face and hovers, looking right at me. It's a purple shade, one of my favourites. It gestures for me to turn and I follow its order.

One the wall is a framed 3D picture of the living room, with stuffed tiny bodies in it. The Flowers stood by the window, Mother ironing, Alexa and Brad chatting on the sofa and the Teacher and Tony sulking together in the corner. I'm not there.

'Where am I?' I call out to the purple butterfly but get no response. It fades away into a multitude of colours. I note the picture's caption: "Sunday at My House, by Lily". The butterflies spin and dance around my face and I slump back into sleep.

Monday

Rain taps against the glass, waking me. Outside, it appears as if the rain is falling without the help of clouds; blue sky and yellow sun shine. My phone's notification screen remains naked, which dampens my morning. I know he's waiting for me to say we're still okay, but I love his messages.

In the kitchen, Mother packs Alexa's school lunch while dressed in what looks like her work uniform. She bids me a good morning, elongating the word 'good', and offers me a cup of coffee.

'No thanks,' I reply. 'Are you going to work?' Something's nagging at my brain, something's off. I just can't place it.

'I know, I know, but I've got a few things which need sorting out. Besides, I didn't go in Friday, so I can't mess them about too much.'

'But you're-'

'I'm what, sweetheart?'

I didn't know. Whatever word ended my sentence fluttered away before I could speak it. 'I can't remember, ignore me.'

'What's your plans for the day, then?' She can't stand still. She's so chirpy.

Alexa bounces into the room, matching Mother's demeanour. Have I missed whatever's in the air? She pours herself a bowl of cereal and eats it with a small spoon.

'No proper spoon?' I query.

'All dirty.'

'Sorry, Mother, what did you say?'

'What's with you this morning? You look like you've seen a ghost.' No response comes from me. 'Anyway, what're your plans for the day?'

'Oh, nothing, yet. I may check out the catalogue for a hobby.'

'Have you still not decided?' She speaks in jest and laughs as I shake my head. No lecture about being lazy. No talk on me wasting time with Brad. No talk about me living a life of misery and boredom.

'I will,' I plea. 'I'm sorry, I just-'

'No need to apologise, you'll find one when you find one. No use rushing into something you'll regret next week.' An attitude I always argue. She *always* says doing something outweighs nothing.

Mother rushes Alexa into finishing her cereal, grabs a stack of papers for her office and rushes out of the house, kissing my forehead as she goes. Her boss, Yvonne, is a sweet, old lady, who doesn't mind her lateness, or so Mother says. Mother always says she's quite pally with Yvonne, more so than anyone else in her office.

I take my confused brain upstairs to again check my phone. Empty. I know I shouldn't, but I long to speak to him. The little green phone icon above his contact calls for me to press it.

'Hey,' he sounds groggy. The clock on the wall mocks me for calling so early.

'Sorry, have I woken you?'

'No, no, it's fine. Besides, your voice is a nice alarm call.' I know it's cheesy, and probably a line he's used on many girls before, but I do love hearing it.

'You're silly. Fancy hanging out today?' What am I doing?

'Of course, but I thought your mother didn't want us seeing each other?'

'She doesn't. But, she's in work.' Confusion replaced with glee. 'You can come here?' The same glee turns sour. What am I doing? I cover my mouth to stop myself vomiting at the sound of the words echoing around my head. Don't be so fucking stupid, Lily.

'Lily, we can meet in public, I don't mind-'

'I trust you.' I *want* to trust him. I always *want* to trust them. Mother trusted Tony. Why are you so fucking stupid, Lily?

I gave him the number and told him I'd need an hour to get ready. I don't know if I'll even have the courage to answer the door when he knocks. Should I set up cameras? Catch him in the act. No, he won't do anything. But, I could have video proof. No, he won't do anything. Nobody knows him, I'll be another girl crying wolf with no proof. Mother won't care; she'll blame me.

Because you were so fucking stupid, Lily.

To her, I'll simply be suffering the consequences of my stupidity. She'd be right. She's always right. Maybe I should tell someone? A neighbour or the police. They could check on us at a specific time; and if they hear me struggling, they'll know I'm in danger.

But who would believe little Lily Hill would have a man over? Showers always calm me, so I allow the water's hands to massage away the fears. I'm barely washed and dried by the time he knocks; a playful, delightful knock. Everything he says and does makes me smile. Would I smile if he raped me?

I slam my head against the wall to knock the thought away and answer. A shaking hand thankful for the steady door. 'Hey,' I beckon him in. No neighbours around, nobody knows Brad's here; nobody even knows Brad.

This is fucking stupid, Lily.

He takes his shoes off straight away, something Mother would *love*. A gas-man or someone came here once and didn't take his shoes off. Muddy boots walked throughout the house, with each black footprint on her new carpet causing her pain. She appeared all kind and considerate while he was there but berated him as he left. She threw his clipboard into the street and swore as loud as she could. But Brad's taken his shoes off. He walks so far into the house and turns to see me, back-to-the-door. In fear? In worry? In disbelief? What is this I'm feeling?

'Where shall we go?' He asks. Can he sense my unease? I gesture to the kitchen and he walks ahead and sits on one of the chairs. His movements mirror *his*.

Brad's not like that. Brad's a genuinely good guy. I believe in him.

I need wine.

I tell him I'll be there in a minute and sneak a mouthful of wine from a bottle in the living room. It soothes my body so much.

'What did you tell your mother in the end?'

'I tried telling her the truth,' I return to the kitchen. 'But she slapped me.' He gets up as if to hug me, but I shove my hand out to say I'm okay. 'She's not normally like that, she's just worried about me. It's her way of caring.' I've repeated that so many times. To teachers, to friends, to The Monday-Lady: I always accept her ridiculous behaviour as her *way of caring*.

The house phone blasts its ringtone aloud and halts our conversation. Its ring echoes around the house as we sit and wait. Wait for it to finish. Moments later a flashing red light appears. I excuse myself from Brad and press play: 'Hi, it's Yvonne. I was just wondering if-'

Static filled the rest of the voicemail, blocking everything she said. I tried playing it again but the same static repeats.

'You know,' Brad says as I walk back into the kitchen. 'You're eighteen, you should be able to make up your own mind.' Thoughts I've buried deep, deep down.

'Mother knows best, and I'm not all-right in my mind, because of what's happened, so I don't mind following her orders from time-to-time. But not this one. I want us to be friends.' I want so much more.

'So, she's ordered you to stay away and you invite me here. She's not waiting for me or anything, is she? Ready to off me with a hammer or something.'

'Of course not,' I giggle. 'She's at work. And Alexa's at school.' It's like I'm advertising my isolation, inviting him to rape me. Fucking stupid, Lily. 'Thirsty?' I race to fetch two cans of store-branded cola from the fridge and place them on the table. 'She can be really nice. Like last night, we watched films all evening. She's not always this bossy figure I make her out to be.' She's not *always* a witch. Frankenstein's monster didn't mean to kill Maria.

'If you want, I could call around and introduce myself-'

'Honestly, Brad, she wouldn't give you the time of day. The worst part is she'd probably love you if she knew you. Her childhood friend, from what I've read, reminds me a lot of you.'

'He sounds like a good guy.' I stay silent. He opens his can of cola and takes a mouthful. Jealous eyes watch as the cola freely touches his lips; something which I cannot do.

'He's the one who raped her.' The air thins.

'Oh, maybe not so much of a good guy. Sorry.'

'It's fine, you weren't to know.'

'Hey, what's in there?' Brad points at the basement door, and I reply matter-of-factly with what the door's protecting. 'You have a basement? Man, that's so cool. Do you keep anything exciting down there, like you see in horror films? Is the Babadook chained down there?' I shake my head, a wry smile across my face.

'Just rubbish, rats and empty space.'

'I've never been in a basement, mind if I take a look?' My body freezes. Words struggle to leave my throat.

'You can't.' He looks disappointed. My heart forces more words out. 'Mother locks it and she has the key. Honestly, nothing's down there of any interest. It's just cold and damp and boring-'

'Okay, okay, I understand.' His understanding grants words to flow easier from me. 'How about a tour of the rest of the house?' I can't hide the rest of the house away behind a locked key. But should I show him everywhere? What about my room? That would be fucking stupid, Lily. 'Hey, what's that sound?' He says, looking around for the source.

I lead him to the living room and show him the crack in the window, which looks like it's got bigger: a cockroach on the glass. 'Shit,' he says. 'That looks dangerous.'

'We've only just discovered it,' I close the curtain over it. Something about it frightens me. 'As we're in the living room already, this can be the first stop in the house tour.' I point out all the features of the room, and he nods and smiles at everything. He only returns a compliment towards the television. Back in the hallway, he stops and looks at a photograph on the wall: Mother and me at a water park.

'I'm about thirteen, there,' I say. 'About six, maybe seven months before the incident.' Her smile's honest. Her life's still in one piece. It breaks my heart, knowing what lies in her future.

'Your mother's a beautiful woman.' I agree. She hadn't even hit the dreaded thirty by that picture, and she was still taking care of her appearance (she stopped after The Teacher came into our lives). Nothing more than a drained fountain of youth. Against this picture, I cry over my former self. Mother probably does the same, too.

I stretch my arms for him to walk upstairs, with the bottom of the house explored. My heart races. Stupid. Stupid. Stupid. This will be the scene in future visions where I lose all sympathy for my former self. In the first tale, it was the wine, in the third, it was the lies. In this tale, it's leading a man upstairs. Upstairs towards three bedrooms and a bathroom.

The first room we come across is Alexa's; Brad doesn't spend too long looking inside (it's a young girl's room, I don't blame him). After that door closes comes Mother's. 'Are those wigs?' He asks, seeing three mannequin heads with two sporting hair.

'Yeah; Mother got ill some time ago.' I don't want to go into any more detail, and thankfully he understands. Mother's regular rushes to the hospital happened when I was ten. Neighbours would look after me, but everyone refused to reveal what was wrong. Mother survived but lost her hair in the process. 'If you see her, don't mention it.'

A rule issued on Mother's behest. Don't compliment it, don't criticise it. She was such a proud and beautiful woman. A bald head was the consequence of an illness she didn't want to speak of again. I can't even remember the last time I saw her without a wig on.

Brad accepts my advice, and we arrive next at my room. My hand shakes as it reaches for the handle. 'We don't have to,' Brad whispers. But I want to. Why should the worst parts of my past influence what could be the best part of my future? I need to do this for myself as well as our friendship. I'm not fucking stupid.

'Wow,' he says as he spots the butterfly collection. 'Not something you see every day.' I smile and sit on my bed, leaving him free reign over the room. He admires the mirror and rests his hands on my drawers. 'Don't worry, I won't go rummaging through your underwear.' He has a way of speaking, which makes even the silliest of things sound charming.

He sits on the bed as well (with enough distance between us) and looks up. 'That's cool,' he says. 'I can't even make out Earth.' I watch as his eyes scour from planet to planet.

'That one.'

'Why are there ten planets? I thought there were only eight?'

'Well, I've got Pluto there. Team Pluto all the way,' I got up and search my wardrobe for my "Team Pluto" shirt, with the planet reading a book of "Rules to be a planet again" with a sad smile. Brad laughs at the shirt. 'And the tenth is Planet Lilian.' A wash of shame comes over me upon speaking its name. 'When I was younger, I wanted to get away from time-to-time, so I invented my own planet out there. Some others were too warm or too cold for humans to live on, so I made Planet Lilian perfect. And only the best-of-the-best are allowed there.' I smile, shame replaced with passion.

'Am I allowed there?' He smiles. Little does he know he reigns by my side. His anointment will come. For the first time since he stepped foot in my home, I feel relaxed. I was right: he's not a threat. He's in my room, he could pin me down, but instead, he's asking questions about Planet Lilian. Asking questions about *me*. 'So, back to the kitchen?' His question shocks me. Was I *expecting* him to rape me? I lead the way and we pick our cola drinks as we sit back down. 'Nice house,' he says. 'Good size. I bet growing up here would've been ace; big house, park around the corner.'

'It was all right, I guess.' It was more than all right. This side of our street was the only place within half-a-mile to have three-bedroomed houses. Mother always used to warn me against bragging, as some people had bigger families than ours and would've been better suited to the bigger houses.

'It's mad, though.'

'What is?'

'I could throw a stone at my old house, we're that close, yet mine is tiny by comparison.' He would have lived in the two-up two-downs which surround our three-bedroomed street of luxury. I've never been in one of them, but they look small from the outside.

'Believe me, with Mother's rules, there are times when this house feels small.' He laughs, probably a little uneasy. 'So, how come you moved away, anyway?'

'My mother struggled to pay the bills after my father killed himself. She couldn't hold a job or anything, and I guess I didn't help by moving out. I suppose I was a bit of a daddy's boy. In hindsight, we both made mistakes.' I reach my hand out to stroke his. 'It's fine,' he reassures. 'Life happens.'

'Yeah, but to lose both your parents at such a young age.'

'I guess that makes me an orphan,' he giggles. My hand retreats. 'Being an orphan worked out for Harry Potter.' Laughter escapes me, too. 'Looks like neither of us had the perfect childhood,' and the laughter ceases. Silence speaks, interrupting the gulping of cola and the pattering of rain. His eyes look around the kitchen, and a wash of embarrassment comes over at seeing its mess.

It's always been Mother who has taken dominance over cleaning the house, however, the dirty dishes and cobwebs wouldn't be providing her with a brilliant reference. And that smell Alexa pointed out, Brad must be able to smell it. Should I pretend it doesn't exist? Make an excuse for what it is?

If only this room contained nothing more than me, Brad and our colas.

He probably grew up like everyone else nearby and assumed the people in the big houses were posh or rich; not living in the slum which he's presented with.

'I should probably get going before your mother sees me.' Is he too embarrassed to be here? I would be. There's only so much of one person you can take. Maybe a disgusting house is the final straw.

He gulps the last of his cola and makes his way out of the house, stopping only to look at the picture of me and Mother. 'You look really happy in that picture.' I was. Life wasn't perfect, but I *was* happy. 'Hopefully one day I'll see that smile.'

Hopefully one day I'll wear that smile.

He takes off after a quick survey revealed no onlookers, and I lean against the door as it closes. I know all-too-well inviting him here was a stupid thing to do, but he passed the test. One day Mother will find out, and I'll tell her he was a perfect gentleman the whole time. He even took his shoes off. And Mother *will* accept him.

In the living room, I hug the cushion on the couch, the punch of his aftershave still floating around my nose, the picture of his smile still etched across my eyes.

I wasn't fucking stupid.

Freezing water interrupts a rare, visionless sleep.

'What? What's happening?' I struggle to speak against the water slapping my face.

'Who has been in this house, Lily?' The water bottles tossed away, granting my eyes sight. The sight of Mother kneeling next to me.

'What? No-no one. Why? I-I promise.'

She picks two cans of cola from the floor and thrusts them into my face. 'One of these has a different scent to the other,' she breathes in both open cans as if to prove her point. 'So, Lily, I will ask again: who has been in this house?' She drops the cans, resumes a standing position and unclicks her belt buckle. Never has Mother gone for the belt. I cower into a ball. Defeated.

'Brad,' floats out of my mouth.

'Brad. The man I told you never to see again?' I nod, hiding my face away. Ashamed. 'And instead of obeying your mother, you invite him here, into our home? How could you be so fucking stupid?'

'You did the same thing.' My arms wrap more tightly; sometimes you just know when you've made a massive mistake.

'So, that's how it is. It's my fault. You whore yourself out to any man who looks at you, despite everything that has happened, and it's my fault.' My eyes leak. 'Tony happened once. And never again have I been so fucking stupid. I learned my lesson. Have you?' I shake my head. 'After the first time with The Teacher, why the fuck did you go back? Or invite him to our house? Talk.' Again, I shake my head. The belt acts like Mother's bodyguard, waiting for the order to attack. 'You're such a child. I try, and I try, and I try, and I *try* to protect you, to make you better, to help you survive in this selfish, cruel world. But, clearly, I needn't bother. Come on,' she grabs my hand and drags me off the chair and into the hallway. She opens the front door and looks back at me. 'Why don't we just invite all the rapists, all the paedophiles, all the murderers and Satan-worshippers and thugs here, into my home. Or, better still, straight to your room. Maybe they'll form an orderly queue; I can make them coffee while they wait.' Her arms flail around, and she slams the door shut, shaking the walls. 'Why bother with the hassle of being duped? Let's just skip straight to the formalities like the slut you are. Pervert special offer: one stupid, pathetic child, yours to do with as you please.' A sinister laugh lets out. 'You're no saint.' I nod. 'I know I was duped, but *you*, you went into the house of a rapist. You invite strange men into our house.' I go to defend Brad but she cuts me off. 'Do you have any idea how irresponsible that is?' Pain overtakes anger as the driving emotion. My mind hosts a roaring headache, preventing movement. I deserve this. 'I know you think of me as some law-creating witch put on this planet to ruin your life, but there are people, like Tony and like The Teacher, all over this world. And I've tried my best to never allow another one near *my* child.' A softer voice enrages my headache. 'What story did Brad use? His house run out of cola?' She ignores my shaking head. 'What was it with The Teacher? Oh yeah, he wanted to use the toilet. This fully grown man who had been molesting you for God-knows how long, who knew *I* wasn't home, needed a piss. Sure, I can't see anything wrong with that what-so-ever.' My heart pounds against my shirt, desperate to escape the fire in my head. Mother sighs. 'Aren't you going to say anything?' My body still froze. 'Typical. Right, get in the basement.' She points towards the kitchen and a scream from my mouth blurs the world away.

'You know what you've done.'

An electric blanket warms my body back to life as I wake inside the living room.

'Oh, Sweetheart,' Mother calls. 'You're awake.' I look to my side where Mother sits with a borrowed clown's smile. 'Would you like a cup of tea? You must be feeling rough. Do you have a headache?' I nod. 'Okay, I'll fetch some tablets to ease that away.' Her speed almost that of running as she takes off, eager to kill my pain.

She returns and forces two tablets with water onto me. 'What happened?' I say, my throat lavishing the water.

'You passed out, Sweetie; you've been out for hours. Oh, Poppy called round before. We had a nice catch-up; she's such a lovely girl. She had to take off, though. Do you need anything? Are you hungry? Are you too warm? I could turn the blanket-'

'I'm fine, honestly, no need to stress.'

'Brad also called while you were out.' My heart sinks. I don't have the energy to deal with this. The kettle's click takes her away from me, but the belt lies still on the ground; gloating about how soon it will touch me.

Mother's cup of tea is not to her usual standard (say what you want about her personality, the woman makes a damn good cup of tea), but it will suffice. Anything will right now.

'I think it's time I tell you the whole story.' I know she's referring to Tony. She's mentioned the act in the past, but never in detail. Unfortunately, though, I know the details from her diary. I cried for weeks after reading it. To me, it brought us closer together, even if Mother didn't know it.

'You don't have to-'

'No, no, it's fine. I know you know I was raped, but you should know everything.' She takes a sip of her tea and prepares herself. 'As you know, Tony and I were best friends. Your grandmother and grandfather both liked him, all the boys at school liked him, all the *girls* at school liked him: he was sweet, he was charming, handsome. Everything those rom-coms try to emulate in their lead, that was Tony.' Her words quote her diary exactly. 'He was two years older than me, so he was more mature than the boys in my class. You remember how boys were at school, always farting and being stupid; Tony wasn't like that. And you should have seen

200

the looks some girls gave me. Why was this handsome, popular guy hanging around with the class weirdo?'

'Mother, you're not-'

'I know, I know, but I was a little weird in school. Too thin for my own good, not especially good at anything. But I had a best friend, so, I didn't care. We were inseparable: The Terrible Twosome, the adults coined us. But there were never any romantic feelings between us. Obviously, he could do better than me, and I just saw him as my childhood best friend from next door.' Her tea rests on the floor, prompting a change in her demeanour. 'Well, one day your grandparents and Tony's parents went out for the day; we were obviously too cool to be seen with them so we stayed home, he came round and we chucked a film on. We put the film on in your grandparents' room, as their television was the biggest in the house, and climbed in bed to watch it. I know what you're thinking, but we were so comfortable with one another it didn't bother us being in the same bed.' The room sits silent, respecting her performance.

'This time, though, about halfway through the film, he starts stroking my leg.' She looks down at her thigh and gulps. 'I slide his hand away and giggle, as if it

201

were some joke I didn't understand. He'd done silly things like slap my behind before as jokes. So, in my naivety, this was the same thing.' She's desperate to cry but fights off the tears. 'Then he grabbed my crotch.'

She sets off out the room and returns with a kitchen towel for her eyes. 'Mother,' I say as she walks back in. 'You don't have to-'

'No, you need to know. You deserve to know.' She sits the soaked towel on the arm of her chair and readies herself for the rest. 'I stopped laughing and pushed his hand away again, but he just returned it. When I went to push it away again, he climbed on top of me and pinned my arms down. That's when he,' her words become inaudible through tears.

"That's when he pulled my pants down and ripped off my shirt." Her diary filled in the words in my head.

'He was bigger than me, older than me.' So was The Teacher. 'He did it, got changed and left without either of us saying anything. He never even kissed me during it.' Neither did The Teacher.

'What happened afterwards?' No words of comfort came to my mind.

202

'I told your grandparents a couple of days later, and they marched around there and confronted his parents. Guess what happened?'

'He lied?'

'He lied. In his version, I was "horny as fuck" and practically threw myself on him. I invited him round to an empty house, I invited him into a double bed with a film on. To your grandparents it made sense. When they got back home, your grandfather punched me and broke my nose.' Never have I been more grateful for Mother not resorting to that form of punishment. 'I remember having to lie to the hospital about falling down some stairs, or whatever.'

'And they believed that?'

'Was easier than asking questions. And a month or so later I found out I was pregnant,' she rubs her stomach. 'When I told Tony, he denied any involvement, and then your grandparents kicked me out.'

'Bastards.'

'It all kicked off. Tony's parents threatened us with all sorts of lawsuits and shit to keep it quiet, and then they moved to Brushwood. Flogging their house to the first bidder to get away as soon as.'

'But they threw *you* out?'

'Yeah; I was a slut who had sex with the neighbour kid in their bed. They were old fashioned; they didn't want an underage pregnant daughter. I slept rough for a few days until Ms Woodfield took pity on me. She had no family of her own, a history which isn't mine to tell, and the rest is history.'

'Did you ever see Tony again?'

'A couple of times, years later. I was about 20, I think. There was this social media thing called Myspace, and I found him on that. He came round a few times, even played with you a bit. I thought he was mature enough, but he still denied fatherhood and that was that.'

Her meetings with Tony weren't in the attic's load of diaries, but in a special few locked away in her bedroom safe. It took me weeks to pry it open, thinking of any combination of numbers Mother might have used to lock it. I eventually found the combination written and shoved inside a sock and found a couple more diaries. These detailed how she found Tony again, the weeks of messaging back-and-forth before meeting, and all the stuff they did together. She admits in them it was awkward, but natural.

'That was not long after Ms Woodfield passed away; she was lovely, but she wouldn't have ever allowed him here.'

At the back of my mind are some vague recollections of an older woman caring for me, but most of my knowledge of Ms Woodfield came from Mother's diaries. She sounds wonderful. She wrote from time-to-time how Ms Woodfield would sometimes be *too* involved, but she never raised it with her. Two broken souls united in chaos. There's a picture of her upstairs; such a happy woman. I've always wanted to research what happened to her family, but nothing good can come from digging up graves.

Mother's attitude went from sad to serious. 'That's why I'm so protective of you. When I was young, I believed the world was good; and it punished me. There are men everywhere, across every generation, that want nothing more than to hurt. Teachers, best friends, it doesn't matter. Brad seems like a nice guy, but they all do at first.'

'I'm sorry,' and for once, I felt it. Bringing Brad here was stupid. But he didn't do anything.

'No need to apologise. Look, Brad and I had a quick chat, and I've read some of the messages on your phone, and he does seem like a decent guy, but I'm not comfortable.'

'How about he comes round for dinner and you can get to know him?' Regret hit me the second I spoke.

'I don't know. We don't need more stress in our lives. But I do love you, so let me sleep on the idea.'

It's been so long since Mother has said she loves me, that it almost breaks my heart. 'I love you, too, Mummy.' My body squirms to prevent tears; now's not the time to appear childish. 'I just know if you meet him-'

'Lily, I said let me sleep on it. Right,' she stands and yawns. It looks fake, but I'm not going to object. 'It's been a long day, and I'm going upstairs to relax. You sleep down here, take it easy.' She kisses my forehead and walks away. It's a shame Mother swore away men because she wouldn't struggle for a suitor. Age has treated her kindly from the awkward-looking girl she appeared as in her teens.

Mother's body barely leaves the sight of the living room before the phone blasts.

'What day is it?' I ask, my teeth chatter.

'It's Monday.'

'Shit.'

'It's fine.'

'She called earlier, too.'

'It's fine.'

The phone continues to demand attention with its cry.

'We didn't tell her.'

'We don't need her.'

The phone gives up and rests, allowing Mother to slither away upstairs. The flashing on the phone signals another voicemail. Press it. Delete it. Press it. Delete it.

'One new message: Hi, sorry to bother you this late, but Lily didn't turn up this evening-'

I stop the message, unhook the phone and throw it into the kitchen. Its beady eyes can't watch me from there. The blanket offers protection in the living room before the wind taps my shoulder.

I open the curtain. The crack's bigger: a centipede.

207

I close the curtains and return to the blanket's protection and warmth. But a bright light pokes through a gap, garnering my attention. It beams into my world: demanding. Each blink brings the source closer. Blink. Across the street. Blink. Outside the window. Blink. Inside the house. Blink. Standing, hovering, towering over me. Watching me with its bright, orange light. Blink.

I'm outside. The wind massaging my neck as the orange light retreats away.

No houses awake, no cars alive. Darkness.

No animals barking, no voices calling. Silence.

The muffled cry of a little girl appears; a gentle cry, caught between wanting attention and fearful of asking. A weak cry. A victim's cry.

The sound leads me down the side of the house, and a little girl sits on the cold, damp floor huddled up. Her jet-black hair covering any sign of flesh. I know this girl. I know this evening.

'No, not this,' I beg.

Four days ago, she had her first encounter with The Teacher. Her mother doesn't know she sneaks out of the house in the early hours to cry in peace. Nobody ever checks to see if she's okay. Why would they? This picture has not appeared since.

'Does he do it again?' She asks.

'I'm sorry?'

The girl looks at me, stands and walks closer. 'Does he do it again?'

How can an adult explain such horrors to a child? I want to say no, to fill her heart with promise and hope, but I can't. All she wants is her mother to offer a hug and to make everything better, but she doesn't get it. The Teacher instead offers that hug.

'You're so young,' I whisper, more to myself than her. She needs someone to tell her it was a one-off act, and she'll come to terms with it one day and move on with her life. I can't be the one to lie to her.

'Why me?'

I can't answer that, either. I stroke her hair back into the style it once wore proudly, and she embraces me with a hug. This needs to be a moment of hope she lives with. She needs hope. She needs friendship.

'Is he punished?'

Blink. The living room. The warmth of her body still nestles on my chest.

'No.'

Tuesday

'Good morning, Sleepyhead,' Mother announces as she pokes her head into the living room. 'You're waking up later and later, these days.'

The clock informs midday has passed by, yet my eyes remain unsatisfied. Mother's right about my sleeping: since the incident, any resemblance of a sleeping pattern has long since been a pipedream. In the weeks which followed, my body became more nocturnal, finding safety in sleeping while the sun woke. What do I have to wake up for? I don't have a job. I don't have regular friends. I don't have freedom. Mother's manipulation causes her own ire.

'Sorry, I had a rough night's sleep.' My go-to excuse. Most of the time it was true; between nightmares and fear, sleeping became as unbearable as waking. It's an excuse wearing thin.

'No need to apologise, Sweetheart. What's troubling you at night? More bad dreams?' She walks fully into the room and sits on the pouffe near the sofa. She looks lovely. But I know she's just feigning interest. If she cares, why would she pay *other* people to listen to my dreams?

'Yeah.' I couldn't elaborate.

'Listen,' she grabs hold of my hand with hers. 'I know they feel scary and real, but you need to remember it's just your mind playing tricks. While unconscious, it opens doors to places you wouldn't dare go. I used to have these lucid dreams *all* the time after Ms Woodfield died, bringing back memories of your grandfather and Tony and you-wouldn't-want-to-know what else.'

'How did you get them to stop?'

'Ms Woodfield taught me a trick: Right,' she stands and gestures me to follow. 'I'll show you.' I'm not dressed for this, wearing just a bra and a pair of short-shorts, but she doesn't allow that as an excuse. 'Hold your hands to the sky, keeping your palms straight and together, relax your heartbeat and declare your name.'

'Declare my name?'

'Yes. Say it with conviction and belief: "I am Lilian".'

'I am Lilian.' I'm so pathetic.

'I'm not buying it. Again.'

'I am Lilian,' this time my voice raised.

'Better. This grants you control over your mind, and your nightmare should fade away.'

'Does it work? It sounds silly.'

'It did for me. Eventually, my mind gave up trying to project scenarios on me because I'd developed this control.' She gives me a quick hug and sets off out the room. 'Why don't you go for a walk?' She calls from the kitchen. 'Exercise also clears your mind. Plus, it's a beautiful day.'

The wind's whistling, louder daily, makes me suspicious about the weather, but a walk regardless could go me right. It is, after all, how I coped when I finally left the house after telling Mother about the incident. The castle's woods offer a beautiful and peaceful space to walk and admire life. Life freer than the one I was caged in.

The wind reaches out and rubs my bare back, jolting me forwards. Maybe going for a walk will erase the demons. Even if only for a while.

Alexa's showers take longer than mine; after all, she cares about her looks more than I do. I wait on the landing for her to finish. The décor upstairs, much like downstairs, is very Ms Woodfield. Mother's tried her best inside the rooms; apparently, Ms Woodfield's bedroom had this horrific yellow wallpaper, and my walls were pitch black when Mother moved in. Outside

214

the rooms, though, everything is cream. As it was when Ms Woodfield was born, or so Mother says. A colour which never goes out of style.

Ms Woodfield, who lived the entirety of her eighty-eight years inside these walls, actually called each of the three bedrooms her own. She was born into Alexa's room, upon her brother moving out she moved into the bigger bedroom (allowing her and her younger sister freedom from one another) and when her parents died, she moved into the main bedroom. I've only ever called one of these rooms mine. Maybe when Mother dies, I'll double that tally. Maybe my children will go to Alexa's room. Maybe, like Ms Woodfield, I'll live my entire life inside these walls. These cream-coloured walls.

As I stroke the cream, a heartbeat emanates from behind the paper.

'Hello?' I whisper, hoping neither Alexa nor Mother hears. The heartbeat is slow, but there. I press my face harder against the walls.

'I know what you've done.'

The words jolt my body back, slamming against the bannister. My breaths double in pace, as does the heartbeat. Louder, faster. It's walking towards me. Whatever it is.

'There you go, Your Highness,' Alexa says as she opens the door, silencing the heartbeat. 'It's all yours.' She bows, offers me a strange look and waddles off to her room. Despite her sarcasm, she's so elegant. Her towel wrapped around her skin perfectly, her hair spotless despite its recent washing, her skin glistening against the lamp's light. With me, I hold the towel with one hand, my hair with another, leaking water across the carpet like an absolute mess.

I don't know where she gets it from.

By instinct, I walk to the bath and turn it on, watching as the hot water crashes against the tub. The steam paints my face. My hand leaves my body as it races for the water, ignoring the burning sensation as it rests. My eyes don't care, either, as they watch the water pour out. The water entices me. Begs for me.

My breathing grows erratic.

I want water. I want to be one with it. I want to wrap my face in its warmth, as my hand is doing. I rid myself of the clothes holding me back and ready myself.

Black liquid spews out of my mouth and darkens the water. More down the toilet. Minutes pass by before the sound of water trickling onto the floor remind me to turn the tap off; the sight of vomit nearly brings up more.

I run the shower, not even pulling the plug in the bath, and rest. I'm not well enough to wash yet.

Soft knocks at the door avert my attention. I redress and jog downstairs, opening the door to two police officers.

'Good afternoon,' the first officer, an older gentleman, says. 'May we speak to Ms Hill?'

'Me or my mother?' The shower continues to pour.

'Whoever works for Brown Dale & Co.'

'That's my mother. What's wrong? She's sleeping at the moment.'

'We certainly don't mean to disturb,' the second officer, one who looks in his thirties, says. 'It's just her boss is concerned she's not been turning up for work; apparently, it's quite out of character, and they haven't been able to contact her. They're a bit concerned.'

'She's fine; she's just been ill the past few days. That's why she's sleeping.'

Mother's been going to work; are they lying? Is Mother lying?

'Okay, ma'am,' the first officer returns. His eyes survey the house. 'If she's feeling up to it when she wakes, can you have her call her office, please?'

I accept and bid them farewell; my acting performance Oscar-worthy.

'Who was that?' Mother calls from her room.

'The police. Your boss is worried.'

'I don't turn up for one day and they phone the police? Bit extreme.'

'One day?' I reach the top of the stairs and talk through Mother's open door, the shower still begging for use. 'They said you've not been in since Friday?'

'And you believe them? They've obviously got their facts wrong,' Mother walks out of her room and kisses my forehead. 'You know what the police are like.'

'You look nice,' Mother says as I enter the kitchen. She didn't look away from the dishes to notice, otherwise, she may not have agreed. Unsure of what mood I'll be in today, I don a grey top with light black trousers. Bland enough so nobody will notice me. Her compliment, however false, raises my spirits.

'Thanks,' still no glances at me. I grab a few bottles of water from the fridge, not feeling the desire to eat, and wave goodbye to Mother.

A jacket was a sensible decision, as Mother's weather report is far less accurate than the crack's; but it's still a comfortable day. Plus, cold, fresh air kissing my lips brings me to life.

The wind's arms guide me along as Mother used to when I was a child. I never worried when mother held my hand. I was safe; she was my protector. Now, the wind has that role. The sun isn't smiling down as much today, but the grass is still greener than ever. Such a deep, luscious shade of greed. The blades flutter in the forest's direction, working in tandem with the wind. My heart bathes in kindness.

The deeper I get, the more trees I encounter and the more I marvel in their dancing; they're in tune with the blades' flutters, wanting to party. The wind offers itself as a DJ, its whistle-based song not a favourite of mine, but everything else loves it. I partied with the blades and the trees and the plants a lot after the incident; they cheered me up when I was at my lowest. Mother had Ms Woodfield, I had nature.

They provided entertainment, a shoulder to cry on or simply a reminder The Teacher is an anomaly in a world of beauty. Although, one evening I was out later than I should've stayed, and it got really dark. While I wanted to go home, my body was so afraid it begged for nature's help. Nature doesn't help at night. Nature scares. I remember hiding for hours because a group of lads came here to drink and talk about girls and sports. Fear forced me to urinate on myself, to avoid them knowing I was here. Mother found me after they left and banned me from ever coming here at night. One ban I happily adhere to.

I walk an alien along a familiar path; once a daily ritual before that evening, terrifying this stretch of land from my days. I come across a tree's stump; a memorial to a once-proud tree which comforted me in times of severe depression. I kiss the stump and apologise for not being there in its last days. Its name was Everest: he was the tallest tree in the land. He was magnificent, and I can only imagine what it was like in its prime. Guarding the woods and all its kith and kin from harm. And me. One last goodbye to Everest and my walk resumes.

The wind tickles my body as I walk. 'Stop it,' it says through laughter. There isn't any conviction in my voice. The tickles fade away, as it grabs my arm and leads me down the path: I duly follow.

We're all skipping together; the blades of grass, the wind, the trees and me, and they're all waving as I pass. Even the pollen in the air sways from side-to-side, smiling. Pollen which normally causes allergies. Never have I felt such laughter, such calmness, such a sense of being one with the world.

The wind releases my grip and the sounds of splashing water greet me; the latest addition to the party. I didn't need to look to know where we are: at the end of the woods there's a cliff, overlooking the lake which flows to the river. The lake is a good ten-metres down. On the other side of the lake are farms, as far as the eye can see. For hours I used to dangle my feet over the edge of the cliff and watch the sheep and the horses be free;

221

free from worries and stress and work. They didn't care. They had farmers who cared for them, some had mothers who cared for them, people would walk by and say hello. Free. My darkest days mixed with breath-taking views.

The lake is narrow, but it's *intense*. Beer bottles, crisp packets and sports balls litter an otherwise clear-blue sight. Rough-looking rocks protect it from dry land. This is worth a photograph. As a child, I loved taking pictures, with many of our family days out recorded with me behind the camera. I always loved capturing the world, even if I wasn't in it.

'Come party, Lily,' the wind whistles in my ear. The wind grabs my right hand and we dance. For so long I've clamoured for the day when they introduce me as the new Mrs Whatever to this party, and me and my husband would take the first dance. Chris de Burgh would serenade us (if Cindi Lauper is busy). Crowds of faceless people would watch and gawp at how perfect we are as a couple. The wind would act like my father, the ocean a background choir, the trees ushers.

The wind and I dance and spin, the water providing backing vocals with the sun smiling down.

The trees shade parts of the sun's smile, offering a romantic setting. Maybe one day Brad and I will have this chemistry.

The wind spins me round and lets go. The water splashes higher, forming an arm to reach out. It wants me to dance with it. Bored with being the vocals, it wants to take the lead. The wind offers a gentle nudge, it's fine with me partying with the water. The water's melody enchants me into opening my arms. The wind guides me to the water, the father passing the daughter to the husband.

It leads me to the cliff's edge and stops me as my toes dangle. The water's arms retreated into a comfortable bed for me to land on. I can feel the rest it's offering, a rest I so desire.

The blades have calmed their dancing. The trees not rocking as much. They're waiting for me to descend to the lake and resume the party on a lower floor. The bed looks so comfortable.

'It looks amazing,' I whisper aloud, silencing the nature around. My toes dangle further off the edge. A horde of sheep stand side-by-side, all watching me. Maybe they'll come party with me in the water.

'You know what you've done.'

The words dagger through the picture. My feet recoil away from the cliff's edge, falling over a rock in my careless walking. The water's lullaby turns frantic, its splashing no longer enticing. It's trying to grab me. It splashes above the cliff's edge, reaching out.

The wind pins me to the ground; its hand wrap around my throat. The trees and the blades cheer on the wind, the water ordering it to choke harder.

Footsteps scare away the wind's choke, as the rest of nature retreats. 'Lily?' I hear Brad's voice. 'Is that you?' My knight in shining armour.

The chattering of birds in the distance wake me. 'Welcome back,' Brad's voice drowns them out. 'You've been out for hours; I was getting worried.'

He was worried about me. A smile erects on my face. 'Wh-where am I?' My words mumbled as my eyes struggle to open.

'In the woods by the castle,' his voice soft. 'You passed out.' No recollections come to mind. A coarse cough lets out, nearly bringing vomit with it. 'We should get you home, you should rest somewhere a little more comfortable.' I sit on my knees, my senses slowly returning.

'That's probably best.' Brad helps me to my feet, but the thought of Mother freezes me. 'Mother's going to be so worried-'

'It's okay, don't worry. I phoned her earlier and kept in regular contact. She knows what's happened and knows you're safe.' Brad's safe arms guide me home, a feat more impressive considering how little my spaghetti legs help, and Mother embraces me as I pass the threshold to the house.

'Oh my God, I was so worried, especially when Bradley called. Are you okay? What happened? Were

225

you attacked or something?' Her frantic speech not allowing any reply. 'I'm never letting you out of my sight again,' she hugs me tighter. 'I can't think of what I'd do if anything happened to you.' Is she crying? I don't think I've ever seen her worry so much.

Thankful faces cover the living room as Mother guides us in. The Flowers and Alexa each offer a hug and thank God I'm alive. As they sit me on the couch, Mother hugs Brad. Something I've longed to see, but still weirds me out.

'Thank you so much, Bradley,' she says; if she's not crying, she's fighting as best she can to prevent them.

'No need to thank me, I care about Lily, too, and I wasn't going to let anything happen to her.' I knew she'd like him; they just needed an introduction.

'Why d'ya faint?' Alexa asks; her look uneasy: does she blackout, too? 'Was it your fault, or?'

'Honestly, I can't remember,' grass patterns still crisscross on my palms. 'I went for a walk, and the next thing I know Brad's there waking me up.' He rubs my shoulder and smiles. Did he attack me? No, he wouldn't.

'Well,' Mother announces. 'It doesn't matter what caused it, all that matters is you're safe. Lily,' her voice dims, 'can I have a word?' Mother takes me into the kitchen, leaving The Flowers to open the celebratory wine they had brought. 'A pretty girl lying alive but unconscious on the floor in a secluded area could have been prey to most men.' I hope it's not another lecture; I can't handle another one. 'You could have been murdered or kidnapped or,' her words fall shy of saying raped. 'But, Bradley didn't take advantage. He kept you safe, *and* he kept me informed. I respect that.'

The urge to say 'I told you so' slaps against my mouth, but I refuse it life. When I was younger, about six (maybe seven), we had a cat called Hermione (I got to name her). I loved her. We'd have hour-long conversations about our days (mine spent at school, hers cleaning, sitting, sleeping and watching television). I think Mother only got me Hermione to stop me pestering for a holiday (at the time I was desperate to go abroad, anywhere abroad, but Mother kept refusing). We had her for about three years until someone ran over her. The man who ran her over brought her to our home and footed the vet bills, and Mother thanked him for his kindness and honesty. I didn't thank him: he killed my cat. A couple of years later I asked her why she was so calm about it (I assumed it was because she didn't even want a cat), and she said because she respects those who pay for their sins before death. 'He could have driven off and got away with murder,' she said. Instead, he paid for everything and owned up to his actions.

'He is really nice,' I say, as close to 'I told you so' as I could get.

'I'm still not happy that he's a man, but if everything you say is true, coupled with his actions today, I am willing to give him a shot. *If* it's what you *really* want.'

I damn-nearly jump on her to give a hug and thank her. Mother ordered pizzas, and the seven of us partied. I know she wants to study Brad more, and I'm fine with that. He'll pass the tests. He's even taken his shoes off; I know she's made a mental note.

'Excuse me,' Brad takes Mother to one side, my ears double in size to hear. Any wrong word said could be the end of this. 'If my being here makes you uncomfortable, I have no objection in leaving. I know how you feel about Lily and my friendship-'

'Nonsense,' Mother offers out a hand. 'Any monster could have been walking through those woods.

Not many men would have passed the opportunity to attack a helpless girl, but you did, and you waited for hours with her. Any man willing to do that for my baby deserves a chance.' He shakes her hand.

I excuse myself and head to the bathroom, dropping to my knees over the toilet as soon as I enter. My stomach feels wrong, vomit's on its way.

Only, it isn't water. The unusual texture scratches my mouth as it rises through my throat. Not until I'm near-finished did I realise: I'm vomiting grass. Another retch brought more blades into the toilet, as grass appears around the room. I back against the door, horrified at the sight.

In my early teens, I became aware I was not what lads wanted in a girl: I was scrawny, had oddly coloured hair, fingernails bitten to random lengths and my female features are nothing special. But, one day I was eating my third bag of crisps and a few of the girls called me a pig. Probably other names, too. It made me so self-conscious about what I was eating I started throwing up after meals. The Internet called it bulimia. The Internet wasn't very keen on the idea, but it helped me. I was eating more and lost about half a stone.

Vomiting is nothing new to me, but this feels different. Wrong.

Another retch and this time water came out. Red water. The sight inside the toilet horrific. Green grass and red water. Comfortably ignoring any attempt my tears made to change it back to normal.

After a few minutes of sobbing, I flush the toilet and brush my teeth. I'll keep this quiet; Mother would only stress. The flush works, the water back to its normal state.

My vomiting wasn't quiet, but nobody mentions it as I enter the kitchen, with everyone acting as if nothing's wrong. Nothing *is* wrong. Ivy's chatting with Rose, Poppy's speaking to Alexa, Mother's still studying Brad. If van Gogh could paint the best sight my eyes have ever seen: this is it. My life. All my favourite people in the world under one roof.

'Hey, Lils,' Ivy calls. Poppy joins us, too, as Alexa darts out of the room. 'You'll *never* believe what happened to me last night.' I giggle. This is my life.

'Ivy,' Poppy sighs. 'I don't think Lily wants to hear one of your stories right now.'

'No, please, I insist.' Anything not about me is a welcomed story. 'I want to hear it.'

'Good. So,' Ivy rests her glass of wine to enable full enunciation. 'I meet this guy, Jeremy, and one thing leads to another and we're in his room.' I love her casual 'one thing leads to another' attitude. She's met people at football stadiums, college, supermarkets, weddings, funerals and even at the castle, and it's always 'one thing leads to another'. I'd love to be a fly on the wall to see how she does it. 'So, we're going at it, and I'm doing reverse cowgirl for a change, right? Then, his phone goes off.'

'Don't tell me he answered it,' Rose begs.

'Oh, he answered it. As it's going off, I can feel him slowing down. So, I'm like, "dude, you're not answering that, are you?" to which he replies, "it might be important".' We all shake our head in disbelief. 'I spin around and see it's his sister calling. So, I'm safe, right? No way he'll answer the phone to his sister, right? So, I go harder. Then he answers.'

'Oh my God,' Rose's voice dances between anger and shock.

'So, I slow down again, because this is weird. I'm expecting a quick call and he'll tell her he'll call back or something. But, no, he has a normal conversation.'

'Oh, please tell me you're kidding,' Poppy's voice horrified.

'Deadly serious. He's chatting away with his *sister* about some birthday party they're planning for their dad while he's fucking me. And he's not rushing the conversation along, he's offering ideas and all sorts.'

'Please tell me you got off and ran away. That's gross.'

'Well,' she pauses and sips her wine. 'I was *already* on him.' Several groans greet her.

Mother brings me a glass of wine and tells me to join in; I try to decline because of the vomiting, but its sweet taste is heaven against my lips. 'Excuse me, everyone,' Mother stands at the head of the room. 'Lily and I have been through a lot together, and I'm not ready for that journey to end just yet. Thanks to Bradley, our Lily is safe, and I get to spend another day with my daughter. So, I'd like to raise a toast: to Lily.'

'To Lily,' everyone replies, embarrassing me. I'm not grateful for whatever caused me to collapse in the woods, but I'm grateful for the happiness it's brought. I'd happily sleep in the woods every evening if it meant having this night over and over.

Happiness fades somewhat as the wind squeezing its way into the living room grew louder. On my way to check it out, the front door's letterbox flaps back-and-forth. My feet walk back into the kitchen, as the wind tries opening the back door. Is it circling the house? Nobody else notices.

The party moves from the kitchen to the living room, all still unaware of the wind's whistling. The sound rises in volume, before Poppy and Rose's laughter wipe it away.

Seconds later, I casually place a cushion over the crack, hoping to soothe any attempt at breaking in.

Throughout the evening Brad was getting along with most of The Flowers (Rose still held suspicion), as well as Mother and Alexa. Everyone was so happy. So merry. So cheerful. So full of laughter.

This is *my* mother. These are *my* friends.

'So, Lils,' Ivy's speech slurred. 'How come you never told us how cute Braddy is?' She has to stroke his arm to stop from falling over. I'd warned Brad about Ivy's sexual adventures.

'Thanks,' he replies. He words grateful, his eyes embarrassed.

'Don't, Brad,' Rose pulls Ivy to one side and sits her down. 'If you accept her compliments, she will track you down, and she will sleep with you. It's like her superpower.'

'There are worse superpowers to have, I suppose,' he replies, making us all laugh. Ivy's body slumps more into the couch; she's done for the night. 'Although, honestly, it's got to be a villain's power. Imagine Blofeld had a woman able to seduce Bond at will.'

'Bond is an easy example, though; he'd probably seduce her first. What we need is an arch-nemesis for Ivy.' Her passed-out state prevents any ability to listen.

'Surely any married man would rebuff her advances?'

'You'd think that,' Rose rolls her eyes. Most of the time we laugh and joke about Ivy's encounters with men, but sometimes it has rubbed us the wrong way. Such as the time she slept with Kevin. Kevin was a married man with two children, yet 'one thing led to another' and he is no-longer a faithful husband. That was one story she never elaborated on: who initiated sex, but we were still disgusted by her actions. I can't imagine sleeping with a man in another woman's bed.

'Okay, so we need a villainous monk who's vowed celibacy and world domination, and-'

'Veganism,' Rose interjects.

'Really?'

'Oh, yeah, our Ivy *loves* steak; there's no way she'd date a vegan unless her hands were tied.'

Rose leaves for a minute, and I apologise to Brad for their behaviour. I love them, but they can appear a bit much. He has none of my apology, though. 'No need to apologise, I'm enjoying their company. They're fun. Although, to be honest, I was expecting more hostility.' Me too. 'I've had a lovely evening.' He takes my hand in his as nerves flutter around my body.

'Me too.'

His holding of my hand only lasts about a minute; a glance from Mother ends it. It's probably wise we don't push it too hard. My hand yearns for his. I love the feel of him holding me, guarding me, protecting me.

I want him nearby all the time. But, I also want my skin to be my own. One day I'll be able to relax around him.

Needing an early night (with a meeting to sort out funeral arrangements planned for early tomorrow), Brad leaves just before midnight. Everyone (bar a still-passed-out Ivy) hugs him goodbye. Mother's hug, though, turns his smile upside down. A jolt of anger rickets inside of me: what has she said? Is she teasing me?

I'm reading too much into it. I have no proof. Brad doesn't tell me what she said as he hugs me on the doorstep. I watch as he walks off into the moonlight. Is he on Ivy's radar? Is Mother *really* accepting of him? Another sip of wine calms down my mind's erratic over-analysing.

'I accept him,' Mother says to me as I slump next to her on the couch. I smile and thank her, and her stroking my hair lulls me to sleep against her shoulder.

An icy shiver brings me back to life. No longer on the couch, I awake to the planets orbiting my ceiling. The room in near darkness, aside from the glow of Planet Lilian. A place where I belong.

My childhood wasn't the worst; I had a mother who loved me in her own way and I found ways of entertaining myself without friends. But I've always felt I didn't belong. A poster of Supergirl protects my bed, a character I resonate with. Sent from her home planet to live on Earth. I need sending from Earth to my home planet.

Planet Lilian is the largest of the planets, narrowly edging out Jupiter for the moniker, with five moons orbiting it. When I was younger, as part of a science project, a study on the planets and their rotations, I realised how minuscule I was in the universe. Humanity has walked on the Earth's moon. And that's it. I'm one person on a planet of over seven billion, amongst a sky of planets and moons we've yet to explore.

I close my eyes, hoping for sleep, but they open to a new scene. No longer the planets on my ceiling. I'm back in the classroom. Stars replaced with countries.

Planets with flags. Darkness with life. Calm with fear. Silence with his voice.

'So, I hear you've been off school for a few days.'

Something's different. Normally, when my mind recreates these nightmares, I'm watching the past. This time, I'm living it. 'Yeah, I felt weird,' my voice says. I have no control over it.

'You haven't told-'

'No, sir.' I can feel how hollow she feels.

'That's a good girl.' He walks to the door and looks down each corridor. 'So,' he returns to me and unbuckles his belt.

'What are you doing?' My mouth asks. Confusion and worry reign.

'Well, now I know I can trust you; this can be a regular hobby.' That smile. That malevolent smile. 'Now, get down on your knees and open that pretty little mouth for me.' She shakes her head, but he grabs it by the throat, reminding me of the power in his grip. 'Open.' Malevolent smile, malevolent voice.

We sink to our knees; eyes closed, mouth open. I'm unable to force her to do anything different. His trousers unzipping flashes me back to my room. Back looking at the stars. Back dreaming about life amongst them.

The nightmares are all-too-regular and all-too-real. I can feel the warmth of his breath as he speaks, the splinters on the tables, how unusually warm the classroom was after school. I used to think it was time-travel, how real everything felt.

I get out of bed and fetch the pink bra again. 'Why me?' I whisper, tears falling next to his stain. The bra still feels tight. The girl in the mirror smiles back at me.

'It's all your fault,' she says. She's me, with about ten years added on, by looks of it. Her appearance cocky and confident. Much more menacing than the fear-soaked mess I offer. 'You were too weak, too easily led, too *easy*.' She winks.

'No, no,' my head shakes. 'He manipulated me. He abused me.' A conversation I've had with Mother during one of her vodka-induced rages.

'Even Mummy doesn't believe you.' Her voice carrying no more weight than a whisper, but it stings with ferocity. 'She doesn't believe you were the victim. Bless. You're pathetic, you know that, right?'

239

Tears spew in every direction as my head continues to shake.

'Want to know a secret?' She leans closer to the glass. 'He didn't even enjoy it.' Her words pierce my skin. 'A man like him has much better taste than what your sorry state offered. No wonder he moved on.'

'Stop, stop, stop, stop, stop,' my hands slap at my ears.

'I'd forgotten how much of a mess you are. Look at you, still wearing that bra like it's a badge of honour. Still ignoring what you've done, I take it?' Anger takes over, and I grab the mirror, rush it out the room and toss it over the bannister. 'You know what you've done,' cries out before it crashes against the floor, shattering glass in every direction. The sound brings peace to my ears.

'I'm not a mess, I'm not a mess,' my body sinks to the floor and into a ball. 'I'm not a mess, I'm not a mess, I'm not a mess.'

The bathroom door opens, and the woman from the mirror exits. 'There's the little slut I remember,' she says, my eyes widen.

Alexa's door opens, and a pair of early-thirties versions of me come out.

240

'Whore.'

'Bitch.'

Out of Mother's room comes a 21-year-old me, whose face mirrors mine, but with fewer worries. 'Slag.'

Out of my room comes the teenage victim. 'Liar.'

'No, no, no, no, no,' I rock back-and-forth, trying my best to ignore them all.

'We're not alone,' the twenty-something version says. The walls to the house fall back, leaving the hallway floor to rest in the middle of a dark room. Countless past-and-future versions of me stand in a circle.

'You're a disgrace to humanity,' calls out from Amanda, an insult she threw in the first year of high school.

'You're such a loser,' Barry repeats his insult from when I was 13.

'You're ugly and pathetic,' Henry repeats himself from prom night.

'Leave me alone,' I shout out, barely audible amongst the sea of voices. 'I'm the victim, I'm the victim, I'm the victim, I'm the victim, I'm the victim.' My voice dimming with each repetition.

The twenty-something me stands over me and holds my head. 'Listen to them, Lily. Listen to their words.'

'No one likes you.'

'No one cares about you.'

'No one will ever love you.'

'No one wants to touch you.'

'No one will cry at your funeral.'

I squirm and wriggle as much as her hold allows, but it's not enough to shake away her grasp. The voices become louder and louder, fanning a fire in my head. A fire built based on anger and hatred. But not at the voices.

I try again to plead my innocence, but it's nothing more than an inaudible mess.

'This is your life,' the twenty-something me shouts in my ear. 'This is what you've accomplished. Ask yourself, Lily: was it worth it?' The words dance and echo around my head: slut, whore, bitch, slag, liar, disgrace, loser, pathetic. Each one that little bit closer to my body. Dancing and spinning. Repeating. Chanting. 'Because I don't think it was.' The fire burns, and, as the first insult touches my skin, I pass out.

'Lily'? Mother's words return my senses, and I wake seeing myself in Mother's room. Standing over the threshold; my body facing Mother's bed. 'Lily?' She speaks more carefully – no; more cautiously – but I cannot find my voice. 'What are you doing there? What time is it?' Her eyes assess my intentions.

Why must Mother glance at me so; as if I mean her harm? I understand the peculiarity with which my presence at this hour brings, but there is no call for such a look of horror; such a look of shame.

'Lily, Sweetheart, what's wrong?' Her eyes may hex me, but her words comfort.

My shadow creeps in her room, independent from its host; unseen by Mother. It creeps until it reaches the other side of her bed and mirrors my stance. The shadow steals my voice and speaks: 'Don't worry, Mummy. You go back to sleep.'

Wednesday

The tag team tandem of a roading headache and cold air resuscitate me. The upstairs landing not offering any of the same comforts as the bed. My mind struggles to reason why I'm here, without a quilt, especially as I fell asleep downstairs. With an angry thud, the cold air's pathway to my room closes off.

'Good morning, Sweetheart,' Mother's chirpy voice rings around the room as I enter. Again, she's washing the dishes, and kisses the air near me to avoid soaking me with the water. The never-ending amount of dishes. Why is she always washing the dishes?

'Morning,' my voice nothing more than a croak. 'Where are the headache tablets?'

Mother stopped circling the plate with the sponge to offer a sympathetic look. 'Are you feeling rough again? Maybe we should speak to someone about it because it's becoming quite regular.' The headaches and nausea *were* becoming regular visitors. But, it is a routine I'm more than used to. I nod in defeat and follow where she points to retrieve the tablets.

Mother turns her back, her attention switching to the plates, as a bottle of wine, with about a quarter remaining, sits close to the headache tablets. Its sweet,

sweet taste pulling me in. After ensuring Mother wasn't watching, I take both pills with the wine. 'You shouldn't drink before 2pm,' Mother used to say. She never had a reason for *why* that is a rule.

Wine was one of my closest allies in the first year after the last incident, and it never bothered me what time of day. But Mother caught me drinking from a bottle with morning cartoons and she lost it. She probably understood, at least I think she did, but she still banished me to the basement for two days. The only light coming from when she opened to give me food. Since that punishment, I've never risked drinking before her arbitrary times. Thankfully, she doesn't notice today.

Alexa hops merrily into the room, her footsteps seemingly heavier by the day. She and Mother kiss each other's cheek and she pours herself a bowl of cereal, ready to embrace another fun-filled adventure in school. Even at the peak of my school enjoyment (not a tough bar to meet), I never wore such genuine happiness. 'So, was the floor comfortable?'

'The floor?' Mother spins.

'Yeah, I must have fallen out of my bed and slept on the floor.' Embarrassment encompasses me, and

Alexa offers a look of bewilderment, which neither of us address.

It only takes a few minutes for the headache to float away, with only a small remnant remaining to remind me it was ever there. The wrestling ring in which my emotions fight for control crowns a new champion: Happiness. It pins Pain, with the image of seeing Brad again at ringside.

A better girl than I could conceal her emotions better, but Mother spots my smile. 'I take it you're seeing Brad today?' She raises her eyebrow in a comical style.

'Probably,' my behaviour growing more and more into those cliched tropes I hated at school. 'I've not spoken to him, yet.' I'm trying to play it cool, but I have such little experience and control it fails miserably, and Mother laughs. The angel on my left urging for me to one day become the new Mrs Brad winning in its fight to maintain a safe distance away. The angel desires love; the demon fears humiliation.

'Well,' Mother looks back at the plates. 'If you go out, make sure to message me everywhere you are, so I know you're safe. A mother worries, you know?' A smile and a nod offer her the satisfaction she seeks. 'Oh,'

Mother's voice darkens. 'Are you going to apologise for last night?' A forgotten memory returns; standing beside Mother's bed in the dead of night.

'I'm sorry. I must have been sleepwalking. I have no idea what I was doing there.'

I grab a bottle of water, rub Mother's arm and return to my private cave. The sound of Mother washing the dishes and Alexa chasing her belongings for school soon fade away into a vacuum of silence. Nothing but my chest rising and falling to the beat of my breath. The Monday-Lady was mostly full of crap, but the breathing techniques she offered were quite useful. To her, it wasn't just the breathing, which was important, it was embracing all of my body. My hands interlock across my stomach, supposedly adding weight. And, instead of your nose being the most valuable player in the process, it's actually your breasts. Apparently, leading with your chest brings health benefits. Whatever the science behind it, it's something I've kept up with during moments of stress.

The radiator and the breathing soothe my body, cleansing it of any nasty auras. The sunlight peeks in, a rare occurrence, and a group of birds fly around together. So happy. My heart still aches for their lives, despite mine coming together. They don't have a warm bed to sleep in at night, or friends to talk to, or Brad to look at, but they're free: free from their conscience, free from judgement, free from Mother when she's cross, free to be wherever they so wish, free to unload on anybody they want to. I know if I were a bird, I'd be aiming at certain people.

My phone receives a message, interrupting the birds and the world outside, and Brad's name fills the screen. Is having Brad in my life better than their freedom?

"Good morning. Fancy the cinema tonight? Whatever you fancy. Xx".

Each word plays its part in the orchestra of emotions partying inside my head. Texting is impersonal, so I call.

'Good morning, Sweetheart,' he speaks after barely half a ring.

'And good morning to you, too.' I grab a handful of hair and start twirling it around my fingers. I used to mock girls for doing this. 'Cinema sounds lovely.'

'Excellent. Anything takes your fancy?' Just hearing his voice raises my breath.

'We'll just meet and see what's on.' It's not the answer he wants, and the brief pause which follows screams that, but I'll be with him. If the film bores me, I'll watch him. If the film scares me, I'll hug him. If the film arouses me-

'Yeah, that's fine.' The conversation enters small-talk territory until Mother's calling brings it to a halt. A quick kiss from my lips to his name captures all the lasting moments of Brad's time with me. One day *I'll* kiss *his* lips for real.

Mother stands motionless over the table which houses the house's phone. The flashing button thinning the air. Mother and I look in each other's eyes for a sign, but none of us so much as blinks. Without control, my body hits play.

'You have *one* new message,' the woman on the machine announces. 'Message one: "Hello, again, it's only me. I'm just checking in to make sure you and Lily are okay, seeing as you didn't turn up on Monday. If there are any problems what-so-ever, do not hesitate to call the office. I hope I see you next Monday." Press one to repeat, two to delete-'

'We *should* call her.' I've only once failed to see The Monday-Lady on a Monday, and we called the morning after to clarify what happened: or, Mother called to complain about how I was apparently so crazy I refused to leave the house. The Monday-Lady asked me the following week why I was kicking and screaming, but I didn't know. I still think they were lies. I didn't hate The Monday-Lady, nor those pills she made me take, but Mother comes out with lies to keep me there.

'You don't need to. She was a voice when you didn't have anyone: now you have me, Alexa, Bradley and The Flowers. We don't need her.' Mother *always* needed her. Mother needed her more than I did.

'I know, but we can call and explain how everything is fine, maybe she'll stop calling.'

'Sweetheart, she's never going to accept you as normal, because it fuels her bank account. And she's greedy. She lies to keep you there, you know that. She's poison. For the last nine months, she's been poisoning your mind, feeding your head full of nonsense. Even The Flowers knew she was bad news.'

251

'Excuse me? What do you mean by that?'

'They saw through her façade. They knew she was poisonous and were uncomfortable with you seeing her.'

'So,' a jigsaw slowly piecing together in my mind. 'You sent me there every week, knowing full-well The Flowers might abandon me as a result?'

'I'm sorry, but I thought at the time The Monday-Lady was more productive for you than The Flowers, and how in the long run you'd be better for it,' her tone matter-of-fact. 'You aren't, she's gone, they're back: I was wrong.' Her tone one of finality. 'Anyway, what film are you going to see? Sorry, I overheard you on the phone.' Her eyes full of curiosity, a fresh look for her.

Mother's said her piece, and when she's finished, there's no use attempting to continue the conversation. 'Yeah, we don't know, yet. We'll just turn up and see what's on, you know?'

She laughs at our plan (or lack of one) and harks back to when she and Tony did something similar and ended up watching a film called The Blair Witch Project, which was garnering all manner of attention at the time. Tony loved it, citing it as one of the scariest films he'd

252

ever seen, but Mother was more bored than anything else. Since then, she's used The Blair Witch Project as the barometer for all awful films. All the child-friendly films I subjected Mother to when I was growing up, she'd remark, 'Well, it wasn't as bad as The Blair Witch, so I'm fine.' I've not seen the film, but I guess after years of hearing how bad it is, I'm in no mood to go out and find it. Her story about watching the film is something she's never told me before, but again it was in her diaries. I'm getting pretty good at pretending to not know the story beforehand.

Mother left afterwards to get ready for work, leaving some dishes to rot in their strawberry-flavoured washing-up liquid. I follow suit and jump in the shower.

The warm water eases me into a relaxed state of mind. The pitter-patter of water hitting the plastic base or the glass door a tickle to my ears. My mind fleas my body to join the flow of droplets hammering down and Brad's face once again appears. Smiling through the sparkles. The water's constant pinching ensuring this is not another dream waiting to turn sour.

'Hi,' I mouth to his face. He watches my eyes. My lustful, wanting eyes.

I lean back against the wall and fixate on the image of his face. My hand joins the water coursing down my body, stopping at its destination. My breath paces harder as his eyes shine ferociously into mine.

'My Lily,' he whispers. I close my eyes, but the picture remains. 'My Lily. Listen to my voice.' I nod, my breathing's intensity increasing. 'I'll soon know what you've done.'

My eyes shoot open as I fall to the floor, my head slapping the wall as my bottom bounces forward. The water no longer a tickle, but a scratch. His face retreats from wherever it came, leaving my body frozen. Fifteen minutes elapse before I rush through cleaning and escape.

The confines of my prison become too much, and I ignore my body's demand for food and head out for a walk; no destination in mind, just freedom. Every time I've left my house over the last few years I've turned right at the first junction: right leads to the park, which leads to the castle, which leads to the shop (which summarises the bulk of my walking), but even getting to restaurants and supermarkets, turning right is easier. This time, though, my legs steer me left. A journey not taken since the week after the final incident with The Teacher. A journey once so familiar to me: a journey to West Drive High School.

It's changed since I was a pupil. Most of the graffiti has gone, and the lines on the ground and the car park (which were fading when I left) have been repainted. Did they wait for me to leave to improve the school? On first glance, it's a whole new school.

Midday hasn't yet arrived; all the children tucked away in their classrooms; their minds blown away by various subjects on offer. Maths. English. Science. History. Art. Cooking. *Geography*. All the children safe. All the teachers protecting them. A well-oiled machine working to perfection.

I walk along the school grounds, watching all the lives through all the windows. Then The Teacher's room comes into view. Any desire to be twelve again and back in the innocent world of high school fades. The blood inside me replaced with little anger capsules which my heart is all-too-willing to pump around my body. The desire to invade and announce to all the type of monster he really is surges through me. It could even save another girl's life. In the weeks after the final incident, my mind created a girl, Kelly, who was the next victim. She used to be everywhere I went, begging for me to do the right thing. Brad was right: I should have gone to the police. How many Kellys forced into secrecy and violence? How many Kellys abused because of my uselessness? Is their blood and sadness on my hands?

Mother wanted to protect me from the abuse of the townspeople and the interviewers and the police and everything else which goes with a high-profile case. And he would've been found innocent. I would either have been the girl who seduced a teacher and cried rape, or the girl who invented a rape story and ruined the life of a respectable teacher. Either way, he wins. He's too clever for prison.

I move around the rest of the school and bask in a series of memories; not all of which are bad. Some are nice, in their own way. Most aren't: the wall where Rebecca pinned me against before cutting off one of my ponytails (and, out of fear, forced me to tell Mother I did it myself as I wanted a new look: she was not happy); the grass where Chloe tripped me and rubbed mud on my trousers and leading the class to mock me for shitting myself; the little pond where Tyson threw my bag into. Some, though, flash an image of the innocent girl who still tried her best to smile against the hostility: the little girl who picked flowers in the summer as a present for the teachers; the little girl who was feeding the fish in the pond (before Tyson came); the little girl who spent break times trying to take the best photograph of the school's nature.

The little girl who died the moment The Teacher kidnapped her innocence.

I wave at a few teachers along my walk (those who *did* care for me, or, at least, pretended to), but they either ignore me or don't recognise me. A few strange looks follow as I arrive at the front gate again, looks which inform me I should leave.

A sense of freedom keeps me from returning to my prison, and I head further into West Drive. Our street is probably one of the most south-western places you can live in. A train track splits West Drive in half, with everyone either living 'above the line' or 'below the line'. Those above are generally richer. And they know it. The school is about a twenty-minute walk from my home, but I loved the walk.

A couple of streets away from the high school, a family gears up for a holiday. The car packed with several suitcases before the father has to squeeze another in. The mother, meanwhile, cares for her two children (both girls, I'd say about three and five), who are both running around the garden. She tries chasing them, but she's not got their energy. I ache for that life. The parents, the holiday, the sibling, the smile. Then the mother spots me.

'It's her,' she says to her husband, who jams the suitcase in with more power. After it's forced in, they rush the girls into their seats.

'Should we get her?' He pauses before getting in the car, looking with fierce eyes.

'Well, we would be doing this place a favour.' She pulls out a lighter from her pocket.

'Look at the state of her.'

'And why is she just staring at us?'

'Let's get her.' They both step to the side and slam their car doors. I run.

Street after street passes by in a blur as I run, not knowing if anyone is even following me before my body demands a rest. My heart relaxes to its normal rhythm as the tears dry up. An old woman in the house next to where I stand closes her curtains with hatred in her eyes. A dog barks in a nearby garden. I don't need to explore West Drive. I need my prison.

Street after street pass by, but my gaze aims at the ground; I don't need to see anybody, nor do they need to see me. My walk comes to a halt as I bump into a man stood with pamphlets about Jesus Christ.

'Oh, I'm sorry, my love. The Lord only gave us eyes in the front of our heads.'

'No, I'm sorry, I wasn't watching where I was going.' I shouldn't talk to strange men. I shouldn't talk to strange me. 'Sorry, bye.'

'You seem lost, my child,' he shouts as I walk away. 'God will look after you if you need him.' I used to pray for his help, but he ignored me. He didn't care about me. Why would he? I'm a lost cause, and he knew it. 'He will help eradicate your sins and will allow hope back into your heart. Which, I suspect, has been lacking some.'

I stop and face the man. 'And how is he supposed to do all this?'

'By blessing you, my child. As he blessed me.' He takes two steps closer. 'These hands have seen and caused so much hurt, but God opened his arms and showed me the path to righteousness. And he can do the same for you if you need him.'

260

'He wasn't there when I needed him the most.'

'My poor child, do not let that deter your faith. If God didn't help, it's because he believes you did not need it. You're strong. Stronger than you give yourself credit. He knows.'

'I disagree. But, I guess I'll go speak to him in the morning, see if he really can help.'

'Why wait, my child? The sun's alive and our time on this Earth is precious. Besides,' a strange look comes over his face. 'You know what you've done.'

'Excuse me?' My lip shakes. My mind pleads for my ears to be playing the role of the trickster.

'You know what you've done, Lily. You need forgiveness,' his body nearing mine. 'You need *his* forgiveness. He knows what you've done. Seek his help, Lily.'

As he reaches touching distance, I scream and run, darting and diving through streets until I arrive back in the sanctuary of my prison. My castle. The door stays open as I run to face the basement door.

'How does he know? How do they all know?' My forehead drips with panic; its odour fills the room. 'I'm sorry, I'm sorry, I'm sorry,' I drop to my knees, ignoring the pain of skin bouncing against floor. 'I'm sorry, I'm sorry.' The door thumps, and I fall back. 'I'm sorry,' I scream, but the thumping continues. Each thump roaring in my ears. My body froze. 'I didn't mean to. I didn't mean to. I didn't mean-'

'You didn't mean to what, Sweetheart?' Mother interrupts, and the thumping ceases, bringing an eerie silence into the room. 'And why are you on the floor? Are you okay?'

'I'm sorry, Mummy.' I wrap my arms around her as tight as possible. I never want this moment to end. I don't ever want to be alone without Mother.

'Don't be daft,' she returns. 'You have absolutely nothing to be sorry for.'

'I do, Mummy, I do. I didn't mean to. It was an accident. I'm sorry.'

'No need to apologise, you've done nothing wrong. You look exhausted, why don't you take a nap. It'll do you good.' I don't want to let go, but she pulls away. Her shoulder drips with my tears.

'I suppose.'

'Lily,' a soothing voice echoes. 'Lily, it's time to wake up.' An engine brings me to life; an engine belonging to The Teacher's car. My eyes widen, but my body refuses to move.

'This isn't the way home,' my mouth speaks. The radio plays Duran Duran's Planet Earth. The chorus making me desire Planet Lilian all the more. My eyes glance at The Teacher; it's all too real: the stubble on his chin, the watch on his wrist, the chocolate-scented deodorant. My heart aches.

'I know; I'm sorry, but I really need the toilet, so I hope you don't mind stopping off for a moment at mine. It's so close and I couldn't wait any longer.' He's so genuine, it's frightening. Nothing in his voice screams about the atrocity he's about to commit. He's the soothing, gentle, caring teacher who wanted to help me with my geography work. Edward Hyde needed a potion to become the villain; The Teacher needs privacy.

We arrive at the driveway of his large four-bedroomed house in a posher area (far north, something I didn't realise until he pawned me off into a taxi home). 'Come on in,' he says, opening the car door. 'People might ask questions if they see you waiting in the car.

Probably best to wait inside.' It's not a suggestion. My body follows without any hesitation.

I can feel her fear. It's not something I noticed the first time this happened, but he stands street-side, hiding me away from any possible neighbours. Has he brought anyone else to his home, before or after? Or was I special?

He locks the door as he closes it ('Just a habit', he tells me), and he heads upstairs to the toilet. I can feel her emotions: afraid, but confident. He's genuinely gone to the bathroom, so this could all be a perfectly normal detour (she doesn't know how far his house is from the school).

She's also confused, as am I: how can a paedophile live in such a pleasant, family home in a lovely, affluent street? Everything looks so normal: a normal-sized television, normal family pictures on the wall, normal furniture in the living room, normal wallpaper patterns. It shouldn't be the home of a monster.

My body walks to a picture of his family, and both of our hearts break. The ache turns to fear as heavy feet walk down the stairs.

'Is this your family?' My body asks.

'Ignore it, Lily.'

'Your daughters are so pretty.' The picture is of his wife and daughters at a theme park, all with cotton candy in hands and smiles on their faces. His daughters look about seven and ten in the picture. His wife, maybe early thirties, beams with pride at the lives she's created with the love of her life, the father of her children, her best friend. I've always wanted to meet her in person, accidentally, of course, to see what she's like. To see what type of person can marry a monster without realising. She looks too nice to be stupid. Was she manipulated, as I was?

'Don't talk about my family.' In another world I talk about his family so much he realises what he's risking by having me here. In this world, I look away. 'Come, let me give you a tour of the house.'

My head shakes, but he grabs us by the throat and pulls out a knife. 'I don't think you heard me correctly. I offered you a tour of the house.' My body nods. 'Good girl. This is the living room, which leads to the dining room.' Everything is so normal. 'Down the corridor is the kitchen. It's nothing special, so let's go upstairs.' The knife rests at his side, a soldier ready to strike on command. I've watched myself take this journey a multitude of times during the night, but now I'm living it again. And living it means I cannot look away.

Everything I normally hear, I feel: the thin sole of my shoes against the wood, the creek of the fourth step, the chip on the bannister by the seventh, the pen mark by the eleventh.

At the top of the stairs, he leads me to the only open door. Again, he locks the door behind him. 'We don't want to be disturbed, do we?' He unbuttons his shirt. 'Sit, make yourself comfortable.'

I can feel her following his lead, unbuttoning her shirt. 'Please, sir,' we beg. 'Can we not?'

He whips his belt off and folds it tightly in his hands. 'Turn around and bend over.' Through fear, my body obeys.

My trousers and underwear are ripped off; my naked body forced into the position he wants. I've tried to convince myself in the past these nightmares are just visions, hallucinations my mind creates to scare me, but as the belt slaps across my behind, I can feel it. I can feel the pain. I can feel my knees wanting to crumble. Belt shot two is worse. Belt shot three worse than two. We're writhing in pain, but the knife still watches. Waiting for its order.

He pauses and brings my face close to his. 'Any Thursday you want more of this, we keep a spare key in the back garden. I always enjoy the company of *dirty* girls like you.' The smell of stale beer wafts from his mouth.

He pushes me back to the same position. 'You have a cute behind,' he says, rubbing the marks left by the belt. I can feel how soft the fluffy pillows are. This is the bedroom of a married couple. A bed designed for comfort. 'I wonder how tight it is.'

I can feel each of his fingernails, all cut to various lengths, scratching my behind as he grabs. I can feel the bed deepen as he kneels behind me. I can feel my eyes tightening at what's to come.

The flapping of my bedroom curtains save me.

I bounce down the stairs, two at a time, and spot Mother reading in the living room with Alexa watching cartoons.

'What'cha reading?' I ask as I walk in, drawing both of their attention.

'Well, aren't you feeling better?'

'Much better,' I sit, and my body relaxes into the sofa's arms. 'I've not been eating much lately, so maybe I've been a little on-edge.'

'Good job I found some biscuits in the cupboard, then, isn't it?' Mother closes her book, not even saving the page she's on and rushes off to fetch a packet of custard cream biscuits. 'Eat as much as you want; you look like you could do with some sugar.' I don't want to get into another argument about my weight loss, so this is one order I'm happy to fulfil.

I do feel thinner, though. Can she tell? 'I love custard creams,' I say between the first few mouthfuls.

'Yeah, The Monday-Lady told me, so I make sure we always have a packet in the house.' She does care.

'With her, though, I had to "earn" them,' I roll my eyes and finish the biscuit. Custard creams were the

268

best part about visiting her, even if she did present several stupid hoops for me to jump through before I could get one.

'Don't attack me, and you get one.'

'Be honest, and you get one.'

'Admit the truth, and you get one.'

'Take your tablets every day, and you get one.'

I lied. She didn't care about whether what I said was real.

I head over to the window and look at the crack. 'Jesus, Mother, look at the size of it.' She offers a nonchalant response; the crack a scorpion in shape and size. The point of impact still no more than a centimetre, still gently allowing a stream of air into the room.

A message from Brad lands on my phone confirming the time for tonight (7pm), followed by a list of films. It's sweet he's planning ahead. He's thinking about me, right now. I reply with a smiley face.

'Mind if I put the news on?' I ask Alexa.

'Yeah, that's fine. I'm feeling tired myself.' She leaves, and Mother returns to her reading.

West Drive at Five is the main news show for the area, with their journalists well-respected across the whole north-west region (many have written for other papers, and Samuel AG Smith even became a famous author after starting as a journalist. I've not read any of his books, but he wrote quite a few before his death).

The two lead anchors introduce themselves as Emmaline Garratt and Alexandra Daniels. Alexandra's relatively new to the station, having transferred from The Roskell Mirror newspaper (quite a coup for West Drive at Five when it happened, as Roskell is the largest city in Wednesbury. West Drive a small town by comparison, only narrowly larger than East Drive and Millbank City, the two smallest places). Emmaline, though, has been anchoring the show for as long as I can remember. She's seen many co-anchors come and go across her tenure, but she's never wanted to leave. I met her once, and she was lovely. Alexandra runs through a quick preview of the top stories before passing back to Emmaline.

'Thank you. Our top story tonight: police in West Drive are searching for a fourteen-year-old girl, who has accused a well-respected teacher of rape. Described as a "vindictive, petty girl," who is "desperate for attention", she has a history of sexual promiscuity. Unfortunately, we cannot name her for legal reasons. We now go to our reporter, Lyla Thompson, who is at the scene. Lyla.'

The screen shifts from the studio to The Teacher's street. 'Thank you, Emmaline. Yes, here we are on Bakers Lane where the teacher lives, and, as you may be able to see behind me, hundreds of residents have gathered together in support of the well-respected teacher, who has shaped so many lives in this city. I would also like to apologise for any offensive chants or signs you may hear or see. Earlier today I spoke to Ms Fedder, and here's what she had to say.' The scene switches to a middle-aged blonde woman.

'Why have I come here today? To help protect the name of an innocent man from the sadistic mind of a pathetic child. If she wants to whore herself around, she can't blame other people afterwards to ruin their life. She's a slut, and she deserves to rot in Hell.' The scene shifts back to Lyla in the present.

'Again, apologies for the language, but it shows just how angry the residents are towards the girl. I, along with everyone else, hope she gets what she deserves when they catch her. Lyla Thompson, Bakers Lane, West Drive at Five.'

'Mummy,' my voice coarse. 'Can you believe this story?'

'Huh?' She finishes her sentence, before diverting her attention to the television. '"A fifth woman has been stabbed in Thynwych Woods". I know what you mean. I hope you never go there; he could be anyone.'

'What?' The teacher appears as I look at the screen.

'Thank you for digging to find out the truth about these nonsense allegations. I'm fuming. I have a family in there, and they have to go to school and work tomorrow knowing and hearing these malicious allegations flying around. My youngest is just ten, how am I supposed to explain to her what this all means? This could ruin my chances of promotion and haunt me for the rest of my life. The lives of my wife and kids ruined by some stupid, pathetic child with an axe to grind. And that ugly bitch better hope I never see her again. Otherwise-'

'That was the teacher at the heart of these baseless allegations of rape, and I have to agree with everything he said.' Emmaline and Alexandra stare with venom in their eyes.

'Lily,' Alexandra begins. 'We're coming for you.'

'You know what you've done.'

I turn the television off and toss the remote across the room. 'Woah, woah,' Mother says, startled. 'Calm down. What's riled your cage?'

'The story about the girl.'

'The one who got stabbed? Poor girl. I wasn't paying much attention, but I hope everybody watches, so this monster can't get to anyone else.'

Custard cream in hand, I walk to the kitchen and pour a glass of wine. Its sweet taste brightens my body as it shoots down my throat. Glasses two and three further clear away any unwanted stress, as I relax on the chair in the kitchen.

Brad arrives dead on 7pm, knocking the door with a musical pattern. It's silly, but it's cute. Mother welcomes him in as I finish touching up my make-up (I'm not generally one for wearing make-up, which The Monday-Lady says is a way of remaining unappealing to stave off male attention, but today feels like a good day to start again). 'Won't be long,' I shout.

Brad rises to his feet as I walk in the living room. 'You look incredible.' He speaks with honesty. My make-up makes me look a good five years older (and more mature than my normal child-like appearance) and combined with a sophisticated beige knee-length dress (which Mother bought me for a cousin's wedding last year, but we never went in the end), gives me rare confidence in my appearance. Brad could be lying for all I know, but I feel pretty. For once.

'Shall we?' Brad gestures towards the door; he must be eager to escape Mother's presence because I am. She means well, but we don't need a third party involved in this.

'Remember, you two,' Mother stops us as we leave the house. 'Be safe, and, Lily, message me. A mother worries, you know?' We each laugh, I agree and we walk away.

We have to take the bus to the cinema (it's on the east side of West Drive); it's been so long since I've last ridden on a bus. I sit with my head secluded, hiding away from the army of protestors eager to lynch me in defence of The Teacher.

Throughout the journey, I marvel at how beautiful this city is; its age adding charm to it. One day I'll explore everything West Drive has to offer. A day when I'm not afraid. Wednesbury is quite well-known for being a beautiful county, with the fields of Brushwood, the lakes of Roskell, the flower gardens of Primrose and the cleanliness of Millbank City all unite to create a popular attraction. I haven't visited many of them, but I do have a book on famous landmarks in Wednesbury. Not all are worth exploring, though, as Brushwood homes a giant statue of a foot. No reason why. The biggest puzzle about Wednesbury, though, is its lack of cinemas, with only two in the entire county (one in West Drive and one in Millbank City, in the north-west and south-east of the county, respectively). A girl, Lindsay, started West Drive High School one day and was quite friendly towards me (she didn't realise I was the freak at the time), and she told me how she came from Roskell and they had to drive over an hour to Princeton (in Taylorshire, the neighbouring county) to go to the cinema. Our twenty-minute bus ride is a drag, but it could be much worse.

Normally I wouldn't dare walk to the cinema from the bus stop alone, but having Brad here alleviates all stress. I know Brad's harmless, but his physique is quite tough-looking, which can intimidate others. My beautiful bodyguard.

The list of films at the cinema means nothing to me, and I offer Brad the choice of what to watch (we often mute adverts at home, so I have no idea what any of these films are about). 'Well,' Brad says, glossing over all the names. 'I'm not too familiar with most of these either. There's a big poster for a film called Sorry; we can check that one out?' I nod and he reads the synopsis from his phone. 'Apparently, it's based on a true story of a man who believed his family were conspiring against him, which led to him murdering them all one-by-one. Sounds chirpy. We can give that a pass if you want?'

That *really* doesn't sound like a film I'd be interested in. Another poster about a policeman grabs my attention, and we look up that one.

'That is apparently about a detective trying to track down a serial killer who is terrorising their town.'

'Spoilt for choice with all these happy films.' We both giggle. 'Witches and Ghosts? Aside from the obvious, what's that about?'

'That's a biography on Samuel AG Smith and his work. Fewer serial killers, by sounds of it.'

We settle on Witches and Ghosts, despite it being the busiest line in the cinema. He's a bit of a legend in Wednesbury, so no wonder it's packed. We choose our seats in the fourth row and marvel at the parts of West Drive presented on screen. I don't even remember them filming this.

The story wasn't anything spectacular; Smith's childhood home was haunted, which led him to investigate the paranormal. A few jump scares were out of place and ending with a brief examination of the apple tree in Brushwood, the last paranormal location he wrote about. The film had a horrible ending, though, with him, his wife and their two sons all found either murdered or having committed suicide, weeks after he released his last novel. Their death was big news at the time, with people split on whether he murdered them before taking his own life or if something supernatural finally caught up with him. I think a crazed fan attacked them, and he couldn't live without his family. I don't think I could live without Mother, even if she is a pain. In his autopsy, Smith's diagnosis revealed Chronic Traumatic Encephalopathy (a head injury which can cause nightmares and episodes). Poor man. Brad loved the film, but the ending was too sad for me.

'What a gorgeous evening,' Brad offers as we step out of the cinema. The sky a cloud-free picture, painted in a beautiful shade of grey. Stars glisten in every direction. The moon even appears in a slightly more unusual dark orange. Brad offers out his hand for me to hold, and enchanted by the night's sky, I accept.

The journey to the bus stop, the ride back and the walk to my house we held hands non-stop. Never have I been this comfortable with someone.

The lights are all off by the time we arrive back at my front door (it's after eleven, and I think Mother has work tomorrow), but I don't invite him in. I don't want to test Mother's patience. He takes my other hand and looks into my eyes.

'I've had a wonderful time.' His words melt any bravado I could offer, leaving a shy puddle behind.

'Me too,' I say, my eyes forced downwards.

He lets go of my left hand and lifts my chin. 'You truly are one of the most beautiful girls I've ever met.'

'Thanks,' I can feel my face burning. 'I'm not, but it's sweet of you to-'

His mouth meets mine, stopping my words dead. His right-hand ruffles through my hair, while his left arm lets go of my hand and cups my waist. His lips want more from mine, but my lack of experience prevents my ability to accept. Suddenly, he's The Teacher. Suddenly, he's a predator forcing himself onto me against my will. Suddenly, I'm begging to be free. My body freezes; his lips locked on mine.

Stress and anger and fear all party together inside my head, shaking my body on the spot. My brain's orders to run lost amongst the chaos. My entire body, hairs and all, feel uncomfortable. I want to run. I *need* to run. But I shouldn't.

Brad is a perfect gentleman. He has been nothing but amazing to me, but I want my own space back. I want Mother to open the door and rescue me. Like the pathetic, weak *child* I still am. I can look grown-up all I want, but I'm still just a child. My hands shake, wanting to push him away. But I want this. I want to want this. I want to be comfortable with this. The fire in my head roars to be free. My heart beats venom around my body.

'Oh, here she goes again,' the voice of the twenty-something me appears from my left. 'Woah is me, woah is me. A cute boy is kissing me. Poor, innocent me.'

'To men, kissing is just a prelude to sex,' replies the teenage victim.

'Then *fuck* him, Lily. He's cute.'

'Lily, don't. Think about what happened. Remember how you *felt*.'

'You'll feel great. *Trust me*.'

My head's the centrepiece of a tug-of-war game, swinging from side-to-side with each argument. He is cute. I do fear feeling how I felt again. I feel great around him.

'If he respected your desire for time and space, he wouldn't be forcing himself onto you.' The teenage victim takes advantage.

'If you respected him, you wouldn't be forcing him away. He's the best thing to ever happen to you, and, what, you're going to give that up because you feel a little uncomfortable?' Twenty-something pulls it back.

'If she's uncomfortable, she should say no.'

'She only thinks she's uncomfortable, because of *you*. And how *you* acted. And how *you* felt. Brad isn't The Teacher. He's different. So, Lily, kiss that pretty face for all he's worth.'

'Lily, don't. You still need time. This will only set you back.'

The fire roars louder and louder as the rope pulls from side-to-side.

'Embrace your sexual fantasies with him.'

'Respect your body. Run away.'

The rope snaps, leaving nothing more than a screaming mess. I scream. Scream and cower. Mother violently opens the door and my body falls into a world of darkness.

'Please.' Brad's begging brings me back. 'Please, I didn't do anything. I'd never do anything to hurt Lily. I swear.'

'Quit lying,' Rose replies. 'You've been playing us all since day one.'

As picture returns to my eyes, I'm presented with a frightening reality: Brad tied to a chair in the middle of the room, The Flowers and Mother surrounding him. Poppy and Ivy have a more hesitant attitude, with Mother and Rose each stood armed with a knife.

'Oh, Sweetheart,' Mother rushes over to me, examining me as if she were a doctor. 'What did this sick man do to you? Don't worry, we'll make him pay for attacking my baby girl.' She rubs my head and speaks in a soothing voice. Completely contradicting its meaning. A quick kiss to my forehead and she returns her attention to Brad. 'We're not afraid of men like you. We know all too well how you pray on the weak and vulnerable.' She grabs the knife and holds it aloft. 'Tonight, the man fears women. Bradley, Bradley, Bradley: *you should fear us.*'

'What the Hell is going on?' I demand. The bruise on Brad's body shines into my eyes as I stand. 'Mother? Girls? What's going on?'

Mother rubs the knife across Brad's legs and shoulder as she circles him. 'Well, we warned Bradley to treat you right or else. Now it's time for the or else.'

'Lily, please, tell them I didn't do anything. For God's sake.'

'You don't deserve to talk to her. Had we of done this to The Teacher after the first incident, there wouldn't have been a second.'

'Hear, hear,' Rose chimes in.

'Please,' my body aches to cry. 'Brad's right, he didn't do anything. I overreacted over nothing. Please.' The knife still writes imaginary number eights on Brad's legs, warning me against physically trying to stop it.

Mother walks towards me, knife still very much in hand, and moves her mouth close to my ear. 'I would sooner slit your throat right here, right now, than let another sick man have his twisted way with you again. So, for your sake as well as his, you better be telling the truth.'

My bottom lip quivers, my teeth chatter together. Never has Mother spoken with such darkness in her tone. 'I'm telling the truth,' I whisper, barely audible to even my own ears.

'Fine,' Mother says. 'Today's your lucky day, Bradley,' she turns to him; relief slaps his face. 'But, let this be a warning: if there is even a slither of evil in your mind, we will hurt you.' Brad nods, desperate to be free from the ropes, as my head burns.

I race upstairs and vomit into the toilet, my chest in agony with each retch. Poppy is the only one who follows and wipes my hair out of the way.

'It's her way of caring,' she says. 'In her own way, of course.' Her kind words can't overtake the vomit retching out of my body. Downstairs, I hear Brad running out of the house in a panic. I'll never see him again.

'I'm sure he'll message you in the morning,' Poppy tries to reassure. 'It's probably just a lot for him to take in.'

'Why would he want to stick around after that?'

'Hope. Hope it was just a one-off from a protective mother. He seems like a good guy, if there's a chance he's still yours, you should fight for him tomorrow.'

I wipe my mouth and hug Poppy. Of all The Flowers, Poppy was the first I told about my ordeal with

The Teacher, and I loved how understanding and sympathetic she was. She never judged me, or blamed me, or pitied me; she hugged me and told me everything was going to be fine like caring people do. Rose was vengeful, and Ivy speechless (probably the only time we've ever seen Ivy speechless).

'Sweetheart,' Mother calls. 'Bradley said he'll message you tomorrow, but everything is fine and he understands our anger.' She's lying, I know.

'Thanks,' I call back. Either she's lying or he is. Anger overwhelms me, and I wipe my mouth again and storm downstairs. 'How dare you do that to Brad?' Bravado I've never experienced before races through my body. 'Before even asking what happened, you threaten him with a knife?' Poppy joins, and looks dejected, mirroring Ivy's face.

'Sweetheart, I saw him kissing you, you were shaking and then you screamed. What is a mother supposed to think? Now, get some rest and we'll have a more civilised conversation about this tomorrow if you wish. But, for now, we're all a bit on-edge, so let's leave it for tonight.'

286

Hidden behind the wall of lips, my teeth press hard against each other, trying to break anything in anger. Mother and I look at each other for a good minute, neither of us blinking, as I try to assert dominance I've never held before. Mother wins. And I storm off like the petulant child I am.

The bedroom door, though, feels my wrath as it's slammed shut, vibrating the walls of my room. Alexa's sitting on my bed. 'What are you doing here?'

'I heard screaming and shouting, and I got scared.' Anger floats away as I mother Alexa.

'Don't worry, it's all over. Tomorrow, everything will be fine, I promise.'

'You really promise?'

'I super-duper promise.' We saved super-duper promises for the very rarest of occasions when Alexa was feeling scared and I had to comfort her. I'd super-duper promise Mother would stop drinking, or Mother would stop shouting, or Mother would stop swearing. I didn't always keep them, but she knew I was trying my hardest.

'Can I sleep in here, tonight? With you.'

'Of course.' I tip-toe to her room and fetch a blanket for her. As an adult, I sleep on the floor. The bed is too small to fit us both in any form of comfort, and I've spent many nights on the floor (and many more mornings waking there).

Alexa lasts about five minutes before she's sound asleep, as I sit against the bed listening to the innocent breaths coming out of her mouth. The Flowers by now have left, and Mother has locked herself in her bedroom (not even saying goodnight to us). With Alexa asleep, it's my time.

A smashing plate interrupts a fine sleep, and I wake to muffled screaming coming from the kitchen. I check on Alexa (she's still fast asleep), before heading downstairs.

'I can't do this, Lilian,' Mother shouts to another version of me. 'Every time you get better, something happens and we're right back to square one.' I edge closer into the room, neither of them noticing me (or caring if they had). The other version of me is the same age as I am, and she stands towering over smashed plates.

'I don't know what the problem is,' she replies.

'You never do. Everything is perfectly normal to you, but there's only so long I can keep up the charade.' Mother walks towards a counter and collapses her face into the palms of her hands. 'You're getting worse, Lilian.' In the sink rest a bunch of dirty dishes, while my pink bra sits on the kitchen table. The centrepiece of the conversation. Lilian cries and tries to escape, but Mother forces her back and slams her against the floor. 'No,' she points. 'We need to fix this here and now. Otherwise,' she wipes tears from her eyes. 'Otherwise, we'll need more professional help.'

The basement door swings open and darkness envelops the room, leaving me stranded. 'Hello? Hello?' I call out to no avail. As the darkness fades, I'm back inside The Teacher's classroom.

'Well?' He stands over me, waiting. 'Shall we phone your mother and ask to do this lesson at your place?' I remember this. The geography classroom needed cleaning for some reason, and no other room was good enough (I'm sure he had a compelling argument against staying in school). My mind screams 'No', but my body reaches for the phone and dials Mother's name.

'Pathetic,' Ivy's voice pinches from my left. 'You're so desperate, you'll do anything for him.'

'No, no, I'm not, I'm scared.' Nobody else has ever appeared in these nightmares. 'He's threatened me before.'

'Well, you could have phoned your mother yourself,' Poppy's matter-of-fact voice comes from my right. 'Then lie and say she's home, or that you have plans. Or, you could have excused yourself from the room and phoned the police instead. You always claimed to be the victim, but I don't see a victim, here.'

Poppy's doubt hurts: she's never questioned my innocence.

'He would never allow me to try anything, and then he'd hurt me again.' Am I trying to convince myself or them? 'He's in control. He's always in control.'

'Power is relative, Lily,' Ivy interrupts. 'He's powerful because you *give* him that power. Face it, Lils,' Ivy leans in and whispers. 'You *want* this to happen.'

'No, no, no, no, no,' I rock back-and-forth, desperate for them to believe me. My rocking interrupted by The Teacher.

'Your mother is fine with it; she's working late so we'll be able to study in private, without any distractions.' He grins that predator smile; his prey right where he wants it.

The four walls of the classroom fall back, a stage prop no longer needed. The scene replaced by the interior of a car on the dual carriageway. The dual carriageway which separates the school from my house. He holds one hand on the wheel while the other rubs my right thigh; I'm powerless to do anything. There's a knife in the driver's side door.

'Look at her,' Ivy's voice comes from behind me. 'Practically begging for it.'

'You've willingly got into an older man's car twice,' Poppy says, next to her. 'And we blamed him.'

'I don't blame her,' Ivy replies, smirking. 'He's good looking, you could do a lot worse, Lils.'

'Wholesome family man who cares enough about you to waste his Thursdays helping you with extra classes. Where's the problem?'

'The problem is,' I scream. 'He's raping me.' Neither girl reacts. 'I don't want this. I don't. I don't.'

'Willingly goes to an after-school class with a man who wants to have sex with you. Willingly hands over your phone to allow that man access into your home. Willingly gets into his car. Lily, you've been lying to us all along, haven't you?'

'No wonder she didn't go to the police.'

The car's engine doesn't roar loud enough to eclipse their laughter. The car driving over 80mph. The first time, I was afraid of going this fast (Mother never even drives at the speed limit, let alone ten miles over), but since it's become the best part. He can't rape me while he's driving. The walls again fall back, and we're closing the door of my house.

'Shall I take my shoes off?' He offers. 'Cute house. Want to give me a tour?'

'We can study in the kitchen, and the bathroom is just through there.' I walk towards the kitchen, praying he follows (but I know all-too-well he doesn't).

'Hold up, hold up, there's plenty of time for studying. This the living room?' A slight nod from me permits him to walk in. 'Your mother has great taste,' he marvels at the ornaments on the walls, ranging from a collection of thimbles to a random assortment of fancy, tiny clocks. 'Is there a story behind these?' He's Doctor Jekyll again.

'They were left to Mother by a friend. She used to travel a lot and collected them.' My voice robotic. I should have kept him talking; delayed the inevitable long enough until Mother came home to rescue me. The sad, monotonous tone doesn't make him further the conversation.

'I bet they're worth a fortune,' he says as he walks around more, stopping at a family picture. 'Now, this is cute,' he takes it off the wall for a better look. 'I see where you get your looks from; your mother is stunning.' He looks at me, waiting for me to accept the compliment. 'I can't wait for parents' evening; I can tell her what a fine daughter she's raised. She's single, right?'

'Yes.' Single mother. He must have had criteria of what he looks for in his victims. How many boxes did I tick?

'Don't you just look adorable with your little pigtails? They suit you.' The picture was of me in year five in primary school; not long before Rebecca cuts off one of those pigtails, forcing me to adopt the shoulder-length hairstyle I've had since. Near that picture were ones from theme parks, hiking in Brushwood's hills, pictures around the house and one of me and Ms Woodfield. The only picture where I'm not smiling is one with The Monday-Lady. Why does she get the honour of being on the wall of pictures?

'I'm too old,' my voice quiet.

'Nonsense. You're never too old to look cute.' He hangs the picture back and walks towards me. 'Well,' he says, his voice darker. 'How about that tour of upstairs?'

'Shouldn't we be studying?'

'Plenty of time for that. Go on, lead the way.'

'Yes, Lily,' Ivy speaks. 'Lead him into your bed. You know, I'm a bit jealous. I have to work to get a man into my bed, but you: you've got some skills.'

'Finally,' Mother appears on the sofa. 'I can see the truth of what *really* happened in *my* house.'

'I don't think you're going to like it,' Poppy says, appearing next to mother. 'From what we've seen already, we've all been fed a pack of lies.'

My body desperately clambers to protest my innocence, but the right words struggle to come out. Even the crack in the window looks at me with judging eyes. All the faces in the pictures have turned their back in shame. The tick-tocking of the clocks come to a halt. The Teacher awaits his tour. Poppy, Ivy and Mother await proof of my victim status. Everyone looking at me.

My body leads the way, through fear, and walks up the stairs. I can feel how sad and hopeless I felt back then; I had no idea this was the final straw, the last nail in the coffin, the snapping of the last string holding aloft my sanity. After tonight, I had a complete breakdown. I leave school with no qualifications. Even St. Andrews kick me out after the way I acted in my first week. I hide away for nearly a year before I can start piecing my life back together. 'Good girl,' he whispers. In some ways, the worst is yet to come for the version of me who walks up the stairs.

'This is the spare room,' I say, my heart breaking at the thought of him knowing about Alexa.

'Nice.'

'This is my Mother's room,' I say to a closed door, but he walks in against my weak protests.

'Now *this* is a bedroom.' He drapes his hand across the quilt as he walks around the room.

'My room is next.' She should stay here. Confine the abuse to this room. A plethora of nightmares avoided. Mother would probably have been angrier, but her mind would be free from hauntings. He follows me to my room; Mother stands as we enter.

'Look at you,' she says. 'Just walking him to your bedroom. Not quite the same story you made it out to be.'

'He's forcing me, Mummy,' I beg. 'He has a knife, and he's bigger and stronger and-'

'How could I have raised such a liar?' Her voice full of pain. My protests continue but fall on deaf ears.

'Cool room,' The Teacher says, closing the door behind us. I know he doesn't mean it. He checks himself in the mirror before rummaging through my drawers. What is he looking for? What could be in the drawers of a teenage girl? 'Take a seat,' he orders as he finishes looking. He walks towards the window and draws the blinds. He wants privacy. 'You're a very good girl, you know that, don't you, Lily?'

'I don't think I am-'

'Nonsense, nonsense,' he strokes my hair. 'You're *my* good little girl.' Little girl. 'Perhaps even my favourite.' His face twists from nice to sinister. He drops his bag against the floor and leans against my wardrobe. 'And, because you're my favourite, I thought we could play with some toys.'

Poor naïve girl. There's a tiny part of her which cheers at the mention of toys. A tiny part of her which hopes he's got toy cars or something in the bag. She's not mature enough to understand. The two hearts beating inside of us beat at different rhythms. Her hope makes mine beat sadder.

He kneels and pulls out a pair of handcuffs from the bed. Handcuffs which will haunt her nightmares in the next few evenings after tonight. From Planet Lilian's invasion by handcuff-shaped beasts, to my hands becoming handcuffs. A dream journal would have made for some bizarre stories.

I told The Monday-Lady about the nightmares, and she didn't mock me. Mother did, although she was angry at the time and didn't care about silly stuff such as dreams. The mother-daughter bond breaks tonight; it's been hanging by a thread for some time, with Mother more annoyed by the day at my behaviour (and the lack of interest in anything) and the messier I was becoming. Her finding me naked, handcuffed to the bed, her final straw.

'It's perfectly natural for your mind to substitute one frightening image with another,' The Monday-Lady said about my nightmares. 'Regardless of how unusual the new image is. I've seen many cases such as this over the years, whereby a victim, such as yourself, creates a new villain to fear. They're usually villains less scary than facing the truth. Perhaps these handcuff beasts eager to invade Planet Lilian are a representation of The Teacher invading your home.' She spoke rubbish most of the time, but that session helped. Since I've not created new beasts in my head; I just re-live the ones I've already faced.

'Now,' The Teacher says, holding a whip, his handcuffs and something which vibrates. 'Why don't you lie down for me?' My body does as it's told, and all the Flowers and Mother stand, smiling.

'Handcuffs, handcuffs, handcuffs,' they chant and clap in unison.

'Please help,' I beg to deaf ears.

The Teacher removes the last item from his bag: the knife. He places it on the side, out of my reach, and handcuffs my hands and feet to the four corner bedposts. 'Oops,' he says with a grin. 'We forgot to remove your clothes.' He tuts, a façade of drama. The knife returns to his hand and they embrace eye-to-eye. The Teacher wanting to abuse my body, the knife wanting to calve it open. The chanting silences as the knife moves towards my body. 'Now, should we rip them off,' the knife caresses my body, from the collar of my school shirt to my belt. 'Or should we *cut* them?' The knife strokes my face, forcing our eyes closed. The cold feel of the knife's edge sends shivers down our body. 'But first,' the knife presses against my cheek. 'Why don't you give the knife a little kiss?' The knife walks across my jaw back-and-forth until I finally kiss the flat side of the blade. 'There's my good girl.'

He cuts open my clothes.

I'm squirming as much as possible, but I can't move. The version of me I'm inhabiting frozen on the spot. There's no way to free ourselves from the handcuffs, despite how small our wrists are.

'You know, girls,' Mother says. 'She invited Bradley into our home while I was out, and she was surprised at my anger. But, he could very well have done this, too.'

'I would have,' Brad's voice joins the room. 'Had I realised she was into all this.' Brad is the last person I want to see me like this. Especially *this* Brad. He's not *my* Brad. They're not *my* friends and family. I'm not a criminal. I'm the victim. 'To think I wanted to kiss you. I bet you play victim with *all* the boys.'

'She did,' the twenty-something me joins, resting against the window. 'Although she didn't properly know *how* to play it. The head-teacher of St. Andrews was surprised when she bent over the table after being called into his office.'

That was the final straw in my tenure at St. Andrews. Mother didn't allow me enough time to recover before sending me to find God in another school, but I was not ready to be out. All my teachers were female, but that didn't stop me. I accused two male teachers of being rapists and stripped in the head-teacher's office. I also attacked a girl; an article published last year noted how she was still recovering from having her eye scratched out. They blamed me, but I don't remember doing it.

As I scream my innocence to the world, The Teacher removes my clothes and climbs on top. Everyone watches with hardly a shred of fear or concern. At fourteen, my way of coping was to look at the planets and pretend this wasn't happening. At eighteen, it's looking at my friends and family, begging for help.

'Let's just assume,' Rose says. 'That this *is* non-consensual and all that, and Lily *is* the victim. His DNA will be everywhere in this house. Why didn't you go to the police?'

'Because she was too weak,' the twenty-something me answers. 'Too weak, too scared. She used to cry to herself at night at the thought of strangers knocking on her door, calling her a liar and God-knows-what else. Selfish, selfish girl.'

'So, in your mind, you allowed a criminal to get away with his crimes because you were afraid of being called names? My God, you're pathetic.' I try my best to ignore her words, but she brings up Kelly, and how she's the victim. She also brings up how his wife and kids go to bed at night respecting their husband and father, without knowing the truth. Thoughts which have caused me to cry before.

The twenty-something kneels by my face. I don't recognise the confidence in her eyes; they're not my eyes. They don't have such a tragic history behind them. 'You know what you have to do, Sweetheart,' she whispers. 'Look at him,' we both look up at his face as he continues to thrust back-and-forth. 'How many more young, innocent girls must have to look up and see that? Or stare constantly at the ceiling, waiting for this to be over. How many more victims will be made because of your idiotic pride?' Such sinister confidence. Whatever I must do, she's done.

'It's been too long for the police to do anything.' Evidence to support my allegations long since cleaned away. Except for the bra. But there's no guarantee that's mine. The police would assume I've robbed it from his wife's drawer and throw it away. I don't stand a chance, and he'd be soon back teaching.

'Who said anything about the police?' She kisses my cheek and winks before standing. She takes Brad's hand and walks away with him. Acceptance I can only dream of.

The Teacher's grunting and sweet nothings quieten as he comes to a finish. 'Seriously, Lily,' Poppy says. 'You need to end his reign of terror on the young girls of West Drive. No school student should be *forced* to behave like this.' Her eyes replace pain with hate. 'Unless, of course, you enjoyed being *his* favourite girl, and this is one big lie.'

'Why would I cry rape?'

'Maybe he dumped you. Maybe you want more.'

'He stopped because I found her handcuffed,' Mother adds. 'Imagine if he had the nuance to let her go beforehand; they could still have been going at it right now.'

'I was going to tell you, Mummy, honestly,' I cry.

'What a sorry sight it was, girls,' she turns to Rose. 'All piss-soaked and shivering. I've never been more embarrassed to be a mother in my life.'

'I'm glad I wasn't the one to find her,' Rose replies. 'She would *never* have been accepted as a Flower.'

The bed held me captive for over five hours. My torment ending when Mother came home from work and rescued me. My phone was downstairs, so I missed her messages warning me she was running late. The Teacher read all my messages, and even a replied to them. Those five hours were the longest of my life. Worrying about how Mother would react, worrying about how the police would react, worrying about how the people of West Drive would react, worrying about how the kids at school would react, worrying about how The Teacher would react. All while feeling weak and pathetic and in pain. I wanted him to come back and end my life.

He didn't.

Towards the end, I created laws and rules for Planet Lilian and ascended my position on the throne as

Queen. I created laws on teachers, technology and people, and harmony reigns.

Mother screamed as she walked in the room, and I broke down in tears and confessed everything. She released me and retreated in anger (I can't remember if it was at me, herself or The Teacher), and pulled me out of West Drive High School. She didn't do much else until I bumped into a policeman in the supermarket with a pair of handcuffs on him and had a mental breakdown. I have no idea what happened, but Mother tells me I shouted and knocked everything over in a blind rage. She refused the policeman's help and had a few choice words to say at the watching eyes.

After she found me, I slept in the living room for about a month until a big argument between Mother and myself forced me to sleep in Alexa's room for the majority of a year. She always wanted me to go to the police but accepted my reasoning not to, instead choosing to punch The Teacher.

'So,' Rose says. 'The Teacher got away with four counts of rape with no repercussions to his social standing, no repercussions to his family life and no repercussions to his career. Only the people in this room know the truth. He should have had imprisonment forced upon him; as far as possible from innocent girls. Instead, he teaches them, he inspires them, he nurtures them, he controls them. A never-ending conveyor belt of victims.'

'I know, I know.'

'You know what you have to do.'

The room collapses and I wake on the floor, safe-and-sound, with Alexa's breathing from my bed filling the room, and nobody else in the room.

I walk downstairs and down a bottle of water before opening the living room curtains. The crack has widened: a small snake.

I know what I have to do.

Thursday

Panic sets in as I wake to Alexa's presence no longer in my bed, but her laughter ricochets from downstairs, easing it away. The sun shines warmer and brighter through my window. Just for me. I take a shower and dress in casual attire, and even offer to make breakfast for Mother and Alexa. A perfect morning routine.

'Don't you look happy, today,' Mother says. Is there worry in her voice? 'Look, about last night-'

'Forget about it, no need to apologise,' I return. 'You were trying to protect me; I'm sure Brad will agree and understand.'

'Has he messaged you, yet?'

'Not yet.' Fear returns, but as if banished away by a spell it doesn't have the chance to reside permanently in my mind. 'But, it's still early. He's probably still nervous after it all. Everything will be fine.' I mean it. Everything *will* be fine.

The scrambled eggs are nothing to gloat about, but they're eaten with little criticism (the last time I made any meal, Mother said it was disgusting, and until this morning I've refused to cook ever since). Alexa and I make plans to go clothes shopping when she returns from school and Mother says she needs to nip into the office.

As Mother left the house, taking a merry Alexa with her, my phone rings and Brad's cute face pops up on his contact information. 'Good morning, Sweetheart,' I say.

'Good morning. Someone woke up on the right side of the bed today.'

'The sun is shining, the birds are singing, what's not to be happy about?'

'That is true, and, speaking of the sun shining, how about we go for a picnic in the park later?'

Small talk and flirts fired back-and-forth after we agreed on having a picnic, and the call ends with me smiling as wide as my face allows. I've never had a proper picnic before, so that's something new to look forward to, and Brad's fine with everything that happened last night. He understands. I've told him Mother is very protective. She cares, in her own way. As does Brad.

I change to a summer outfit (switching the black tracksuit bottoms to a white skirt with rose-coloured lilies on them). The roses remind me to call Rose and ask if The Flowers can come a little earlier tonight. For encouragement. For back-up. For common sense.

The crack has widened more overnight: the same length snake, but thicker; with the wind still whistling through the opening. But, if Mother sees no problem with it, who am I to argue with her? I'm sure she has already made plans to fix it. Hopefully, before it breaks completely.

Twenty more minutes dance by before Brad's knock jolts me out of my seat. 'Come in, come in,' I stand aside and direct him through. He's more nervous than he should be. 'Don't worry,' I seek to reassure. 'Mother isn't here. Besides,' my tone softens. 'She understands it was all a big misunderstanding on her part, and I think she wants to apologise when she next sees you.' He's actually brought a picnic basket. He's so sweet. Does he picnic a lot? He hugs me before saying anything, releasing well before my body repulses.

'That's fine. Look, I'm sorry about-'

'No need to apologise, I should have told you I was uncomfortable, rather than screaming. That's all in the past.' I don't think I'd scream if he kissed me.

We walk to Thynwych Park, the most beautiful park in all of Wednesbury. Aside from the recent attacks on women in the evenings, anyway. I don't have that fear; I have Brad. He'll protect me against any predator who wishes harm against me. My guard. My soldier. My hero.

Allergies make their presence known before too long, but a few sneezes here and there will not take away from how cute everything is. Brad sets a blanket on the grass, surrounded by beds of flowers of all colours. The purple ones to my side are my favourite, and I pull a few from the ground to add to our blanket. I'll water them when I get home. We should have more flowers around the house. I think Mother would appreciate them.

'So,' Brad says, still unpacking the picnic basket. 'Are you seeing your friends tonight?' It's sweet he remembers.

'Yeah, I can't wait. Assuming there's no repeat of last night.' It's healthy for our relationship (are we in a relationship?) we can laugh and joke about what happened. 'How's the funeral arrangements coming on?'

'The police suspect foul play,' his eyes close. 'Possible blunt force to the skull. They're performing an autopsy on the body, so we can't have a burial until that comes back.'

'Murder?'

'Yep,' he's opens his eyes, but I can't read his body language. He must be going through so many emotions. 'I don't know why anyone would want to: she doesn't, didn't, have any money, she's not been involved with anyone for a while and I'm her only child. My aunt says she didn't have much of a life outside of work. The police reckon it'll be back by Sunday, so I guess we'll find out then.' I hope it turns out to be an accident. I couldn't bear the thought of someone murdering Mother.

Sadness wearing false bravado.

'Well, I hope you get the outcome you want.' What would that be? Why did I say that? There's no outcome for him on Sunday which he wants. There are outcomes which are better than others, but none he *wants*.

He smiles, probably aware there's nothing to say to my stupid comment. Instead, we each watch the park; what a beautiful scene. Mothers and fathers chasing their children, older people walking their dogs, people gossiping about the world and its faults, teenagers racing on their push-bikes, all with the sun watching over them. Blessing them. Blessing us. It's sad to think some predator is using this park as his hunting ground; how many more families would be here today if it were not for him?

'You know,' Brad says. 'In a warm spring's evening, this place would be amazing for a wedding.' He looks around for the perfect spot and settles on a plot near the tallest tree in the park, sitting isolated on its own. I've seen plenty of movies where people get married outside, and this place is nicer than any of them.

'Do you want to ever get married?' I word the question so it doesn't sound like I'm proposing. Does he want to marry *me* here one day?

'Someday, yeah.' To me. 'I'm not one for dating girl after girl, you know? I'd rather meet my soulmate and live the rest of our lives together.'

'Unusual attitude for someone your age.' An attitude I share. An attitude I love hearing him share.

'I dated girls in high school, obviously, but it's superficial. Like, I'd rather spend 35 years with my soulmate, than 25 with her and ten years dancing from fling to fling.' He smiles *that* smile. 'How about you?'

'I've always thought I wanted to get married, but you hear and see so many stories of people cheating on their families, or couples growing to hate each other, that it makes me think twice. I want the romance, but I worry I'd be constantly watching over my shoulder.' I've never had a loving couple to aspire to emulate. Maybe if I did, there'd be more hope in my heart. 'But, I guess it depends on the man I marry.'

Topics switch from the upcoming election to aspirations (Brad wishes to write screenplays, with one idea focusing on an old man who no longer wants to live in a world without his wife, who passed away a month prior).

He walked me home after three hours (safe from the Thynwych Park predator) and offers nothing more than a handshake goodbye. I reject in favour of a hug (I'm not quite ready for a kiss, just yet).

I wave like an idiot as he walks away, but I don't care. I'm his idiot. And I fear I always will be.

After Alexa finishes school, we shop for a couple of hours (only having to stop due to the shops closing), with me buying some new black clothes (for tonight) and two new dresses (for Brad), while Alexa bought some new tracksuits and trainers. Mother gave us her credit card before we left and told us there was no limit. With our meals bought, too, we exhausted that credit card rotten.

'Lils,' Alexa says on our way home.

'Yeah?'

'Have you noticed how quiet town is?' She's right. I don't recall seeing many people out and about: shops normally jam-packed full of people lie barren of souls; car parks normally full to the brim with vehicles beg for attention; streets normally full of people rushing are clear for us to navigate stress-free. Even the female cashiers working didn't offer much in the way of conversation while we paid.

'You're right. I hadn't noticed, but how weird is that?' The world silent. A silence which allows my mind contemplation.

'Come on, girls,' Mother says as we arrive home. 'Show me those new clothes.'

Alexa and I spend about thirty minutes putting on a basic fashion show for Mother's approval (she doesn't approve of the black colour; 'You need to be brighter: brighter clothes, brighter soul'). Our fashion show ends with The Flowers' knock.

I escort them upstairs, bidding goodbye to Mother and Alexa, and close the door as tight as the wood allows.

'Right, girls,' my voice hushed; Mother would disagree with the plan, even if she'd approve of the result. 'You know I have nightmares about what happened to me?' They nod. 'Well, they're not as uncommon as I make out.'

'How common are they?' Rose asks.

'Every night.' Six eyes look on in disbelief. 'Whenever I fall asleep, I see *him*. I see what he did. Sometimes I don't see it; instead, I *live* it.'

'Okay,' Poppy's sympathetic tone out of place. 'Tonight, we'll help you talk through these, if you like.'

317

'No,' I giggle. 'I know why my mind haunts me with these images: because there was never any retribution. He got away with it.'

'Lils, we've been telling you this for years. He needs to be arrested.'

'But does he? Sure, he can go to prison for five years, but he'll come out the same horrible monster who went in. And that's if he even gets arrested, with the lack of evidence and his social standing. The legal system will not help me. We need to pay him a visit and send him a little message.'

'What type of message are we sending?' Ivy asks, leaning forward.

'And how little?' Rose's fists clench. She'll be on board even if the other two aren't.

'A rough one,' I say. 'His family are out of town, and I know where the spare key is. His Facebook status says he's getting an early night for classes tomorrow. Seems like the perfect mix.'

'And what will this achieve?' I don't think Poppy has ever got into a fight with anyone, she's such a pure soul.

'Peace of mind. A night where I can go to sleep without a regular reminder of the worst time of my life. If my mind knows I won overall, it'll leave me alone and I can *finally* move on with my life. I can get a job, I can settle down with Brad, I can repair all the damage he's done to mine and Mother's relationship. If nothing changes, I can't go on. I'm exhausted.'

'I'm in,' Rose stands and holds out a fist. I replicate and our fists touch. We look over to Ivy, who joins with a brief look of caution. Poppy refuses to stand. 'Look, Pops, I get it, and if you don't want to, that's fine. But Lils *needs* this.' She looks at me. 'Besides, we're only gonna slap him a little bit.' She winks, away from Poppy's view, before Poppy accepts her role and joins her fist with ours.

Mother and Alexa both went to sleep around ten, which allows us to sneak out of the house with no reason for doing so. Our first port of call: West Drive High School.

'What are we doing here?' Ivy asks. Midnight nears, with the school and most of the surrounding houses fast asleep. We climb over a fence and walk towards the back. After the first incident with The Teacher, I was in-and-out of the head-teacher's office every week. While there, I watched the CCTV cameras: ensuring no pupil suffered mistreatment. The music classroom was the only one where I saw no cameras.

I grab a small rock and tap away at the glass until it cracks and collapses in. No alarm goes off, and I rush us all inside. 'If he doesn't heed our message,' I say as the others sneak in. 'Then maybe others will see it and listen.'

With our hoods up, and dressed in all black, we walk from the music class to my old geography room. On his desk is a picture of his wife and daughters. How could he pick and choose his next victim with their smiling faces watching? Rose tapes a piece of paper over the camera, allowing us to remove our hoods.

'I sat here,' I stop at my desk and lift the lid to reveal where I'd scratched "Help" in the corner. 'Nobody ever helped.' Perhaps it was a bit too vague. Perhaps nobody cared.

'I wonder how many,' Ivy trails off, stroking each desk as she walks up and down the classroom. Her unfinished question goes unanswered.

Poppy sits at a random desk and reads aloud the markings. '"Cutest teacher ever", this one says. Poor girl.'

It was a common thought among girls in my year, with them gossiping in toilets or changing rooms about who the best-looking male teachers were. The Teacher was always top of the list.

'He could have had any girl he wanted willingly,' I say. 'They all liked him. Geography was the only class where the girls were in no rush to leave. Which annoyed me, because they walked so slowly, and I wanted to leave. Even before he became a monster.'

I walk over to his cupboard and smash open the lock with a hammer I brought. An expensive-looking Welsh whisky bottle greets me with four glasses. I pour us each a drink as silence threatens to take over.

'The scariest thing,' Rose breaks the calm. 'Is this could be any classroom across the country.' Rose looks at all the normal geography posters on the normal classroom walls in a normal school. She swirls the glass in hand, with its liquid soaking every bit of the glass, without any falling out.

'So,' Poppy's nerves evident for all to see. 'Are we just l-leaving his alcohol exposed for other t-teachers to see?' She's not a whisky drinker, but she's drinking faster than any of us.

'That would be too easy. He's a professional liar.' I look at the whiteboard at the head of the classroom and grab a black marker. 'Besides, that's nowhere near serious enough.' I write "I AM A PAEDOPHILE" as large as I can for the world to see. 'And he needs punishing for this,' the black marker taps on the last word. 'Not the whisky. And tomorrow, *everyone* will know. One way or another.'

Poppy's glass the first to need refilling.

'Pops, he needs to be punished.' Ivy sits by Poppy and holds her hand. 'We're the heroes of this story.'

'I'm scared,' Poppy sobs, before Ivy embraces her.

'I know, babe. I'm scared, too. But, think, tonight we can all sleep easier knowing this monster will never strike again. Think of all the lives who can sleep easier and safer.'

'How are you?' Rose whispers to me, ignoring the giant letters written in front of her. 'I can't imagine it's easy preparing to see him again.'

According to a suspension notice I once received, I screamed "I hate you" at The Teacher, among other people, in one of the last times I saw him. That was nearly four years ago, but my mind has recreated his face almost nightly. 'I'm ready,' I reply. I've seen him in my mind so many times, this evening will be like any other. Albeit with the victors switched.

'You seem nervous. If it's too much, let me take over.'

She's right about my nerves, but not on seeing him. I'm petrified about how far I'll go. Or that I won't go far enough. I've seen torture-porn films (the modern I Spit on Your Grave my favourite), and they always murder the villain. Is that too far, or not far enough? All I know is, I'm the hero. And this is the ultimate level of our game. The princess rescued; the villain banished.

Poppy leaves the room, complaining about feeling sick, and Rose and Ivy escort her to the toilet down the corridor. Leaving me, whisky in hand, reading the words on the board over and over.

'You win,' a voice speaks from behind me. I turn, the twenty-something stares at me, sat at my desk with a glass of whisky.

'Do I?' I seek reassurance. I beg for reassurance.

'He goes to prison, and you're free to live your life.'

'Why does he go to prison?'

'He confesses,' she downs her glass and stands. 'You make him realise how bad he's treated other people, and tomorrow he'll go to the police. They'll lock him away, and you're free. You get a nice little job, nothing special, and you sleep. You sleep so much.' She walks up and down the classroom, tapping on each table as she passes. 'I know how you're feeling: nervous,' tap, 'excited,' tap, 'afraid,' tap, 'delirious,' tap. 'Embrace all of them.'

324

'I need to know: are we doing the right thing?'
My mind races to another solution: find other victims
and jointly accuse him of raping us all. He could silence
me, but not seven of us altogether.

'Ask her,' she gestures towards a sniggering 14-
year-old me, cowering against my desk.

'Why did he do that to me?' She sobs, unable to
look either of us in the eye.

'It's only happened to her the once,' the twenty-
something me speaks low enough, so she doesn't hear.
'Do you have the heart to tell her it gets worse? How her
home will no longer feel safe? Because I couldn't when I
was you.' Standing in front of me, she adds the fire I
need.

In her time, she's sat in the bath, fully clothed,
with the water mixed with tears. Her mother is out
shopping without a care in the world. The water soon
pulls her under to end the suffering, but it fails. 'Ask her
if you're doing the right thing.'

'Does he do it again?' The teenager's eyes stare
into mine.

'Don't worry, Sweetheart,' the twenty-something
me says, still manoeuvring around the room. 'Lily, here,

has a plan for revenge.' I nod towards them both. 'That if, well, if revenge is the *right* thing to do.'

The teenager stands, wipes away the tears from her cheek and marches towards me. 'Of course, it is. Slit his throat. Break his fingers one-by-one. Gouge his eyes out with a fork. Don't you dare give him a pass.' Her hatred is still very raw, still animalistic, whereas mine is tired.

'I won't.' For my past. For my present. For my future.

The Flowers return, Poppy, feeling better, and I declare my readiness and we set off, leaving the alcohol cupboard open. If nothing else, there's one more rule he's broken.

As the day was, so too is the night quiet, with nothing more than the sounds of our footsteps and breathing accompanying the fresh air. Rose and I walk in front, both ready and determined, with Ivy and Poppy still holding hands, walking at a slower pace. The lengthy journey passes by without much time, our minds ignoring the miles.

My heart stops as the house of the monster welcomes me. The driveway only houses one car, confirming his wife is away, and the four of us sneak around the back. The spare key still sits underneath the same plant pot, granting us access into his home. We tiptoe as quietly as possible (we even take our shoes off), through the kitchen, through the living room, through the hallway, up the stairs (mindful of the creaky one), across the landing and into his chamber. I stop and growl at the monster sleeping peacefully. Dreaming of more sadistic ways of hurting innocent children.

Rose pulls out a cloth and chloroform from her bag, soaks it and hands it to me. I stand over him. The monster of my mind. The rapist. The man who broke my soul. Now I'm in charge. The smell of disgust wafts with the chloroform. The cloth nestles over his face, forcing him to wake before passing out.

The chloroform took a few minutes to administer its effect; it's not as easy as they make out in movies. While passed out, we tied and handcuffed him to the four bedposts. After that, the rest of The Flowers left me alone with him and went downstairs. While he slept, I didn't move, I barely blinked, I just sat. Watching.

'What the,' he trails off. I watch as life returns to his body, only for a horrific realisation to set in. 'Lily?' Confusion. Fright. Everything I felt when he first attacked me. It's nice to know he still remembers me. 'What's going on?'

'Hi, *sir.*' I wear that predator's smile. I've got that abusive wink. I've got that power.

'What are you doing? Why am I tied up? What is going on?' Silence. 'Untie me, or else.' His empty threats bring about laughter. He wriggles and tries to force his way out, but the knots are too tight. As he sinks his head back in defeat, the noose wrapped around his throat greets him. 'Seriously, let me go.'

'I will, in time. Maybe.' I lean over and pick up a kitchen knife; I think it's the same one which threatened me. I stand as it strokes his pyjamas. 'Wanna kiss the knife, *sir?*' The tip of the knife caresses his lips before he

328

puckers up and offers it a kiss. 'Good boy.' The knife gently rips his pyjamas away from top to bottom, until just his boxer shorts remain. Are there tears in his eyes?

'Please, Lily, don't do this.' Definitely tears; the urge to taste them rages.

'But, *sir*, you don't know what I'm doing.' I walk back-and-forth around his bed, the knife gliding along his body as I go. 'Yet.'

'Please, I'm a married man-'

'When it suits.' The knife moves from his lips to his naked ring-finger on his left hand. 'I see we're not married tonight.' The power I exert orgasms throughout my body.

'Okay, Lily, let's be grown up about this. You're not stupid. What do you want? We can settle this amicably.'

'Maybe I want to be stupid.' The knife removes his boxer shorts; he's a shivering, naked mess on the bed. 'Maybe I want more of this,' my hand grabs and squeezes his penis; the look of discomfort on his face tells me when I've gone too far. 'Or maybe,' my hand lets go, and the knife takes up residence. I lick my lips.

'I'm sorry, okay? I'm sorry. I don't know what else you want me to say. Please.' His attractive muscles work overtime to get free; they fare better than my scrawny arms managed.

I stand on the bed and slam my pelvis onto his penis. A groan flies out of his mouth, sweeter than any tune instruments can offer. 'Or maybe I just want to talk.' I cock my head. I can look childlike when I need to be.

'Okay, okay, okay, let's talk.' The look of fear in his eyes turning me on.

'Why me?'

'Because we were friends-'

The knife shoots to his throat, stopping his lies. 'Why *me*?'

'I-I-I don't know. You're pretty, we were alone-'

'But you're sometimes a married man,' my voice teetering between seductive and villainous. 'How many more *pretty* girls have you forced yourself onto, *sir*?'

'None, I swear, I swear. Please, please.' More tears. More licking of my lips. This is everything I've ever wanted, and so *much* more. Maybe this is how he felt. This power he exudes over young, innocent girls. This power is sexy.

'Want to know what I think?' I don't wait for a response. The knife caresses his right nipple. 'I think you're sick. I think you like *little* girls. Little, innocent, *young* girls. Girls you can rape and manipulate and scare.' He winces. 'What's the matter?' I lean in. 'Don't enjoy being called a *rapist*?'

'I'm not, please, just let me go.' His voice cradles anger and sorrow. His pain such a rush.

'A paedophile *and* a rapist.' I lean in closer, my lips touching his ear. 'That's a bad combination.' I sit back, watching the greatest movie I've ever seen.

'I'm not, I'm not, I'm not.' His quick-paced repetitive responses mirror mine. His eyes close as tight as his eyelids allow. His limbs still trying (and failing) to escape their trap.

'I wonder how your mind covers the rapes you've committed. I am impressed, *sir*. There's so many parts of my life I'd like my mind to erase, but I just don't have the ability.' I raise myself from him and move towards the base of the bed. 'Buy you: if I wasn't raped by you, I'd believe you were innocent.'

331

'I am innocent. I'm not a rapist.' Is he trying to convince me or himself? My eyes bathe in his misery.

'You know what, *sir*? You have a *cute behind*,' the knife crawls up his legs until it reaches the parting. '*I wonder how tight it is.*' I know he remembers those words. The knife pokes in, before retreating down the other leg.

'Please, I'm a good man, I have a family-'

'I think we may disagree on the validity of you being a *good man*, but I suppose you're free to believe it.' The knife takes a break as I grab his left foot in both of my hands. 'Perhaps in your mind, you are a good man.' My nails scrape the base of his foot. 'Maybe at times, you behave quite well. You do charity events at school,' my right thumb's nail stops scraping and digs. 'You volunteer with after-school clubs,' close to drawing blood. 'You take your wife and daughters away for the weekend.' Blood. 'You even offer to teach girls privately after class.' I suck my thumb dry, swallowing the taste of his blood.

'Do you want money? Anything, just; please.'

'I could do with some money,' my optimistic tone resonates with his ears. 'I don't have a job, you know?' I sit on the corner of the bed. 'I don't get on well with people. The Monday-Lady says it's because I'm afraid. Go figure. But,' the knife's break ends as it raises to my lips. 'Do I really want to end this here-and-now for a few quid?'

Cars driving by alert me to the window, but they're not his family. They're people without a care in the world, who will read about this on the news and report to the police what they saw. They'll say anything to get themselves attention.

'Right, *sir*, let me ask you a question: that night at my house, would you have stopped *abusing* me had I offered you some money?' I close the curtains and turn to face him; my smile indicates he doesn't need to respond. Neither of us needs more lies. 'I had to suffer, physically and mentally, so I think it's fair you have to suffer, too. Quid pro quo. Honestly, if there was another way I'd be all for it.'

'Don't you think I've suffered enough? Your mother-'

'Oh, no, no, no, *sir*,' over-the-top laughter highlights his delusions. 'I've not even started yet. And as for Mother's assault, that was fun, but I never got to get my licks in.'

'Okay, hit me, and we'll call it even.'

'If only it were that simple. So, tell me, which of the four times you *abused* me was your favourite?' He offers no answer over his whimpers. I sit on a chair beside his bed. 'I imagine your favourite was my least favourite, but I'm curious.'

'Please, Lily, this isn't you. You're better than this.' His lies are so obvious he can't even look me eye-to-eye.

'And who am I, exactly? The stupid girl who struggled with basic geography? The poor child from a broken home? The vulnerable fourteen-year-old you *violated*? Or the girl whose mind couldn't cope with the abuse.' The knife back caressing his nipple.

'It wasn't abuse,' still no eye contact. 'We were just having an affair.' He struggled to make out the last word; is it because it's such an obvious lie, or because he's ashamed? How can a man do what he did and go home to his wife and daughter without a care in the world?

'An affair? Well, silly me.' My hand glides across his body as I walk around the bed again. 'Of course, we were having an affair. How could I resist you? You're handsome, you're smart, you were kind.' I sit back on him, softer this time, though. The blood in his body confused at where to go. 'Maybe I'm annoyed because you ended our fully consensual affair.' His face fears that isn't true, despite the blood wanting it to be.

'Whatever you want, I swear.'

'So, if I wanted you to leave your family,' my eyes lead his to a picture of his two daughters by his bedside. 'Never speak to them again, run away with me and start a new life far away, would you be willing?'

'If that's what you want.' His tone defeated. Would he commit to a life with me to avoid the true horrors coming out? Better a cheat than a rapist, I suppose. 'Please.'

'Your daughters are so pretty,' I reach over and grab the picture. 'And your wife, she's beautiful.' A picture on the other bedside cabinet shows the four of them together. 'What's her name?'

'Leave her out of this.' She lays with a rapist; she's very much involved.

'Your eldest looks about fourteen. What's her name?' Nothing. I don't care. 'She is very pretty. Nice and slim, like me at her age.' A train of thought quickly put to one side. 'Have you ever wondered if any of her teachers are locking the door after class and pulling down her trousers? If any of those *grown men* you trust to take care of your darling, baby girl, have come into this house and tied her to the bed? It must be a parent's worst nightmare, that feeling you've failed the same humans you've brought into this world and sworn to protect.' His teeth clench. 'I bet you'd want to kill anyone who raped her, wouldn't you?'

'Shut up. Please, leave them out of this.' His mind must work overtime in trying to find the right balance between anger and caution. 'Look, call me names and whatever else, but they haven't done anything.'

'You have such a wonderful life, *sir*: this house is amazing, your family are gorgeous, you have been blessed with looks yourself and have the brains and energy to forge out a decent career. Yet you risked it all on an underage child.' My pelvis rocks back-and-forth. 'Even now, you're still keen. What's the matter, *sir*? Your wife not doing it for you, anymore? Is she too old?' Any desire for balance in his behaviour ends as he spits on my shoulder. 'Now that's just rude.' I use the ripped-up boxer shorts to wipe it away. 'That's five minutes of quiet time for you, *sir*.' I roll away from him and fetch some duct tape from my bag and tape three pieces across his protesting mouth. 'Now, if you don't mind, you promised me a tour a few years ago which I'd like to take.'

He squirms and muffles inaudible sounds as I leave, with the first bedroom I encounter belonging to his eldest. Topless pictures of actors and singers cover large parts of her walls, and a pin-board proudly displays a catalogue of pictures of her and her friends in various scenarios; ranging from concerts to school trips. She's smiling in every picture; she must be a naturally happy person. It saddens me how people can have such ridiculous childhoods, while I had to make do with insults for company.

Her wardrobe is full of stunning dresses, fashionable skirts and expensive-looking designer brand shirts. Nothing here is from the £1 section at the local discount store like you'll find in mine. She gets to wear these daily. I could have only dreamed of wearing such fashion at her age.

On her bed lies her diary: her name is Ashley. I flip to a random date and read it aloud.

September 20th

When I was younger, I always hated sitting alphabetically boy-girl, but now it allows me to sit next to Robbie. He's so cute. We have a year 9 dance coming up soon, I want to ask him but I'm too scared. If he says no, the entire school will know I fancy him. I wish I could talk to my parents about this, but Mum doesn't care and Dad would flip his lid if another lad came near me.

'Another lad, Ashley? Naughty. What would your dad *do*, exactly?' I rest the diary back and return to her wardrobe. An overwhelming urge to *borrow* one of her pretty red dresses takes over; I deserve pleasant things, too. Besides, it's the least that monster owes me. He can afford to buy her a new one, if she'd even notice this one random dress missing. I don't stop with the dress, as I *borrow* some underwear (leaving my pink bra on), socks and a scarf. I'll happily wager everything I've chosen each costs more than the sorry outfit I came wearing. The girl reflecting at me in the mirror is the girl

I should be, the girl I was born to be, not the shell I inhabit.

Wanting to show off my pretty new dress, I skip back towards The Teacher's room and do a little twirl for him. He knows it's her dress straight away; it's nice he recognises the clothes his children wear. 'I hope you don't mind,' I spin again. 'But I borrowed some of *Ashley's* clothes.' My voice speaking her name slaps his face. 'They fit me perfectly; how crazy is that?' The duct tape covers what would be a tirade of abuse. 'She's got good taste; I'll give her that.' I offer a seductive smile. 'In clothes, that is; I don't know about boys.' There's recognition in his eyes; something has happened with a boy before. 'Be right back, *sir.*' I dance off and explore door number two: the all-girl bands and pretty-colourful creatures across the walls scream the room of the youngest. She's at that strange age where everything is so clear, yet you know it's confusing. Are you a child or a teenager? Do you want to act like a child or a teenager? Cartoons fade away, replaced by more live-action shows (whether they're on the same channel). Pop music plays less as their library features other genres (I dabbled in rap at her age, much to Mother's chagrin). Clothes become important; in fact, your overall looks become important. *Boys* become important. Boyfriend-girlfriend at this age means nothing, but they're the building blocks for what comes later in life. This girl is the poster child for her age: Pokémon posters on one side of the room with heavy metal CDs on the table by her laptop. I zoom in on a poster of a professional wrestler and read its autograph: "To Amy, keep on winning". Amy and Ashley. Pretty names.

I can't fit into Amy's clothes; her wardrobe a bizarre mix of dresses and tracksuit clothing. She doesn't know how she'll dress, yet. So, for a souvenir I take a teddy bear from her bed; I have a blue one like this at home – and walk back to The Teacher's room. 'This teddy of *Amy's* is so cute; would she mind if I borrowed it?' Seeing the teddy bear replaces anger inside him with tears. I know he's adding two and two together and producing seven, but I'm not going to correct him yet. His mind is creating the worst-case scenarios, as mine did. I wondered if he'd kill me, I wondered if he'd kidnap me, I wondered if he'd hurt Mother. Now, he's wondering all of that.

Somewhere in his mind I've murdered his family and staged it to look like a murder-homicide. Somewhere else in his mind I've exposed his secrets, and he's gone to prison, disowned by his family. Somewhere else in his mind I've set him free. It's the hope that kills you.

I rest the teddy bear by his face, positioned so they can watch each other. 'It might get messy, later, but you can think of the teddy as Amy.'

The children's rooms done, now time to rummage through this room. The room of a monster. On the outset there's nothing too out-of-the-ordinary: her underwear more motherly than wifey; his suits grouped, as are his casual and posh-casual attires (how much time must he waste organising this); but in the corner is a box. I open it to see a dildo inside. Holding it aloft, I turn back to face him. 'She pleasures herself with this, you pleasure yourself with children. In the future, I'd advise you borrow this instead; less chance of prison.' His eyes confirm my humour fails its audience. I've borrowed something of Amy's and Ashley's, so I pocket the dildo and place the box back.

'Isn't it funny,' I stop hunting and sit on the corner of the bed. 'What you can find when you search through someone's house? In just a few minutes I've found out your wife's unsatisfied, your daughter is afraid to confess she has a crush. Oh, ignore that last one, that was supposed to be a secret. Sorry, *Ashley*. Then there's you. You have respect from your neighbours, your colleagues, your friends; they all believe the wholesome family image you present, without realising it's all a façade. A show.' I grab the knife. 'A lie.'

I march out of the room, leaving him confused, and go downstairs for a glass of water.

'How's it going?' Rose asks, the only one standing, ready for when I need her.

'It's fine, shouldn't be much longer.'

They're drinking wine they found from somewhere, and I grab a glass, too. Water and wine make for an excellent combination. I return to The Teacher's room and place both glasses out of his reach. 'I'll leave these here, in case you're thirsty.' Again, my jokes are not welcome.

I place down the knife and pull out a hammer from my bag. 'I saw this film once,' I say. 'Misery, I think it was called. Have you seen it?' He shakes his head. 'It's about some crazy stalker lady who kidnaps a famous writer and holds him prisoner for ages.' The hammer mimics the knife's stroking of The Teacher's body. 'But, as he healed, oh, he was in a car crash so couldn't walk or anything. Anyway, as he healed, she broke his ankles with a sledgehammer.' The hammer spins in my hand. 'I couldn't find a sledgehammer.' His pupils wince. That corner of his mind which is hoping to be released grows smaller and smaller. 'I can't believe you haven't seen it; it's based on a novel by Stephen King. You should check it out.' The hammer hops down his right leg. 'It is pretty disgusting, though, when she breaks his ankles; they swing in such an unnatural way.' An icy shiver hugs both of us and the hammer hops on his ankle. 'Even just thinking about it gives me the creeps; that's how good the film is, you know?' The flat side spins around, allowing the claw to scratch its way from his left ankle to his waist. 'I don't think I could do that to someone.' The flat surface bounces on his stomach. 'I'd probably vomit afterwards.' Each tear which falls lubricates my mind's desires. 'Honestly,' the hammer rests on his stomach, as I watch it rise and fall with quick regularity. 'I'm not

343

entirely sure what I'm going to do with you, yet.' A thought falls into my mind: 'You have a gun in this house, right?' He shakes his head, but I know he does. 'That'd be quick and easy: bang, bang, you're dead. I imagine it's pretty painless, too; a quick shot and it's over. Whereas the knife approach,' the knife returns to my hand and softly outlines the hammer around his stomach. 'This is much slower, much more methodical. So, you suffer more. You could take *hours* bleeding to death; perhaps *five* hours? Five hours where you have to sit and contemplate your life; five hours where you worry about how your family will react when they finally find you like this; five hours of crying and feeling worthless and begging for a God you don't believe in to rescue you. All to no avail.' The knife shoots up to his throat. 'And I know that because I waited those five hours.' More tears. More lubrication. 'Or,' the knife backs off and sleeps next to the hammer. 'I could take my clothes off,' I adopt a more sensual tone. 'And continue our *affair*.' His emotions flick like the changing of a radio. 'You never let me on top.' I climb back on top, rocking gently. 'Only this time, we'll record it.' A strange look takes over his face, but I don't press it further.

'We'll send a copy to your wife and you'll be free to run away with me. I might even send it to young Ashley as a warning against men, because she's at that age, *sir*, where someone needs to talk to her about the birds and the bees and the monsters.' Muffling sounds indicate he wants to speak, and I lean over and remove the duct tape.

'Please, please, I'm begging you. I'll do whatever you want. I'll pay whatever you want.'

'But you're just saying that now, but when I set you free, you'll leave me.'

'I won't, I promise.' There's hope in his voice. It's the hope which kills you. 'You and me, Lils. We can get married, we can have children, we can buy a house together. You'll be in charge; I'll do whatever you say.'

'That sounds tempting. The man who broke my soul can be the man who fixes it.' Hope. I lean in and kiss him. Hope. Both of my hands wrap around his face. Hope. They glide down to his chest. Hope. Then to his stomach. Hope.

Then they pick up the hammer and the knife.

It's time.

I toss the bag, along with its insides, into the darkness of the catacombs as soon as I enter the house. The Flowers parted ways with me not long after we left The Teacher's house, with Poppy and Ivy more shaken than Rose, and the walk home was long and quiet. Too quiet. Streetlights guided me home as my body searched for a way to feel; relieved, anxious, powerful, scared.

I race to my bedroom, to my quilt, and cover myself from head-to-toe from the world. I don't deserve Planet Lilian; my violence and revenge breakings its laws. The breathing exercises The Monday-Lady taught me cease working; the speedster inside my chest continuing to race.

The walls cave in, crushing furniture in its path. The window turns into a vacuum and sucks out oxygen. My body a frightened mess, clamouring across the floor; trying to find spare oxygen. Claustrophobia rising with every passing heartbeat. Every wasted breath. My body shaking, naked in frozen waters. I'm sucking and sucking but no air fills my lungs.

Sick laughter fills the room, shooting pain to my stomach.

I race out to the bathroom, narrowly escaping the clutches of the shrinking room. The stairs no longer face downwards, instead, they raise to the ceiling and end. Preventing any escape. I stumble inside the bathroom and vomit hurls into the sink, followed by the bathtub and eventually the toilet. The window here also sucking out oxygen, through a crack similar to the living room.

With what feels like the last of the black sludge hurled from my mouth, the taps all turn on and pour out a thick, red liquid, which splashes against all the basins and flicks itself across me and the walls. It covers the lightbulb and a dark, red glow covers the room, with silver added from the moonlight. Sick laughter still rings through my ears.

I fall out of the bathroom, just as the walls cave, and drape the red liquid across the carpet. The stairs still facing up, the dimensions of each room constantly changing, churning my stomach from side-to-side as the walls fall backwards and forwards. Doors swing open and shut as if rocking in a storm, with water still gushing from the bathroom. Air sucks into each bedroom, through their respective windows, as I sink to my knees.

347

The red liquid crashes its way out of the bathroom, painting the carpet. It races up the stairs and covers the walls, as my vision encompasses nothing more than red. A thick red. Every glass pane, every mirror, every shiny surface: red. The crack from the living room's window inhabiting all those places. The same crack. The same sick laughter ringing out.

'Mother,' I call, but the lack of oxygen doesn't travel my sound far. 'Alexa,' even less so.

The stairs fall back to their normal place, and I near-fall down them, as more gushes of red liquid mounts every surface downstairs. The oxygen here delicious, but fleeting. More windows, more mirrors, more surfaces cracked, sucking oxygen for themselves. The front door locked; my prison.

My body throws me into the kitchen, as red replaces white. Serene moonlight mocks me through the windows, its silver sparkling on red. The back door taunts me with its lock. The guards will not allow their prisoner to escape. As with upstairs, angles and dimensions soon cease. Walls rise and fall, the floor's surface bounces. All except one place: the basement door.

It flings open and roars, knocking me onto the uneven floor.

'Come, my child,' it beckons.

The door leading out of the kitchen slams shut, as the sick laughter still rings. I refuse the basement's call before a hand reaches out. A black, shadowy hand. I stumble and fall in a failed effort to escape it, and it wraps its long fingers around my left leg and pulls me in.

I'm screaming for help, but my words fail to leave the room. Closer and closer it pulls me. I'm grabbing onto every surface, every object, every floor tile to stop. My efforts all fail.

Once inside the basement, the door slams shut. No more red. No more silver. No more rocking.

Just darkness. And laughter.

Friday

'Sweetheart?' Mother's call the first thing my ears hear. For the first time in years, my sleep was perfect. No hallucinations, no memories, no monsters; a safe passage from night to day. I wake refreshed, before the solid flat surface below me brings confusion. A shudder jolts across my body. Darkness provided by my eyelids replaced by the darkness of the basement. 'Why are you down there?' She calls again, the door providing a beam of light to allow my eyes sight. I have no reply.

I skip up the stairs one-by-one and my hand dances on the handle as it closes the basement away. I shrug and offer a look of bewilderment to Mother, and she laughs. She offers me breakfast but I refuse; there's a stench on me from the basement I need to wash away first. It matches the stench of the house.

'Hey, Sis,' Alexa greets as we pass on the stairs, high-fiving for the first time since she was a baby (although back then I had to force her tiny hand to high-five).

'Beautiful day, today,' I say and skip into the shower. Is this life after a good night's sleep? I need more of this.

The soap needs to work harder to clean my skin, but no images greet me during my time. Not from the bath or the shower. I return to the kitchen after drying and putting on the dress I slept in (where has this come from?), where Mother and Alexa chat away.

'You seem well,' Mother acknowledges. 'I don't know why you slept in the basement, or where that dress came from, but whatever the reason, it's worked wonders for you.' And she isn't lying. My hair has extra volume, my skin looks more alive; not only my demeanour, but my body's healthier.

Mother and Alexa had both changed their outfits while I was away in the shower; Mother wearing her own summary dress while Alexa dons a red and blue shorts-and-shirt combination. If the three of us went out, *everyone* would admire how amazing we all look as a family. Mother is a beautiful woman when she tries, and Alexa is the spitting image of me at her age (although with more life).

'You look pretty, Mummy,' Alexa says, saving my mind the need to compliment her.

'Why thank you, young lady, but I get my prettiness from you.' Alexa's old enough to know that's not how genes work, but she welcomes the compliment, as I once did when we went caravanning when I was about Alexa's age.

'We should do something together,' I say. 'Perhaps go away for the day?'

'Your sister has school and I have a few things to sort out at the office; how about tomorrow? We could go to the lakes of Roskell? Perhaps you can even invite Bradley?' Alexa bounces, desperate for me to accept. I'd much sooner we all go now, but tomorrow's fine. 'Perfect,' Mother and Alexa say in tandem as I accept. 'I'll put it in the calendar.'

The calendar. She's the type of mother who always puts things in the calendar which hangs on the wall in the kitchen. School trips, work meetings, appointments with The Monday-Lady, shift changes; nothing exciting, but always written in. Mother writes "lakes of Roskell" by Saturday's column and a wave of happiness takes over.

'Fancy a cup of tea?' Mother asks, and I accept as I head to the living room. Alexa dashes off to get ready for another fun-filled day of learning. The television awakens to the news, and I watch as stories flick by.

Nothing catches my eye (stories about how care homes are seeking donations, the local sports team has lost their manager and the closing of the longest-running pub in West Drive). 'Are you seeing Bradley, today?' Mother asks as she enters the living room, setting the cup onto the table.

'Probably, yeah. We've not made plans, yet, but it's still early.'

'Is that your phone?' Mother asks, directing my eyes to the floor. It is, strangely enough, and I retrieve it to see a message from Ivy: "Today is the first day of YOUR life. Xx". A smile greets my face as I tuck the phone into my pocket. It *is* the first day of my life. No longer living in fear. No longer susceptible to mental torture. No longer a victim to my past. No longer the helpless little girl. I am free.

A slow knock on the front door interrupts my proud chest's heartbeat.

'I'll get it,' Mother offers. My heart works harder, fearing who could be on the other side of the door. It's too early for the mailman. Brad would message first. Neighbours would ring the bell. 'What on Earth are you doing here?' Mother spits.

'Please, I need a minute of your time.' The voice stabs my ears. Mother walks back into the living room and pulls out a handgun from her safe. She stands in front of me, my human shield, as The Teacher enters, rightfully holding his hands in the air.

'Speak what you have to say and *get out*.' The gun ready, willing. Why is he here? Part of me wants Mother to pull the trigger. The pitter-patter of feet on the stairs frighten us both. 'Alexa,' Mother says. 'Stay upstairs, Darling.' The feet retreat.

'Okay, okay, you won't have to do anything stupid.' Shooting him wouldn't be stupid.

'Speak.'

'Okay, okay. Look, I've come here to apologise.' Neither of us moves a muscle. 'Not just to you two, but the town. May I sit?' The gun permits him, providing his hands remain aloft. 'Thanks. I know what you two think of me, and, quite frankly, I deserve it. I'm a horrible, horrible person. I'm diseased. I'm sick. Only, my sickness is that I like young girls.'

'That doesn't give you permission to *touch* them.'

'I know, I know. And it's not why I became a teacher, honestly. But, being around them every day,

355

unfortunately, emphasised feelings I tried to avoid. I hated myself for having them-'

'Maybe you should have killed yourself. I would have if my mind was that sick.' Is that how Mother thinks?

'I tried, but I couldn't go through with it. Then, I fell in love with a student. It was consensual, I swear. She was fifteen and fancied me. Having girls fancy me was all new to me; I've been with my wife for over twenty years, and the affection they showed was like a drug. A drug to ease the sickness.'

'This gun can also ease your sickness.'

'Please, hear me out. She came onto me one day after class, and I didn't know how to react. I was stupid and gave in to her, and when I realised what I'd done, she bribed me to continue sleeping with her by threatening to go to the head-teacher. It would've ruined my career, my life, if it came out.'

'Are we supposed to feel sorry for you? A grown man who couldn't say no to a *child*?' The gun still staring a hole into his chest.

'No, no, certainly not.' His presence in my home has sent my tongue into hiding. 'I'm just trying to explain the entire picture. I became hooked: hooked to the excitement, the naughtiness, the youth. And, as time went on, girls, sadly, became less and less consensual. And the more I got away with it, the more I craved it. I never once stopped to think of those I was hurting until last night, Lily, when you came to my house.'

'Excuse me?' Mother shoots me a dirty look, the gun confused where it should point. 'Last night?'

'I was horrible to you,' The Teacher resumes, spinning Mother back to him. 'I betrayed the trust of your home and the trust your family placed in me as a teacher. And, for that, I'm truly, truly sorry.'

'This is wonderful and all,' sarcasm oozing out. 'But, what's your point? Why shouldn't I pull this trigger?' Her index finger strokes the trigger – no; caresses the trigger.

'If you want to shoot me, that's fine, but I'm going to the police. I'm going to explain publicly to the whole town and take the punishment I deserve. You won't need to testify; I'll refuse to give names. I deserve to spend the rest of my life in prison.'

Mother's finger refuses to leave the trigger. The crack in the window sucks time out of the room, freezing the monster on the couch. Jekyll's conscience besting Hyde's wants. 'Then why come here?'

'I wanted to apologise to you both; and, to rest your fears. Here,' he gently takes his phone from his pocket and tosses it towards my feet. 'I've saved all the evidence to another phone, but you deserve that one. There's a girl called Janine in my contacts. She's the most recent. She's taken it quite badly, and if you're up for it, I think she could do with a friend.' Fellow victim, he means. 'Her address and contact details are saved; she doesn't deserve what I've done to her, as much as you didn't, and I will do everything I can to atone for my sins. Both in this life and beyond. Shoot me if you wish, or let God and the police judge me.'

He stands, closes his eyes and waits. Even when confessing to his crimes, he has a charm about him. 'Let him go,' my tongue speaks from its retreat. 'Let the courts punish him properly.' He offers a half-smile and opens his eyes to thank me.

'Fine,' Mother asserts, stopping his eyes from gazing at me. The gun lowers its aim. 'Get out.'

He bows and leaves. Only time will tell if he's being honest or not. The walls shake as Mother slams the door shut behind him. She'd sooner shoot him, or let him rot to death. I'd sooner imprison him; a fate I've suffered.

'It's finally over,' I perk up with, my tongue waggling in its freedom. 'We're all free.' Mother and I embrace Alexa as she comes downstairs; all the suffering of the last four years now over. Four years of crying, four years of arguing, four years of anger and sadness and fear and hatred, four years without hope. Now, I have hope. Hope for life. Hope for a future.

'You best record the news, Sweetheart,' Mother smiles. 'I don't want to miss a second of them publicly shaming him.'

This day will be one I tell my kids about. This day will be the one *Brad and I* tell *our* kids about. I press record and wait. My mind is at peace. Watching through all the undercard, waiting for the main event to break.

An hour passes without the story breaking; it's probably too soon for reporters to know the full story. Maybe the police haven't told them yet, still gathering evidence. Maybe they're on their way to his house to collect everything they can find; I wonder if his family will be home, blissfully unaware of what their future holds. Maybe his wife won't believe them, despite all the evidence which cements his guilt.

His phone sits by me, waiting for its previous owner's guilt to appear. Its call ignored by me throughout the hour. As another nothing article breaks, I succumb to the phone's call and look through it.

I start with pictures, and scroll through his immaculately arranged folders: folders such as "Holiday Pics" (filled with a variety of holidays, from Britain and abroad), "Castle Quests" (looks like he was one of those on a quest to snap a selfie in front of every castle; West Drive's being the only one I recognise), "The Pets" (pictures of the family with their dogs and gerbils, none of which were present last night) and "La Familia". The first picture is a selfie between The Teacher and his wife. A selfie which brings tears. That poor woman will soon have her entire life destroyed by the very man she wedded. The very man who promised to protect her no-matter-what in front of his friends and family will be the very man who ruins her life, and the lives of their children. Children bullied for having a rapist as a father.

Further in the album are pictures of all the family, with an uncomfortable about of them in bikinis. Ashley's skin is so pure, so elegant, so regal. She has no idea of the horrors inside the mind of the man she's posing half-naked for. At the bottom of the folder are topless pictures of his wife; her body hiding any sign of delivering two children. She's a full-chested woman, doing well to stall the effects of her thirties and looks after her body. Yet she's not enough to satisfy his cravings. Nor does he satisfy hers.

The next folder is "School Stuff", full of pictures of the classroom and projects the kids have done in class. Towards the bottom is a sub-folder called "Misc."; housing the photos he keeps secret: photos of his victims. The girls who look at the camera scream for help, those who don't have no idea he's taking their picture. All of them topless, for his sick mind to leer over. Despite their screams for help, help never came. Towards the bottom are girls happily posing topless *with* him. One of those triggered the carnal desire in him. They got to choose their fate. I pray I don't pass her on the street.

None of them named; Janine will remain a mystery. One girl I recognise, though; a recognition which brings vomit close to the surface: me. I never realised he even took pictures (nor has any nightmare of mine pictured him doing so). Visions can skew facial expressions to suit the vision's desires, but this was a photograph of my abuse. The eyes of a girl I wish wasn't me. Seeing them cloud the room in darkness. My legs noodle, my heart decays.

The rest just more evidence against a monster, but those three pictures are better deleted. Better never seen again. I don't need reminders, and nobody needs proof. Before I hit delete, I stroke her face. 'Everything will be all right.' It may take some time, but she'll get there. For better or worse, she'll survive.

I'm not *just* deleting evidence; I'm deleting *him*. Deleting the rape. Deleting the memories. Deleting the visions and nightmares. Deleting the cage trapping the girl I was a mere twenty-four hours ago.

With confirmation, nothing remains to show I was once a victim.

With the pictures explored, I move on to his messages, with the most recent coming from his wife (Abigail): "Grandad had a slip, won't be home until tomorrow evening!! Sorry babe. I'll make it up to you. You know how. :) Xxx."

She never needs to apologise to him ever again.

The second conversation thread is from the head-teacher, confirming a morning meeting. Who will be the first person to discover the message on his whiteboard?

Next is Ashley, with his messages containing more words than her replies. "Hi, gorgeous. I'm working late today. There's money left in the house for you and Amy to order takeaway. I'll try not to be too late. Okay, babe? Love you. Xxxx."

She simply replied "Ok. Xx."

Is *she* a victim? Or a teenager embarrassed by her father's love?

Further down is Janine's thread. "Shut up. Or else." The last message sent by The Teacher, in response to her begging to talk to someone about the abuse. Was Abigail sat by his side watching television with him while he threatened a child? Was Abigail cooking tea while he messaged Janine saying "I can't wait to see you again. You are so fit. You're my darling. My baby." Was Abigail at work while he perused through his collection of victims?

Janine's contact does have her address and I jot it down on a piece of paper. Any plans with Brad can wait, I need to see her. I need to reassure her. And countless others. They all deserve to know their ordeal is over, as much as I do.

Janine lives a few streets away from me, in another poor area: he chose his victims well. It's frightening to think of how much effort went into targeting me. Would he browse through the register and cross-reference against his checklist? Broken home: tick. Poor area: tick. Lack of friends: check. Inability to grasp basic geography: check.

Did he have back-up options? In case I refused after-school tutoring. How many girls have *narrowly* escaped his abuse by having a more unfortunate classmate?

My eyes hide away a wanting tear. A random surge of masculine adrenaline is one thing; premeditated stalking is another.

Images of what I could witness flood my head throughout the walk. If she's anywhere near as bad as I was, I may not want to stay too long. What if her mother doesn't know? What if she doesn't want to talk to me?

All those thoughts pushed aside as I knock on her door.

'Hello?' A middle-aged, rather round lady opens the door, narrow enough to just about see my face. Her fidgeting confirms she knows about Janine's abuse. 'Whatever you're selling, I'm not interested.'

'No, no, sorry. My name is Lily. May I please have a word with Janine?' My body assumes an answer and takes a step forwards, but her fidgeting turns anxious.

'What about? She's not feeling well today.' Mother used that excuse on the phone. Firstly, with the school, then with anyone who came to the house (one girl, Katy, actually came to see if I was okay, which surprised me as we barely spoke). All of this is all-too-real and all-too-scary to see from an outsider's perspective. Actors re-enacting my story. The house is different, the faces don't match, but the story and the beats remain the same.

'It's about *him*.' I cock my head and allow an air of silence to hang, filling her with all the information she needs.

'You're not a reporter or anything, are you? I'm not having my baby harassed by you lot and-'

'No, no; I'm another *victim*.' My voice quietens to save us both from the word. My tone is confident, despite its volume. A fully recovered alcoholic addressing an AA meeting. Aware of the pitfalls and the trials those in attendance will have to endure, but proof they're doable.

'Come on in,' she closes the door first to unlock the chain, before opening and gesturing for me to come in. Would Mother have accepted Janine in the immediacy of my suffering?

'Thanks,' I whisper as I step into their world. It's smaller than ours, but also cleaner. And without the smell which hangs around our house. Pictures on the walls of happy times and bright colours everywhere; it has a homely feel which mine doesn't.

'Want a cup of tea or water or coffee or-'

'I'm fine, really, thank you.' Her fidgeting on full effect. Her behaviour so familiar, mine so alien. 'She's free, by the way.'

'Free?' Hope clouds her eyes, dispelling bags of tiredness and stress.

'I visited him last night and scared him enough that he's confessing everything to the police as we speak. His arrest should be on the news today.' Such confidence. The chains really are off. She rushes over and embraces me in a hug.

'I would have killed him,' she whispers. I believe her. 'Janine's room is upstairs, the last door on your right. I hope you can help her.'

'Me too. I've survived him, I'm sure she can. In time.' I take one last look at Janine's mother, who takes a picture of the two of them off the wall and strokes her daughter's happy, smiley face, and ascend the stairs. I want to be the girl who mends the pieces of all the girls The Teacher has broken. I want to be the hope in their lives, allowing them the willpower to survive. As I knock on Janine's door, I realise the first day of my new job is about to begin.

'Come in, come in, come in,' the ramblings of a girl I used to be. I walk into a plain-looking room, with walls barren of posters or pictures. Remnants of wallpaper appear here and there. Ripped clothing of what the naked beige wall once donned. I moved room; she has erased hers.

In a corner sits a green chair, with the only electrical items inside the room resting on it: a phone, a tablet, a television and a games console; the latter two unplugged; the rest of the room free from modern life. The red curtains drawn creates an almost stereotypical lap-dancing-club style of red throughout the room. Janine sits on a wooden chair, leaning over her desk. As I get closer, I notice she's drawing circles on dozens of sheets of paper. A shattered mind needs no rhyme or reason.

'Hi, Janine, I'm Lily. I've come to have a brief chat, if that's okay?' I stand dead-centre in the room and offer my best motherly voice; this will be the voice of the professional me. The voice I use with all future victims whom I'll mend.

'Lily, Lily, Lily, nice to meet you, Lily. How are you? You. You. I'm fine, Lily. I'm Janine.' Not once did her gaze leave the circles on the page.

'I'm very well, thank you, Janine. What are you drawing, there?' This entire new persona I'm performing will be the owner of Lily's Healing Service (the name can be finalised on a later date), and she will be caring, and considerate, and kind, and sweet, and understanding, and strong: she'll be everything I'm not, but nobody will ever know.

'The world, the world, the world, as I see, I see: hallow. World nothing: no good; no life; just hallow world.' Was I this bad? Was I this broken when The Monday-Lady tried piecing me back together?

'I am a sufferer, too.' Every word enunciated for effect. The words alien for me to say, and I'm not sure if she's at a stage where she wants to hear them: I know I wasn't this soon afterwards.

'He, he, he: monster. He abused Janine, and, and, and hurt, and pain. He, he, he over there. I, I, I, I-'

'Calm down, calm down, it's okay, I'm here.' I race and kneel beside her, watching the creation of a constant stream of circles. Am I even helping?

This close reveals the true nature of her broken state; a vile smell erupts from her, her nails bitten too close to the skin, her hair tied, but damaged, her eyes are absent as she stares without blinking at her circles. 'I know what you're going through; I've been through it, too. He came into my home and did the same to me.'

'My, my, my bed; he abuse Janine there. And, and, and pain. Suffer. Hallow-'

'I know, I know,' the strength of my new persona tested by her ramblings; my inexperience visible for all to see. 'But, he's gone to prison. Forever.' I pause, hoping for a reaction, but still, her eyes remain unfazed. 'And

370

he'll never hurt anyone ever again. You're free. We're both free.'

'Bad man, prison, bad man, prison; free Janine. Need bad man, bad man need Janine. Prison, no Janine not free; must be bad girl, bad man said so, so, so, must be-'

I grab her arms to help soothe her, and her entire body thrusts in my directions as her eyes lock on mine. 'I know it's scary, but you'll eventually be free to live your life without the fear of him.' Her lip quivers with each word, as her hand still tries to draw its circles, sans paper. No life exists in her eyes. She must be about fourteen (it's hard to tell with her appearance being so broken) and knowing how much she must fight for her sanity punches at my heart. He must realise when he's pushed his victims to their breaking point; perhaps that's why he left me tied to the bed. His abuse had broken me beyond repair.

'Janine, Janine, Janine dead. Janine needs bad man; bad man need Janine. Janine dead, dead, dead-'

'No, Janine, you're alive: alive and free. No one will ever hurt you ever again.' My inexperience in my new role shines over the room's red, as I continue to fail to garner any response from her body.

Strands from her hair drop in front of her eyes, and my motherly instincts kick in and I push them back behind her ears. I can see why he chose her: she's pretty. It's a prettiness she's done a superb job in hiding, but it's there beneath a layer of fear.

Her arm slows and rests on her lap. A calmness drifts over the room as I try to picture what her life was like before he came in and hollowed-out her world. Nails stick out of the wall indicating pictures once stood with pride, remnants of yellow show what her wallpaper may have looked like, stuffed animals all lumped in a corner could have provided the room with a cheery atmosphere. Instead, it sits in darkness, with Janine a shell of who she was. Who she should be. Who I was.

Another rogue strand of hair pushed back; my fingers run down her cheek: feeling the dirt resting on her skin. Her pupils shake, and she leans forward and kisses me.

It startles me and lasts longer than it should have as our mouths move in sync. As our tongues touch, she pulls away, allowing a glimpse of life to flicker in her eyes. A glimpse of the real Janine. It's only a glimpse, though, as the look fleets, allowing the stoic look residence.

She walks backwards, knocking the chair against the floor, and walks zombie-like towards the bed. She sinks to her knees and kneels across the bed. 'Our Father, who art in Heaven, hallowed be thy name. Thy kingdom come, thy will be done, on Earth as it is in Heaven-'

'Janine, Janine,' I whisper, trying to understand her confusion. 'You don't need to do this anymore.' Her hands clasp together as she buries her head into her pillow.

'-and forgive us our trespasses, as we forgive those who trespass against us, and lead us not into temptation, but deliver us from evil-'

'Janine, stop, please.' She pulls her trousers down, revealing pink underwear. Stained as much as the rest of her attire. 'That's not why I'm here. You don't need to do this. He's gone.'

'-hallowed be thy name. Janine purpose must be for bad man. Bad man lives for Janine; and needs Janine. Janine needs bad, bad, bad man. Our Father who art in Heaven-'

'Janine,' I call but get no response. I rush to the side of her bed and rub her back. 'You're free. Free to be yourself and not his slave. Free from his dominance and cruelty.'

'-give us this day our daily bread, and forgive us our trespasses, as we forgive those-'

Her rendition of the Lord's Prayer repeats over and over as my words cannot bring her out of this behaviour; Lily's Healing Services may take a while longer to get going. I've failed my first mission. I'm not at the level of The Monday-Lady. I'm not even at the level of Mother, who helped nurse me back to health. The ceiling matches the walls' emptiness; mine has stars and planets to look at while trying to forget; she must have delved into faith. The faith in a God who will save her.

By her sixth full rendition, I realise I'm not bringing her back and retreat out of the room. I bid her farewell, but her mind is too far gone.

I trudge with heavy steps downstairs, stopping as her mother desperately hopes for good news. 'Well?' Her eyes widen, her smile hopeful. It's the hope which kills you. She wants good news; she *needs* good news.

My pathetic skills bring for none. 'Did it help? Please say it helped.' If anything, I've made it worse.

'I'm sorry,' shame bows my head for me. 'I couldn't get through to her.' I soldier through the tears threatening to attack my cheeks. 'I've not seen anything like that.' Even at my height, was I *that* bad? My pain put into perspective, but Janine's mother doesn't care about my pain.

She lowers her head and stumbles against a wall. 'I don't know what to do,' she whispers over a sad heartbeat. 'I just, I just don't know-'

Her words, and my desire to escape the after-effects of my pathetic offering, are interrupted by a thud and a scream from outside. We rush out and her mother screams at the sight of Janine's body, bent and doubled, on the floor. Her window wide open. 'My baby,' Janine's mother screams and rushes over to cradle the mangled corpse. Her blood painting the garden's grass red with every passing second. 'My baby, my baby, please, no, my baby.' Whispers and shocked voices circle the garden as more onlookers gather. 'What did you do?' She turns to me, still cradling her baby. Eyes filled with venom. She needs someone to blame. 'What did you say? What did you say?' Her tone increasing in anger. 'What did you say?' By now a scream. 'You murderer. You murdered my poor baby. Please, Lord, please save my baby. My poor baby.'

Janine's face wears the same expression as it did in her room. No doubt the same look created and wore during his abuse. A look which highlights the very worst of her life. Not the look she should have to end her life with. 'My poor baby,' her mother still wails. 'My poor baby, please, come back to me.' More and more onlookers gather, as one rings for an ambulance. My eyes fixed on Janine's.

Her eyes as empty as in her room. Her soul has long been dead, with her body catching up. Any punishment the police throw at The Teacher will not be enough. How many more victims are still suffering? How many more ended theirs this way? How many more mothers are cradling their daughters, begging for life to return?

Her eyes, her mother's screams, the onlookers' whispers; it all becomes too much and I run. Run away like the coward I am. Her mother calls me a murderer as I run, a claim I don't know if I can deny. Nobody chases me, and a couple of minutes later, once out of sight of my crime, I collapse on the floor and cry. Crowds of attention-craving idiots rush pass me to see what the commotion is about, none bothered about the girl crying in the street. None aside from Brad.

'Lily?' His voice confused. He kneels by my side. 'Why are you here?' The street empty by the time I offer a reply.

'I killed her.' My eyes hallowing out, as hers did. 'She was fine. Then I killed her.' My voice stoic and low. 'It's my fault.'

'Don't you dare think like that.' Brad wraps his arms around me. '*He* killed her. Not you. Some people just can't be saved.'

'But she was alive. She was so young.' My eyes focus on a brick on the wall in front of me, a circle carved into it. 'So pretty. Now she's dead.'

Brad lifts me and walks me away from the scene. I turn as we reach the corner, Janine points at me. The same hollowed-out look in her eyes.

I wake on the living room sofa, the room inside and the world outside in complete darkness. 'Mother? Alexa? Brad?' No answer. As I reach over to turn the lamp on, the television comes to life, startling me.

'Ladies and gentlemen,' a loud, brash American begins. 'Welcome to Earth's Worst; the game show where we show you the very worst of Planet Earth. On today's show,' the camera zooms in to his face as he adopts a more sinister voice. 'Do you know a murderer? Do you know a torturer? Do you know a rapist? Well, today is your lucky day,' he raises his hands and the audience claps and cheers. 'Our special guest on tonight's show is Lilian,' the audience woo as the scene transitions to reveal the twenty-something me standing at the podium. The loud American appears next to her. 'Young Lilian here is either a murderer, a torturer or a rapist. Are we excited?' He raises his hands again to more clapping and cheering.

The camera zooms in again on his face, as all the goofiness about the show fades. 'Then come on down to Lilian's house and find out which one she is.' He winks and the television dies.

Fear freezes me to the spot; my ears perched. Silence fills the room. The final hum of the television long gone. Scratching appears at the window.

Against my better judgement, I walk over to the window, brace myself and draw back the curtains. Behind the crack, several snakes covering most of the window, are hordes of people scratching against the glass to get in.

'Torturer, torturer, torturer,' they chant in unison. Highlighting every syllable. I close the curtains as fast as my arms allow and collapse to the ground. 'Torturer, torturer, torturer.' The anthem of my death.

Their voices raise and I run into the hallway. Loud knocks attack the door, thumping it nearly from its hinges. 'Who is it?' I shout.

'It's Janine's mother,' a voice returns, lifting the letterbox open. 'Come out here and fight me like a man, you murderer. Let's see you try to murder me, you bitch.'

I recoil into the kitchen and the door slams. Rain strikes as more people scratch and claw at the windows in here, too. As I turn around fully, Ashley, Amy and

Abigail sit around the kitchen table, arms crossed, watching me.

'My daddy is in prison, thanks to you.'

'My friends have abandoned me, thanks to you.'

'My husband has lost his freedom, and I've lost my trust, thanks to you.'

Their hurt and anguish slap me back against the counter, the clawing nears me. Desperate to reach me. 'No, no, no,' I repeat. My tone mirroring Janine's. 'He deserves it. He deserves punishment.'

'Did we?' They reply.

'Did you even think of us?' Abigail asks. My silence is my guilt.

To fix my life, I've had to break theirs. The clawing at the windows close to breaking point.

'Torturer, torturer, torturer.' Louder. Closer.

'I'm sorry, I'm sorry,' my head hides in my hands. 'I thought I was doing the right thing.' The three of them stand, and I run out of the room before they could reply. In the hallway, Janine's mother still demands a fight, as the clawing nears ever still to breaking through.

I walk back up the stairs, watching and waiting for the inevitable break, and retreat to the sanctuary of my bedroom.

The room dons a red hue, and the Lord's Prayer sounds as I enter. The wallpaper ripped in unnatural ways. On the bed, Janine and The Teacher are having sex; he thrusts inside her maniacally, while she begs for rescue from a higher power. The same look on her face. The last look she ever gives. They both stop and look at the window.

The wind breaks through, shattering the glass outside, and wraps itself around my arms. The rain and the clawing stop; my body draws to the now-open window. Hope is on the outside. Hope of a freer world. Hope of a life free from pain. The wind nudges me a little closer, as smiles etch onto Janine and The Teacher's faces. Silence forms outside.

As my body's nudged to within touching distance, my senses return and I refuse its embrace; waving away the wind's grasp and retreating out of my room.

The rain returns.

The clawing returns.

The grunting returns.

The Lord's Prayer returns.

I run into Mother's room; I *need* my mother. 'Mother? Mum? Mummy?' No reply. Clawing reaches the upstairs windows. The wind filtering through from my room, sucking out the air from Mother's room.

'Torturer, torturer, torturer.'

I race out of the room, as a crack forms on Mother's window, and try both Alexa's room and the bathroom doors. Both locked. The wind sucking air out of the hallway. I race downstairs to the open door. Janine's mother stands at the threshold, with hordes of people behind her. All waiting. All wanting.

The sounds of whipping lead me to the living room. All the eyes of the outside world watch me walk.

The man on the television is back on, but silently watching the events unfold. In the living room, The Flowers, Mother, Brad, Janine, Janine's mother, Ashley, Abigail and the twenty-something me are all handcuffed to a pole running across the ceiling. All stripped down to their underwear. All facing the wall. The Teacher stands in the middle of the ring of bodies, preparing his long, thick, black whip for another lash.

The window in here smashed, and the crowd all watch, no longer chanting. No longer clawing. Their phones record the events; one day they'll tell their children how they witnessed this. They'll photograph every whip. Record every sound. Catalogue every victim.

'Lily, Lily, Lily; you were my favourite.' The Teacher says. 'You were always such a good girl, who always did as she was told.' The audience on the television woo. 'You really should have stayed as that cute little girl.' The ten victims all sob for their release. Their sobs fall in the minority of people wanting that outcome. 'Just look at all the people you've got involved in this pit. Tell me, weren't they healthier *before* meeting you?'

He's not real. He's not real. He's not real. I shake my head, trying to erase this from my mind. Each lash rejects any ability to forget.

'Firstly, you want to torture me,' Ivy's whipped across her upper back.

'By drugging me with chloroform,' Brad's whipped across his right ankle.

'Then, you threaten me with castration,' Rose's whipped on her right leg.

'Then, you want to gouge my eyes out,' Abigail's whipped across her neck.

'Then, you call me a rapist,' Janine's whipped on her lower back.

'Then, you blame *me* for *your* mental breakdown,' Poppy's whipped across her left arm.

'Then, you pull a gun on me,' Mother's whipped on the back of her head.

'Then, you want me to go to prison,' Ashley's whipped on her behind.

'To be locked away forever,' the twenty-something me's whipped across her left thigh.

'Or to be executed,' Janine's mother's whipped vertically down her back.

The Teacher rests the whip on the sofa and bows; the audience, both outside the window and in the studio, applaud. Their cheers loud enough to trick the mind into thinking hundreds were residing inside these four walls. The crowd outside add chanting to their applause: 'torturer, torturer, torturer.'

All the cameras turn and face me. The ten bodies writhe and scream in pain, before silencing and turning their attention to me. Their face menacing. They join in the chants: 'torturer, torturer, torturer.'

My mind freezes, my body glued to the floor. The Teacher stands gigantically in the centre of the room. Amy's touch brings warmth to my mind. 'What's my daddy doing to all those people?' She asks. 'Why are my mummy and sister tied up and crying?' She cries.

'Break it to her,' The Teacher says. 'Break that little girl's heart. Tell her the truth, before she becomes old enough to learn it from *me*.' There's movement in his trousers, a sight which strangles me. 'Come here, *Sweetheart*.' Poor, defenceless Amy walks into his world and I break down.

The chanting still ringing in my ears. Amy's voice part of the mix. 'Torturer, torturer, torturer.' Every single chant in perfect unison. 'Torturer, torturer, torturer.' Every single chant aimed at me. 'Torturer, torturer, torturer.'

'Embrace it, Lily,' The Teacher kneels to my level. 'You know what you've done.'

Each body disappears into a cloud of smoke. No more people outside, no more inside, no more live studio audience. 'That's all from us here at Earth's Worst,' the loud American begins. His picture engulfing the screen. 'Remember, Lily, we know.' And with that, the television dies.

The living room returns to normal. And with a blink, my soul returns to the sofa where my body sleeps.

Brad's snoring wakes my body. I stand and hear Mother washing the dishes. 'Brad,' I whisper, trying to avoid Mother's attention. He doesn't hear me, so I crawl over to him and shake him gently. 'Brad, Brad.'

'Hey,' he wakes, his voice groggy. 'Are you okay? We were worried-'

'I am now.' I embrace him in a hug. His heart strokes my face, as I nestle against his bare chest.

Saturday

Hushed tones of Brad and Mother greet me as my eyes return me to life, and I rise and open the curtain to grant the beautiful sunshine entry into our living room. As a kid I used to love waking up on a Saturday; it was the only day of the week where there's no bedtime or reason to rise early; the entire day was one big adventure waiting to happen. Adventures at the park, adventures at the castle, adventures at the lifeboat station (to the right of the castle), adventures in front of the television. Whichever I went with, they made Saturdays worth waiting for.

After the last incident with The Teacher, I locked myself away in Alexa's room for just shy of a year, as her window faces off towards the park; I'd spend all day watching them playing, mourning the time when I could have joined. They'd frolic around, kicking balls and riding bikes, not knowing or caring about the mad woman in house number 29.

Despite 10am having not long since passed, plenty of children are outside running around. Countless news stories have lambasted about the problem with obesity and laziness among British children, so it adds a smile seeing those facts and figures haven't derived from these streets. I'd like to think my children would be outside, playing, running, enjoying life. Not locked away.

Brad and Mother both embrace me as I enter the kitchen, before returning about their business. My mind slaps a picture of Abigail, Ashley and Amy over the scene before I shake the remnants of it away. 'Feeling better today?' Brad asks, his voice soft.

'Much.' I grab a bottle of water and sit beside him at the kitchen table; in the seat where Amy sat.

'We've been thinking,' Brad looks over towards Mother, who's washing dishes. 'We could all do with a day away. Away from the stresses of life, you know?'

The thought of a day away strokes my ears. 'What's the idea?'

'Well,' Mother retrieves her laptop and sits it down in front of me. On it are a series of waterfalls, lakes, couples kayaking and other welcoming pictures. 'How about a trip to Roskell? It's so beautiful there, I think you'd love it.' I've never been to the lakes as an adult; Mother has told me we went as a child, but my mind has long since deleted those memories. It's the last memory Mother has of Ms Woodfield, as she passed away the following evening from a sudden heart attack. Mother swore we'd never visit them out of fear.

'That sounds amazing,' my voice barely above a whisper, but the passion screams across the room, and Brad takes off.

Mother races upstairs for a shower; and to drag a still-sleeping Alexa out of bed. I tread back to the living room and turn on the news, keeping its volume low. A hand grabs my heart and squeezes it as The Teacher's house appears. The property cordoned off with yellow tape, and police escorting away onlookers and passers-by. The reporter across the street, herself unable to get close.

I hit the record button; this will be a story I'll savour for the rest of my life. It'll be in the promotional video should Lily's Healing Service ever open its doors again; an example of how the company's leader bested her own monster.

Aside from nosey neighbours and police, men in suits bring out bags of evidence; all collected to prove his guilt. His phone cries out to me from the floor, and the weight of importance it can carry to this investigation settles on my mind. Even if he's made a copy, this is the original; but I cannot bring myself to part with it. I pick it up and scroll back through the pictures of his victims; a sick obsession forces me to seek Janine's photos.

If the pictures in this album follow a chronological order, then four girls separated my abuse and Janine's, with Janine the penultimate victim. The current victim saved from any more abuse, thanks to my hands. Janine's pictures follow a similar pattern to mine; starting in the classroom, followed by his house and what looks like hers. A fourth picture taken in a wooded area. A fifth picture taken in his car. She suffered more than I did. Did she suffer the most?

The first of her pictures, in the classroom, shows her barely facing the camera; but her prettiness shows. How pretty she *was*. Her skin full of life. Unaware, as I was, he snapped her picture. By the last picture, she wore the same facial expression and assumed the same position as when I left her. Evidence of whipping striped down her back.

I scroll back to the top to the first girl; I believe his story: they were having a genuine, honest affair; even if she forced his participation. She's smiling and posing next to him (she looks older than fourteen, but she still wears her school uniform). The next picture also shows a girl willing; pictures clothed and topless. The third girl (of eleven total), the first to not consent to her picture.

Her appearance more rugged than the two pretty girls who preceded her, and her body language screams for help. I was girl number five, the first to have a picture taken in his home. Perhaps the more girls he got away with abusing, the more risks he needed to take to satisfy his urges.

After scrolling through all the victims, I take one last longing look at a picture of Janine and hide the phone away in the coffee table's drawer. The reporter has changed locations, probably detailing another aspect of his cruelty, but he's still plastered across the headlines.

"BREAKING NEWS: High school teacher found-"

I don't want to watch this alone. Mother deserves to bask in the glory of victory, too.

A brisk walk to the train station prevents Alexa from her usual whining about how long journeys can take. She moaned about Roskell (she wanted to spend her Saturday catching up with a new series on Netflix and playing with friends; friends we've not met before). But Mother and I both know she'll love Roskell when she gets there.

The train journey wasn't as kind, with it taking just shy of two hours for us to arrive at the quaint train station in Roskell. A short taxi ride brings us to our destination: the beautiful lakes of Roskell.

Fresh cut grass greets my nose as we walk through the gates, as waves crash against their shores in playful fashions. The sky in its prime, defending itself against attempted clouds, allowing the sun a clear route to the ground. Trees either side a luscious shade of green, brimming with life. Large groups of flowers decorate the park; reds and yellows and purples and oranges and whites please watching eyes. Benches rest at various parts along the path's trails, each filled with families such as ours, enjoying their day out.

The crashing waterfall echoes around, leaving the issued map meaningless. The waterfall's mouth is several minutes away, with a large pool of water at the bottom full of people, splashing and laughing and playing. The mouth high into the sky, leading towards a mountainous region which divides Wednesbury from its neighbouring county and Wales. The blue of the water contrasts perfectly with the green of nature.

We find a spot and relax, soaking in the sun. Mother and Alexa soon run off into the water, while Brad and I watch on.

'Maybe one day,' he says. 'That'll be you and your daughter.' His eyes suggest a desire to be the father, in this imaginary scenario.

'Maybe.' The smiles painted on Mother and Alexa's faces bring about a yearning for this future. They're splashing and racing back-and-forth; a dream mother and daughter duo. Genuine happiness which shouldn't belong to a victim. Seeing it, though, allows hope Lily's Healing Service can prosper, despite my initial failure. If Mother can be happy in this new world we live in, that is something I can aspire to match. If I can aspire to match it, so, too, can other victims. On Monday, I'll try and work out the latest victim, and reassure her she's free.

As free as I am.

An hour passes and we move to the second lake; a shallower, more intimate setting contrasted with the family dynamic we brought. We set up here, and Mother and Alexa run off to relax in the water, again leaving Brad and me to watch on. Dogs and children and families and beautiful couples with kites and balls and bikes and laughter roam across every acre of land. The mountains, more in view from this lake, tower over us with their masculinity.

I try to capture the *spirit* of life here; were a famous photographer to capture the shot, immaculately, no doubt, it would fetch thousands, as it would accurately convey the happiness felt on every face. My shot offers none of that.

When I was about twelve, Mother took me to the underground caves in Brushwood. They're about a mile underground, formerly used as mines way-back-when, and house the locale of many ghost stories of the town. Brushwood itself is full of ghost stories. There's an eeriness around every corner. But at the core of the cave is a room full of calcite crystals, covering the ceiling. It was landmarked as a national treasure many years ago, so signs everywhere ordered us to not touch them (or the walls) to preserve their mysterious heritage.

While Mother and I were part of a tour group, I tried to capture the remarkable views we could see with our eyes, hoping one picture would be worthy enough to hand on the wall at home with pride; none of them came close to replicating what we saw. While the pictures themselves were beautiful, as are the ones I take of Roskell, they don't capture its spirit, its beauty, its passion.

'Life can be beautiful, sometimes,' Mother says as she and Alexa return. I couldn't think of a response and simply smile. For once, though, the smile isn't fake; I feel happy, inside and out. She grabs hold of my hand and we watch as the lakes glisten against the sun. If of the three lakes one is its heart, it's this one.

The third lake offers activities (with swimming prohibited), as kayaking and canoeing take centre stage. The ban on swimming isn't working to significant effect, with some lawless humans in the waters.

'You would love kayaking,' Mother says to me. 'Your grandfather took me once as a kid, and it was so relaxing.'

'I suppose I can give it a try.'

I can watch the water's beauty from afar all day long, but my mouth dries at the prospect of being atop it. Despite Mother's refusal of my protests, I walk into the office and book a kayak ride for one.

'Have you ever been in a kayak before, ma'am?' The man behind the counter easily doubles my size, in weight and height, with a long beard down to his belly button.

'Yeah, once in school.' It lasted about two minutes until some bullies rocked my kayak and it tipped over. Apparently, it was my fault; apparently, I was reckless, and I endangered my life and others.

She didn't care for the truth.

After I sign a form, filling in my name and address and contact information of my next-of-kin, I grab a life-jacket and head out with the man to the kayak.

'Here,' he hands me a small flare gun. 'Any problems, fire this in the air.' A sign behind him warns about misusing the flare gun and how it can result in a police conviction.

I place the gun by my side and drift out into the calm waters, leaving the rest of the world behind me. Everything which has ever bothered me ceases to be of importance. The gentle rocking of the water against the kayak takes me back to infancy, rocking to sleep in Mother's arms. The stroking of water against kayak worthy of having its own studio album, full of songs to soothe and lull someone of their fears.

The silence, the weather, the tranquillity; everything is perfect. Had I come here the day after the incident with The Teacher and allowed my body to drift then, as it is now, on this Heavenly cloud, I would have gone to school the next day as if nothing had happened. I thought I needed wine to reach this high, when all I needed was the outdoors. The sedation caused by wine nothing in comparison.

The kayak needs no rowing, as clear waters push me along a predetermined route. My eyes close, further locking away all feelings of ill will: The Teacher, Janine, Mother's erratic behaviour, Brad's forced advances; nothing bothers me. This is the feeling everyone on Planet Lilian lives with every day; carefree and happy. Not emotionless robots. The key, locking away dark memories, lost forever in the lake. Here, floating across the watery cloud, I'm just an ordinary girl: no baggage, no history, no bullies, no worries. I'm the Lilian I've always wanted to be. And if my body were to cease living in this very moment, I would go out with a smile on my face.

My hand trickles into the water, as my kayak drifts further into the lake. The water's strangely cold, but it offers a nice counter to the blazing heat of the sun. West Drive's news preoccupied with The Teacher; Roskell's news probably gloats about the warmest spring in recorded history. Because it feels like it should be.

In the distance, fish swim in harmony with one another, not fazed in the slightest by the constant stream of kayaks passing them by. Pushed aside by the ripples, but reuniting with their friends and family on the other side. They all play together in such joyful fashion.

The other side of the lake houses land full of luscious green trees. Their shadows cascade a stunning image on the water; with clear blue water abruptly turning dark. Yet the fish still swim as if nothing's changed. To them night is day, and day is night. The only difference being the warmth of their habitat. The greens, the blues and the oranges all form together to create a wonderful work of art.

A surge of desire creeps over me to lean over the kayak and meet my reflection. A rogue horror who escaped its capture presents itself: the baths in the aftermath of the incidents. I scrubbed and scrubbed for hours at a time, with the boiling water turning ice cold by the time my shrivelled-up body finally left. And I still felt as dirty as when I went in. Nothing worked in cleaning the remnants of him away from my skin. After the second incident, the water began enticing me in, promising me freedom and cleanliness. By incident three, Mother had banned me from taking baths after I drank a bottle of wine (or two, or three) and fell asleep while washing. Mother had to kick the door off its hinges to rescue me (after she worried when I never returned her calls). She caught me as my head fell under and nursed me back to health. She ordered me from then on to take showers, as if I were to fall asleep in a shower, the water would slap me for being an idiot, not bathe in the bed the bath offered.

The reflection smiles, an alien picture for me to see; the only times I ever *see* myself smiling are futuristic

400

or prehistoric versions of me in my dreams. But this is *my* face, showing *my* smile.

'Come on in,' her voice speaks. A combination of my inflexion and the water's waves. Her words create sweet ripples in the water, teasing the fish's path. 'The water's lovely. Much better than being on land.' Her words comforting, her smile enticing, her demeanour urging.

'I like land,' I jest back. My hand subtly tries to trickle the image away by drawing circles in the water, but she remains. She looks so at ease.

'Feel this water, Lily.' She allows her arms to float around. 'Come on in, dance with me and the fish. Dance with me and the Earth. Listen.' The sounds of other kayakers fall silent. 'Can you not hear its rhythm? Its beat? Come party with us.' As if on cue, the rhythmic beats of water and the merry sounds of all the creatures which inhabit it descend upon my ears. They're all enjoying their party.

'I don't think I should.' I want to. 'Brad and Mother and Alexa are-'

'They'll understand; after all, they only want what's best for you. There are no worries at this party.

401

No reasons to stress. Come live with us and you'll never have to visit those nightmare-filled streets of West Drive *ever again*.' Her face so genuine. I look back where Brad stands, the reaction of Mother and Alexa the after-effects of a joke told by him, before looking back at my reflection. Free.

I want the life she's offering.

I wake coughing water inside a chilly hospital room; its white décor matching our kitchen. Machines beep and people acquiesce to their lonely beds. A nurse sits by my side. 'Here you go,' she hands over a bucket as I cough up more water. 'You've had a rough day.' More heaving.

'Where am I?' My entire body feels weak.

'You're at Roskell General Hospital. Do you remember why you're here?' She walks over to the curtains, revealing the late-afternoon sun.

'No, not really,' my mind too weak to create memories. The urge to heave more water forces me to cradle the bucket tight.

'You were out kayaking at the lakes and you fell in. A coastguard and another kayaker brought you back to the surface and rang for an ambulance. Does any of that ring familiar?' Her voice delicate, deserving of an answer, but nothing comes.

'Where's my mother and Brad? And Alexa?'

'I'm sorry, nobody has arrived. Should we be expecting them?' Is she telling the truth? Has she refused Mother and Brad entry here, for some reason? Her words sound soothing and genuine; she's had to deal with friend-and-family-less people before.

'They were all with me at the lake.'

'I'm sorry, but the ambulance brought you here alone. Perhaps they've made their own way and just haven't arrived, yet?' She's offering anything to reassure me. Or to force me to believe her lies.

'I suppose.' I need to leave.

'Your phone is on the bedside table if you want to call them to say you're okay.' Has she gone through my phone?

'I suppose.' She offers a sympathetic smile and takes off to speak to a doctor in the distance. I dial Brad's number and he picks up before the first ring rings out.

'Oh, thank God,' he says through panted breaths. 'How are you?' I can hear Mother fretting in the background. 'We've been worried sick.'

'Where are you all?'

'Us? We're back at your house. The ambulance wouldn't let us come with you, so we came home to wait as we didn't know what hospital you were being taken to.'

Why wouldn't the ambulance take them? Why didn't the nurse mention that? 'So, you've left me?' The weight of the words sets in my head.

'No, of course not. Here, your mother wants to speak,' a muffled sound appears before Mother takes over the phone.

'Lily, Sweetheart, take a taxi and get home as soon as possible. A female taxi driver. We're all so worried about you.' Not worried enough.

I accept, and, after a bit of small talk, end the call. Just in time to see the doctor walk over to my bed. I wonder if he'll be more honest with me, unlike the nurse. I need honesty.

'Glad to see you're feeling better, Miss,' he elongates the last word as he searches for my name.

'Lily,' I help him.

'Right, Miss Lily. There seems to be no lasting damage; thankfully, you weren't under the water for too long.'

'Am I free to go, then?' Speaking as if in prison.

'Certainly. Although I would recommend you visit West Drive's St. Christopher's hospital tomorrow, just to be on the safe side. I've already called a colleague there to let them know the circumstances.' How does he know where I come from? I need to escape.

'Yeah, yeah, I-I will do. On Monday. Anyway,' I jump out of bed, ignoring the grogginess my body feels, and grab my clothes from the nearby radiator. 'I'm busy tomorrow, so.' I'm not, but his face needed a reason for it to be Monday.

'Lily, is everything okay?' He half-sits on the bed and rests the clipboard on the table. 'You're more than welcome to spend the night here if something's-'

'My family are waiting. I'm-I'm fine,' my behaviour anything but that of a fine woman. 'I'm fine.'

The doctor makes some notes as I remove the hospital gown, not even caring about onlookers; although the doctor respects my privacy by looking away. I ask him for a few taxi companies and begin calling. I need to go home.

Thankfully, I still have Mother's debit card, so I have the means to pay. A train might be a quicker route home, but there could be too many people on a train. I need privacy. I need solace.

A taxi journey spent in-and-out of consciousness; the driver thankfully respected my desire to sleep. She tried talking to me whenever I woke, asking about the accident and why I was so eager for a taxi (her company, ABC Taxis, were the third I tried, with the first two refusing to drive from Roskell to West Drive). She made me pay in advance (a ridiculous sum of £150), so there was no need for her to take a longer route or drive as slow as possible to extend the meter; I know they do that. Mother told me; they always take the longest routes possible in hope you don't notice. Anything for a few extra quid. She tried telling me at one point about how taxi drivers prefer small journeys (easier to rip off the client, no doubt) to long ones. I don't care; I want to go home and cuddle with my family.

As I open the door, Mother and Brad were seemingly waiting on the other side and embrace me as soon as I cross the threshold. Alexa is apparently asleep, after worrying so much. They both hug me individually and together, before escorting my still-weak body to the sofa, where it collapses in a heap. Mother announces the evening's plan (takeaway and a movie), and despite my urge to sleep, I'm in no mood to disagree or argue and accept.

'So,' Mother starts after ordering the food and sitting by my side. 'What happened out there?'

'I don't know,' my voice solemn. 'One minute I'm enjoying the p-peace and quiet, the next I'm sat in a hospital bed coughing.' Brad, sitting on the other side of me, grabs my hand. Mother doesn't object. My body too weak to crave its own space. 'I wanted you guys in the hospital.'

'I know, Sweetheart, but we didn't know which hospital you were at. There are loads in Roskell, and we could have been driving for hours.'

'You didn't ring me.' During the taxi ride home, I noticed there were no missed calls on my phone, no unread text messages or notifications.

'Bradley tried,' Brad nods. 'And he messaged. Did they not come through?'

I shake my head and grab my phone, confirming my story, but there sits a text: "Hey, hope you're okay. We couldn't come to the hospital in the ambulance so came home. Call me as soon as you wake. I miss you. Xx."

Where did that text come from? Did the nurse read it? They knew where I came from. Why would she read it?

'Are you okay?' Mother stops my racing mind.

'Yeah, sorry, I guess I didn't see this.' Once again Mother's right, I'm wrong.

Brad chose an adaptation of a Stephen King novel (he's still trying to confirm King is better than Poe, but he's not). I would have preferred an easy rom-com, as would have Mother (who hates horrors), but I'm in no mood to play the victim to get my way.

Silence, aside from Mother's nervous screams when the music changed in the film, was, for once, a welcome visitor. Her fears escaped the film into reality; with Mother making the pizza delivery man drop the pizzas on the floor and back away before she'd open the

409

door. Which was quite funny. He was so confused, bless him.

The adaptation wasn't great (I've read the book, and they missed so much out), but it was fine. Upon its conclusion, Mother grabs a blanket and places it on the spare sofa for Brad to sleep with. She's growing keener on him day-by-day. I knew she would. Seeing him accept her offer brings a merry little dance to my heart.

'So,' Brad says as the sound of Mother's bedroom door closing confirms we're alone. 'How are you really feeling?'

'Sad, weak, scared.' I giggle at how much is wrong. When they rescued me, they obviously found the key to those locked away feelings and opened the door. I long to be the girl on the lake again. I long to have that freedom from worries. Instead, they're all back, all running wild inside my body.

'Anything you want to talk about?' Brad changes the channel to the news and my eyes glimpse The Teacher. Smiling. A picture victims get, a picture good men get, not criminals. Criminals should have mug shots, not ones depicting him as a happy-go-lucky family man. My stomach swirls.

'*Him,*' I spit out, my eyes fix on that stupid, smug grin. Even when I think I've won, somehow he still beats me. Will I be the villain?

'Who is he?'

Brad knows about my rape, but now he has a picture to go with the tale. He joins in my anger at seeing the man portrayed in uplifting spirits, not slaughtered for his actions.

'I went to see him on Thursday.' Brad looks over with confusion, splitting his time between me and the man praised on national television.

'Why? Why would you do something like that?'

'Every night I'm haunted by what he did to me, and what he might be doing to other people. And they're getting worse.'

'Why haven't you told me about this?'

'Because I thought nothing of it. These nightmares are nothing new; I've had them for over three years.' The crack in the window visibly widens as the story goes on. 'And on Thursday, The Flowers and I decided I needed revenge before I could move on.' Brad understands, but I still feel the need to defend myself. 'Because he got away with everything, with no

411

repercussions to his family, friends, nothing. Whereas I was left scarred for life.'

'You should have told me,' he holds my hand in his. 'I would have come with you. To protect or help.' His honesty shines. I was wrong to ever doubt him, or to accuse him of not caring enough to come to the hospital.

'I know, I know, but it was fine. Anyway,' he speaks honesty with such ease; my mouth struggles. 'We tied him to his bed and I-I tortured him.' I fight back a tear wanting to pity him. Maybe that's why they're praising him; he told them he's the victim of torture. He knows his confession's under duress. He's outsmarted me again. 'Only a little bit, I promise, nothing too-'

'Define "a little bit".'

'Barely anything; it was more m-mental than physical; like, I called him a rapist repeatedly. Once I realised I was going too far, we stopped and went home-'

'He didn't chase you or anything, did he?' His fists clench.

'No, no, nothing like that. But I wanted to torture him more. I felt I deserved it, you know? He deserved to

412

suffer. He deserved to feel pain. Feel misery. Feel weak. Feel helpless. Feel lifeless.'

'Lily, what did you do?'

'Nothing, I told you, I promise. I just wanted to hurt him. But I didn't. I didn't. He came round Friday morning.'

'He came here? Lily,' his voice roars. 'Why didn't you tell me any of this? We've spent all day together; I think I deserve to know if you're in danger.'

'I'm fine, I'm fine. He came round to apologise and to tell us he was going to the police. That's why he's on the news. And he left me his phone.' My eyes divert to the drawer housing all the evidence the police need to wipe that stupid, sadistic grin from his face. 'He told me to contact Janine using her information from it.'

'Who's Janine?'

'Another victim. She lives over in Blueferry way.'

'That's where I found you yesterday.'

'Yeah,' my eyes close; trying to hide the image of her face. 'I went to see Janine, to help her, to heal her. To confirm she's no longer a victim.' The window more crack than glass. 'Afterwards, she killed herself. *I* killed her.'

His arms yearn to hug me, to comfort me, but my posture warns against it. 'I told you, *he* killed her, not you.'

'I know, I know. But last night I had another nightmare, this time where I was the villain.' I stand and walk to the window, watching over the sleeping street.

'Don't do that to yourself-'

'I am, though.' He stands, his face's reflection rests on my shoulder. 'There are now two children and a wife whose lives have been ruined, thanks to me. There's now a young girl with the rest of her life to live who's dead, thanks to me. Three innocent girls forced to torture a man, thanks to me. Mother's life is a misery. Everyone at school bullied me. You tied up and tortured; all thanks to me. What is the point in me? I *am* the villain.'

Brad walks closer and rubs my shoulders gently. I allow my right hand to cross over and rest on his left. 'Everything that has happened, is *his* fault. You're a victim, like everyone else in his web of cruelty. All you did was remove his mask, but he's still the monster who wore it in the first place.' Brad holds me as we watch the night pass by, the town sleeping like a baby. Even drunkards refrain from stumbling by our house.

414

Somewhere in this town are nine girls who are victims of his abuse. I wonder what their reaction to the news is. The news has largely ignored Janine's death; perhaps suicide isn't as fascinating as it once was. I wonder if a clever journalist will piece the articles together.

Brad's presence eases away the guilt.

Brad drifted off to sleep with relative ease, while my body refuses sleep whenever it requests an appearance. Giving up, for the time being, I resume my position in front of the window and trace my finger along the crack, leading to the centre where it momentarily stops the flow of wind entering the house. A simple flick could send this window crashing down.

If this glass shatters and kills someone, the glass will be the villain. Not the man who threw the stone which created the original crack.

I kiss my fingers and tap them against Brad's forehead as I walk outside. The chill in the air slices against my exposed skin, contrasting against the serene sky cascading down. The town still fast asleep, oblivious to any of the horrors. Oblivious to the victim who lives in their street. Oblivious to the villain who lives in their street.

Brad's right, I'm the *victim*.

'Psst,' a voice whispers. I look around to no faces. 'Walk,' it speaks through the wind.

A strong sensation shivers my body, and I walk, with no end destination in mind. It's soon clear enough where I'm walking: the castle. I've been too frightened to visit the castle at night since that group of lads trapped me. Those fears dispel as I reach its consecrated land. Fortunately, the castle's grounds are free from yobs, allowing me a safe passage through the war-torn gate. Mother and I once walked passed the castle in the early evening, and a group cat-called and whistled at her and asked her to join their party. She ignored them; a power I've never been able to possess, but I can still remember the anguish on her face.

The moonlight shines over the town's oldest resident; another picture I could never capture. Waves crash against the shore in the distance, greeting me as I enter the castle's forecourt. The air whistling to the beat of every step my feet take. There's a full moon in the sky, radiating a silver glow. Planet Lilian's moon *always* glows silver and is *always* full.

A kicked stone lands at my feet as Mother marches. 'You didn't talk to her? Hey.' I scan the scene to see the version of me from two weeks ago storming off. 'Don't you dare just walk away from me.'

'Just leave me alone,' she shrieks.

'I will not leave you alone. I am your mother, whether you like it or not. Now, get back here.'

The pair march into one of the castle's chambers, but as I enter after them there are no signs of life; just the echoes of an argument two-weeks old. The chamber with the dungeon, or bedroom, or kitchen. I climb down and sit against its stone walls. A pile of pebbles sit by my side, and one-by-one I throw them against the opposite wall, watching them ricochet in every direction.

'Poison.'

I lift my head but again see no faces. 'Hello?' I call out to silence.

'It's poisoning me.'

The fretting version of me from a month ago stands. She's walking around the railing in continuous circles. 'Hello?' My words don't even resonate with her.

'Poison, poison, poison, must stop.'

'It's not; stop being such a hypochondriac. Nobody's poisoning you.' Her mother tries to reassure her, appearing in the chamber with us, following her around the room.

'Poison, poison, poison.'

They both disappear into smoke.

I climb back to their level and scour the area, but no bodies exist. As I look round, I see, carved in stone,

"Free Colin". I grab a nearby stone and scratch it away. I will not. I will not.

'How was your decision any better than theirs?' Outside of this chamber is a version of me from a year ago, screaming in her mother's face. 'They both resulted in a broken family.'

'You weren't prepared.' She backs away; is her mother wrong? That's the body language of someone conceding defeat.

'And you were? You're such a hypocrite. I hate you.'

A slap from her mother causes them to disappear into smoke in the night. I sit on a stone pillar and watch the moon. Why is it showing me these images? On the moon, the same crack pattern from my window appears. It then appears on the stone I'm sat on and in the sea off in the distance and the clouds in the sky. The same crack. Everywhere.

A baby's scream jolts me towards another dungeon, but the room's empty. Empty of body and sound. Soft laughter trickles over my shoulder. But nobody claims ownership.

As I leave the chamber, the castle fades into darkness, dropping me in the park. I walk to the swings and take a seat. 'That's a nice thought,' Brad's voice begins. I move from the swing where Brad speaks to a version of me from a week ago. 'But my mother wasn't the nicest of people, so I can't imagine they would've talked for long,' he laughs.

'How did she, you know?' The version of me replies before the scene evaporates.

'Mummy,' a voice calls out. 'Look at me.' I spin around, a six-year-old me runs across the random building in the park. Mother sprints from her grown-up conversation to order her to come down. Her mother frets and worries, as more parents come to reassure her nothing is wrong.

The sniggering laughter of Barry soon appears from behind her, and he pushes her from the roof. Scenes and times beginning to blend. Barry pushed me from the school roof when I was eleven, after he tricked me into helping him retrieve his phone. I broke my ankle on the fall, and Barry got away with it. A lesson I've endured time and time again. The six-year-old me screams as parents rush to her aid before the scene vanishes.

A baby's cry sounds out from my left, where Mother hands over a baby to a familiar-looking woman. A dark ghost from a past my mind has buried. I cannot place her to a time or place, but I know something horrific happened with her. 'Are you sure?' She asks Mother, taking possession of the little girl.

'We're sure,' Mother replies. 'She's not ready.'

'Hello, Sweetheart, nice to meet you.' She rocks the baby, speaking in a motherly tone, before they disappear.

'I know how you feel.' The twenty-something me leans against the gate. She walks towards me, not removing her gaze from my eyes. 'In your heart, I mean, not your head.' She sits on a nearby bench and gestures me to follow. Feeling duty-bound, I oblige. 'You feel like you're the villain because fewer hearts are beating.' She lights up a cigarette and inhales a deep drag, before releasing smoke into the clear air. 'And tomorrow, you have to decide whether you're a villain who seeks redemption, or one who should be defeated.' Another drag; she makes it look so appetising. My mouth unable to speak. 'I sought redemption. The memories never go away, mind. The memories of what you've, we've, done. The memories of those hearts which no longer beat.'

'You said I win.'

'You do.'

'This doesn't feel like a victory.'

'What were you expecting victory to feel like?'

'Freedom.'

'You'll never be free. Not truly. Not in a world haunted by its ghosts. Every year we honour the dead, we celebrate their lives, we give thanks to their contributions. But we can never forget. The good and the bad. If you're strong, you'll mourn them every year. If you're weak, they'll mourn you. Should one deserve happiness, it shall be thrust upon them on Earth. Should one deserve penance, it shall be forced upon them in Hell.'

This time it's my turn to fade away into smoke, as I reappear in the comfort of my living room, lying on my sofa, hugging my pillow, watching the crack expanding.

Redemption or defeat: tomorrow I'll make that choice. Somehow.

Sunday

Brad's chair sits empty as I wake, with laughter coming from the kitchen; Alexa's cartoons screaming on the television. I never noticed it as a child, but those programmes are so loud. Do they have to be? They grab your attention, though; maybe that's their grand plan.

A desire to check the news springs forth and I ask Alexa if I can borrow the television for a moment. News of The Teacher's arrest has fallen down the pecking order. Another woman, attacked by the Thynwych Park predator, takes over the mantle of the top story. Pictures of The Teacher and his family still occupy the sidebar, with the sun shining behind them, smiling as wide as God allows. They're still flattering him even in prison. I should turn the volume up to hear their words, how they praise him so, but Alexa doesn't need to hear it. She's still young and innocent. Besides, we don't need to hear their lies first thing in the morning.

The television returns to its colourful world of cartoons and I storm into the kitchen, wanting to free my mind from their twisted ways of reporting a rapist's arrest. Brad and Mother each embrace me as I enter. Their laughter silencing on command with my presence.

'Good morning, Sweetheart,' Mother says. 'Your Bradley is so funny; he's just been telling me this charming story about his mother.'

My Brad.

'A story I know, or?' I grab a bottle of water and drink it in one elongated gulp.

'I don't think so.' Why is Mother hearing *charming* stories I haven't heard? 'It was back when I was younger, my mother used to take me to work with her; she cleaned caravans and rooms at a holiday park in Richmond, when we lived there.' He's never mentioned living in Richmond before. More information Mother knows what I don't. 'Well, she used to cut down brushes and mops and things to half their size and make me and my sister help out.' A sister? What sister? Why has he kept so much from me? Is he really *my* Brad? 'So, there's this picture in my house framed on the wall of a little four-year-old me with a tiny broken brush sweeping the floor.'

'I was telling Bradley,' Mother continues. 'You used to help me when you were little.' My memory of that vaguer than *my* Brad's; with Mother working as a teaching assistant in a primary school. She'd take me to school earlier, have me set up the kids' desks and then take me to my school before darting back. That must have been tiring for a single mother, but I guess you never really think about how much work a parent needs to put in. I null the desire to hug Mother.

'Yeah, I did,' I reply. 'Although I can't really remember it.' The empty bottle placed in the recycling bag.

'It's such a shame she passed away; I would have loved to have met her.' Mother flicks on the kettle and takes *my* Brad's cup for a refill. 'Have they sorted out the funeral, yet?' She knows about that, too. She knows too much. How long have they been awake gossiping?

'Not yet,' his smile fades. 'The police are dragging their heels with their investigation. But, the funeral isn't something I'm looking forward to, so they can take as long as they like.'

'As the eldest, I image a lot of responsibility falls on your shoulders for the arrangements.' She knows his sister is younger than him.

'True. I didn't know her too well later in life, but I remember a few songs she loved and a poet she liked, so I've got some things sorted.'

'You're going to be in charge of my funeral, aren't you, Lily?' Her words dagger through my chest. Why are we talking about Mother's funeral?

'What? Am I?' Am I still asleep? This feels like another nightmare.

'Of course, silly. Unless you die, first.'

'What? What did you say?' Fear produces sweat.

'I said unless you don't want to.' No, you didn't. Why is she lying? Why are they both conspiring against me? And gossiping behind my back.

'Oh, of course. Sure.'

The sun's rays shine through the kitchen window, for once warming the house enough to not need the radiator. Birds serenade the morning from the outside. The trees sway from the slight breeze on offer.

'Right, time to feed the animals.' Mother takes a jug of water outside and pours splashes over the plants and grass in the garden. A couple of years ago, Mother and I set a weekend aside to clean the garden (to distract me from my misery), and in the process, we mowed over a family of frogs. It did *not* help my misery. More hearts who no longer beat thanks to me.

427

The sight of frogs fleeing for their lives against the anger I was bringing forced me to break down and cry. I can't remember anything else from that day. I remember the frogs mourning their lost loved ones in the days which followed, though. Since then, Mother has tried to care for any wildlife who ventures into our garden, as well as developing green fingers herself. 'Beautiful garden, beautiful home, beautiful smile,' she used to say in the weeks after she started gardening. It became such an annoying catchphrase.

I rarely explore the garden, choosing instead to merely observe. It has a couple of bird's nests, a small pond (built especially for the frogs), plants all around the garden's parameters and animal statues honouring those who inhabit the land. As she pours water over the flowers, I can't help but notice how wilted the plants look. She's been neglecting her motherly duties. Their demeanour is sad. Drooping over their homes. Even the taste of water fails to resurrect their happiness.

Even the white lilies have wilted somewhat.

She's always been regular as clockwork in keeping them alive. What's changed? Have I made her too angry with seeing *my* Brad? Is she too distracted by *my* Brad? The plants are but more hearts who aren't beating because of me. How many more hearts must I break?

'Hey, Lils,' *my* Brad says to me. I join him in sitting at the table. 'I know yesterday was a bit of a disaster, so how about we have another day out, today?' A roasting pot of emotions bubble inside me. The sound of Mother's watering and singing still echoes through the back door. 'Nothing too crazy like going to Roskell again, but, like, bowling, or the cinema, or the racetrack.' The racetrack, located in east-Richmond and one of the most well-known horse racing tracks in England, attracted interest of people from all over. Mother and I have never been; a distaste in horse racing is something we share. Even if our reasons differ.

Mother hates how her father was a *huge* gambler and would spend hours upon hours at the racetrack. According to her diaries, if he won they celebrated as a family. If he lost, he drank. And when he drank, he got aggressive. The diaries talk about one particular occasion where he lost nearly £10,000 collectively over one summer, as his addiction reached its zenith. Mother and her mother tried to stop his excessive gambling, but each received a back-handed slap for their troubles. Later that night, he dragged Mother's mother to her room. The diaries don't state what happened, but Mother reckons he beat her, as she was heavily make-upped the next day. I hate horse racing because of the horses' mistreatment; killed due to their failure to win. No wonder The Teacher refuses to die.

'Bowling sounds fun,' I return, realising my time without speaking was bordering on unnatural. We both agree on needing a shower and a change of clothes, so he sets off home (a home I've yet to see), as I head upstairs to run the shower.

'Hey, Lils,' Mother says as she knocks on the door. I don't reply. 'He's really cute.'

I swing open my door, standing in nothing but my underwear, and gaze into her eyes. 'Hands off,' I jest. There's an undertone of malice in my voice which I hope she detects. 'He's mine.' I know Mother would never date again, but her words frighten. He's *my* Brad.

'I know, I know,' she smiles. 'Look, I know I give you a hard time about men, but you do seem to have found a special one. He's charming,' *he's mine*, 'he's cute,' *he's mine,* 'he's funny,' *he's mine.* She pauses, waiting for me to interrupt.

'But?'

'Just be careful.' I roll my eyes. Noticing this, she sets aside her basket of laundry to focus solely on me. 'That's all I ask, as a mother. Please don't be too blinded by love to see the truth.' An agreeing nod satisfies her enough, and she kisses my cheek before heading away with the laundry basket.

She means well, I know that. Especially after everything we've *both* been through. But her constant repetitive warnings come across as annoying, more than caring. I return to the bathroom; the windows steamed from the rushing warm water. Unease trickles up and down my stomach around the sight of water. One blink and I'm back on the lake. Another blink and I'm in the bath. Another blink and I'm back watching the shower.

'Come,' a voice whispers through the water.

I recoil.

'Come, Lily,' it whispers.

Despite my body's demand for cleansing, I race out and into my bedroom.

'Wow,' *my* Brad says as he greets me. 'You look amazing.'

An old red dress of Mother's adds an air of freshness, despite my dirty body. It's a dress Mother no longer wears, and she notices as soon as I appear. 'Nice,' she smiles.

'Thanks,' I say to *my* Brad, before turning to Mother. 'I hope you don't mind.'

'Of course not. You look fantastic in it.'

Whether I look amazing, I'm not sure, but I appreciate the comments.

'Thanks,' my face blushes. I rarely receive such compliments; part of me still believes it's all one big conspiracy against me, and one day soon *my* Brad will reveal his grandiose plan to humiliate me in public. I twirl my hair in my fingers as silence befalls upon the room, before realising how I'm behaving like every stereotypical girl. I'm more than that. 'You look good.' Inexperience at compliments shines for all to see. Is that the first time I've complimented him? An overwhelming wave of embarrassment directs my attention downwards, which prevents me from seeing his reaction. I hope he's smiling.

Static from the television squeals around the room. 'What's up with the television?' I ask, directing everyone's attention towards the haze of black-and-white lines.

'Nothing,' Mother replies slowly. Does it behave like this regularly? Regular enough for Mother to not see its oddness?

'Come,' the television whispers, before dying. The lines condensing into a white circle before blackness takes over.

'Are you okay?' Mother asks. I shake the television's behaviour from my mind and nod.

We arrive at the bowling alley having taken the bus to the east side of West Drive. The bowling alley is next to the cinema, which is next to an action-adventure playground for teenagers, flooding the adjacent streets with moviegoers and thrill-seekers alike.

Within seconds of sitting down on the bus, *my* Brad grabbed my hand, and I didn't prevent him throughout the entire journey. He never let go. Even as we arrive at the counter, his hand holds mine, his fingers interlock with mine, his palm touching mine. *My* Brad doesn't need the baggage I carry, but he sees something in me. Something I don't see. Maybe one day I will.

I'm not attractive (he can do better), I've not got a body to be desired (he can do better), my personality and history are a mess (he can do better), my family and friends are crazy (he can do better); yet he sticks around.

The desire to swash away his hand still rings, but with The Teacher locked away for good, I'm trying. I'm trying to be a girlfriend. I'm trying to be less pathetic. I'm trying to be the type of girl who gets the boy. I'm trying to be the Lily I've always wanted to be. The Lily he cares about. The Teacher never cared about me as a person; he cared about sex. Mother never cared about me as a person; she cared about having a daughter. *My* Brad cares about *me*. So, against the lessening desires to run, I hold his hand.

With lunchtime having not long trickled by, the bowling alley is largely free from the groups of families or teenagers or teams training which are commonplace. They're probably all at home enjoying their Sunday dinners. Or living more exciting lives than we are. But, their lack of appearance grants *my* Brad and me more seclusion. More privacy.

My Brad sneaks off to make a phone call, and I pay for the lane; booking three games of bowling (that should last us a good few hours). The only thing missing are two glasses of chardonnay, but a nearby bar informs it will not be an issue for long.

'Sorry about that,' *my* Brad says upon arriving at the lane with me. 'Police stuff, you know? Anyway, what are our names going to be?' He gestures towards the two blank names: waiting. Long gone, it seems, are the days when people came and used their God-given names. Mother and I came here last year and used Mother and Daughter as our bowling aliases. The lane by our side still broadcasts Easy-E's victory over Chalky. 'I think I'm going to be Mr Bradley.' The name echoes from one ear to another, shivering my body. 'And you?'

'Ms Lilian,' I say, freeing my body of the coldness. He smiles, showing perfect teeth. Mine are a dentist's dream: oddly positioned, full of plaque, needing fillings and probably an extraction or two. They'd make a fortune out of me. They don't care about people like *my* Brad, whose teeth are immaculate. Brad doesn't pay their bills. Until the day comes where the pain is too unbearable, though, I refuse to sacrifice money to their greedy wallets.

Mr Bradley (the name spiders down my spine with each glance) vs Ms Lilian. A battle as gigantic as Godzilla vs King Kong. As romantic as Romeo and Juliet. A battle depicted in future novels and movies. The outcome written in song. A romance deserving of a better female lead.

My Brad playfully mocks my need to throw the green balls (the lightest and smallest available) as he uses the purple ones (the second heaviest, of the five colours) with ease. This after jesting about my need to have the railings up. Our score is closer than the odds beforehand would've suggested; he beats me by forty points in round one, with *my* Brad recording three strikes in a row (a feat impressive to a love interest, but frustrating to a competitive rival), seventeen in round two and fifty-four in round three. Our first sporting event ends in his victory, in all three rounds. Eventually, we'll lose track on who's winning overall, but *my* Brad takes round one.

My Brad runs to the toilet as I take my shoes back to the guy at the counter who asks how my game was. 'Fine,' I reply. I shouldn't fear *all* men.

'Surprised they let torturers play bowling.'

'Excuse me?' The radio quietens.

'I said, I'm surprised you paid for two lanes, playing alone.'

'What?' Anger and confusion. I slam the shoes on the counter and back away.

'I said, I hope you come back soon.' No, you didn't. Why is he lying? Why does he keep changing his story?

I meet *my* Brad outside, desperate to get away from that *man*. That weirdo. That *liar*. 'Well,' *my* Brad exclaims. 'I think I need to refuel after that victory.' It's funny seeing his gloating ways; it feels natural. He's not hiding who he really is. He could've been respectful to my defeat, but instead, he's behaving honestly. A trait oft rejected so far today.

His burger dwarfs mine; with him keeping the lettuce and onions and cucumber and bacon and sauce. A burger dripping with everything available. Mine, on the other hand, stands more diminutive, comprising just the buns, the patties and cheese. Mother tried her best in my youth to steer me towards healthy eating, but she always failed. One time she tried to bribe me with a brand new computer game if I just ate a banana. I refused. I have this special ability to know whether I like something based on its appearance alone. Nobody believes it's possible, but *I know*.

'Mine's like, forty points bigger,' *my* Brad jests as we dink our burgers together.

Despite the news' warnings against coming here, *my* Brad and I talk a walk through Thynwych Park on our walk home. We decided against taking the bus back, despite it being a long journey, to enjoy more time walking and talking. The sooner we get home to Mother, the sooner a wall stands between us. Here, we're free to be who we are. Free to explore what this could be. Free to allow my hand home within his.

Attacks here are becoming far too common, but I have *my* Brad here with me. My soldier. My knight. My protector. With him by my side, I have nothing to fear.

The attacker's MO is to sneak behind his victim and rub their bottom. The majority of stories began this way, followed by how he wrestled his victim to the ground before assaulting them. He can't sneak up on me with *my* Brad here. I'm safe.

Much like the fields of Roskell which surround the lakes, Thynwych Park is very well protected and cared for (despite the numbers visiting its domain diminishing, according to an article on the news). The grass, sharp and to attention, stands a beautiful green, ice cream trucks station far enough to satisfy a craving at any time and mini-bars prop up to fill adults with alcohol. The sun beams down, cascading shadows from the trees.

The sun shines hotter than yesterday, creating large queues at each little shop.

'Just think,' I say after we find ourselves a patch of grass to settle on. 'If we were part of The Truman Show, everyone here would be an actor, pretending to ignore us,' we gaze out at the plethora of people in all directions. 'Each trying to be in the shot, with hidden cameras everywhere.' Children and dogs run, boyfriends and girlfriends rub cream on each other, elderly couples talk on the benches. All of these would be fake.

'Question is: which one of us is Truman, though? Because that would mean the other one of us is also an actor.'

'Me,' we each giggle. His eyes enquire why. 'I've got the backstory, we've only been to my house *and* you're better looking than me, which makes me think you've been cast.' He laughs, taking another sip of his drink.

'True, but you can write a backstory to a character. I'm the one preparing to attend a funeral, and they don't give extras that much of an arc.' He winks, taking the lead.

'Okay, okay. However, you've met my friends, my mother and my sister. Why would an extra deserve that many associates?' Advantage: Lily.

'I see your point, but I have a job.' Does he? Since when? 'Why would an extra be forced to spend several hours a day working? Not exactly quality entertainment.'

The argument comes to a mutual conclusion, as we watch the sea of actors going about their role, greenery working as a majestic frame to capture their presence.

An hour passed by before we released our seats for the next group to take ownership of, as we continue our walk around the park. His body leads the way, twisting and turning left and right, steering me where he wants to go. He must know this park well.

The beauty of the world minimises as we enter a secluded area, blocked by trees and bushes. We're isolated from the world. 'Today's been really fun,' he says, stopping me. His voice more serious than comical, which dominated his speech in the walk prior.

'It has,' I try to keep the comedic tone. 'It's just what I've needed, especially after yesterday-'

His soft lips press against mine, and this time our lips dance together with effortless choreography. His tongue makes a brief appearance, leaving me wanting more each time it retreats. His right hand lessens its grip on mine and strokes its way up my body to my cheek, his left arm mimics its movement on the other side. My body presses closer to his, our lips still locked in a dance. His right hand slides down my cheek to my neck. Down my neck to my chest. Over my chest to the nipple. The focus of his lips lessens as his thumb circles my nipple.

His hand climbs and eases off one of my dress' straps, dangling it over my shoulder before returning, hand inside the dress, to my nipple. Our lips no longer dance. Mine a teacher whose pupil has given up. My body is my temple.

His left-hand glides around my body to my back and up to my neck. Forcing me closer to him. His tongue, once a welcomed visitor, now an intruder. Settling permanently when it once left. His thumb still swirling around my nipple, a shark around a small island. My bra acting as the final barrier.

He's panting: he's enjoying this. I *should* be enjoying this. But my nipple feels trapped. My mouth invaded. Invaded like when The Teacher sat me down on my knees and forced me to open wide. 'Let's go over there,' he breaks away to whisper, and leads me against a nearby tree. More privacy.

Any protests disregarded as he takes the lead, and presses my back against a tree, before returning his body in its position against mine. I *should* be enjoying this.

His left hand grabs my right and moves it down to feel the bulge in his trousers. Despite its urge to ignore his orders, he forces it to rub up and down. His right hand still circling my nipple. So many girls would enjoy this. My body is my temple. I *should* enjoy this.

His hand lifts my bra and returns to its circling. Now, skin on skin. Now, I'm exposed. The bulge inside his trousers forcing itself in thrusts against my hand. I *should* be enjoying this.

Any sign of effortless choreography well-and-truly gone, as his mind has lost interest in anything his lips are doing. My body is my temple. His tongue paints my lips with its saliva. My body is my temple. His left-hand frees mine and widens my legs apart. My body is my temple. His tongue back inside my mouth. My body is my temple.

My body is my temple.

My body is my temple.

My body is my temple.

My teeth bite down on his tongue, jolting him away from me. 'Woah, woah, woah, what's up?' He asks through a half-working tongue. He tries to take a step closer but my eyes refuse. My teeth etched in his tongue.

'My body is my temple. My body is my temple.' My body shakes, desire explosion. Falling back against

444

the tree, I slouch to the ground. My eyes distant. My body raging. Burning. My hands dig piles of dirt from the ground. My body is my temple.

'What's wrong? Lily?' Brad asks, kneeling beside me.

'Leave me alone, leave me alone,' my tone starting to rise with each repetition. 'Leave me alone, leave me alone,' the words shout from my throat. 'Leave me alone.'

'Calm down, calm down, people are looking over. I'm sorry, I didn't mean to. I just thought-'

'Is everything okay, over there?' A woman's voice yells. She sounds strong. Very, very strong. Her voice what mine needs to be. A voice I need to own. To say no. 'Hello? I heard shouting.' She slowly walks into view, but by the time her forty-something body arrives, *my* Brad has left. Left me shaking and shivering on the ground. Fists full of mud. 'Oh my God, are you all right, my dear?' She rushes over. 'Did you get a good look at him?' She thinks it was the Thynwych Park predator. Not Brad. Not *my* Brad. Not him. Never. He wouldn't. He wouldn't hurt Lily. Not Lily. My teeth clatter together. Inaudible, noncoherent words escape my mouth.

'My dear, don't you worry, you're safe now. Shall I call someone? Your parents or a friend or something?' She takes her phone out, but no response comes. My body is my temple. Why would *my* Brad attack me? Silly woman. She's wrong. She's wrong.

'Is this yours?' She grabs my phone from the floor and waves it across my face. I can't tell if it's my phone or not. Is she lying? She's wrong about *my* Brad. 'I'll call someone, let's see,' she tries Mother, all three of The Flowers and *my* Brad (the five most recently messaged contacts in my phone), but none answer. 'Bloody Hell,' she says. 'Right, my dear, I'll call the police. Hopefully, you got a good look at the pig.' Not a pig. *My* Brad. He's not a pig. Why is she calling him a pig? I don't need the police.

'Hello? Wednesbury Police, please.' She waits while the operator transfers her and watches me. Maybe she's the attacker. Perfect disguise. Nobody suspects a woman. 'Hi, I'm in Thynwych Park, and there's a girl here who screamed and seems to be having some sort of episode.'

More noncoherent words escape my mouth; my mind immediately erasing them upon speaking.

'No, no one's around,' she continues. 'No, she's not making any sense. No, she isn't responding to anything. Okay, I'll keep an eye out, thanks.' She returns my phone to my pocket and strokes my arm. 'There, there, my dear; the police are on their way. Everything will be all right, don't you worry.'

My mouth still babbling, my brain still refuses to acknowledge it. My body is my temple.

'Don't stress yourself out, my dear. The police will be here any minute, so just calm down.' Her lack of experience is obvious. As a carer and a detective. Why does she have my phone? Does she know?

I wrap my arms around her head and move in close, our noses touching. 'I did it. They'll never know. Never know. No one will ever know. I did it.' Of course, of course, of course, of course, of course. She doesn't. Policeman might. The policeman will ask. I shouldn't answer. Really. Should I? No, no, no, no, no, no, no course not. I shouldn't. I should go. I should.

She pulls me into a hug and whispers repeatedly how everything will be fine.

Lily should go. Go. Go. Go. Now. The policeman is here. Flashing lights arrive in the distance, causing people to look on with more nosiness. They want to know the story. They want to watch the news tonight and claim they were there. They want to interview and question. He'll ask where I was. Won't he? Yes, he will. He'll want to know what I did. Why I was there. I did it. He'll know that. This woman will tell him. I did it. They'll arrest me. I should no. Now. Lily. Go home. Run, run, run, run. Go.

She shushes me politely and tries in vain to calm me. I settle back against the tree. My body is my temple. Spotting the policemen, she waves them over. 'What happened?' The lead policeman asks.

'I don't know,' she begins. She doesn't know. She's wrong. Not *my* Brad. 'I heard a scream, but nobody was here, and she's just rambling.'

'The policeman is here. He knows. We're done. Mother knows. This woman knows. He knows. I did it. They all know. Don't go with him. Don't go with him.' Don't, Lily. Be safe. They're not safe.

'Ma'am, I'm officer Donald, and this is Officer Winchers. Can you tell us your name?'

Don't, Lily. He doesn't need to know. Don't. He'll follow us. He'll follow us home and will find out. Does he already know? Not *my* Brad. Confess. Be careful. Be careful. I was stupid. I'm the victim. I don't know these officers. Fake names. They're lying. They crave information. They know and want our name. Don't tell them. Donald, Winchers.

'I've not been getting anything, either.' Just babbling.

'Thanks. Ma'am, we're going to take you down to the station. We'll get you a nice warm drink and we'll find a doctor. He'll be able to help you. Is that okay?' His baby-talk doesn't suit his rugged physique. He's a man's man. He wants me. He's taking me. I should assume the position. I'm the victim. He wants me in his car.

Don't go, Lily. He wants you. I know. Handsome man. Wants you. You. You. You. Like The Teacher. Bend over. Take it. Don't go, Lily. Safe.

Officer Donald backs away, allowing Winchers, a female, to take the lead. 'Ma'am, I understand some people have trust issues.' More baby-talk. I'm not a baby. I'm an adult. 'So, would you like to come with me? We'll

449

take you somewhere safe.' Safe. Need safe. My body is my temple.

'She knows, Lily.' She knows.

'Come.'

Steel greets my shivering body as I come to inside a prison cell; confusion and fright reign. The walls are too narrow, too small, too basement-like. The window shows freedom, but its bars prevent it. The air chills. I'm trapped. Centimetre-by-centimetre, the walls close in. Forcing my body to the heart of the room. Stone slabs scrape along the floor, closing in on its destination. Beads of sweat race down my brow, stinging my eyes with its salt.

I bang on the door and yell for freedom as the walls close in. A guard releases me; that nightmare left behind.

'I see you're awake,' his thick voice surprises me. 'Officer Winchers,' he speaks into his walkie talkie. 'The young lady is awake.' Exhaustion sinks my body to the ground; the sound of voices from the cells swirling about my head.

'Officer who?' I ask, but my words carry so little weight he doesn't hear.

A lady arrives about a minute later (is she Officer Winchers?) and helps lift me from the floor. 'Come, follow me.' She leads me to what looks like an interrogation room (what have I done wrong?), complete with an obvious two-way mirror. Someone's watching me. Someone's watching *us*. Why?

'Glad you're feeling better,' she says, pouring me a glass of water. When was I feeling worse? 'I am Officer Winchers, or Carol, if you'd prefer. Shall we start with you telling me your name?'

'Lily,' I whisper. She writes it down.

'Good evening, Lily. I'm an officer of the Wednesbury police. Can you describe to me the events which took place at Thynwych Park earlier this afternoon?'

The park's name brought everything back; everything I didn't want to remember. 'I-I was out with my boyfriend.' *Boyfriend*? How will *my* Brad look by the end of this story? I stop, unsure of how to proceed. I need to be clever. Whoever's listening in is waiting for information.

'Okay, and what's your boyfriend's name?' The pen waits.

'Brad.' She writes it down.

'And his surname?'

'We ha-haven't been dating long; I don't know.' Her eyebrows raise, offering a sceptical look, but she writes it down, anyway.

'Okay, fair enough. And where does he live?'

'I don't know,' my voice diminishes. Every word her pen writes a knife carving into my head. Her a butcher wielding it. Carving for information.

'Okay. And his age?'

'Maybe twenty, twenty-one.'

'Do you have any photographs of him on your phone?' She slides the phone across the table inside a plastic bag. Is it evidence for something? The butcher readies her knife.

'No.' She moves the bag to the side and slices more streaks in my head. Each streak adding towards my growing headache. 'Brad hasn't done anything wrong.' I don't even know what she's accusing him of, but she's got the wrong guy.

'What happened with you and Brad in the park, Lily?' Her pen sharp and ready.

'We were kissing, and I got nervous,' how must I sound to her? 'And I screamed. That's all. Nothing, really. I'm just a nervous person, because of,' my words

453

trail off. She doesn't need to know that. The Teacher could be behind the two-way mirror fuelling his campaign of innocence. 'So, I screamed; a mild panic attack, I guess. But he hasn't done anything.' Her knife carves every line, enraging my headache.

'I appreciate you feel that way, ma'am, but I'm sure you're aware of the recent spate of attacks in the park, so when an incident such as this comes up, we like to investigate every potential lead.' Her tone motherly. 'And, if I may sound unprofessional for a moment, an incident where a man hasn't told you his full name, his age, his address, has not allowed any pictures to be taken of him and who ran away from the scene of the crime sounds like the type of guy we should be questioning.' Her unprofessionalism wades as the pen readies itself for my reply.

'Questioning about what? Brad's not the attacker. He's a good man, I swear.'

'Lily, you haven't known him too long, how can you be so sure before meeting you, he wasn't someone else? I'm not saying he is, by the way, this could all be one big unfortunate misunderstanding, but I would like to speak to Brad to lay any possible erroneous concerns to rest.'

'His number's in my phone,' the words of a defeated victim. A role I've played enough to act it to perfection.

'Yes, we know.' She opens a folder and retrieves another piece of paper. 'I hope you don't mind, but we saw a few messages from him and tried to trace his number, but it's connected to a burner phone. Burner phones, in case you aren't aware, are notoriously difficult to track. Are you aware he uses a burner phone?'

'Y-yes. His old ph-phone broke.' Her knife carving right through me. 'My Brad is not the man you're after. Can I please go? I want my mummy.' A fully grown woman begging for her mummy.

'Just a couple more questions, if you don't mind.' She waits for approval, before continuing. 'We tried contacting your mother with the number on this phone but couldn't get through.' She produces another piece of paper. I'm not looking at their lies.

'She d-doesn't use her phone t-too much.'

'We also received a phone call from her boss last week concerning her apparent disappearance, as I'm sure you're aware.'

'Yes. Some officers came around. She's been ill: that's all.'

She takes a deep breath. 'So, you're in the park with Brad and you're kissing. You're boyfriend and girlfriend. Everything seems normal. What happened which made you scream for help?' Her notepad and pen ready to further rage my headache with its slicing.

'He,' a sigh escapes me as I realise what I'm about to say. 'He put his hand up my shirt.' Slice. Slice. Slice.

'Did he force his hand there, or was it an action in the heat of the moment?' Is that what people normally do *in the heat of the moment*?

'I think it was the heat,' my voice shrinks. 'But I've had terrible experiences in the past and got frightened.'

'Okay. Any idea why he would run away when,' she searches through the notes, 'Ms Hollis came to see if you were okay? Surely if it's all a misunderstanding, he would be happy to be interviewed to clear his name.'

'Because she thought he was attacking me, and maybe he got scared. I don't know. I don't remember too much afterwards.' All memories end with the strange woman arriving. My mind transitions her appearance with that of a police cell. With nothing in-between.

Her knife slices deeper into my head: my headache burns. 'Do you have many panic attacks or blackouts?'

'A few, from time-to-time.' The Monday-Lady asked these questions. Why can't they just ask her? 'Sometimes my experiences get the better of me.' The fire in my head roars.

'Have you ever screamed because Brad has made advances on you before?' The blood from the carving drips down my face. In the mirror, I'm the final girl in a horror movie. Covered in blood, but still alive.

'Yes. Mother was angry. But we settled it. Can I go, please? I want my mummy.' I *need* her.

Her disappointment clear to see, but I don't care. She's holding me against my will and accusing Brad of things he hasn't done. She should be ashamed of her career. 'Yes, okay.' She speaks, resting the knife on the counter. 'The rest of your things are on the desk, our there to your left.' She gets up and taps against the door. 'An officer will take you. If you can wait five minutes, I'll give you a lift home and explain to your mother what's happened.'

The uniformed officer leads me to the desk and I smile at Winchers as she walks off in the distance. I retrieve my things and take off. Mother doesn't need her lies. Her faceless, fact-less, everything-less lies. I dread to think about what I'll tell Mother. Or *my* Brad. If I ever see *my* Brad again. He's done nothing wrong, yet the news tonight will paint him as the attacker Winchers so obviously wishes he was. She'll explain how they're talking to a survivor who can identify the man. I'll never succumb *my* Brad to her manipulation. So what if I don't know *my* Brad's full name, age, address, family background, whether he has sisters, what school he went to, what job he does, who his friends are, why he doesn't allow pictures taken or anything at all. He's still not the attacker they'll falsely accuse him of being. He's *my* Brad. Not theirs. He's the Brad *I* know and like. Not the Brad they don't and hate.

Ghostly streets accompany my walk home; which I accept. I don't need people seeing me and questioning me. I don't need their lies. Everyone's tucked up in bed: safely getting ready for their jobs; or preparing their children for school; or watching the latest Sunday-night programme to sweep the nation. Because normal people do things like that. Nor me, though. I've never had that luxury. And when I had the chance for it, Mother gave it away.

The easiest and quickest route from the police station to home involves walking beside the park. Alone, I'd normally try to avoid it, but today I embrace it. Bring on the attacker. Bring on the predator who roams the trees. Because the predator will *not* be *my* Brad; freeing him from suspicion. *My* Brad is waiting for me at my house; waiting to apologise for abandoning me.

Again.

He abandoned me yesterday after my fall. And now after my screams.

I'm sure he has a logical and perfectly rational explanation for both, and he'll tell me when I get home and everything will be fine. I mustn't let Winchers' scathing indictment of *my* Brad poison my mind.

Dusk has settled on West Drive, with the streets dimly lit and the majority of houses sitting in darkness;

bar the occasional yellow hue of light from a house's sole waking occupant. Dark rooms full of people energising themselves for their fun-filled day ahead. Some will sleep alone, some will sleep with those who've promised their lives to them, some people will sleep with those whom they've barely known a week. Everyone contempt with their lives. Then here I walk. Alone. Fresh from the police station. Walking home to a dominating mother and a boyfriend wanted by the police.

That same yellow hue glows from my house as I near, with the shadows of bodies pacing back-and-forth confirming a full house.

'-She's home-'

'-Thank God-'

Mother and The Flowers rush into the hallway the second the sound of the door opens makes its way to their ears. All four of them wrap their arms around me in a panic.

'I'm fine, I'm fine,' I whisper, not returning any arms to the group hug.

'Why did the police phone us all?' Mother breaks away. 'Has something happened? We haven't been able to contact Bradley, either. Is he involved?' How quickly do people jump to the conclusion *my* Brad is heinous?

'It's all right, I'm fine, just a misunderstanding.' I free myself from their hug and collapse on the couch in the living room. 'So, has no one spoken to Brad?' They all shake their heads. 'I'll phone him later. I should probably warn him the police want to speak to him.' Fatigue prevents further movement. The crack completely covering the entire window; one strong gust of wind away from caving in.

'What happened, then?' Rose pipes up, ignoring an unspoken desire to leave me in peace. 'You don't get taken to the police station at the same time your boyfriend disappears for nothing.'

'Fine,' I let out a large sigh. 'We were kissing in the park and I got freaked out again. And a lady thought I was being attacked and phoned the police.' Every time I retell the story, I hear how pathetic I am.

'And Bradley?'

'He left once the woman thought he was the predator. And, because of the attacks, they're putting two and two together and producing seventeen.'

'So, they think-'

'Yes.'

I recount each question the policewoman asked, felling the room into a stunned and confused silence. Mother and Rose err on the side of caution, with Poppy and Ivy willing to give the benefit of the doubt. Silence joins for about twenty minutes before the need for sleep takes over. Thankfully, they grant my release.

I check my phone one last time, but no messages were showing up. He must know I trust him. "I trust you. Xx", I message. He needs to know I trust him.

462

Hopefully, that'll lead him back to me. Back from wherever he is. Whatever he's doing.

Because clearly I know so little about his life.

Scratching – no, sawing – greets my rise at an unknown hour. The clock, who once proudly ticked away, shuns its face in shame. As vision returns, branches outside my window try to break in. They're sawing the window off its hinges. Nervousness takes over and I flee downstairs.

As the penultimate step meets my foot, a woman's giggle resonates from the living room. My feet tread lightly, fearful of whom the laughter belongs. I arch my body around the part-open door and gasp at an ungodly sight: Brad and Mother having sex.

'Mother,' I shout, slamming my back against the wall. 'What are you doing?' The horror prevents my teeth from clenching, gasping my mouth open. My eyes forced to stare against their will.

'Oh, hi, Sweetheart,' she tips her head to see me.

'All right, Sweetheart,' Brad cocks his neck backwards, still thrusting inside Mother.

'He's *really* cute,' she smiles; the satisfaction of honest sex is unknown to me, but her eyes, to mine, show victory.

'And she's not so shy,' Brad wears those same eyes; that same look.

464

I retreat; my stomach knotting around. The Flowers stand in the kitchen, all holding hands; six eyes watching my entrance.

'What's the matter?' They say in unison. 'We're all getting a turn.'

'No, no, he's mine. He's *my* Brad.' A stronger woman wouldn't need to resort to wailing.

More branches scratch – no, saw – at the window; the sound in every room. The volume louder.

'Maybe you should torture him.' The Flowers still speak in unison.

The wind's nightly howling now laughter, which floats in and dances around me. It mocks my situation with its laughter; its shrieking laughter. It mocks my mind.

'Who's next,' Brad's voice calls through. Poppy breaks formation and walks towards the living room.

I give chase, harassing and pleading with her to stay away; to no avail. In the living room Brad stands, his penis erect; Mother, by contrast, lies flaccid and motionless on the floor.

'I was too good,' Brad jokes as he lies Poppy on the couch.

'Mummy,' I cry and rush over to her body. 'What did you do? Please, no, Mummy, I need you. Please, no, please come back.' My tears fall in hope of containing healing powers, but the coldness of death refuses to release its grip. 'I can't live without you.' My words but a whisper over Brad and Poppy.

I recoil against the wall, cradling myself; watching Mother's body. Hoping, praying, she comes back to life. Never has a nightmare killed Mother.

'You're on your own, you're on your own,' the wind sings and dances around the room. 'You're on your own, you're on your own.' Its melody enchanting; enticing. Must more laughter mock me?

My arms cradle tighter.

'Good evening, ladies and gentleman,' the television springs to life, hushing the wind's chimes somewhat. A man, again with a loud American accent, addresses the camera in a news-like show I've not seen. 'Our top story tonight is the death of a mother from West Drive. The poor mother wasted her life mothering a pathetic excuse for a child and has finally given up.'

'You're on your own, you're on your own.'

'Let's go to our broadcast colleague at the scene.' The scene transitions to a woman standing in front of my home; as if on cue, lights appear from behind the living room's curtain.

'Thank you.' Her voice coming from both the television and the window. 'I'm here at the scene where the mother lives. Rumour has it, she's finally ended her life to avoid the shame and misery of mothering such a torturer. Back to you.'

The scene transitions back to the loud American, taking the lights from outside with it. 'Thanks. Goodnight, ladies and gentleman. Be safe.' The screen blackens, leaving just a reflection of my cradled body.

'You're on your own, you're on your own.'

'Look, Lily,' Brad stops thrusting; my eyes hover towards him, trying their best not to see Poppy. 'This is what *normal* people do: they fuck. They don't run away screaming like a little victim. They don't torture a man for showing an interest. Your mother was up for it, your friends are up for it. Hell,' his voice lowers. 'I bet in a few years Alexa will be up for it, too.'

'No, no, no, no,' my body rocks back-and-forth. My eyes observing nothing more than the ground

467

beneath my feet. Despite its proximity, no picture is in focus. 'No, no, no, no.'

'You're on your own, you're on your own.' Its melody haunting; yet beautiful. Swirling effortlessly and cheerfully around the room. Were it not for its message, I'd join in the merriment it offers.

Rose and Ivy enter the room and stand against a wall adjacent to where I cradle. 'First your mother, now your friend; are we going to torture him, then?' Still, they speak in frightening unison.

'We can't, we can't, we can't-'

'You won't,' Brad asserts. 'You're such a pathetic excuse for a human. Oh, woe is me, a naughty man touched me,' his force stations away from dominant to sarcastic. 'I must torture him. Now, the lad I refuse to sleep with is sleeping with someone else: I must torture him. Oh, Mother grounded me, oh, the weatherman promised sunshine, but it rains, oh, the shopkeeper overcharged me by ten pence, oh, the old lady I helped across the street didn't thank me, oh, an actor gave a terrible performance: torture. Must use torture. Torture solves everything.'

Still the branches scratch – no, saw – at the window, desperate to join the wind's merry dance. Every item in the room faces me, from the photographs on the wall to the angle of the dead television. All looking at me. All condemning me. All laughing at me.

'You're on your own, you're on your own.'

Rain taps away at the window, aiding the branches' attempts to break-in. A sound so familiar – of droplets in the shower, of images so bright and cheerful – now so dark. I'm right to be fearful of what they would do, were they able to enter.

The fireplace erupts in a mesmerising soiree of colours; reds and yellows and oranges blaze. Their brightness destroys the dark which longed held reign over the room. The radio joins the fireplace in coming to life; Evanescence's My Immortal plays. Mother's favourite songs. Amy Lee sings with more bite.

'You're on your own, you're on your own.'

'First your mother, now your friend; are we going to torture him, then?'

'Go on, Lily: reveal your true colours. Stop hiding who you really are from the world. Be a torturer. Be the torturer you were always destined to be.'

'You're on your own, you're on your own.'

'First your mother, now your friend; are we going to torture him, then?'

Your face it haunts my once pleasant dreams, your voice it chased away all the sanity in me.

'You're on your own, you're on your own.'

'First your mother, now your friend; are we going to torture him, then?'

These wounds won't seem to heal, this pain is just too real, there's just too much that time cannot erase.

The rain taps.

The clock ticks.

The fire laughs.

The door slams.

The radio mocks.

The wind dances.

The branches saw.

The pictures judge.

The walls condense.

The television pities.

The ornaments gossip.

It's all too much – the noise, the belittling, the claustrophobia; I run out of the house: screaming.

470

The garden trips me, and I land facing the house. What once may have been a castle offering protection now nothing more than a prison. A morgue. Only mildly illuminated by a nearby streetlamp. Its dark windows pierce through my soul. The rain lashes against my forehead. The grass forms itself into little knives, cutting away at my skin. My attempt at standing halted by the brutality of the wind's push. It taunts me. My legs and my back bleeding from the knives as rain continues to missile down.

'Oh my God, oh my God; are you okay?' A pair of old ladies rush me to my feet. 'Are you okay, my dear?' I nod; my throat unable to form coherent words. 'You want to stay away from this house, my dear. A torturer lives here. It said so on the news.'

'She's a cruel, vindictive witch, I heard,' the second old lady pipes in.

I nod, force out a 'Fine,' and walk off.

'Torturer, torturer,' they chant at the house – priests mid-exorcism.

The sadistic desire to watch them waggle their fists and splash their holy water nearly causes a car to hit me; which needed to swerve dramatically to avoid me.

471

'You stupid cow,' he calls out after slamming his car to a halt.

'Should have run her over,' a woman's voice speaks. Their words silenced by the roar of the car, and they vanish into the night.

One-by-one doors open, and families of all shapes, sizes, colours and wealth descend upon my home, wearing clothes not befitting the weather. 'Torturer, torturer,' they all chant. They stand outside the grounds – the grounds of my prison – without stepping foot inside. The rain illuminates my house above all others; as if a spotlight needed shone upon it. A sea of easily a hundred people, all chanting and raising their fists, flood around my home.

I fall to the floor, the pain of my knees clattering against the concrete ignored; the rain feels more condescending than sinister.

'Lily, Lily, are you okay?' *My* Brad's voice soothes away my worries as he wraps his arms around me. 'What's going on?' I crumble into his chest. 'Come with me.'

We arrive at the castle minutes later; with *my* Brad suggesting the peace it offers would be a welcomed ally. During the day, the battered remains of this 750-year-old castle look almost pathetic; but at night you can feel its history; you can feel the souls who fought between Wales and England still wandering; still preparing for the enemy to attack. Each of the four buildings more solemn at night.

'What on Earth was going on in your street?' *My* Brad asks as we stop in the castle's forecourt.

'I don't know. There was a news report,' I pause. 'It doesn't matter. Where have you been?'

'I went to the police to explain everything. I realised afterwards how I must have looked, and I think they believed it was a misunderstanding. If it *was* a misunderstanding, that is?'

'I'm sorry?'

'What brought it on?'

'The way you acted, the way you moved,' I sit on a nearby rock. 'It matched the way *he* moved. It just brought back flashbacks.'

'God, I'm so sorry.'

'You weren't to know,' Brad sits next to me. The thunderous might of rain eases off, allowing us to talk in a calmer volume.

'Still, I went too far. I just got carried away in the heat of the moment.'

'I wanted it, I still do; I just don't know if my mind and body will ever allow me to have it. I've got too many scars, too many dark thoughts, too many fears. I'm a mess-'

'Don't say such things,' his hand grabs mine. 'We all have shadows in our closets; we just need somebody to help open the door and let the light in.'

His words soften feelings of anger as we sit motionless, absorbed in each other's eyes; the souls from the war and the mob outside my home all irrelevant as I lose myself in his blue eyes. A shade of blue which radiates in the moonlight.

'Will your mother and sister be okay with all that ruckus going on?'

Mother. This Brad is real; he's not the apparition which murdered Mother, which means Mother may well, too, be an apparition – the real her sleeping soundly in her bed.

Hope.

'I'm worried about Alexa,' I reply. 'She's probably terrified.' She must be; Mother can handle a raucous crowd, but Alexa is far too timid to cope. I must protect her; I must *mother* her.

The wind no longer dances to the rain's beat, as silence resonates around the castle's grounds. 'I'm getting pretty chilly,' Brad's word tear away silence. 'Fancy going for a walk? Get our body heat up.'

I accept; the desire to protect Alexa wades somewhat – after all, Mother is there. West Drive is not a massive town, by any means, so it doesn't take long before we arrive in the town's main street. While you need to travel to the outskirts or a nearby town to do your proper shopping, the street houses everything I've ever wanted or needed: Pokémon cards during my childhood; makeup kits in my early teens; DVD rental stores (albeit their number is dying out) and a whole host of food shops, each trying to better their competitor. In between various shops are pubs, whose clientele stumble outside of, and takeaway restaurants, where those who stumble out of the pubs soon venture.

It's a generic town, but it's home.

'Look at the state of that,' Brad says, gesturing towards a woman whose dress wears a cesspit of stains. She's sat outside a pizza place with a bottle of cheap wine, shouting for someone called Tony. 'Poor Tony,' Brad jests.

'You, sir and madam.' As we turn, a homeless-looking man holds a bible. 'Bless your youth and romance. Bless your future prosperity.'

'Thanks,' Brad returns.

'Bless your torturer ways. Bless our Father who sent his Son to save our souls.'

'What did you say?' My voice infected with venom. 'Bless our what way?'

'Lily, calm down; he's just a drunk old preacher talking nonsense.'

'No: he called us torturers. I'm not a torturer, I promise. Brad, I'm not. I'm really not. He's lying. He's-'

'Calm down, calm down, I believe you. As I said, he's talking nonsense.' Brad turns to the old man. 'Thank you, sir, for your kind words, but we must bid you goodnight.' That's professional Brad. That's the Brad who speaks in whatever job he has. We move on, leaving the remnants of his utterings behind as he fades into the

476

night. 'Find all sorts of characters at this time, don't you?'

'I rarely come out at this hour. But, I have read books about those who come out during witching hour.' His confusion doesn't surprise me, but my body still too shaken to explain. 'I think I want to go home; sorry, but I don't enjoy being here at this hour.'

Upon the completion of my words, all the lights of the stores turn on together. The street lights glowing a brighter shade of yellow. Music from passing-by cars create a carnival-like atmosphere to the locals waiting by the takeaways. The traffic lights no longer working, instead flicking at random between the colours.

'I wonder what's going on,' Brad's demeanour opposes mine. 'Should we stay and join?' Party fever has enveloped around him.

'I'm sooner go home, to be honest. I'm tired, and a little worried.' Worried about Mother. Worried about Alexa. Worried about *me*.

'Hey, hey, you two,' a flamboyant man addresses us, dancing over with two short-skirted ladies behind him. 'Did y'all hear about that torturer who lives over *there*.' While my house is not visible, he points in its direction. 'News says she's cray-cray, if y'all know what I mean.' I don't. 'Come to think of it, my dear,' his eyes meet mine. 'She looks a lot like yaself. What'ya say, ladies?'

'She's got those torturer eyes, all right.'

'And those hands ain't made for holding dick.'

'I'm not a torturer,' my cries ricochet off their skin and drift off into the night. Am I begging for their understanding, or my own? 'I'm not, I'm not. I'm innocent.'

'Y'all claim that, Sweetheart, but we here disagree. I say y'all the torturer the news warned us about.' His tone not as flamboyant, as the surrounding party atmosphere dies down. I survey the scene and notice the crowds slowly converging around us. 'We all think you're the torturer,' he pulls out a knife from within his trousers and licks the blade. 'We just don't know your method; me, I like to cut off as much flesh as possible. In small increments. That way they suffer until they *beg* for death, y'all dig?'

I recoil backwards, but shadows approach from behind. 'I haven't done anything, I promise.' I protest in vain. 'Please, Brad, help.'

'Your dick ain't gonna help ya, he knows it's true. Don't ya? Y'all been sleeping with this torturer? Better watch out.' The flamboyant man nears and runs his knife gingerly from Brad's neck to his waistline; Brad froze in fear. 'So, what shall we do to you two Bonnie and Clyde wannabes?'

'Torturer, torturer,' the crowd chants. More bodies appear from the direction of my house, joining in the chanting. 'Torturer, torturer.'

My hands slam over my ears; a headache wakes within me. The knife creates shadows on the ground, pointing in my direction. Amongst the sea of people are policemen and nurses and electricians and shopkeepers and journalists and butchers and teachers. All eager to get me. All with that look of contempt. All chanting.

'Come to daddy, baby girl,' the flamboyant man says, wearing The Teacher's smile.

He takes a step forward and my body screams. Loud enough to drown out the chorus of chants. A slight opening in the crowd allows me to force my way through – thankfully without anyone grabbing me – and I run. I run home to Mummy. I *need* my mummy. She'll protect me from this army.

479

Their chants follow me, despite no footsteps follow. I circle the back streets and run home; the crowd have dispersed from here, allowing me sanctum.

'Mother? Mother?' I shout, running straight into the living room; no remains of her body or any sign of Brad and Poppy exist. Despite everything, a huge weight lifts from my shoulders.

Whispers ring around the room, with no source. The closer to the walls I get, the louder they are: are they coming *from* the walls? I can't hear what they're saying; there are too many voices. All speaking at random. I hear one speak my name, and I lean in close: 'You know what you've done.' My body jolts back; the whispers fall silent. Except one: 'You know where she is.'

I run upstairs to check Mother's room, but it's empty. All of her wigs still sitting on their mannequin heads, her nightgown still placed across the bed. As if she hasn't slept here in days. *Weeks.* I run into my room and all is as it should be; aside from the whispers. 'You know what you've done. You know where she is.'

I run into Alexa's room and find it barren of life. The walls full of cobwebs, her wardrobe empty of her pretty little dresses, the mirror reflecting nothing but dust. This isn't Alexa's room. This is the spare room from all those years ago; which held my imprisonment for all those months. A force pushes me towards the lone cabinet in the room. Fear urges me not to open it, but the force is too strong.

Inside is a book titles The Big Book of Baby Names, with a bent-over page leading me to Alexa's name, highlighted in yellow. Tears fall above her name, drowning Aletta and Alexandra. The book lays dormant next to the trilogy of pregnancy tests, each hitting home reality a little harder. For me and Mother. Three tests I passed.

Next to the tests is a picture of me with a newborn baby; the only picture I have with Alexa. There's happiness on my face, one so rarely seen since. That poor baby has no idea about the woman who birthed her, or the circumstances. I hope she never seeks out the truth. A small blue teddy hides behind the picture; its name is Marcey. A gift from Mother, as a way of remembering Alexa; but it was too sad.

I never even signed my name on her birth certificate: what kind of mother does that?

The walls interrupt my reminiscing with more whispers: 'You know what you've done. You know where she is.'

The tear in the wallpaper which vexed me throughout my time here still stands; a tear Charlotte Perkins Gilman no doubt would've hated. It still holds something disgusting in its appearance; I never did figure out what was so vile about it, but it mocks me still.

I trudge back downstairs where The Flowers wait at the bottom. 'It's time,' they say in unison. 'Open the door, embrace your reality. You know what you've done.' They open the downstairs kitchen door and hand me Colin: a sledgehammer.

The urge to fight drains from my body. 'I know what I've done.'

In the kitchen, I retrieve the set of keys which unlock the basement door. The black gateway to Hell.

'You've fought so bravely.'

'I've fought so bravely.'

As the creak of the door swings, I stare at the stairs. 'Go,' The Flowers whisper. Always a guiding light in my darkest moments. Each step down needs more weight; my body repulsing the idea of our destination.

Standing in dead-centre of the room, the tragedy which houses here screams. The sledgehammer thunders against the wall, dropping chunks of rock the ground with every swing. More and more bricks fall, until rotting corpses reveal themselves.

Mother stands, Jesus-like, her body rotting. Maggots and flies and other insects have nested on her body. To her right is The Teacher's head. Dried and drained of life. To their left, the skeletal remains of Tony, alongside Mother's hidden diaries. The very ones where she described meeting Tony; once he refuted her claims of being the father, she killed him. She killed him and she buried him. She didn't know I found the body. Mother and Father buried together: forever.

'Forgive me, Mother,' I drop to my knees, praying against the God she is. 'I did what I thought was right.'

The corpse doesn't speak; its face contorted from the impact.

'She didn't believe in us,' Poppy speaks. 'She said we were all imaginary. Illusions. But we're your friends.'

'And she was poisoning you with those drugs,' Ivy steps forward and kneels over to meet my look.

'Those drugs kept us away. That was *her* doing. Because of *him*. But we're back, now. Back with you forever.'

'We're the good guys,' Rose inserts. 'We save the world from people like these. Never doubt your sanity; we're here.'

'Lily?' Brad's voice echoes through to the basement. 'Lily? Are you home?' His tone in a panic.

The silhouette of his body appears at the top of the stairs, but I'm too tired to prevent him from entering. His phone drops to the floor in shock as he sees the bodies.

'Is that?' I nod. 'And she's?' I nod again. 'And what is that?'

'Daddy.'

The Flowers step to my side. His eyes white. 'What the Hell, Lily?'

'She was so miserable; always miserable. So, so miserable. Always complaining; forever complaining. Now, she doesn't complain. She's happy. She's at peace.'

'She's dead.'

The word stabs me. 'She's resting; reborn in my world. As did *he*. Their sins and transgressions forgotten. Their behaviour perfect. They're happy; not miserable

Mother, anymore: nice Mother. Happy Mother. *My* Mother.' A fit of giggles breaks out. Her eye, larger and stoic, watching the scene. 'Are you unhappy?' I ask the eye. 'Miserable?' I rise from my knees and face Brad: 'Maybe you need to be purified. I can write away all sins; make you the man you should be. You can live here forever with me. We can run, we can dance, we can fuck, we can love. Mother would accept this version of you. The Flowers, too. The world would accept us. All you have to do is kneel.' The sledgehammer readies itself over my shoulder. 'Kneel and be mine in Planet Lilian.'

'You're insane.'

'That's what The Monday-Lady says. I don't like The Monday-Lady; she doesn't believe in my Utopia. She makes me take disgusting tablets. Tablets which scare away my friends. Her purification is nigh. She'll be a doctor who listens to the realities their patients experience. No longer miserable; no longer diseased. No longer poisoning the minds of perfectly healthy people.'

'Perfectly healthy like you?'

'We're all a little unhinged, are we not?' The sledgehammer slams against the floor. 'We all have our ailments, do we not? If we're all broken, we're all *normal.'*

'We're not all murderous lunatics,' his voice offers confidence his body doesn't have.

'No one has been murdered; they're merely purified. And Mother agrees; she's back to being a mother. And The Teacher agrees; he finally confessed for his sins. And you'll agree.'

He walks backwards until his foot hits the bottom step. 'Please, Lily,' he begs, but the sledgehammer raises back over my shoulder. He runs.

Laughter consumes my body; be it so that madmen laugh, yet I am not mad: for this be the laughter of the powerful. 'The doors are all locked, *Sweetheart,'* I roar. 'Accept purification. You'll be happy.'

Flanked by The Flowers, I exit the basement, sledgehammer in hand, and walk with a soldier's rhythm to the living room. Despite searching every corner, there's no sign of Brad. 'You can hide, my love, but we will find you. This is, after all, *my* house.'

We march up the stairs and rummage through the entire bathroom, secret hiding places and all: nothing. Next comes Alexa's room: nothing. Next comes

Mother's room. Mother sleeps soundly with her blonde wig on, oblivious to the world around her; we look around but see no sign of Brad. Next comes my room: nothing. 'You're so cute, Mr Bradley.' The name no longer holding its sting. 'Come be purified. Come be *mine*.' The sledgehammer scrapes along the floor, waiting for its mission.

We return to Mother's room, all-too-aware she doesn't sleep in wigs. 'Oh, Sweetheart,' I say as the sledgehammer's head pushes the door wide open. Rose, Ivy and Poppy flank the bed, as the sledgehammer raises in excitement. 'Purification can be simple: one teeny, tiny tap and you're free.' He turns, removing his pathetic disguise. Mother would never be so careless as to *sleep* in a wig. And I *know* that. Does Brad take me for a fool? His lip quivers.

'Please, Lily,' he begs, but I pucker my lips and blow him a kiss.

'It'll be over, soon.'

I stand close to the bed, but he kicks out. It knocks me down and he runs. More chasing. Must he delay the inevitable so? The Flowers demand my stance, and we give chase once more. At the bottom of the stairs,

Brad punches me after springing out of hiding, again knocking me down.

Lightning crashes against the front door; its temper matching mine. I stand, blood dripping from my nose, and growl. 'Although, some purifications can take a while.' The sledgehammer returns to my hand and I again give chase. The Flowers behind me, cheering me on.

'Lily, please, don't,' he says as he runs to the kitchen. 'I don't want to hurt you. Please, it's me.'

His legs retreat as I limp closer; the sledgehammer still crawling across the floor. Brad's resistance spurs me on, like a drug in my veins. I can feel it. Coursing. Flowing. Filling me up. I need more.

So, too, does the sledgehammer; it roars with its addiction. Begging.

My speed more methodical than his. He retreats into the basement; why must he choose there for his death? Buried with the man whose name he wears.

'You know what you have to do,' whispers the wallpaper.

'I know what I have to do.'

The crashing of a dinner plate changes the picture, as I spin, greeted by Mother entering the kitchen. The moon's hue replaced by the sun. 'I found them,' Mother says, and in storms a version of myself from ten days ago.

'Why are you rummaging through my drawers?' Her petulant behaviour on full effect.

Mother slams her tablets on the table and walks towards the sink full of dirty dishes. 'Lilian.' Another plate slams to the ground, its shards ricocheting to my feet. 'Lilian, stop it.'

'I don't need them,' she says. 'I don't need them. I don't need them.'

'I know you think you don't, but the doctor-'

'That stupid woman?' Another plate crashes. 'You're not in there; she asks me stupid questions and doesn't believe anything I say. Those tablets aren't doing anything for me other than poisoning my mind; Ivy told me so.'

'Ivy,' her voice harkens to a whisper. She hides her eyes from the window's reflection; hiding the shame she feels. The shame of what her daughter's become. Of what her daughter refuses to change from. 'I can't have

489

this conversation again.' Her voice struggling against the sadness. 'I just can't.'

'Fine; I'll have this conversation with Brad. I met him by the park earlier; his mother is lovely and kind.'

'Sweetheart,' she is so tired of this. 'You haven't left the house today.' Her wet hands meet her eyes. The lapse in tablets is over a week; the longest span since the doctor issued them. 'There is no Brad. There is no Ivy, or Rose, or Poppy. How many times do we have to have this conversation, Lilian? If the doctor isn't working, we need some serious help, because I can't-'

Her words end abruptly as the sledgehammer kisses the back of her head. Blood flies over the dishes as her body slams and flails its way to the floor. Her daughter breaks down in tears and cries over her mother's still spasming body; as the life dries out.

'Please, no, Mummy,' she cries. 'I need you. Please, please come back to me.' Her voice almost genuine. 'I don't think I can live without you. Mummy please.'

She stands and looks at the blood across the room. The bright sunshine dims into an evening shade before she comes back to life. 'Yes, Mother,' she says. 'I'll clean up, Mother, don't worry. I know about the wall in the basement. I'll even clean the basement, Mother. Okay, Mother. I'll dispose of this.'

I watch her drag the body; it thumps down each step as it descends out of my view. My heart aches. I slump to my knees, the sledgehammer bouncing against the ground. The picture returns to this night.

'Lily,' The Flowers speak in unison. 'We're waiting.' As if controlled by an outside force, I reassemble myself, and retrieve my weapon.

'Lily,' Mother says, entering the kitchen. 'You were named after the most beautiful flower in the world. The soul of the innocent, they're said to represent.'

'Am I innocent, Mummy?'

'Of course, Sweetheart. And you always will be: my sweet Lily.'

'This house, it's cursed me.'

'And the doctor has poisoned you. You are *innocent*.'

'I am innocent.'

After locking the basement door, I race upstairs, passing The Flowers on my way, and storm into my room; my prison chamber. With almighty swings of the sledgehammer, I destroy remnants of my life. The drawers which house my clothes – including the pink bra – splintered across the room. The television which offers distractions smashes and shards. The window – whose crack mirrors the living room's – broken. The mirror – which so often has reflected a weak child – smashed into hundreds of tiny pieces. I'll take seven years of bad luck. The stars and planets – so often offering comfort – ruined.

Next is Mother's room. The mannequins, the window, the wardrobe: all feel my wrath. The toilet, the shower, the bath, the sink, the walls, the bannister, the photographs, Alexa's drawers: all feel my wrath. Roars and groans accompany every swing.

In the living room, the pictures, the television, the sofas, the tiny ornaments: all feel my wrath. Except for the window. The window, who's more crack than glass, needs no help in smashing. The sledgehammer rampages throughout the house; smashing holes in walls and ceilings.

'Okay, Brad,' I say, stumbling back into the kitchen. 'One more room, and you're next.' Silence returns from the basement. The dinner table, the microwave, the fridge-freezer, the back door, the window: all feel my wrath. The sledgehammer smashes the basement door open; ignoring the key in my pocket. The Flowers join me in the kitchen. 'Come give us *both* a little kiss.' I can hear him whimpering; his cries need no syringe to inject me.

'Help,' he calls out. 'I'm at 29 Sovereign Drive, West Drive, and a mad woman is trying to kill me.' Bless, he thinks the police will help him. Those good-for-nothings won't help anyone. They eulogise monsters to reporters, who respect them on the news. 'Please, be quick, she's coming and I'm trapped.' *Trapped*. Yes, you are, my love.

'They won't help,' I say as I reach the bottom. 'They'll listen, they'll pity, they'll *understand*; but they won't solve the crime.' The sledgehammer headbutts the ground. 'They'll sympathise and tell you the criminal is a monster, and you were just *unlucky*.' The sledgehammer smashes against boxes of unknown rubbish in the basement. 'But, the criminal will get free.' It raises its head and points at Brad. 'Plus, they'll be too late. I'm tired, Brad; let's finish this and we can sleep.'

In the graveyard of those who wronged me.

'Okay, okay,' he says. 'I'm yours.' The sledgehammer falls to my side in defeat. 'Forever.' His body appears from the shadows of the basement; covered in sweat and dust. 'I just went a little mad. I'm better, now.'

Lies. He lies.

Or does he?

He walks closer, closer, his pace slow; not wanting to frighten. Until his lips meet mine. The sledgehammer drops to the floor as I wrap my arms around him. Lost in his mouth's movement. His tongue cheeky, his hands comforts; our lips designed to pair off. 'I love you,' I whisper. 'I'll always love you.'

His hands glide up my neck and hold both of my cheeks, as mine glide down his body to his belt. 'I love you, too,' he whispers back. Before slamming my face against the wall.

My blackout lasted for what feels like two minutes, but in the basement, time paces to a distorted rhythm. My vision upon waking blurred.

'What happened?' I muster.

'I'm sorry, Sweetheart,' Brad says, as the picture paints a clearer colour. He's standing over me, sledgehammer in hand. Looking down with malice.

'It's funny,' I say. 'I made you everything I wanted in a man, and everything I wanted to be.' I pause to catch my breath, and sit up against the wall, with his permission. 'Good looking, smart, funny, strong, dominant, clever, cunning. *Nice*. The opposite of what *he* was. I guess I just got a little lost along the way.' He doesn't say anything; the sledgehammer sits agitatedly: waiting. I change position to kneel before him. 'You know what I've done; you know what you've got to do.'

'I'm sorry, Lily.'

Brad raises the sledgehammer above his head, gripping it with both hands. 'My name is Lilian Alexa Hill. And I will pay for my sins.'

And the sledgehammer comes down and kisses my head goodnight.

Steve James graduated from the University of Chester in 2016 with an undergraduate degree in English Literature and Creative Writing, before a postgraduate diploma in International Journalism at Liverpool John Moores University in 2019. *The Flowers of West Drive* marks Steve James' debut within the self-published community (ignoring the failed attempt several years ago with an unedited mess of a book: spoilers: an edited version will be coming soon).

A lover of psychological horrors/thrillers and time travel, Steve James' stories all centre on characters and their journeys, whether combating haunted apple trees, their own inner demons or time travel. Spoilers: those are the first three novels.

Contacts:

Feel free to follow me on any of my social media platforms; I'd love to hear any feedback, comments or suggestions on my work. And fellow indie authors, if your work matches the genres of mine, I'd love to read them.

Facebook:

Personal profile:

https://www.facebook.com/steven.w.andrews.7/

Writer's page:

https://www.facebook.com/SteveJamesOfficial

Twitter: @SteveJOfficial

Instagram: OfficialSteveJames

Come say hi. :)

If you enjoyed reading this, please consider leaving a review on Amazon. It greatly aids aspiring authors such as myself. :)

– Steve James

Printed in Poland
by Amazon Fulfillment
Poland Sp. z o.o., Wrocław